THE ARIADNE CONNECTION

Sara Stamey

Book View Café
www.BookViewCafe.com

THE ARIADNE CONNECTION

Published by Book View Café Publishing Cooperative, March 2015.

Cover design: Dave Smeds.

Cover art: Glowing Earth & DNA, Johannes Gerhardus Swanpoel, Dreamstime.com; Beautiful Woman, Aridom Chowdhury, Dreamstime.com; Caduceus Medical Symbol, Jgroup, Dreamstime.com.

Greek Key Patterns, Techlogica, Dreamstime.com

Production Team: Katharine Eliska Kimbriel, Sherwood Smith, Vonda McIntyre, and Leah Cutter.

ISBN: 978-1-61138-453-6

Book View Café Publishing Cooperative

P.O. Box 1624, Cedar Crest, NM 87008-1624

http://bookviewcafe.com

THE ARIADNE CONNECTION

Sara Stamey

Part I. SEED
Part II. FACETS
Part III. LATTICE
Addendum: A Guide to the Major Players

A CYGNUS Award Winner

Also by Sara Stamey

Islands, originally published by Tarragon Books; ebook edition by Book View Café.

"Cybers Wild Card" science fiction series originally published by Ace/Berkley/Putnam Publishing; look for new ebook and print editions from Book View Café:

Wild Card Run

Win, Lose, Draw

Double Blind

This one is for Thor,

with love and ongoing amazement.

With thanks to:

–My writers group—Katherine Trueblood, Gary McKinney, and Margi Fox—once more into the fray!

–Mary Alice Kier and Anna Cottle, for valuable feedback and support.

–My brilliant fellow authors at Book View Café, and my editing and production team for this novel: Katharine Eliska Kimbriel, Sherwood Smith, Dave Smeds, Vonda McIntyre, and Leah Cutter.

–Dr. Leslie Conton, anthropologist and shamanic practitioner.

–My go-to science guys Dr. Thor Hansen and Dr. Bernie Housen, Geology Dept., Western Washington University. My forays into speculation are entirely my responsibility.

–Stelios Mamalakis, for his gracious Greek hospitality to two wandering strangers. *Chairete!*

Part I. SEED

In the wilderness of the stones, in the power eaten away....
Where they spend much time in dying.

—George Seferis, *Mythistorema*

LEEZA CONREID, HOSTESS OF "Celebrity Smackback," plops her well-honed tush onto a stool at the production console, hooking her stilettos over the rung. Violet fingernails flick open a popper beneath her nostrils as she inhales with a hiss, and focus sharpens into max clarity. She snakes out two leads and snaps them into her lower-back spinal insert. Slips on the goggles.

"Showtime." Reaching into deceptively empty space, her long pale fingers spider the air to cue the file:

> *NLNE* REQUESTED FIELD ASSIGNMENT: 5 March 2027
>
> LEADLINE: *Where is Ariadne? Who is Ariadne?*
>
> SUBJECT: "Saint Ariadne," rumored healer of New Plague leprosy victims.
>
> MEDIA SATURATION: 53% and growing.
>
> QUOTABLE:
>
> Gaea Speaks cult leaders: "Mother Earth is fighting back against the pollution of the patriarchal corporate technocracy. Only Ariadne can save us now."

Behind the goggles, Leeza smirks. "You said it, bitches. And I'm the one gonna nail her." Another finger-twitch through the file, images cascading across her retinas.

> ASSIGNMENT DANGER RATING:
>
> High. No data on risk factors for illegal penetration of Med League border. No weapons or training provided.

She licks her lips and shimmies on the stool, running a fingertip over her thigh. Leeza Conreid doesn't need a gun.

INITIAL FIELD CONTACT:

None established. Field agent Conreid advised to search Athens' Piraeus Harbor taverns for one Peter Mitchell, AWOL NorthAm Navy. Current occupation: smuggler.

Part II. FACETS

Things fall apart; the center cannot hold;
Mere anarchy is loosed upon the world....
Surely some revelation is at hand.

—William Butler Yeats, "The Second Coming"

1

GEOMAGNETIC PALSY HIT THE satellite navigation again.

Peter Mitchell scowled at the rebellious LEDs and the radar static, rubbed his chin stubble, and watched the compass in its plexiglas bubble dip and spin aimless as an oracle. It was built-in and he hadn't seen any point to removing it. Anyway he liked it, part of the old bucket of bolts, like the crude mermaid some forgotten seaman had painted inside *Nereid*'s wheelhouse.

He pulled off his shades, rubbed bleary eyes, and squinted into morning-after sunlight over the purple-blue Aegean. The "wine-dark sea."

With a groan, he groped for his binoculars and scanned, wincing at the sun dazzles. Was that a distant froth of boat wake? A border patrol? Or worse? He shook his head—all he could see now was glare. He lowered the lenses and fumbled through a bundle of old paper charts. More solar flares were hitting, amplified in effect by a geomagnetic null phase, garbling navigation signals. All the satellite systems getting damn shaky. And with the accelerating geomag field wobbles, the communications blocs weren't bothering to maintain the satellite grid, so the gaps even during stable intervals were getting bigger. A lot of useless junk in decaying orbits up there. Like the "Peace Shields" the Reds and Feds had sucked their budgets to launch.

Scanning the charts and his scribbled updates, he snorted. Big boys had their horns clipped now, down to ground level with the rest just trying to read the maps. Momma Earth not a hell of a prize any more, what with the pollution and global warming, rising sea levels, quakes, ozone holes, and solar radiation showers—not to mention the human hordes on self-destruct.

Fire and brimstone. Retribution? Daddy Reverend righteous-right after all?

Peter shrugged. Looked like *nobody,* meek or not, was going to inherit. Just keep paying the price of progress right along with one of the geomagnetic polar alignment reversals that had maybe happened last time to herald the Flood. This time it was a new pandemic, Rapid-Proliferating Hansen's— leprosy on fast-forward. He'd seen them go, like the guy at the shipyard. You start with a rash, some bumpy "sunburn blisters," and the next thing you know your fingers are just lumps, your face a horrorshow blob choking the breath out of you. No cure in sight.

On the plus side, the powers that be were too busy to worry about one Peter Mitchell, "freelance import expediter" and NorthAm AWOL from the latest un-greatest war, or a missing Turkish spy boat dressed down as a fishing trawler, impounded during that same illustrious Gulf War Three. All things considered, he was sitting pretty to watch the world go to hell in a handbasket.

A lopsided grin cracked his stubble. He checked the radio and radar again—still nothing but static. Could be anything out there, he was cruising blind. And he couldn't shake the itchy feel of something closing in, a sort of useful sixth sense from his Navy days, much as he hated to admit it. Unrolling another chart, he swore, then leaned down to rummage in the console cubby for the right tube. He straightened, clipping his head hard against the wheel. "Son of a bitch!"

He slammed the cubby closed, flinching as the clatter tromped spike-shod through his hangover. Frowning at the nav readouts, he popped the heel of his hand against the tried and true spot on the console. Gauge needles jumped, but the digitals kept up their drunken dance.

Terrific.

Clutching the charts and a coffee bulb, he left the wheelhouse, sucked in a fresh salty lungful, and hauled himself up the ladder to the flying bridge. He nudged its wheel, dropped into the pilot seat, pulled off his shades and lifted closed eyes to the morning sun already simmering. He stifled another groan and rubbed his throbbing temples. Reaching for the fifth-liter in its handy slot, he thought better of it, took a sip from the lukewarm coffee, and made a face.

Peter grasped the wheel. "Captain Mitchell surveys his domain."

Up here on *Nereid*'s bridge, bathed in light shimmering over the distant stark-stone islands of the Cyclades and skimming closer above the purple-blue depths, he could almost forget looming Doomsday. These islands had been honed to the bare bones for centuries. They'd somehow gone beyond time and change, despite the recent earthquake and volcanic upheavals rearranging map contours, like they'd survive anything mere humans could throw at them.

He peered edgily from his chart to an approaching scatter of bare islets. Hadn't taken this route in years, not since the big Number Three. Most of the old drifting mines, at least, had been cleared out by pukes like himself—ex-puke—but he didn't like running unknown waters without his depth-sounder. The geomagnetic fluctuations screwed up more than just radio transmissions. Right now, they were getting one of the unstable shifts to null in the global field, as the north and south poles wavered in and out or split into random islands of magnetic charge. Played hell with fine-tuned circuits. And he wasn't in the mood to appreciate the irony that advances in nanocircuitry miniaturization had come just in time to make the electronics even more vulnerable to the electromagnetic field pollution.

He studied the chart, made a course correction, and stood to scan 360 with his binoculars. No sign of border patrols. Or pirates. Or Sons of the Prophet.

He sat, drumming his fingers, still keyed up. Too easy. So why look a gift horse? If he couldn't monitor the patrol radio bands, they couldn't get spotter reports on him. Maybe he'd make it clear. He leaned back, riding the dip and surge over low swells as the twin diesels hummed high. The sea glimmered around him, breeze freshening, sky gem-clear. Off to starboard, toward one of the rock islets, a gleaming curve broke the surface, then two finned backs—dolphins, breaching in a burst of spray.

Despite his jitters, Peter smiled. Greek sailors counted them good luck. He just liked to see them around, liked to cruise in the midst of a rough-and-tumble of sleek dolphins riding *Nereid*'s bow wake, grinning up at him. No hate or fear in their eyes, laughing through it all at the lunacies of *Homo sapiens*.

He wanted to believe the islands and the dolphins would survive after all the wars and warriors were long gone. Somehow he needed to believe that something beautiful and pure would outlast human stupidity. His own Noble Quest had certainly been a roaring farce.

Another leap, a splash, and the dolphins were gone. Peter shook his head, checked the radio and radar. Still no go. His fingers drummed on the armrests. He took another look at the chart, tempted to veer off on a shorter course, but that would put him right through a recent pirate hotspot.

Damn. He wanted to get this run over and done with, gold standard stashed in the kitty, maybe invest in an engine upgrade for a little more edge, and thank you ma'am *Kali nichte Good-bye.*

He blew out a breath and leaned over the spray shield to peer down through the forward deck's open hatch to the bunks.

His client was still sleeping. Pricey fantasy material for certain tastes, the pale, coltish limbs and blond tousle so fair it was almost white. A delicate blue artery pulsing beneath her firm little chin. Face half-hidden, smoothed out in dream, the only hint of color in barely parted pouty lips. And dark-smudged lids hiding the feral glitter of her eyes. Even asleep, she screamed Trouble.

Peter shook his head, gripping the wheel. Sunlight on the swells pulsed hypnotically, rippling through him like the high of the night before….

∞

Taverna Georgios. Smoke and drunken splashes of light from antique neon signs washed over dim faces and scratched plastic tabletops. The insistent beat of bouzouki, Greek sailors on weekend leave dancing and tossing plates onto the floor. Peter and his drinking buddy Chen laughed as off-duty barmaid Viv shouted dirty jokes over the ruckus.

"—didn't tell him he got the wrong end."

Peter groaned. "Jesus, where do you dredge them up?"

"She's an Amazon." Chen raised his glass to her.

Viv punched him. "Lay off that."

Chen reached over to lift the crystal pendant hanging above her cleavage, turning it to display the little plasticized portrait of Saint Ariadne, the trendy new Gaea Incarnate who was supposedly healing RIP-leprosy by laying on hands. Could have been any young Greek girl—braided dark hair, straight nose, level brows over wide-set eyes. Nobody had recent photos, so maybe she was just an urban myth, like the scattered "sightings" and miracle cures.

Chen swung the pendant. "So why the denials? Isn't that what your Corybantes want—blow all us male pigs off the face of Gaea?"

"They're not *my* anything! They're a bunch of extremists." Viv yanked the chain from his fingers. "I told you, those Corybantes aren't the same as Gaea Speaks. We want to use Gaea power to heal, not kill."

"So you say Gaea speaks? Maybe you do better to listen." It was Georgios, lips quirking behind his droopy mustache as he whisked away the empty ouzo bottle and plunked down a fresh one. "Listen, this land, she gives us every kind of death and destruction. For centuries. You do not *cure* her. You endure her angers, as always."

Viv stiffened. "Oh, so it's *her* fault! You think the earth *wants* these Alpha-male assholes with their bombs and germ warfare and ozone depletion and—"

"Remember the old tales." Georgios gave one of those expansive Greek shrugs. "The Furies were women."

He sauntered off as Viv spluttered, "That's the same old macho crap! World-hating, woman-hating male culture and technology destroying the natural order." She was quoting from some Goddess bible now. "Ariadne will never come out of seclusion to lead us if we swallow the same old patriarchal bullshit—"

"Hey. Drink up." Peter grabbed the bottle and sloshed more ouzo into the glasses. Last thing he needed was another goddamn sermon, heard enough as a kid to last a dozen lifetimes.

"Well, if it ain't Sir Galahad!" Now it was Crista, snapping a wad of bubblegum and nudging the other hooker with her, both barely-dressed in the ripped satin babydolls all the rage in the redlight district.

The other girl giggled, under the makeup and bleach another fourteen-year-old refugee.

Crista winked. "Come on, Mitchell, give you a discount."

Peter just shook his head. They headed off to troll the sailors, heads together, Crista whispering and her friend laughing.

Viv smirked. "Hey, Mitchell, *she*'s the one—?"

Chen elbowed her and pushed the ouzo bottle at Peter, who scowled and poured. Big barrel of laughs. So he'd tried to "save" the little snot from her pimp who'd given her a black eye, back when he'd first arrived in Piraeus. Story just wouldn't lie down and die.

Peter tossed back a shot and poured again. "*Yia sas.*" *Bottoms up*—which come to think of it was the perfect conclusion all round: The girls. The drinks.

The North and South Pole flags. He shoved the Pai-gow dice at Chen, and soon the second bottle was ebbing to the point where the sailors' dance on the broken dishes looked like fun.

A ripple of louder excitement washed through the dancers. The ripple wove its way past the hooting sailors to Peter's side, planted spike heels, and tossed back a short fringe of platinum blond. "You Peter Mitchell?"

He didn't know her—definitely not a local gal—but the face and voice were somehow familiar. And those narrow eyes, glitters of oddly pale azure.

Viv gasped. "But... you're Leeza Conreid! *Celebrity Smackback*. We get it almost on schedule over Athens Cable."

"The producers will be thrilled to hear it."

"Yeah, catching shows got dicey when wireless crapped out with all the geomag static. It's cable now, or chip download."

The stranger lifted an eyebrow. "You're wired?"

Viv shuddered. "No implants in this bod, Bless Goddess."

Ms. Conreid rolled her Siamese-cat eyes. "NeoLuddite?"

"No, Gaea Speaks. We're—"

"Yesterday's news, dolly." The gal reached down to snag Viv's crystal pendant, studying its Ariadne icon. Her nostrils flared and her jaw clenched, then she was dropping the talisman with a dismissive flick of her blood-red fingernails. "D'you mind? I've got business with Mr. Mitchell."

Chen, grinning, tugged Viv away into the smoke haze as the Conreid gal appropriated a chair. She was all skin-hugging black leathers and studs and big spiked bracelets and hair spiked out, too, crimsoned lips and pale pale skin, and it was really a ridiculous getup but maybe she was setting some nostalgia trend. He had to admit he liked it.

So he sat back while she made him her business proposition in a staccato spiel that managed to sound bored while her red-tipped fingers moved from stroking the bottle to running over his biceps. "...so all you have to do is get me through the closed Med League border. I've got a pass to interview Her Royal Highness Saint Ariadne." Venom suddenly eating through the cool mask.

Peter sat forward. "You think she really *is* the Demodakis heiress? I thought they'd denied it."

"No shit, Sherlock. But I've got the inside skinny."

He rolled his eyes. "It's a wild goose chase."

"Yeah, for the golden egg. Don't you catch the news feeds here in the boondocks? *'Where is Ariadne? Who is Ariadne?'* Fifty-three percent media saturation with these Savior healer stories. I get the scoop, it takes me up to prime time."

"And?"

"Big bucks riding on it, whoever finds her first—look at that cool million the Sons of the Prophet are offering for the privilege of snuffing her. By this point, they don't care if she's for real or not."

"Planning to cash her in?"

"Aren't you a gem." She shook her head. "But it's all ripe for debunking. Maybe she's not so saintly…." She shrugged. "They said you were the best at slipping through patrols. You in, or not?" Her index finger sidled up his arm, under his rolled-up sleeve as her lips parted for a glimpse of a pink tongue.

Something was off, that venom the only real glimpse under the come-on. A scam? Nobody knew if Ariadne was for real, let alone how to find her. But Conreid had contacts all right. A NeuroLink celebrity, however minor, didn't just wander into a Piraeus bar and pick up a Peter Mitchell. So what the hell, he had a nice buzz going. And he'd made the connection:

The iceberg-blue eyes, the lanky stalk, the promising pout right here in the flesh. That data chip one of his "relocating" clients had left onboard—a pirated Triple-X reissue from before Ms. Conreid had graduated to the networks, when she'd been just another NeuroPorn actress. *"Hot Kitten."*

Now it looked like she wanted to plug him into the picture. He didn't tell her she could stop talking him into the job. He was going stale, settled into the cozy smuggler's milk run, Greece-Italy-Spain, throw in a pinch of North Africa. He did tell her fair enough they had the proverbial camel's chance of getting through the Med League patrols and the Aegean pirates, not to mention he'd heard the Sons were in the area on a purge. Maybe it had to do with those Corybant warrior women blowing up an Arab chem-weapons plant in the name of their "Goddess reincarnate." But for the kind of gold standard Conreid was talking he wouldn't mind giving Saint Ariadne the finger, her and her duped devotees—one more holy scam. Ms. Media didn't need to clinch the deal.

But somehow they ended up at the docks. Grin gone lopsided, he swayed with the bottle and watched her prowl *Nereid*'s cabin in those skintight black leathers. The crimson talons jittered over his stuff on the built-ins. She snapped her fingers, took the bottle, pushed him through the doorway of his dinky stateroom onto the bunk.

And they're playing out the scene. He lets her direct, quick hands and flash of white silky skin beneath the unlaced vest, high little round breasts. He's fuzzy on details, but the flesh is willing, spirit weak, and God knows she's an expert, sucking him in, sucking him up and up and hot red dances behind his eyes. He looks down then.

Crimson lips, devouring him. Her eyes lock his—ice cold.

His gut goes empty and he's spinning into black alien space, up down onto a white cratered moon exploding over him and she's launching herself onto him, launching him into her, thrusting, demanding, her gleaming nails sweep down and a jolt of fire detonates and it's over.

He's blinking in a daze, chill white face of the moon floating over him. A red-smeared exultant smile.

She rolls off and away, watching the ceiling as she arches on her back, dips one businesslike fingertip in his spilled fluids and brings herself to a violent climax. She wipes her hands on the blanket, jumps up, says they'll leave in two hours. She's gone.

2

"FOCUS, *CHICA*..." LEEZA POPPED a criss-cross tab along with an STD bolus, yawned, stretched, and grimaced. "Showtime." She activated the portable senscorder she'd persuaded that horny tech geek back at the station to add to her requisition for this freelance assignment. Last chance now to get a cable news update before checking out of the Athens hotel and going off grid. Snapping the leads into her spinal implant, she Linked in.

*** "*Mediterranean updates for English speakers, with Colin Blackwell.*" And she's zooming through a maze of islands and blue water, swooping up to a talking head superimposed on an old ruin of marble columns.***

"Cheesy visuals." She flicked fingers, scanning. There:

*** *Traveler Advisory. 24-Hour Incident Reports.*

"...despite denials by Mediterranean League spokesman Spiridion Zervas." The image shifts to a photogenic young Greek man. Damn, Leeza would kill for those long eyelashes.

"Last night our forces repelled an attack on our headquarters— our capital—by the Sons of the Prophet terrorists. Eight of our brave soldiers were killed."

"And is it true that the Sons threaten more attacks unless *Tyrannos* Demodakis surrenders his daughter Ariadne—Saint Ariadne—to them?" A faceless voice off camera.

"I repeat, there is no basis to the rumor that *Despoinis* Demodakis is this supposed faith healer. The motive for these attacks is political, attempts to control our shipping lanes."

"The lanes that the Med League has itself seized in the last two years? What about the evidence that your forces were implicated in the sinking of the British freighter *Faraday* two months ago?"

"This interview is over." The Greek begins to turn away, then adds, "Be advised our forces are on high alert, and will not hesitate to defend our territory."***

"Terrific." Just for a second, doubt nibbled. "Fuck that shit." She hit Delete and finished packing.

3

PETER BLINKED AND SCRUBBED his gritty face with his hands. The scream of the turbos caromed inside his skull, glittering sea strobing as *Nereid* churned closer to the islands. He felt like hell.

He shot another look down through the forward hatch. His new client stirred in the bunk, frowning a pretty little frown in her sleep, blond halo gleaming. He shook his head. When those two hours had brought her back to the boat past midnight with her recording gear, to roust him out of his bunk, he'd almost told her the deal was off. But he could use the gold. He just hoped she wasn't planning more fun and games, because once was enough for educational purposes.

"Damn!" Off in the distance, a sharp flash. Reflection off glass or chrome?

He grabbed his binoculars. There. Throwing up a good-sized wake, bearing on his course.

"Shit." Still nothing but static on radar. He swung off course in a steep tilting curve, past a rock reef, got a larger islet between him and the approaching boat. He idled down, drifting. Standing on the pilot seat, he could just sight over the rock. Still couldn't make a flag, but it looked like a fast patrol boat.

"Just what I need...." He checked his chart, decided to chance it, hit the throttles and swung around tight starboard, raced across open water toward a larger, steep islet. Rounding it, he squinted, desperately scanning. There. Almost missed it, cut the throttles back, with a port thrust eased in close to the sheer inward-curving cliff, rocking on his own wake. He peered down side to side, watching for shallows, hoping to hell the chart wasn't obsolete already, but these islets didn't show signs of recent volcanics or quake uplift. And with the rising sea level, he figured he had a margin of error.

"All right." Dead ahead, looking at first like just an outcurved part of the islet, a jagged fang of rock nestled close, maybe a 30-foot wide channel between them. "Easy now, baby...."

Chugging along as close as he could to the surge lapping the cliff, he craned from side to side over the bridge. Thanked God and the mermaids the Aegean was so crystal clear he could see every sharp boulder etched below in cool blue. He held his breath as he eased *Nereid* in.

He put her into idle, jumped down to throw out the twin anchor lines, bow and stern, Greek custom a necessity here in this narrow cubbyhole. He killed the engines, stood staring out the skinny slot past stone walls, straining to hear.

Grinding engine noise, closer. He grabbed his assault rifle, gripped it in his sweaty mitts. Eyed the launcher disguised under a tarp and fishnet, his two wire-guided missiles pretty well useless in the constricted space, obsoleted Navy weapons so pricey on the black market they were only last ditch anyway. Out there, the engines sounded closer still, but no appreciable change in speed or bearing.

He sat up top, sweating it, ready for a scramble to cut the lines and shoot out the other side, speed his best defense. The distant boat rumbled closer. Pirates? That aggressive new Mediterranean League "nation" taking over shipping ports? Should have his head examined for taking this run.

Etse k'etse. A Greek shrug.

The approaching engine noise got louder. Then started to recede. Peter sagged and let out a breath. He took his rifle down to the wheelhouse.

"Any caffeine in this crate?" Ms. Conreid stood yawning.

He tossed her a plastic bulb. "Microwave's on the fritz."

She mumbled a casual obscenity, yawned, and popped the seal, gulping the unheated coffee. With a criss-cross tab for a chaser. She rubbed her eyes, fluffed up her hair, and stretched, nipples thrusting against a man's undershirt she'd taken scissors to.

"Mierda!" Peering into a hand mirror she pulled from an overnight kit. "Eyes all puffed-up, look like a dreck. I could use some ice cubes."

Peter shook his head and put the rifle back on its hooks.

She eyed it, then looked out at the rock walls. "Where the hell are we?"

"Waiting out a patrol boat." He tilted his head. "It's heading off now. Cheer up, you get to keep your speed bonus." He rummaged in the galley and found some crackers for his stomach, aspirin for his head.

She scowled into the mirror, brushing color on her eyelids. He pushed past her, out to the stern deck. He rubbed his eyes, swallowed the crackers, listened to the boat still receding.

"Leeza Conreid, Chip One, March Nineteen. On location: somewhere in the Aegean, on a dangerous race through the scorched-rock islands of the new Mediterranean League."

Peter whipped around. She'd brought out her media gear. Mini-cam on a tripod aimed at her perch on the starboard rail, gritty realismo with her carefully tousled head, makeup, and the sexy ripped T-shirt. Recorder leads ran from the expensive-looking portable master box to the camera, another set running under the rucked-up shirt at the base of her spine. Jacked into the subcutaneous insert his fingers had brushed the night before.

Peter shuddered. She was wired. Literally. Surgically equipped for direct interface with her spinal cord. Electric signals tapping, triggering raw nerves, and she plugged in casually as filing her nails.

Visceral memory jolt: dumb little Petey visiting his uncle's farm, cousin's dare ringing in his ears, and he grabs the live electric fence wire—

Peter jerked his stare from the NeuroLink lines. Ms. Conreid was producing a cool smile for the camera. "Destination: Thia Nea, island fortress of shipping tycoon and 'Emperor of Gems' Constantin Demodakis. He's crowned himself *Tyrannos* of the new nation pieced together like an ancient amphora from shards of Gulf War Three. But it's his daughter Ariadne who's put this bit of old Greece back on the map. Today, for the first time, you'll come face to face, Link to Link with the mystery woman— the inspiration for the Gaea Speaks movement, the rumored miracle healer, the latest incarnation from this age-old cauldron of saints and gods. Today we're going to meet the Med's reclusive new Savior.

"To find her among the still-skirmishing Balkan navies, pirates, Sons of the Prophet extremists, and smoldering radioactive hot zones, we're crossing borders without benefit of passport. Boat and captain have seen better days in the battles of Sinai and—"

"Can that crap!" Peter belatedly got moving as she swung the camera onto him. "That wasn't part of the deal." He thrust his hand over the lens.

"Hands off the equipment!" She glared up at him, pulling the camera unit back. "I'll morph over your ugly mug. Journalistic standards."

"Journalistic standards." He snorted. Serve her right if she did connect with the Demodakis kook. "You said you were out to debunk all that savior crock."

"Me, fall at her feet and kiss the hem of her robe? Not. Cult flea-brains just have to latch. Makes nice copy, all the hacks jumping on it. But they're clueless. Ariadne Demodakis ain't no dizzy peasant saint. Studied structural crystallography at a high-price California University."

"So what's your angle?"

A smirk. "That would be telling." She turned the camera back onto herself, flashed a dazzling smile, and shut it down. She reached to her lower back to pluck the recorder leads free. "So what do you think? Big story, you can be part of it. I won't ID you, but you'd score a fee if you gave me a neuro imprint. Sweating it at the wheel."

She dangled her leads with their spinal probe needles. "I've got electrode patches, you'll hardly feel a thing." Teeth gleamed. "Assuming you're sensate material. But with this baby," she patted the master box, "I can do a lot with even low-level links. I'm *good*."

His eyes fixed uneasily on the swinging leads with their glinting probes, and he swallowed down an irrational upsurge of nausea. "No thanks."

Laughter rang off the rock walls. "Chickenshit." She started to roll up the leads.

"Hold on. I want that stuff about me and the boat erased."

"Not! Freedom of the—"

"You want to get there, that part comes out."

She glared azure daggers, but he stared her down. Finally she shrugged and shook out the leads, pushing them back into her spinal insert with an almost-audible click. Crouching, she pulled shiny black goggles from her case, jacked their lines into the recorder, and slipped them on, pressing their ear buds into place. Hand groping for the recorder touchplate, she leaned back, face gone blank behind the curved black bug-eyes.

Long fingers twitched like a spider over the control spindle as Peter's glance veered to the mocking features gone empty as carved white stone. Before he could turn away she was grimacing, pulling the goggles off and blinking.

"Satisfied?"

"How do I know you erased it?"

Slow smile. "You'll just have to scan, won't you?"

He hesitated. The distant motor noise was still receding. "As long as I'm only receiving." He had to make an effort not to flinch from her fingers as she settled the goggles over his eyes. Which was ridiculous, but after last night he didn't want any part of what was between her and that electronic box.

"Don't worry, I won't steal your soul." She pushed the speaker buds into his ears.

Sealed into blackness, he felt her press a sticky electrode against the back of his neck. The patch was no big deal, just a low-level neural stim, and the circuits wouldn't work without the grounding. "Okay, go ahead—"

***Breath punched out of him, he's whirling backwards into a maelstrom of flashing colors, inward-sucking barrage exploding in his head a mad beast roar as pins and needles and icy heat flash through his body on a surge of nausea. He flails, fighting for balance as panic and numbing dread pour through him and he can't find any sense—

With a jolt, he's in a padded flight chair, acceleration thrusting him backwards under the impact of doubled gravity. Helmet on his head, oxygen mask over his face, his gloved hands gripping the armrests of the copilot seat of a supersonic jet. He vaguely wonders how he knows that. Beside him, the pilot manipulates the controls as the jet screams up and then suddenly reverses and plummets.

They're falling. Down from the high blue air and dazzle of sunshine. Into a rolling floor of dark cloud. A kaleidoscope of computer graphics flashes colors before his eyes, points and lines burgeoning into precise glowing geometries:

The globe is a blue curving grid, white and yellow weather patterns dancing over it. Red sprouting loops of the old, symmetrical geomagnetic field sagging, warping, fading out and in, twisting and flaring. The green ozone asterisks overlying it now, fluctuating, little blips zapped and dying. And the white swirling halos of hurricanes and typhoons curvetting across it all. The patterns accelerate, past and future blurring, strobing, engulfing the blue grid.

Armageddon.

A flare and it's gone. Dark clouds swallow him. A crackling flash of lightning, rain lashing, and the jet's bucking, tossed in the turbulence and sparking electricity—

Another jolt. He's perched on *Nereid*'s rail, feeling the boat's easy sway on the lines, smelling the salt air, a tingle of visceral anticipation building inside, jittering down his impossibly slender, pale arms and legs, hearing himself talking in Leeza Conreid's voice at the same time he's watching her face at a close angle giving him that cool smile.

"...radioactive hot zones and simmering volcanoes, we're crossing borders without benefit of passport—"

A blip, static hiss, flash of Leeza's face, teeth bared at the camera. Empty black grabs him, spinning***

4

LEEZA HAD TO LAUGH as the fucking idiot boat driver clawed at the goggles, his face gone pasty green.

"*Alto!* Let go." She snatched his hands away, peeled the electrode flap from his neck, and pulled off the goggles. "You'll screw up my gear."

He shuddered and scrubbed his face with his hands. "What was that? You turned up the gain on me, didn't you?"

"Big hombre can't take a little reverse stim?"

He shot a look at the recorder box and muttered, "It's warped."

She snorted. "For your information, you just got a free ride on a top-gun prerelease newsstim. So feel lucky."

"Free ride? Like last night? You get off on recording yourself, don't you? Selling the public your...."

"So original, Mitchell. All artists are whores?"

"Artists." He pushed past her. "I don't have time for this." He headed back through the cabin to the wheel.

Leeza rolled her eyes, coiled the leads, and stowed her gear. Typical NeoLuddite, freeze at the sight of a neural probe. She carried her gear into the cabin. Grabbed her embroidered neon toreador pants from a bag and pulled them on. Mitchell was checking instruments as she moved up beside him.

She leaned over the console, deliberately brushing him with a little shimmy.

"You mind?" He spread out some maps, making a big deal out of it.

She perched against the edge of the console and flashed him a mocking smile. "Important stuff? *Que macho.* Sure you don't want to show off your toys? How about an added eight per for some action here, your back only, at the wheel? Maybe fake some emergency."

She still had the crimson polish on. Perfect. Her long nails clicked across digital readouts. Her fingers stroked a knobbed joystick as she shaped her lips into a replay of last night's chill smile.

He clutched. She could see it.

She laughed merrily.

"Jesus Christ!" He plucked her hand from the controls. "I don't have to fake some emergency. That patrol boat's still out there, along with who knows what pirates or Sons of the Prophet. More solar flares with the geomag turbulence, too, screwing up radio reception, radar, satellite nav. So we're running by the seat of our pants here."

She froze for a second. Then she shrugged and hopped off the console. "They told me you were halfway competent."

He started up the engines in a roar and rumble. "We'll be underway again in a minute. Go up top, your victims will like the view through the islands."

"Ha. Ha." But she gathered her gear, wrestled it out and up the ladder onto the top platform, sneaked a shot of him hauling up the anchor lines.

He scrambled up to the wheel, and she edged over on the bench, wrinkling her nose at his sweaty stink adding to the general fishy ambiance onboard. The boat eased forward. The rock walls pinched in tighter, and she gnawed her lip, trying to keep the camera steady.

"Ohh—!" She caught a sharp breath as they broke out of the shade into open water, light pouring over her. The camera swung in a dizzy swoop: cliff towering above, sapphire sea below, razor-sharp white island gleaming off in the distance. The engines roared and with a surge the boat was rushing

Leeza into a dazzle of spray and shrieking wheeling gulls. It sounded like someone else whispering, "Maximal...."

She gripped the camera. "Unreal!" Almost like Virtual Reality. Absolute immersion—that light! Sunlight quivering alive off rock and sea, shimmering, sky intense blue, boat plunging in a throbbing sexual rhythm, all her cells scintillating to old Sol's radiation. *Radiance.* She suddenly groks why those ancient rubes worshipped the sun. It's real here. *Sur*reality. And Leeza's the camera eye, nerve-ends tingling and soaking it in, storing it all to replay forever in the Link.

"Look!" His hand grasps her shoulder.

"Hey! Watch the groping."

He points his chin forward, grins.

She frowns and looks down. *"Madre!"*

Dolphins. Leaping alongside the bow of the boat, plunging right up and down in the frothing wake. A dark eye gleams, and Leeza swears the creature's grinning up at her. Reflexes whip the camera to her eye, and she's got them, two at once arching clean clear out of the sea in perfect slippery curves. Forever. She lowers the camera, sighing.

Mitchell laughs. "Dolphins are good luck around here. Go on down. Hang on."

She remembers her pose then, gives him the frosty stare, but he just waves her on, grinning like an idiot. She grabs her gear, gets it down that ladder and stashed in the cabin, gropes forward gripping the rail, and they're still there.

One of them leaps up, so close she can almost touch that sleek back, and she's laughing, leaning half over the rail, hanging on as the spray soaks her and the boat crashes up and down, racing those beautiful sea creatures dancing the sea and the air. Trying to touch them she nearly loses it takes a header into the sea but who cares she's alive what a rush what a RUSH!

"Maximal!"

A last leap and plunge, and the dolphins are gone into the deeps. Leeza reels back from the bow, dizzy, arms out to the sky, slips and plops right onto her butt on the deck. She's still laughing. She shakes her drenched hair back and squints up. Mitchell's laughing, too, up on the platform, throwing his head back in a real belly-shaker. Laughing at Leeza Conreid? Oh, no, *with* her. Yeah, right, what a crock.

Leeza jerked to her slippery feet, grabbed the rail, flipped him the bird and stalked into the cabin. Shit. She had a job to do. Her butt really hanging out here, if she didn't get at least an interview. Corporate talking cutbacks, axing her show. Dead in the water. She shuddered, glancing at the big rifle on its hooks above her. That missile launcher on the back of the boat, she'd sneaked a peek under the tarp. And maybe a patrol boat after them. Maybe *really* dead in the water...

No. That was Mitchell's job, she was paying him to worry. *Delegate. Focus.*

She had homework to do. Keep her indexes up-to-date, *Madre* she was getting some prime material here. The scenery, the scene. Incredible. Maybe another feature, mysteries of the lost islands, the magic dolphins, Atlantis and all that shit... They might go for it, the mystical angle, fit with the Doomsday hysteria, she could really pull out the stops, stretch the stylistic envelope.

Gear strapped down on the galley bench, neuro leads connected, scanning goggles on. Fingertips on the control spindle, she's flying down the Link into indexed storage:

> ***"...we're crossing borders without benefit of passport. Boat and captain have seen better days in the battles of Sinai and—"
>
> "Can that crap!" Mitchell jerks forward over the deck, square-cut tan face scowling down, dark beard stubble, *que macho* for little Leeza's camera as his ham hand thrusts out and the scene goes dark***

Behind the goggles, she grins. *Gotcha double, Stiff.* She can't believe the nondigerati sometimes, so clueless. All she had to do was transfer the stolen bits to storage, replay him the blank, with a neurotweak thrown in since he's being such a jerk.

She skipped back to the jet sequence she'd thrown at him, rode it for fun down the boiling clouds and jagged lightning, thinking maybe she could clip a few bites for intro on the Ariadne feature, state of the world catastrophe, etcetera. Newsstims the latest candy for the disaster junkies: "*Live* it in the Link." Not that Leeza bought the Doomsday scenarios, eco-disasters and the projections of RP-Hansen's cascading fatalities, cost of the leper isolation camps on top of all the other economic meltdowns and the electrosmog impacts—blah, blah, blah. There was always a crisis. Just part of the media hype, crazy circus watching the scientists scrambling for fixes.

And all the military boyz—situation normal—just wanted to build a bigger penis.

But the Ariadne story, they'd sit up and pay attention. The ticket up for Leeza Conreid. *"Celebrity fluff"*—hah! She could cut it in the trenches. Lips pressed tight, she scanned what little she'd dug out of archives.

Quick series of still-shots: Hazy Greek crowd, the big cheese *Tyrannos* Demodakis raising a hand—handsome dark hard face and max intense eyes—and behind him, just turning away, glimpse of a black-haired young woman, face averted.

And the old one—boarding-school portrait, anonymous rows and that one young face, eyes focused beyond the camera. Amplifying, computer-augmenting and bringing it close on the Link, Leeza's skill morphs the face into something ageless, beautiful, carved marble goddess in a lost temple gazing into eternity. Capturing the image, she can almost make those opaque eyes meet hers, open their secret gates—

Leeza bit down on her lip, tasted blood, and shook her head sharply. She gripped the spindle, leapfrogging into more newsstims:

    *** Tall redhead in a polyply toga holding a big chunk of rock crystal on the shores of the new Death Valley Sea, disciples chanting odes to Mother Gaea. She raises the crystal flashing in the sun, intones, "Hear us, Great Mother. Heal us. Bring us your daughter Ariadne to teach us the way...." ***

    *** Crone face under a dark kerchief, seamed and sunbaked to brown leather, nodding and smiling gap-toothed. She babbles in Greek, and the pretty young man with the mike turns to the camera, translating, "When we brought Stelios to her, he was dying of the evil curse—" He coughs. "That is, Rapid-Proliferating Hansen's, the so-called RIP leprosy. She says that Saint Ariadne touched him and he was cured."

    Behind him, the old woman gestures emphatically, babbling again. The reporter frowns, translates, "The water. She blessed the holy water with her sacred stone and he drank it and the scales peeled from his eyes and face."

    Closeup of the earnest reporter. "Another story of the mysterious recoveries that have triggered more cult demonstrations. The ecoterrorist Corybantes, too, have sworn to enlist Ariadne, and have reportedly made a kidnapping attempt. They must beat the Sons of the Prophet: Fatwa, a death sentence, is declared against the blasphemer Ariadne Demodakis...." ***

Leeza jacked out of the Link and pulled off the goggles. She stared out the window over the restless sea as her hands tightened into fists, nails digging into her palms. Out there, somewhere. *Ariadne.*

Cool blue rippled over shadowed deeps. Monsters down there, nightmares, old fear failure death swimming up to grab her *Madre* no good thinking why what if she was fucked forever. No. She *had* to find her—

The boat lurched over the choppy waves, swung in a tight curve around some jagged rocks, and they were shooting for the open sea past another little island. Leeza grabbed the table for balance.

A sudden roaring in her ears—crashing, echoing. Not the engines. Guns. Bullets. Where? Exploding, splintering the sea across the bow. Leeza screamed and dove under the table.

5

UP ON THE BRIDGE, Peter was just nudging the wheel, taking them past the end of the islet into an open stretch. He whistled, tune stolen by the wind.

A rattling roar off to port. Bullets sprayed across *Nereid*'s bow, ripping over the sea.

"Christ!" Peter flinched down, alarm crisping his hangover. Reflexes took over: Swing hard to starboard. Gun it. Into evasive.

More automatic fire, crashing from portside. He curvetted side to side, shot a look back, saw the patrol boat churning up to speed after him. Must have been hiding behind the islet. Looked like a four or five-inch cannon up front, maybe a 12 millimeter machine gun aft.

"Bloody hell!" He gave it full throttle, bucked forward. More staccato gunfire, off to starboard.

"Shit!" He wove back to port, and bullets shredded the sea off to port. They were driving him, weaving side to side in the scream of turbos and erupting spray. But it looked like they weren't trying to hit, just stop him.

"Screw you!" He yanked the wheel, tilting sharp starboard to a clatter of loose something down below, clinging to the wheel slippery with sweat and spray as they tilted farther too steep Christ don't broach don't lose it but then they righted and shot out toward another islet and cover. Maybe he could return fire if he'd just get a breathing space—

Whumpf. A deeper concussion, and the sea erupted ahead of him.

"Damn!" He squinted over his shoulder. Boat still gaining on them. Whipping flag—dark blue, or black? Pirates? Flag didn't ring a bell, if it was pirates or the Prophet boys he should turn right now and nail them with a missile while he had the chance. If he was over the border, and he fired on the Med League, he'd be signing his own death warrant. "*Damn* it!"

Quick look back. Blue-white flared. Another deep bone-shaking *whumpf*.

The shell exploded right in front of *Nereid*, sea roaring up in a foaming gout, lashing over the bridge, tossing the boat.

Blinded, Peter clutched the wheel. The explosion echoed out of memory:

Enemy destroyers overhead and they were trapped below in the submarine, wallowing tin can among the minefield. The flash and then the screaming—

"Mitchell!" Clattering down below.

Nereid bucked and floundered into the chop, flinging Peter off the wheel and against the rail, razor taste of adrenaline slicing through him. He groped back to the wheel, eased the throttles, got her stabilized.

The patrol boat closed in, flashing a warning light.

"Hang on down there, we're coming around."

"What!" she yelled. "You're giving up? Get us out of here, Mitchell you dreck! *Do* something!"

Do your patriotic duty. Complete the mission at all costs.

Fuck that shit.

He let the engines idle, pulled out a white flag, and waved it overhead. "Nothing *to* do!" he yelled back to Conreid. Then muttered, "Knew I should've had my head examined...." He climbed down to the deck, peered in, snorted at her huddled under the galley table glaring up at him. "Get your ass ready to negotiate, Ms. Conreid. And better hope they aren't Sons of the Prophet, or you'll wish you never heard of Saint Ariadne."

6

SHE STRODE DOWN THE rocky path, her donkey trotting along in the cool morning as they rounded the headland and broke into a spill of sunlight. Below, a cove glimmered clear vibrant blue—mirror for the cloudless sky and white cliffs cutting pure lines against it. The air shimmered, humming electric with the fresh day.

Ariadne Demodakis stopped, filling her lungs with the air's astringent tang, tingling with the brand-new, ages-old promise of dawn. Life surged in her, pulsing with the world's heartbeat.

A shadowy twinge. She knew even as she savored this rare morning that it was only a brief reprieve from all those urgent voices clamoring for attention: the RP-Hansen's victims, the healing experiments her scientists were running back at the lab, the communications conglomerates' announcement that they were raising the already-dangerous transmission power on the remaining microwave towers, the latest plan to capture more shipping lanes by her father the *Tyrannos*—her jailkeeper. And this beloved island, her birthplace become her prison.

She took a deep breath and pushed those strident voices back inside a sphere of silence, summoning the cool serenity of a marble statue to smooth her face. Within that quiet, she had learned to find her freedom.

Today, this fragile glory of the dawn, wasn't meant for shadows and clamor. The world even stricken was such a power of beauty it sounded her depths like a bell and she could only ring with it, send her voice pealing out to the earth and sea and sky in reverent praise.

"Chairete!" Rejoice.

Lifting her face to the sky, she turned slowly with outstretched arms, stepping to an ancient dance of thanks-giving.

A nudge at her back startled her. "Iris!" She turned to her donkey who carried the waterskins strapped to a pack saddle. "All right, no more dawdling." She smiled and gathered the lead rope.

The path took them around another headland, dropping toward the village spread along a pebble beach. An old stone windmill spun its sails in the breeze, pumping water from an underground spring. The climbing sun was already heating the rock wall of Fofoula's garden on the edge of the settlement, stirring scents of herbs and dust.

"Despoina Demodaki! You're out early today." Fofoula, drying her hands on her apron, hurried from her doorway with a glass bottle. "Did you bring more of the holy water?"

Ariadne filled the bottle with her activated mineral springwater. "Don't forget, all you need is a small drink each evening, for the pain."

"Despoina Demodaki! *Despoina* Demodaki!" Two little girls and a boy came pelting down the dirt road.

"The holy water. Mother says can you come?" The boy caught a breath, panting. The girls, suddenly shy, looked at the ground, gripping their skirts.

"Tell them I'm on my way."

The children raced back toward the village square as badly-amplified bouzouki music broke out over the housetops.

"That Nikos!" Fofoula's husband Yiorgos joined them, shaking his head. "He can't wait to start the party."

Fofoula touched Ariadne's arm. "Come to the celebration. It's Nikos's name day."

Ariadne hesitated. How long since she'd been to any kind of celebration? *"Endaksi."* All right. "I'll go."

Low stucco houses closed in around them, laundry flapping from lines and chickens pecking the dry dirt yards. They passed the ruined, blackened walls of the old two-room school bombed during the Sons of the Prophet attack the year before. Beyond it, the new school gleamed in its fresh coat of white, with blue-painted door and lintels.

The villagers were already gathered in the dusty square, in front of the crumbling masonry chapel and the combined *kafenion*-grocery store. Nikos, the proprietor, was spruced up in a garish plaid jacket, mustache waxed to black points. He snapped another cassette into a battered antique boombox, turning up the volume in a barrage of hissing tape and singing voices. Children in patched skirts and shorts wove screaming and laughing around legs as an old man danced by himself, eyes closed. Women with headscarves sat on wooden chairs, whispering and laughing. Plates of cookies and breads, bottles and glasses filled a long table.

"*Despoina* Demodaki! Welcome. Welcome. You honor us." Nikos hurried forward, hands outstretched.

Heads turned, voices dying, and Ariadne braced herself. All those faces, watching her. Curiosity, eagerness, speculation, caution, resentment against the rich crazy Demodakis in her dusty peasant skirt.... And the worst: reverence.

A matron rushed up, then dropped to her knees to grasp Ariadne's hand and kiss it. *"Despoina sancti! Efcharisto." Thank you.*

"No, no, Ksanthi! Please." Ariadne tugged her to her feet.

"You saved my mother," *Kyrias* Mamalakis insisted, clutching her hand.

"The chapel, too, by the Grace of God," a younger woman piped up. "And the children have a new school, thanks to you… And to *Tyrannos* Demodakis, of course," she added hastily.

"Pah! It wasn't the *Tyrannos* who saved us from those filthy Turks." A man in a fisherman's sweater spat to the side.

"We send thanks to God for you," Ksanthi added, still clinging to Ariadne's hand.

"Please. This is Nikos's party." Ariadne managed a bland smile, nodding at the villagers.

"There would be no party, no village at all if you hadn't stopped those boats and their bombs." *Kyrie* Mamalakis had stepped up to take his wife's arm.

Ariadne closed her eyes and took a deep breath, fighting a shudder at the visceral memory:

The Sons of the Prophet attack boats breaching the outer islands's defenses, intent on capturing and executing the blasphemous "Saint Ariadne" and stopping her father's expansionist Med League. Thundering explosions, blinding flares, ground-shaking impacts of the missiles in the night. An urgent voice over the radio, "They've hit the village school, the headmistress is killed!" Her father's calm response, "They're entering the minefield waters now. That will stop them." But it hadn't. The pale blips on radar kept coming, winding through the labyrinthine safe passage past reefs and shallow mines that only the Med League navigators knew. A traitor onboard?

After that, memory blurred to frantic cries, orders, missiles launched but mostly intercepted, screams of wounded soldiers, and suddenly Ariadne was swept into a dark vortex of grief and rage and the force of a hissing subterranean power coiling up through her to explode outward in pulses of fury.

Blinding pain, then darkness. When she awoke, her father was staring down at her, the soldiers crossing themselves and whispering, "A miracle! Saint Ariadne."

They told her that when she screamed and went rigid, the attacking boats veered off course into the mines and exploded, while the defense radar blanked out and the compass spun as if seeking reason....

Ariadne shook her head. It was only coincidence, of course, one of the anomalous geomagnetic fields engulfing the island, though apparently only very locally. She had started tracking her increasing headaches and heightened sensitivity to sound and odd sensations, and now realized that they corresponded with the episodes of geomagnetic null phases.

"...grateful for your holy water. *Efcharisto,*" Kyrie Mamalakis was finishing.

She took another steadying breath. "Please, today is for Nikos." Her bland smile in place, she moved forward with Fofoula into the village square.

A stout, graying matron pushed closer to Ariadne, smoothing her crucifix and necklaces of seed pods. "Well, well, you're going to join in the fun? About time, Ariadne. We'll have some dancing, maybe find you a husband."

"Juliana, please don't—"

"Hah!" A scowling matron rose from her folding chair. "The Demodakis doesn't need a husband, when she can steal another woman's as she pleases. *Magdalena!*" She spat and stalked off.

Ariadne went stiff. Biting back an angry retort, she raised her chin, daring the rest to accuse her.

"Tell that lazy Manolis of yours to eat a dish of bull's balls!" Yiorgos shouted after the departing matron. "Then you won't have such a sour face!"

Laughter broke out among the men, the women hiding smiles behind their hands. Ariadne let out a breath, envying Yiorgos his easy ways.

He was striding forward now, raising his arms, bellowing, "Where in

Hades are you hiding the ouzo, Niko? You penny-pinching old fart! You think that name-saint of yours will bless you for another year if you keep us all thirsty?"

A roar of laughter, the men hustling Nikos into the shop. They emerged clutching bottles, grinning. Someone was pressing a paper napkin into Ariadne's hands, with a powdered-sugar *kourambeade.*

The special cookie her American mother had learned to bake for celebrations, always letting little Ariadne help. She tried to remember her face so beautiful then, before the cancer ravaged it and then stole her away. Blinking quickly, Ariadne bit into the cookie, barely tasting its sweetness.

"*Despoina?*" A teenaged girl in the traditional head-scarf, lips bold with orange lipstick but trembling on a shy smile, was standing before her, holding a half-grown puppy. "Will you take him? He won't eat, he needs your holy water."

Ariadne—bemused in the uproar of music, laughter, shrilling voices, gesturing hands, darting children—found herself with an armful of wriggling fur, a pink tongue licking her hand.

A louder roar rolled over the crowd. A motor launch, speeding to the cove's quay. A shout. Heads turned. Commotion at the cove end of the square, and a line of soldiers in blue strode into the open space, pushing through the villagers.

"*Despoina* Demodaki!" One of her father's lieutenants stopped stiffly before her, the men falling into a row behind him. Sunlight glinted off the geometric white insignia on their shirts.

Voices died. Someone cut the music, echoes fading off the walls.

"A message came from the *Tyrannos.* You're needed at the house immediately." The lieutenant, expressionless, stared past Ariadne's shoulder.

Vague muttering behind her. She pulled back her shoulders, chin lifting. Of course she was needed for her father's schemes, not wasting time with her healing experiments. The soldiers avoided her eyes, stirring uneasily, and one of them furtively touched the holy medallion at his throat.

"Here." Ariadne stepped past the lieutenant, thrusting the puppy into the nearest soldier's arms.

The young man startled, stared down at the puppy, looked at Ariadne and broke into a grin. Stifled laughter from another one. The soldier with his armful shot a look at his superior's livid face and sobered.

Ariadne turned back to the lieutenant. "I'm not done here." She turned to the watching villagers and gestured at Nikos. "Music! Let's dance."

Someone snapped in another antique cassette, mandolin crying over the square, an old tune.

More strings, crescendoing. Ariadne lifted her chin, raising her arms and turning her head to one side. A man stepped up beside her, then two young girls. More of the villagers. A long straggling circle, arms out, linked.

Slowly, deliberately, they raised their right feet, crossed over, dipped. Rose and cross-stepped again. Swaying now, the music picking up tempo, momentum, knees bending, rising and swinging, hands gripping arms as they danced faster. Feet pounding up dust to glimmer in the sunlight.

The music swelled, ringing celebration from the house walls, lapping like the sea on the stony beach. The dancing circle ebbed and flowed to the surge.

∞

An hour later, she stood on the terrace of her father's house, watching the wind shiver cat's-paws over the translucent blue shallows at the foot of the cliffs. Soldiers stood stiffly at attention near the stone parapet, faces carefully blank and gazes fixed past Ariadne as she turned from the view.

Her uncle Stefanos strode past the line of soldiers, breeze ruffling his black slacks and white silk shirt, sapphire ring flashing. Beaky nose thrust upwards, he planted his feet and fixed a dark glare on Ariadne.

"You countermanded Constantin's orders for the laser allocation."

"We need to complete our study."

"Your study." He snorted. "Why can't you accept the hand of God in this plague? Maybe you'd like to take over for the Lord Himself and feed them all with loaves and fishes? Here's more for you." He swung around and waved a contemptuous hand at the peasant boy, perhaps ten years old, and the crone in shabby black cowering on the terrace.

They were still wet from the antiseptic shower the soldiers sprayed on any of the pilgrims picked up by the patrol boats. They'd brought empty jugs in their leaking old *caique*, risking the closed border to beg Ariadne for her "holy water."

She pulled her shoulders back, stepped past her uncle, and knelt beside the old woman, touching her arm. "How long has he shown the signs?" She reached to raise the boy's lowered face, livid with the scaly red scabs and the blisters, the collapsed nose and the terminal-stage nodules swelling around his eyes and mouth. As she touched the boy's face, the soldiers gasped. She had assured them that her researchers' new studies and the epidemiology showed the syndrome was not contagious, though it seemed to build on a formerly inactive presence of Hansen's bacteria. The triggering mechanism remained elusive, but Ariadne was growing more certain it was connected to the increased electromagnetic pollution and NeuroLink technology. The World Health Organization would not publish her lab's results without extensive corroboration, so people still feared contagion and put misguided faith in the isolation camps.

The old woman was making the bottom-up sign of the Orthodox cross over her breast. "He's been cursed for three months, Blessed One." She sighed. "We think he was hiding the rash before that."

Ariadne nodded, took the boy's rigidly curled hands and examined the misshapen finger stubs, the proliferating skin masses turning his hands into lumpy mitts. She closed her eyes, darkness shuddering through her as the boy's dread and heavy numbness invaded her own hands. She forced herself to maintain her contact, willing warmth and sunlight to reach him, but knowing that for this boy it was too late.

Taking a deep breath, she steadied herself, rose and gestured toward the nearest soldiers. "Please take them to the clinic. We'll do what we can."

The soldiers stepped back, away from the boy, and one crossed himself. Farther down the line, a different soldier stepped forward in a glimmer of sunlight catching his shiny purple socks—Yannis, who always flashed her his happy grin when he passed by on his duties. He kissed his holy medallion. "I'll take them, Ariadne *Sancti*. I'm not afraid."

The old woman scuttled forward on hands and knees to kiss Ariadne's feet, and Yannis had to pry her loose, guiding her with the limping boy toward the terrace steps. Ariadne blew out a breath and turned to see her uncle glaring.

"You think what you're doing helps these people? *Poh-poh-poh!* It's only a distraction." Stefanos stepped over to her, pushing his face close. "Now listen. Constantin will be home from Headquarters in a few days, and he expects to see some progress from his technicians on the laser weapon. Your pet healing experiments will just have to wait. He's indulged you so far, allowing your specialists time with the laser, but that's finished now. Constantin has completed security at the new facility and will relocate the laser there. For your safety, he'll also relocate you to Headquarters."

She jolted back from him, from the image of the squat, ugly fortifications he'd built at the port on Naxos. "I can't live there! And what about the Hansen's patients?"

"They'll be moved to a proper isolation camp. You may continue to receive the pilgrims, under guard, and give them your holy water, but this science project of yours has gotten out of hand. It's a waste of resources."

"But I'm paying for the research myself—"

"Enough. You seem to forget it's *you* these pharmaceutical mercenaries are after! And you ought to thank the Lord and the *Tyrannos* those cursed Sons of the Prophet haven't made good on their new threats. You'd better put your heart into helping us build a strong nation that can protect you and our people."

"My heart!" she cried, despite herself. "You'd like to own it, and my soul, too. Weapons and power! Taking over the shipping ports. That's all you men care about." A contemptuous thrust of her hand. "Can't you see, none of that will matter if we can't find a way to protect everyone from the unbalanced global fields and the electromagnetic pollution? This pandemic is only the first, but we're making progress here, and if Father would only let me visit additional sites to test—" She bit it back. She was a prisoner here, if in a gilded cage, and soon to trade her island for a fortress of steel. Was it too late to escape?

"To test what?" Her uncle was eyeing her, close, suspicious. "I swear, Niece, if you're hiding something...."

She summoned the coolness of marble, made her face a stony mask. The wind plucked strands from her braid, whipping them across her uncle's eyes.

"*Christos!*" He paced again, then turned back to her, his lips twitching with a reluctant smile. "*Ariadne-mou....* God in His infinite wisdom has seen fit to entrust such a sacred gift to a mere *koritsi*." A mere girl. "But don't forget it's the men who shelter you, who make your visions work in the world." He strode off, followed by the rest of the soldiers.

The wind whispered, sang, howled. Ariadne stared down at the sapphire sea, waves crashing against the rock cliff at the breakwater. *Lithos Athanatos kai Akinetos* — their family motto, from generations of traders and gemcutters, to the new *Tyrannos*: *Eternal and Unyielding Stone.*

7

A DARK BLUE FLAG with squared Greek zigzags in white snapped overhead as the cutter chopped the waves. Nobody was talking, wouldn't even let the media gal trot out her credentials. The only thing they'd made clear was that Mitchell and Ms. Conreid were now "guests" of the Mediterranean League.

Peter leaned against the stern rail next to the 12-millimeter machine gun and a sailor keeping an eye on him. There was another 12-mm up forward alongside the five-inch gun for lobbing shells, and the twin diesels were supplemented with a pumpjet engine for speed. Poor old *Nereid,* bobbing and wallowing on the tow line, hadn't stood a chance. He'd have to do some fast talking this time.

Etse k'etse. They were damn lucky it was a Med League patrol hauling in their catch, not the Sons. And it looked they were following the same course Conreid had paid for, to the Demodakis home base on Thia Nea. The engines hummed down as they cut speed approaching the bare island, white rock cliffs wincingly bright even through his shades. He rubbed his temples, hangover still throbbing with the engines. They seemed to be taking a circuitous route toward the island, weaving closer in a looping course as the sailor they'd left onboard *Nereid* powered her up and snugged in closer behind the cutter.

"*Siga, siga.*" *Slow and easy.* Another sailor portside gestured up to the flying bridge, and they slowed again, edging starboard before making another sweeping curve and heading for a rocky breakwater where waves dashed themselves to foam against the cliff.

More shouts, gestures, and they were aiming for a narrow entrance to what looked like a cove.

Peter moved to the port rail, craned over the side, couldn't see anything darker in the deep purple-blues. But that itchy sixth sense was prickling his back again, and he could feel them down there. Mines. He closed his eyes, fought off a shudder.

"*Efthia*," the sailor was calling out. *Straight ahead.*

Peter blinked. They were easing through the cut in the breakwater that nearly sealed off a circular cove, into a fishing harbor where gulls swooped and cried. He took a deep breath of the fresh salt breeze.

Vaulting over the side and onto the concrete quay before the cutter touched the bumpers, he raised his eyebrows and gave a humorous shrug toward Leeza for the benefit of the guards on board. Still silent, they gripped their automatics—looked like Chinese design recycled plastic—but didn't stop him as he grabbed a line and grinned at the sleepy-looking reception committee in blue uniforms. Probably hauled out of siesta.

"*Kali spera.*" He waved an arm at the men grappling lines. "*Siga, siga.*" He directed, helped them snug bobbing *Nereid* up against rotting tires.

He took another breath of hot air spiced now with the smell of fish and tar. Sun glared off the quay, shattered across the clear turquoise cove and narrow stony shingle, blazed over stark cliffs and the rock slope zigzagged by a goat path. He tilted his face, tracing the trail up to a gleam of windows. White walls and blue-painted balconies of a low villa shimmered in an impossible patch of green. Mirage?

Above it, at the top of the cliff and real enough, a missile launcher hunkered.

He swiped his forearm over his face, sweating now in the sheltered cove, and turned back to help secure the boat.

One of the guards stayed beside him, young *pallikar* swaggering with his pistol and the plain blue uniform he'd gussied up with a gold sash, cool as long as everybody kept up the pecking order. That was fine with Peter. He played along, politely greeting the young boys and sunbaked old men in baggy pants and cracked boots who wandered over from the taverna at the head of the quay.

He shot a look up at the cutter deck. Conreid had given up on whining, cajoling, and threatening. She slouched against the cabin in a strip of shade, arms crossed, face hidden by a floppy straw hat, one sandalled foot jigging as she ignored the sailors eyeing her skintight tank top and pants. Lucky it wasn't the Prophet boys picked them up. Though her outfit would have been a big hit in the slaver *souks*.

She raised her face and he grinned, giving her a mocking salute. She glared and lowered the hat.

A shout from the head of the quay. Hubbub, voices raised, dogs and chickens scattering, a goat jumping down onto the beach. The crowd broke apart as a stocky middle-aged man strode past the small docked *caiques* at the head of more men in blue. Peter's audience deserted him, swarming for the big cheese.

The man nodded and said a few words to the old-timers, then came on toward *Nereid*. He wore dark slacks and a white silk shirt open at the neck, plain but expensive, with a gold chain peeking out and a blue gem the size of a grape on his pinky. His gray hair was thick and wiry, face weathered brown, dark eyes flanking a high-bridged beak of a nose steady on Peter.

The soldiers moved in to back him up. Peter noted the holstered automatics, the embroidered insignia with the squared zigzag, the childish bright additions like a chrome-yellow cap, a multi-colored woven belt, one moth-eaten fringy epaulet, even a pair of shiny purple disco socks. But they rearranged themselves efficiently behind their leader, eyes alert on Peter.

Before he could start his song and dance, there was a tussle on the deck above.

Ms. Conreid pushed through the guards. "*Carajo*! Just let me—"

Hands grabbed her. A kick and a curse, and the neon-pink legs strode down the gangplank. The leader turned with a raised eyebrow, shaking his head at a soldier who moved to stop her. He flicked a contemptuous eye over her outfit.

She clapped a pale hand over her hat as a gust off the cove licked past. "Take me to Ariadne Demodakis."

At the name, the man's face went from scornful to stone cold. He gestured sharply at the soldiers, and two in the back with rifles stepped forward, bringing them up into ready position as two more reached for Conreid, pulling her back. The leader turned his back dismissively on the woman, eyes locking on Peter with new hostility. The rifles came around to bear on him, along with a row of automatics from the cutter deck.

Sweat broke out on his back. He shot a furious glare at Conreid. Smiling innocuously at the Greek honcho, he spread his open palms. "Now wait. We're all reasonable men, right?" He gestured toward tethered *Nereid*. "You can see, I'm just a businessman, hired to bring the lady here."

"With what purpose?" the man replied in Greek.

Peter shifted gears and language. *"Kali spera."* He bowed his head a polite fraction. "We apologize for the...." He searched for the word, his Greek vocabulary pretty basic. "For the unwelcome arrival. The lady is a journalist, who assures me she has permission to see Ariadne Demodakis." He hoped that came out right. "Could we speak in English, *Kyrie*....?"

The man didn't supply a name. "In these islands, we speak Greek." He glanced back at Conreid, who was looking like she might be warming up for another outburst.

Peter shook his head at her, made a cutting motion.

The Greek turned back to him. "You have violated our borders. We will confiscate your boat."

"Now, wait—" Peter caught himself, spread his palms. "Can we discuss options?" Have to get him into the marketplace mode, most Greeks loved bartering.

"I see little of value you have to offer us, *Kyrie*...?"

"Mitchell. Peter Mitchell." Peter stuck out his hand. *"Kyrie*...?"

"So. American?" The man ignored his hand, again refusing to supply a name, blatantly defying Greek courtesy. Not good. "A spy, no doubt, for the Turks." He tilted his head contemptuously toward *Nereid,* and the missile launcher the sailors had revealed beneath its net camouflage. "They and their Russian allies used such trickery in the last war, and they think we'll believe these fishing nets now?"

Peter raised his hands. "It was confiscated during the war. I... acquired it later."

"Stolen? So you're a thief as well as a spy."

The sweat was drenching Peter's back now, a trickle running down his face. "All right. I stole the boat, but I figured the Feds owed me. They..." He broke back into English. "They were screwing me over on my medical discharge, I'd paid my dues twice over, me and everyone else in that fiasco at Sinai—" He bit it off, blew out a breath.

"Now we make progress." The man responded still in Greek. "So we see here an American who has invaded our waters, a smuggler defying international law, a soldier absent without leave, and a thief. And you want to negotiate with us?"

"Sailor," Peter offered faintly. "Navy."

Was that finally a flicker of a smile? "I see. Very well, Peter Mitchell, what was your specialty in the military service?"

"Navigation. Communications."

The man studied him. "So. We may have a use for you, after all, in the Mediterranean League. We're expanding the patrols on our shipping lanes, and our men need training." He eyed *Nereid* again. "Possibly this old spy vessel could be useful, as well, if you prove we can trust you."

"No, no." Peter shook his head. "I'm done with the military."

"Very well, it's your decision." He gestured toward the nearest soldier, barked out a quick order Peter couldn't follow, but the soldier stepped over and put his pistol to Peter's head, clarifying the whole situation. Things were going downhill fast. "We execute spies in these islands." He nodded at the soldier and started to turn away.

"Stop! *Stomat!*" Peter blurted. "Okay. You… persuaded me."

Again the flicker of a smile. "A wise decision. We will talk later." He gestured to the soldier, who lowered his pistol.

Peter sagged in relief.

The Greek started back up the quay, then paused in front of Leeza, still held by her guards, her pale eyes wide, rolling like a startled colt's from Peter to the honcho. "*Magdalena.*" Whore. He shook his head and said something to the guards, who started to drag her back toward the cutter gangplank.

"No!" Her face suddenly morphed from terror to rage. "Hands off, you gorillas!" Insanely, the twit was struggling again, kicking, jerking forward and wrenching an arm free to grab the head man's arm as the soldiers dragged her back and the man barked an order.

Conreid hung on. "Listen, bub, don't pull this machismo on me. This is Leeza Conreid you're talking to. I need to see Ariadne, and you better take me to her." She waggled her fingers in front of his face. Sunlight caught a thick, engraved platinum ring she hadn't been wearing onboard, kindled the facets of a big sapphire, and flung blue sparks.

Peter blinked. The boss was grasping Leeza's wrist and scrutinizing the setting of her ring.

The identical ring on the man's finger caught the sun, gem flaring cobalt blue. His jaw clamped down hard, muscle jumping as he glared at her. He dropped her hand and swung away, gesturing sharply at his men and stalking off down the quay toward the steep path leading up to the villa.

Peter stood staring as the uniforms reformed to flank Ms. Conreid and escort her after their leader. She paused to smirk over her shoulder, hand flashing sharp blue as she gave him her own mocking salute.

8

"ELA ETHO!" THE OLD witch swathed in black skirt, blouse, and head-scarf beckoned with a clawlike brown hand down the hall, and the two soldiers hustled Leeza after her, barely giving her time to register the polished glow of wood trim, terracotta tiles, what looked like some expensive art on the off-white walls. It was all a blur as they hurried her through a doorway into a bedroom.

"Hey, careful with that!" She grabbed the handle of her gear case as the soldier started to drop it onto the tiles.

The other one tossed her duffle onto the bed and headed back out, still not meeting her eyes. She had to admit they were decorative, but she hadn't been able to crack a smile out of either of them, more of that Greek-statue treatment.

The crone chattered something else at her—didn't they have a clue, English was supposed to be number-one worldwide now? She pulled a towel from a cupboard, and when Leeza stepped over to take it, she jerked back with a horrified look like the American was some kind of creature that might bite or sting.

"Okay. I want to see Ariadne. When do I—?"

The crone hurried out and slammed the door behind her. A click. Leeza tried the latch—locked in.

She puffed out a breath, blowing a drooping lock of her 'do out of her eyes, and wandered over to the open French doors onto a little balcony with a wrought-iron rail. "Whoa!" She stepped out into a sizzling shimmer of sunlight over white cliffs and a dizzying drop to the gemlike cove below. Heat pressed down, flattening the azure shallows, deepening beyond the breakwater to purple-blue. The only sound was the shriek of gulls dipping and rising.

She gripped the rail, anchoring herself against a sudden wild urge to fling herself into that great openness and swoop with the distant birds over the sea. "Down, girl." Maybe she should have skipped that second speed tab. "Showtime."

She was here. The Demodakis villa. And somewhere near, Ariadne. Leeza would see her soon. She looked down at her white-knuckled hands and the engraved platinum ring, its gem shivering blue sparks, sharp memories....

Ariadne's sapphire ring, eight years earlier, flickering deep blue over the keys of the sorority's baby grand. Lisa-not-yet-Leeza tossing her long blond hair over her shoulders, turning away as the Debussy surged around her to ripple out the open window and over the shadowed garden. Liquid arpeggios melting into the whisper of sprinklers, California moonlight shimmering over the distant stretch of San Andreas Gulf and the seismically-shielded towers and domes of the brand New Los Angeles.

Lisa bit her lip and dropped her gaze from the expensive view. Her own pale, long-fingered hands looked so artistic, but could only plunk out the ragged refrain of "Lucy in the Sky."

She watched Ariadne's hands—strong brown fingers commanding the keyboard. Watched, aching, as Ariadne, eyes closed, swayed to the music with that devastating grace she didn't even seem aware of.

She looked up then, as her hands summoned the soothing music, and deep blue eyes met Lisa's. Quick shock of that link, bottomless mysteries, magic to be sounded, if they could stay open to it—nobody but Ariadne—and they were swimming in the blue rippling waves of music forever in this moment.

Lisa flinched. No forever; tomorrow Ariadne would be gone. No good, none of it, if she couldn't hold onto this Now, make it—make her—stay. Her fingers tightened.

Ariadne's eyes flickered, seeing it. Her gaze demanded Lisa's acceptance. Wasn't everything else she'd laid at Ariadne's feet enough?

"No!" Lisa lunged forward and pounded her hands into the keys, killing the music in a crash of dissonance.

Ariadne jolted back, then blinked and took a deep breath, reached out to take Lisa's hands between her own. "Try to understand. I must go home to Greece. If my father has called me back, it means I'm needed."

"But they're fighting again over there! It might be Gulf War Three. What if something happens to you? And you haven't finished your degree."

Blue eyes held steady on hers. "I've learned what I need."

Lisa pulled her hands free."I'll go with you! Who cares about this limp school. Their namby rules and playing 'Greek Row' and attending Reformed chapel so I won't get on the union blackballed list...." She made a disgusted face. "Take me with you, Ariadne. I'll watch out for you, I'd do anything for you, even die, you know it. Please."

Ariadne rose from the piano bench and touched Lisa's shoulder. "Stay and finish your degree. Don't throw your scholarship away. It's important for you."

"Important." She snorted. "Journalism courses are a joke!"

"When you've graduated, you can come visit me."

Lisa turned away. "Sure." She pressed her hands hard against her temples. Her pulse pounded, revving up into one of the blasted headaches.

"Sit down, Lisa." Her resonant alto soothing as the piano music. Ariadne guided her to the couch and sat beside her, gently prying her hands free. Strong fingers moved in the sure, familiar motions of massage. "Let it go, little ouno."

"Donkey?" She'd looked it up. "That's all I am to you?" She sat upright, voice shrill.

"Shush. It means **dear one**, silly. Here." A cool weight was sliding over Lisa's finger. "Wear this, and you will have no trouble when you come to see me."

Lisa looked down at the beautiful clear stone set in engraved platinum. Inscribed inside in Greek, Ariadne's family motto: **Eternal and Unyielding Stone.**

The gem flashed deep blue, and a thrill of gratification flickered through Lisa.

She looked up, not quite believing. But Ariadne's face had gone blank, indigo eyes unseeing. Like one of those Greek statues in the book Lisa had checked out of the library when she met her, carved faces beyond reach, even the chipped ones with noses knocked off by looters. Blank eyes looking through you.

Lisa hated that look, it made her itch to pummel and scratch. "Don't do that! It's not fair." She took a deep breath. "When you're with me, you should <u>be</u> with me." Even she could hear the whining note in her voice.

"I'm sorry this is so hard for you. I didn't mean it to be."

"Didn't mean it! Didn't mean anything, did you?"

But Ariadne was already standing, backing away, eyes impenetrable as the sapphire....

Sunlight jittered through the gem, hypnotic, sucking her deeper, and Leeza realized she was gripping the rough metal rail so hard her fingers hurt. "Shit!" She jerked back and paced across the little balcony, rubbing her hands together. She glanced down at the ring again, tempted to yank it off and throw it over the rail, watch it tumble into the sea and drown.

But it had gotten her this far. Finally. She'd see if it was all lies and false promises. See what Saint Ariadne had to say this time to make it all better. *"Heal the halt and the lame, and those stricken with the plague...."*

It had been her cousin Kenny, why not anyone else in her miserable stinking family? But it had to be Kenny, who'd taught her how to hack, break the code, ride the Link, who'd fronted her the cash for her first NeuroLink implant. He actually cared about her more than the scholarship and the money she'd make to help the family. It had to be Kenny struck down with one of the first cases of RP-Hansen's, though at first they thought it was some weird cancer. But that didn't matter, she'd promised him the money for the best clinic, and they could have cured him early on if Saint Ariadne had just stooped to answer Leeza's messages, had come through like she promised. But no answer ever came. No help.

She strode into the bedroom where they'd locked her in like some kind of zoo animal. She snatched up the first thing she saw, a little glass dolphin on the dresser, beautiful smooth curves and it felt good in her hands, almost alive, and that made it even better when she threw it smashing over the tiles.

That was only the start. Saint Ariadne was going to pay.

9

"...SO WE MUST CONCLUDE before Father returns to relocate the laser equipment. I need to make arrangements for the care of the terminal RPH patients. If we accelerate treatments for the others who are recovering, they may be able to return to their homes." Ariadne swayed, closing her eyes as dizziness clouded her vision.

"Ariadne, enough. Sit down." Teresa Espinoza took her arm and nudged her onto a lab stool. "You need to take some rest."

Ariadne took a breath and touched the quartz pendant on its cord around her neck, the laser-cut facets soothing to the touch. She smiled into Doctor Espinoza's concerned face. "I'm fine, just a bit dehydrated."

"Then drink!" She filled a glass beaker from the carboy of tonic mineral water and pressed it into Ariadne's hands. "All of it. You won't help them if you don't keep your own strength up. I know you've been cutting your sleep short, too." She placed her beringed hands on her hips over her lab coat. "All of it."

Ariadne drained the beaker and stood, setting it on the lab table beside the data printouts. "Now where does this leave us with the study results? Doctor Singh?"

Arun Singh turned from a scrutiny of his computer monitor, swiveling his stool and gesturing at the printouts with a flick of long fingers. "Still inconsistent, though I believe we are on the right track. Clearly, the old chemical model of Hansen's treatment, destroying the proliferating bacteria lodged within the nerves, causes irreversible neural damage, and as we have seen, it accelerates fatality in advanced RPH cases. The pulsed laser treatments are promising at the molecular level for regeneration, as is the electrical neurostimulation for functional recovery, both rates improved with your tonic water. And as for the disease trigger—what can be creating these virtual storms of mutating DNA and cellular growth around the nodes of formerly inactive bacteria? Based on our epidemiological data, there is a strong correlation with microwave and other electromagnetic frequency overexposures in certain populations, as you suggested, *Despoina* Demodaki. However...."

He spread his palms. "We cannot replicate the recovery results unless you are present at the patient trials. Unless you administer the water."

Teresa frowned. "We haven't proved that. You're encouraging her to continue exhausting herself."

He blinked, pinched the bridge of his nose, then raised his gaunt height to tower over the petite Chilean biologist. "May we for once set aside emotion and examine the evidence, Doctor Espinoza?"

Teresa only smiled, waggling an elegantly pink-polished fingernail at him. "Don't try that ploy with me, Arun. Just try to find a flaw in my data analysis." She winked at Ariadne.

"Wait." Ariadne's English was less fluent than theirs, and she took a moment to process the quick interchange. "Doctor Singh, what are you suggesting?"

He stepped closer, hesitated, then touched her shoulder. "*Despoina* Demo— Ariadne." He took a breath. "*You* are the variable in all our studies. There is something happening that we cannot explain, something that your presence—your touch—is doing to help heal these patients."

"No, wait, I—"

"My dear." Teresa was smiling again, gently now. "There is a reason they are calling you Saint Ariadne the healer."

"You can't seriously be telling me you believe—"

"I am a scientist." Teresa reached under the silk scarf brightening the neckline of her lab coat and pulled out a gold crucifix on a chain. "Yet I am also a Catholic and a believer. There are mysteries we may never explain."

"I should say that we cannot *yet* explain them," Dr. Singh interjected. "Regardless, as scientists, we must remain open-minded. How you are doing this we do not know, but our observations clearly show that you *are* doing it."

Ariadne sat back on the stool, reflexively touching the smooth coolness of her crystal pendant. *Saint Ariadne?* No. She refused to follow that path. Clearly she could no longer deny some connection with her strange headaches, dizziness, enhanced perceptions… the way she could increasingly *feel* the illness and pain of those she touched. And more—she was starting to sense the disrupted geomagnetic fields before the instruments registered them. But there had to be an explanation.

Teresa patted Ariadne's hand. "Perhaps it's just as well that we need to draw up our conclusions to date, close the studies before your father returns. We've gone as far as we can here. Given your generous funding, Arun and I will continue our experiments once we return home." She peered closer at Ariadne. "You would be most welcome to join me in Santiago at my home and at the institute, my dear. There is urgent need for help there, too, with the pandemic. It would be fascinating to pursue more tests on your—"

"Father will never let me go." Ariadne gazed past the lab tables at the rough rock walls, part of the complex burrowed into the cliffside that expanded a natural cave system. Usually she found the cool passages a refuge from the drought and the agitated energy outside, but now the weight of stone seemed to crush down on her, trapping her forever in the grip of the *Tyrannos*.

"Please." Dr. Singh was pointing out the printouts on the closest table. "Here is information you requested that may give you a direction to investigate."

As Ariadne rose to stand beside him, he pointed to different pages. "We have collected enough data to explore the correlations you suggested, the higher incidences and timing of RPH outbreaks with locations and frequency of anomalous geomagnetic 'islands' in the larger field." He pointed to different pages with circled conclusions. "Here we see the greatest number of RPH cases coupled with both high-intensity microwave tower exposure and frequency of anomalous geomagnetic zones." He pointed to another page. "The next highest occurrence rate is in areas with frequent anomalous geomagnetic zones. But this"—he shuffled printouts to pull out a different page—"is most interesting. At these three sites in our limited regional study, with data adjusted for relative population densities, there are frequent anomalous geomagnetic zones but *lower* than usual incidence of RPH."

Ariadne leaned closer. "What are the three locations?"

"Here, I've circled them on this map." He spread out a larger sheet.

Her finger traced the circles around the three locations. One on the island of Tinos, one in the mountains of Crete, and one on mainland Greece, at the mountainous site of ancient Delphi. *Delphi*—the "navel of the world," home of the famous oracle and a healing mineral spring. She caught a quick breath and looked more closely at the other two locations. Tinos, the site of a shrine to the *Tiniotissa*, where pilgrims flocked every year for Her holy water and cures. And the site on Crete appeared to be in the mountains where the myths told that Zeus was born in a sacred cave, also an area reputed to generate healing springs of mineral water.

"Ariadne?" Teresa's brow was creased in question.

"I see. Thank you." She folded up the map. "May I keep this?" She slid it into a pocket of her skirt.

"Ariadne!" It was her uncle Stefanos, pushing brusquely through the lab doorway, stepping past the startled Dr. Singh to plant himself close before his niece.

"Yes, Uncle?" Ariadne's fingers were still touching the map in her pocket, luckily hidden.

"What's this?" He spoke in Greek, jabbing a finger at the data printouts on the table.

"Final reports of our studies," she answered in English, knowing it would anger him. She gestured toward her two researchers. "Doctor Espinoza and Doctor Singh are making a special effort to tabulate our results before they close up the lab, as you have instructed. I am very grateful for their efforts."

"Good," he responded stiffly in English, nodding at the two foreigners. "We thank you." He turned to Ariadne, switching back to Greek. "We've captured a boat invading our waters."

"Another mercenary?"

"No, a smuggler. An American, he acts the fool, but he has a military background and may be useful for training our recruits. The woman with him looks like a bleached whore, but she's wearing our family ring. She says you gave it to her." He was watching her eyes.

"I gave—?" She bit her tongue. Could it be? "Lisa."

"She gave that name. She came by the ring honestly, then?"

Ariadne blinked. "Yes...."

Lisa, here, out of the blue? At the worst possible time? She took a deep breath. "I need to finish the patient treatments, but please tell her I'll join her for dinner. She must need to rest after her trip."

"She will remain confined to her room until dinner."

"Please ask Marta to treat her as a guest." She turned her back on him, stepping over to clasp the hands of Teresa and Arun. "I must finish an errand now, then I will return to help you pack up the lab. Thank you, my friends, for your dedication to this work." She turned quickly from their bewildered faces, past her uncle and out of the lab, past the gas canisters, power cables, and hulking metal curves of her father's weaponized laser in its glassed enclosure, past her own alcove of a gem-cutting studio with its small triad crystal laser they had adapted for some of the healing experiments. In the dim light between fluorescent fixtures mounted on the rock walls of the passage, she strode past the turning that led to the RPH patients she had treated earlier, and the exit to the villa beyond. This passage led deeper into the mountain past locked storage rooms for weapons and supplies, to a massive metal door.

"Hello, Stavros," Ariadne greeted the sleepy-looking soldier guarding it.

"*Despoina* Demodakis." He snapped to attention. "You need to go for more springwater?"

"Yes, thank you." She waited for him to signal the soldier on the other side, then unlock the door for her. She had obtained a copy of the key, but did not want her uncle or father to know that.

Ushered through the opening, she greeted the other soldier and continued along the tunnel that soon narrowed into the natural passage opening to a cave where Iris waited in her paddock for another trip to collect water at the mineral spring. This was also an emergency escape route to the coastal trail along the cliffs, but once Ariadne had followed a curve taking her out of sight of the guard, she flicked on a penlight and turned aside, squeezing through a low opening onto what appeared to be a dead-end rockfall. She had a found a way through while exploring these caves as a child.

Pausing a moment to listen and make sure there was no movement in the outer passage, she gripped the penlight between her teeth and climbed up the jumble of rough boulders that provided good traction to her sturdy sandals. Near the slanted stone ceiling, she gripped the top edge of a long boulder, working her way sideways, crouching, until she could swing her legs around the right side of the boulder into an open space. Groping with her toes, she felt a crumbled rock surface on the other side, and lowered herself onto it.

Catching her breath, she edged around, crouching to avoid a jagged low ceiling, and shuffled forward until the opening widened and she could straighten. She wiped her palms on her roughspun peasant skirt that was the ideal garment for her trips through the caves or along the baking rock trails outside. She had found this route from the outside when she was seven years old, escaping her father's stern eye to run with the wild goats over the mountainside.

Now, as then, she needed solitude and at least the illusion of freedom. She needed a space with her thoughts. Her head pounded with the pressures converging.

Following the dim twists and turns past more dead ends or passages that led to sudden drops into darkness, she squeezed through tight openings and clambered over the uneven footing of broken rocks until she finally climbed down another jumble of boulders into a cave where eons of the slow drip of water had created ridged stalactites and stalagmites. But since her childhood, the drought had sucked away many of the hillside springs, and the cave held only a whisper of moisture.

Ariadne threaded her way around the stone formations, following a glimmer of light toward the exit high on the mountainside. Flanking the low opening, two ancient guardians, carved from the white stone in some unrecorded past, watched the distant blue sea. The faces, blurred by time and weather, were little more now than faint eyes and blunt noses, but they seemed to gaze calmly through Ariadne as she obeyed her childhood ritual and knelt to touch their smooth curves in thanks for safe passage through the labyrinth.

She sat crosslegged, taking a deep breath, trying to draw in the cool serenity of the distant sea, resisting the waves of the agitated electromagnetic fields she could feel swirling around her now that she had left the natural shielding of the caves. Her thoughts swirled, too, with worries about the dying patients below, the surging pandemic worldwide, the imminent return of the *Tyrannos* and her imprisonment in Headquarters where she would be denied even this escape onto the mountainside. The wildly improbable implications of the map, in her pocket, connecting the sacred sites. And the calls of the faithful for "Saint Ariadne" to declare herself and give her life to their desperate needs.

And now, Lisa here, too? She fought down hysterical laughter, touching her polished crystal pendant, willing the smooth calmness of the carved guardians to flow over her, seal her into the grace of silence in this place.

It was here she had always escaped as a child from her father's angers, his lectures about the proper behavior of a young lady. She had come on her seventh birthday, fleeing her worry about her mother's illness, her hand clutching the secret gift from her Uncle Demetrios, the carved sapphire crystal that had started it all....

10

"STILL NO RADIO SIGNALS getting through. Thought we might get more about the Sons of the Prophet fire-bombing that RIP-Leprosy camp. " Peter turned from the pilot console to his two shadows, Med League sailors he'd been instructed to give the grand tour of *Nereid*.

"Cursed sons of camels!" Panos, the one with the fringed sash he'd added to his uniform, made a crude gesture. "God will strike them down, if we don't get to them first." He eyed Peter. "You are a true believer?"

"Right, raised Southern Baptist." He added quickly, "That's like Catholic...."

He was doing his best congenial new-recruit act, greasing the skids with some war stories, and it didn't hurt that he was on the outs with the NorthAm bullies, too. Once out from the eye of the Demodakis honcho, the sailors seemed pretty relaxed.

Peter led them out of the cabin to the back deck. "You have weather updates? I should secure the deck... gear?" He was still groping for his Greek vocabulary.

Aleixo, the shorter one, gestured dismissively. "Don't bother. Time for a beer." He tilted his head toward the taverna at the foot of the dock. "You can tell us about the blonde." He wiggled his eyebrows.

"Hey, better, I show you. Let me… find the chip. Triple X." He ducked back into the cabin and reached for a cubby.

"Better I open it." Panos, a little more alert, cut Peter off and opened the cubby, checking for weapons presumably. "Okay."

Peter, moving carefully, pulled out a case and rifled through odds and ends. "Right, here. *'Hot Kitten.'* You will like this." He handed it to Aleixo.

The Greek looked like a kid with contraband candy, as he nervously licked his lips. "NeuroLink is banned here."

"Oh, right. This is just visuals." Peter winked. "It will play without Link-In."

Aleixo looked eager as he stuck the chip into his pocket. "So, we go watch it and toast our new brother in arms, eh?" He swung over the side of the boat, followed by Panos.

Peter headed after them down the quay, then paused. "I could use a swim. A little sweaty after my… job interview. Want to join?"

They shook their heads.

"Okay if I take my dinghy and go spear-fishing? Maybe catch dinner for us and join you at the taverna?"

Panos frowned, but Aleixo just shrugged. "You might find a fish the next cove over. You know better than to try to escape in that little rubber boat?"

Peter gestured seaward toward one of the cutters making a round of the island. "Not a chance."

Panos added, "The Sons would enjoy capturing one of ours. They like public beheading."

"Point taken." Peter raised his palms. "See you later for that drink."

11

"ARIADNE!"

Only seven years old, she hadn't yet learned not to jump at her father's voice. His frowning face had descended on her out of the confusing bustle of the foreign guests in the villa, their bright skimpy clothing and babble of voices. Her father, handsome and stern, eyes glinting in the way that meant trouble as she cringed after dropping and breaking her plate, food soiling her party dress. But then another man had swooped down—brown-baked skin, dark eyes crinkling with laughter as a white grin flashed beneath his long bandit mustache—big hands grasping Ariadne and swinging her up.

"Little Kri-Kri! Oof, not so little now!" Uncle Demetrios chuckled as he lowered her.

"Big enough to start behaving like a lady, Ariadne." Her father scowled. "You shame us."

"I'm sorry, Father." She looked at the floor, turning to go.

"Use your eyes, brother! She's pretty as a young goddess. A fine strong girl, and time enough later for taming her." Her uncle's hand on her shoulder eased Ariadne toward the edge of the room.

Her father shook his head and returned to his guests, letting her go. For now.

Demetrios gently squeezed her shoulder and turned her to face him. "And you thought I wouldn't come?" He raised his shaggy eyebrows. "I had to bring your gift."

"Gift?"

"Something very special, very old. Now where did I put it?" He patted his many pockets, frowning and shaking his head, finally pulling out a polished agate and examining it slowly through his jeweller's lens. Ariadne shifted from foot to foot in an agony of apprehension as he shook his head again, sighing. Mournfully he put the stone away. "No, that's not it. I must have forgotten it."

Ariadne bit her lip, trying to hide the disappointment.

"Wait." He snapped his fingers. "Maybe...."

His big rough hand reached out, touched her ear, and reappeared, filled with blue light—glittering, sparkling, water and fire. He kissed her cheek in a brush of smoky smells and whiskers, dropping a crystal into her hand.

She gasped and stared at the clear sea-blue stone, perfect facets etched with a maze of serpentine lines enclosing designs of a flying fish, a bull's horns like the fabled Minotaur's, a crescent moon.

"Uncle?" She looked up in disbelief.

"Our secret." He winked. "Who knows, maybe it belonged to the original Ariadne. See these lines, like the thread she gave that blockhead hero to find his way out of the labyrinth? Study it and work on your stonecutting, maybe a Demodakis will match the ancient ones yet." He pulled out his amber worry-beads, rattling them in quick flicks as he turned to rejoin the adults.

She stood gazing at the deep blue crystal filling her palm with cold fire.

Somehow she had escaped the party and her father's stern eyes, had climbed to her refuge where she could be alone in the heat and silence. The grotto below the cave opening was a cauldron of light, the one live branch of a twisted olive pointing a shadow finger at Ariadne. She shared this place only with the wild goats, the *kri-kri* as her uncle called her, and their herd leader appeared now atop a boulder, staring at her as his horns carved out a blue slice of sky.

Ariadne swung herself up and over a rockfall to hunker in front of the cave entrance. It was only a narrow gap of darkness, partly blocked by fallen stones, flanked by the ancient carved guardians of the winding passages she had once followed until she'd almost lost the thread of light.

She crouched between the marble faces, letting her heartbeat slow. The sunlight like X-rays laid her bare to her bones, laid the mountain bare to its stones. She narrowed her eyes to slits, let her Ariadne-self melt out of her face so it would look as smooth and almost-erased as the ancient carved guardians. She was stone, hewn from the earth, stretching roots into the heart of its cool shadows.

A loose pebble clattered, dropping through the pooled heat. The goat, still watching, shifted his hooves restlessly. He moved across the grotto, then picked his way up until he stood before the girl, yellow eyes like the ancient god's staring close into hers. She crouched motionless, caught in the spell of something she couldn't name. A silent hum swelled inside her, mounted into a perfect, unbearable pitch as she opened her palm to let sunlight ignite the blue gem.

Light—but it was somehow music—burst through her, blinding sapphire and silver dazzles. She gazed unblinking into the blue-sparked depths of the carved crystal as the music poured through her, vibrating down her spine and humming into the rock beneath her, following a vein of connection far below.

Light danced in the facets, and the designs of twining serpents came to life. Music shimmered crystal-bright all around her, inside her. No, she was inside the music. Inside the gem. Shifting mirrors of lights and tones, looking out through glittering angles, looking out through the magic. And the music telling her how, where. Something sprang open in a rich outpouring flood and she was tracing the secret geometry of dazzling light-gem-music deep inside the crystal, treading its tilting dazzling paths, fearless, into the hidden ways of the maze.

12

LEEZA, LOCKED IN THE Demodakis guestroom—but that's only her bod, the Meat—runs free in the Link. The geomag static has calmed for the moment, opening a slot, and she's hitching a ride on a local Med League connection she's hacked. She prowls, pounces on an active site, and enters:

Auto updates, Athens Register: Smog level 5, full facemask, bottled air recommended. Security level Red—

Leeza scoffs silently and shunts into Search again. When in the past few years has the level been lower than Red?

> ***Breaking News: A secondary eruption of the infant cindercone island in the Cyclades at 13:27 today. Marine and air traffic advised to avoid the area. These images just in from Citizen Link-In:

> A deep, clapping roar shudders down Leeza's spine as a gray cloud rolls over the blue sky, engulfs her in choking heat and the smell of sulfur. Through the ash-cloud, a fiery red pulses. Something big and jagged flies past, there's a splash and she's flinching, adrenaline surging fear. "Oh, shit! Oh Christ, watch out—"***

Static cut in again, and Leeza lost the Link. *Cut and Save: NewsFix 12.* She'd add the datelines later. Throw in some cobbled updates—more ozone thinning and solar flare alerts; politocrats assuring the voter-consumers there was no need to worry about the fringe scientists with their "proof" of mutations from the scrambled geomagnetic fields; more riots and famine zones worldwide; RIP-leprosy on the rise—standard news.

She liked cutting the quickie chips, and she could always use the cash she picked up from local stations for their morning shows, no way to enforce copyrights.

The five-minute newsstim capsules were the latest American addiction: Fast trips through the facts for John and Jane Doe, safely muted without the direct neural links the pros like Leeza used to produce them. Little shudder of doom and ruin for the day, breathless rush of sound/sight/sense and no bogging down to over-process, just a quick catch-me-up on the latest state of catastrophe before running for the jobs they were damn lucky to have, no complaints here, We're Working for the Better Way.

Leeza was vaguely grateful to the gonzo freelancers whose short-range transmissions she pirated, throwing themselves into the thick to record the bullets and the clubs to the head. They tended to burn out fast, or get wasted. But the window of opportunity was Now. What with the satellites mostly useless, networks had to rely on the global microwave towers for their world news, and those got knocked out all the time by terrorists, NeoLuddites, and the wild new storm systems, or their signals got scrambled by electromag interference. On-chip was where it was happening.

People were hungry for it all, the meaner the better, and Leeza Conreid was going to the top. This Ariadne feature would take her there—then she'd blow some minds. Stiffs were clueless where the Link could take them. *Medium the massage.*

She was just about to exit and pull out her leads when she got the Ping. Static breaking up again, a message was coming through. She blinked in surprise when she saw the source, her section boss from NewsEntertainment. The message had clocked in after she'd checked out of the Athens hotel:

"Bad news, Chica, the brass got wind of that gear you stole. You're fired."

"Fuck!" Leeza screamed. She'd blown that horny tech geek so he'd change her freelance assignment database to assign her some decent gear, after they'd nixed any funding. It had all gone slick as snot when she checked out the new *ImmerseTech* X3bt recorder unit before her flight to Greece. Now they're saying she stole it? "That asshole, he ratted me out!"

She took a deep, shaky breath and played the rest of the message: *"Told you to stick to the celebrity game, they all wanna see you stomp the big egos with those stilettos of yours. Who cares about some crazy dame the other side of the world? Anyway, don't say it came from me, but they might file charges. I'd watch that fetching little butt of yours, baby. Ciao and good luck."*

"*Mierda!*" Leeza jacked out, threw down the leads, and stalked across the room to pace the deck, staring blindly at the open expanses of sky and sea, gears spinning. Now she was really hanging it out here, no safety net. She *had* to get the inside scoop with Ariadne.

"Fuck, fuck, fuck!" She picked up the crumpled note she'd tossed on the floor hours earlier:

"Welcome, Lisa. Please rest and refresh yourself while I tend to some urgent business. I look forward to catching up at dinner."

Urgent, right. "Bitch!" Then she shook her head. *Keep it cool, Chica. Got to pull this off.*

A click at the bedroom door, and it swung open without a knock. The old crone was back, beady eyes fixed on Leeza. Black kerchief, black dress, black stockings. *Caramba!* in this heat. Her leathery nostrils flared like she'd smelled something bad, and the dark gaze slid down Leeza's nakedness. She jerked back like the American might be contagious, snatched her lunch tray off the bedside table, and scuttled back toward the hallway.

Leeza strode after her. "*Alto!* When do I see Ariadne?"

The door slammed shut. Leeza furiously rattled the locked latch. Nasty old hag. But she was used to looks like that, she didn't give a shit.

The sapphire ring flickered, mocking her.

"Screw this!" She ripped into her bags, threw clothes over the bed. She had to time this right—get the story first, stick the knife to her later. Hands stupidly shaking, she popped open a bottle and dumped a bright scatter on the dresser, gulped down one of the blue capsules and two of the white criss-cross tabs. She plucked up a sheer blouse, held it over her breasts, and turned to the mirror.

She summoned her best media pose, tilting her face, hand on hip. Icy smile, dagger eyes. Ready to take on Saint Ariadne.

13

THE DESERTED COVE AROUND the headland from the villa shimmered far below, cool beckoning blue, as Ariadne strode the narrow path again, urging along Iris with the empty waterskins. The sun blazed overhead now, baking the cracked earth.

The donkey balked at a switchback, digging in her hooves.

Ariadne tugged impatiently on the lead rope. Then she took a deep breath and reached to scratch behind Iris's soft ears. They twitched forward as she murmured, "Poor little *ouno*. First my pompous ass of an uncle interrupts our work, and now you have to make another trip in the heat of the day. Come now, we'll cool you off at the spring."

The donkey tossed her head and followed, as Ariadne tried to contain her own jittery energy. The fresh clarity of the dawn had vanished, defeated not only by renewed geomagnetic turbulence. An oppressive weight hung in the air, a goading sense of pressures converging.

She rubbed a pulsing ache in her forehead. She had to break free. Escape.

The geomagnetic upheavals were accelerating, and when the normal background fields wavered, the negative effects of manmade electromagnetic fields were only amplified. Few beyond the "fringe" scientists and the NeoLuddites seemed to appreciate the danger to living cells. Her RPH experiments, with the expertise of Doctor Singh and Doctor Espinoza, had been on the verge of a breakthrough, she was sure of it. There had to be some way to explain and perhaps control her apparent ability to heal, erratic as it was. Somehow the map of the three anomalous disease zones held the key, and she needed to visit those places.

It had to be soon, before her father the *Tyrannos* returned. Or would he subdue her to his will once more?

"*Ohi!*"

No. No. No. Her cry echoed off the bare cliffs.

Ariadne urged Iris to a faster pace, striding up the trail that climbed over the headland. A loose rock broke away under her sandal to clatter over the edge, and she threw out a hand for balance, cliff wall burning her palm.

Ignoring the tingle of pain, she climbed higher into searing white and blue. Her breathing settled into the smooth rhythm of exertion as she savored the open expanses of sky and sea, the flex of leg muscles, the faint dry breeze on her face—all that would soon be lost to her if she allowed her father to imprison her in his fortress.

Still tugging Iris along, she crested the rise and headed down between boulders and sparse thorn. A rustling in the brush brought her up short, as Iris snorted and jerked back against the lead rope.

"Nyaa!" A black domestic goat clambered past a twisted olive tree onto the trail.

"Easy, girl." She patted Iris's neck. "*Kali spera!*" She knelt to rub the goat's head. He butted against her, nibbling her skirt, and she couldn't help chuckling. "What's wrong? Lose the herd?"

A flicker of movement farther off the trail. She stood.

Across the stretch of boulders and scrub, an old man in high boots and a dusty jacket glared at her. He whistled sharply, and the goat leaped away from Ariadne. The old man jabbed his crooked staff ahead of him as he drove three spotted goats to join the herd moving over the opposite slope.

Josef.

The goatherder always seemed to appear just when she needed this wild solitude, watching her with his gap-toothed scowl. Outraged, like her uncle, that Ariadne—a mere *koritsi*—would violate a man's domain? The goatherder stopped to glare back at her, raising a hand in the sign against the evil eye. She could feel the old man's ill-will troubling the air.

Impossible to dismiss it any longer. Like the birds with their geomagnetic sensitivity, she had gradually come to sense the tremors of agitated energy fields. She felt like a forked divining-rod, resonating despite herself to invisible eddies, to auras of sickness, imbalance—and not just in humans. At times she was nearly overwhelmed by the visceral pain of the polluted earth.

She turned her back on the old man, striding on, finally pausing where the path dipped to cross a dry streambed.

It was only early spring. The stream should have been lively from winter rains, but it was already parched, stones laid bare and baking in the fierce sun. And where were the swallows? Gone, those wings dipping and wheeling airy traceries over the island.

A silent cry stabbed her. Ears ringing, she felt dizzy, dislocated. Out of blind habit, her hand groped for her crystal pendant, and as she touched its smooth facets, the buzzing in her head clarified into a pure, vibrant tone. Almost a tune, something she should remember…?

She blinked, shaking her head. The pain and the ringing in her ears had faded. She moved on, then paused again at the turning toward a dirt clearing and a low stone structure flanked by olive trees.

Years since she'd visited this ancient shrine, and she'd vowed never to return. It was hardly more than a ruin, fronted by a broken mosaic, pieces of fluted columns scattered before the remaining chamber. This had been a sacred place for thousands of years, the sanctuary built upon layers—crude stonework, broken bits of colored tile, the remnants of Ionic columns, and finally a Byzantine arched ceiling whose crumbling frescoes of dour saints still frowned past stains of leaking rain.

Ariadne gave in to her impulse to visit the shrine one last time. The Church didn't own this place, it had been claimed long ago by much older powers. As a girl, she had believed she might meet one of the Old Ones here. She ducked under the low lintel, stepping into musty dimness.

"Ariadne! Never thought to see *you* here." In the flicker of votive candles, the village midwife turned from the cheap icon and the wooden altar, her black dress and head-scarf melting into the shadows, face eerily disembodied.

Candlelight wavered over the offerings on the altar: fresh and withered flowers, a few dried figs and a small bottle of ouzo, a dusty blue crystal—

"What is it, child?"

Ariadne yanked her gaze from the offerings. "*Kali spera*, Juliana."

"What's wrong? Those strutting soldiers bring bad news this morning?" She stepped closer, peering into Ariadne's face. "Maybe you could use a dose of your own special water. Or some of my herbals. It's a rare day brings you into a chapel."

Ariadne shook her head, backing out of the gloom and wishing she could run away before the old herb-woman launched into a lecture about the Church, and Ariadne's need for a husband in order to follow the "wise ways."

Juliana followed her out, dusting her palms on wide hips. She raised her weathered face. "*Aman-Aman.*" She shook her head reproachfully at the cloudless sky, thick fingers touching the crucifix and the colorful strands of dried seeds over her bosom. "Come now, give us some rain," she muttered.

She bent to pick up a packet near the doorway, straightening with a grunt. "Save me a trip down the mountain. Didn't want to give you this in front of those soldiers." She thrust the package at Ariadne, tanned leather tied with a string.

"But... why?"

"It's not from me, Lamb." Juliana was unaccountably brusque. "Came from... a woman I know on the mainland. In the healing sisterhood. That's all I know. Good day."

"Juliana, wait." But she'd picked up her stick and her gathering basket of leaves and roots, puffing up the path behind the chapel.

Ariadne studied the bundle in her hands. She opened it, then sat abruptly on one of the broken columns, staring blankly into the heat shimmer. She took a deep breath and pulled from its packet the strip of black linen cloth, meant to be tied as a headband, embroidered in white: a single staring eye within a spiral.

The emblem of the Corybantes.

It was the same design on the message she'd found mysteriously pinned to Iris's pack saddle a few months ago, demanding she join the militant feminists as a "wise-woman" in their crusade to purge corrupt technology and patriarchy. To rid the world of the nuclear power plants, the chemical weapons, the microwave towers, and destroy the "corporate hegemony and military-industrial complex." Ariadne sympathized with some of these goals, but not with their violent means. The rebels seemed to believe that more destruction could somehow return them all to a Golden Age of myth and the Goddess, to a benevolent rule of women. She wished she could believe in such a myth.

Ariadne dropped the headband onto her lap, fingers reflexively touching her quartz pendant once more. She sprang to her feet, stuffing the headband back into its bundle and knotting it tightly, carrying it into the shrine. She thrust it onto the wooden altar, refusing to look at the other objects there.

Her second offering at this altar. Lips pressed tight against the bitter taste of that irony, Ariadne strode from the shrine, gathered Iris's lead rope, and hurried down the trail to the cove.

14

SUN SLANTED FARTHER PAST noon, burning the cloudless sky pale, puddling fiery sheets between smooth swells as the breeze died. The bow of the inflatable sliced glittering ripples as Peter pulled on the oars, glancing over his shoulder. He edged out into deeper water, skirting a rocky toe where sunlight glared white off the cliffs, even the suck of sea on stone listless in the heat.

He pulled harder on the oars, working off his hangover and way too many questions, sweat running down his bare back.

One more pull, then he leaned back against the hot rubber, gliding on smooth blue. He took off his shades and winced as the sun knifed in, ultraviolet intensity haloing everything it touched. *Toh phos*—that Greek light. Wiping his face with his forearm, he closed his eyes, letting the salt bake. It was quiet, except a bird somewhere, and the rhythmic shush of water on rocks. He tried to breathe deep and slow with that distant rhythm, fighting the fast hot surge of blood in his wrists and throat as red-tinged darkness behind his eyelids pulsed against the heat pressing down on him.

Ticking like a countdown. To what? Looked like fast-talking wasn't going to get him out of this one—now he was a recruit for the Med League. Could he play along, make a break later? Or was this the new winning side to be on? Was there any "winning" to be had any more?

He frowned and sat up, pushing the shades on. There was a grinding noise now, far engines coming closer. He squinted under his hand and spotted it across the molten glare—another cutter with a big gun, patrolling out beyond the defensive ring of mines. As Panos back at the dock had pointed out, he'd be an idiot to try a run for it.

He let the dinghy drift closer to the rocks, then threw out a weighted line. He leaned over for his fins and slipped them on, threaded the snorkel onto his mask, spat on the lens and rinsed it over the side. He strapped a holster onto his thigh and loaded the pneumatic spear gun.

Peter didn't know much about this new Med League—other than taking over some shipping ports and lanes, complicating his usual routes. And the rumors about Ariadne Demodakis healing RIP-Leprosy with "holy water" while those Corybant wild women were busy blowing up the odd nuke plant or microwave tower in her name, the rest humming peace prayers to Mother Gaea crystals. He snorted. Holy loonie-tunes. He knew that tune too well.

His grip tightened on the spear gun, then he shrugged and slipped it into the holster. He knew himself well enough. He was good in a pinch—direct action, how to make things work, fast reflexes—but notso hotso at thinking out big personal decisions, analyzing strategy. So if he stopped picking at it all, worrying it like a scab, sometimes the right answer would just come clear.

Etse k'etse. He snugged the mask onto his face and eased over the side. A quick, sharp breath and then his muscles eased, salty clean cold closing over him, deep blue washing through him. He took another deep breath and dove.

He kicked hard, straight down into hushed shadow. The water split and reformed around him as he arrowed into it, sharp-edged as flowing crystal. It was bare underneath, too, rock outlined precise below him, not much in the way of fish or plants. Here and there a sparse weed curtsied in the swell, fingerlings scattering in a silver spurt of alarm. But the water: incredible clear blue like swimming in air, and the pure salt cool of it you could almost see forever stay forever, siren voices calling him deeper....

His lungs screamed. A shrill panicky voice sent him shooting for the surface in a cloud of bubbles.

He burst through, gasping in the white flare of sun, skin tingling with the salt chill. He'd never get over this Mediterranean water. The Florida Keys he'd grown up on and under were a whole different thing, softer-edged. He flipped onto his face, finning along the surface, sighting below. He floated face-down closer to the cliff, suspended in the hypnotic rhythm of the swells. Strobing ripples of blue-tinged light drifted him back:

Shadows whispering, pages rustling in the night, taking him away from vengeful Fathers and the rod not spared. Pegasus wings of his secret boyhood hoard, those deliciously pagan books, as he devoured the old Greek myths by flashlight under the covers....

The books burning, his father fervent in the pulpit, red hair burning like the torch of the Reformed Brethren scouring the sinful earth. Reverend's righteous voice ringing out King David and the born-again warriors for the glory of God, the good fight for the Way and the Mideast oil and the blessed U.S. of A....

Haggard faces in the dim glow of control panels, fingers gripped over firing studs, stink of fear and trapped-animal sweat as the stricken submarine plummeted into the purple-blue depths—

Peter jerked his head up from the sea, shaking off a pathetic thrashing urge to scramble back to the dinghy and cling to the sunny surface. He took deep breaths, held the last, and plunged into those flickering shadows.

Clearing his ears, he kicked deeper, touching cold rock. He pulled himself down over the boulders, legs drifting upward as he peered into a crevice to see an eye staring back at him and a snakelike suction-cupped arm coiling back into its lair.

Jacknife reverse and back to the surface, lungs burning, heart hammering. He was going a little soft, not bad for thirty-four, but maybe he should think about working on it, maybe cut down on the booze. Clean up his act? And here he was in another pointless screw-up.

He kicked along the surface, scanning, closer to the cliff. A flash of dull color, fins hovering.

He hadn't really expected to see anything, decades of dynamite fishing had taken care of most anything close in, and the tactical nukes over in the east Med some more, but there was some restocking going on. Now he recalled those *caiques* at the quay, nets on some, they weren't all sponge boats. He grabbed more air and shot down, pulling the gun free.

The fins flickered ahead, disappeared in dark. He churned past a rock edge over a dropoff, almost too far, spotted the crevice to the side, a narrow dark cave, almost gave it up, chest starting to ache with the pent-up breath, saw a faint flicker, was doubling up before he could think and down through it. Dark, then sliding light, flashing strobe from above, more dark, rocks squeezing in, no air, but then he was through into open water. No sign of fins. Lungs aching.

He broke surface and flung drops, gasping. Treading water, dragging in air, he looked around to see he'd come through a tumble of stone slabs into a cove nearly sealed off from the open sea. Down below, a sand bottom and the escaping gleam of scales.

Reflexes took him down and after. The lithe body whipped away, then reversed and hovered. The spear shot of itself in a burst of bubbles.

The fish flailed at the end of the line, fighting the spear in a dark cloud of blood. Peter surfaced, pulling it in, suddenly wishing he'd let it go. Eyes gone dull already. But it was a nice pompano, he'd take it to the taverna and have them cook it up in some olive oil for dinner. If.

He raised his head, gripping the spear, checking out the cove. Over at the other end was what looked like a narrow inlet that might be an easier way out. He slipped under, kicked closer, and reemerged smoothly. Now he could see there was a trail running down this end of the cliff to the narrow beach. And a freshwater spring burbling out of the rocks. A donkey with a pack saddle, head down and blinking in the sun, stood next to it. Then he saw her.

She was bent over, heaving at a bulging water-sack, firm muscle straining in brown arms and sturdy, bare wet legs as the spring gurgled over her feet.

Peter blinked in the glare of white rock, sharp dazzles over the cove, sunlight gleaming off smooth tawny skin. He kicked quietly closer. Her hair was a thick black knot at the back of her neck. She was wearing a white blouse and faded skirt hiked up at the waist that somehow recalled an old snapshot of his grandmother as a teenager, wearing a flowered minidress and peace beads. The young peasant woman had livened up her drab outfit with a shiny crystal pendant, flashing prism lights in the sun.

Peter smiled and touched bottom, pulling off his fins and easing toward shore.

The way her body moved under that skirt had nothing grandmotherly about it. More like one of those old celluloid movies the Stateside art houses showed to be clever and the rundown Kinematographos Hermes in Athens showed because neuro-enhancement wasn't sanctioned by the Orthodox Church and anyway where were they going to get the cash to switch over. One of the big-screen sex goddesses. Sandra—no, Sophie—Sophia Loren in a tight dress shouting laughing insults at some soldiers.

He stopped on the sand. She hadn't heard him over the splashing spring. "*Kali spera.*"

She dropped the water-sack, startled, but turning with a lovely grace like a born dancer. She raised a hand to her breast, clutching the big crystal.

He stared, stunned.

Face off a vase in a museum—the straight nose and brows, generous forehead and mouth. But her eyes were blue. A deep, almost purple-blue. Like the Med where it dropped off from the crystal clear shallows to shaded fathoms. Old Homer had it· the wine dark sea. Couldn't have been blind all his life, the poet, he'd gotten too many things just right. Bright-glancing Athena. Incomparable Helen on the ramparts, and the troops flowing down steep hills for her, gleaming with their shields and greaves and whatnot, rippling over the plain of Troy like waves.

Peter could have drowned happy in those deep blue eyes. But they were watching him. Wary. A surge of desire flushed through him. Damn. She was the real thing.

He swallowed, took a step, pulling the fish off the spear and holding it out in an instinctive gesture, groping for words. "Please.... Don't be afraid. Take the fish, a...." Damn. "A gift. Please. Welcome. Thank you."

The start of a smile flickered over her face, but she got it under control, standing her ground.

He laughed at his own ridiculousness, shaking his head. "Help you with that?" He pointed at the water-sack.

She stood silent, then stepped back, nodding. With another of those fluid dancer's moves, she turned away to the donkey, and he did see a smile flit over her face. Not pretty, no, a more austere beauty that shouldn't have gone with the all female shape of her, but did perfectly. Knockout legs, too, strong and shapely and she even had trim ankles, not like most of the peasant women. A healthy glow like a sturdy little mare. He was giddy, crazy. Struck by that mythical bolt from the blue, Goddess rising before him from the waves, naked glory on her scalloped shell.

He blinked and shook his head, hoisting the water-sack, tying it to the donkey's saddle, gutting the fish and rinsing it and thrusting it at her, babbling nonsense.

"See, it's a pretty one. Peter popped a peck of pompano. But not as gorgeous as you." She wouldn't know English. "I tell you, Aphrodite my girl, your sidekick with the heart-darts just nailed me pointblank."

She threw back her head then and laughed—a rich, throaty chuckle that seemed to dance through her whole splendid body. Peter grinned and moved closer.

But she was stepping back with a surprising dignity, sober now, that bottomless blue gaze steady on Peter. She raised the fish, thanking him with a simple, *"Efcharisto."* Voice low and resonant. She took the donkey's lead rope and turned away for the path.

He stood dripping, holding out his empty hands, wanting to run after her and kiss her battered sandals. "Please.... Could I just—?"

She shook her head and led the animal away.

15

HER FATHER'S SERVANTS KEPT the ebony grand polished to a mirror-smooth gloss. Ariadne sat stiffly at the keyboard, playing Debussy but not hearing it, looking out past open shutters to the sea. The sun was sinking into molten copper and crimson, ash from the latest eruption refracting vivid shimmers. Her fingers summoned arpeggios to echo the rippling colors.

This might be the last time she played her mother's piano. She sighed, letting the old hurt out through her hands, letting the music flow through her. Her mother had loved to play here, where she could see the sea and the gulls, her pale hands moving over the keys like the sweep of wings. Then the music had died for little Ariadne, light dimming in Uncle Dmitrios's magical blue crystal that she'd given to the mountain chapel's altar so God would heal her mother. But it hadn't worked. Nothing had worked. Ellen Barrett Demodakis had become too ill to play the music that first captivated her husband in the concert halls. To the end, the servants carried her daily to this room with the long windows and distant wings.

After Ellen's death, Ariadne's father had ordered her to keep practicing, until she finally stopped hating her mother's piano. And so she had to owe even the gift of music to *Tyrannos* Constantin.

She stood abruptly, echoes of "Clair de Lune" summoning that childhood day—her father's stern voice, her uncle's white grin as he gave Ariadne the carved crystal, then turned to intently watch his brother's wife at the keyboard.

And now Lisa, here? Pretty blond Lisa, laughing, teasing—the sorority's trickster. So brash yet sweet. To Ariadne, she'd embodied the American freedom to explore, challenge the rules, plunge into experience. Maybe her old friend might help lighten these dark times.

She took a deep breath, smoothing her blue silk dress that had also been her mother's, touching the knot of hair at her nape, sliding her fingers over the smooth facets of her crystal pendant. She stilled her nervous hands as the door swung open to admit Lisa.

Blue toenails, high-heeled sandals of colored straps, long thin legs in garish orange prancing past Marta's stiff outrage, pale skin and bright makeup and the gauzy sheer blouse clearly molding high breasts. An American ad come to life. Ariadne had always enjoyed Lisa's free-spirited fashions, and she herself knew too well that look of Marta's.

But as she raised her gaze to Lisa's, her welcoming smile froze. The pale topaz eyes glittered in a painted mask of the face she'd known, wearing an arrogant—hostile?—expression.

Ariadne finally offered her hand. "*Chairete*, Lisa." *Rejoice.*

"It's Leeza now." A wolf's grin. She held out her hand, not taking Ariadne's, but displaying the platinum and sapphire ring. "Nice little souvenir you left me with."

Ariadne stood rigid, struck dumb.

Lisa paced past her. "Figured better late than never. You did invite me, you know, back when you ran off. Even if you never answered my messages."

"But... You didn't receive my letters? When I didn't hear from you, I thought...." She closed her eyes. Of course, the *Tyrannos* would have intercepted them in his campaign to keep her isolated here. She cleared her throat. "Lisa, I've been something of a prisoner here, cut off from the world."

"Right, I can see it's brutal." She snorted, gesturing around the room with its expensive antiques. She ran a finger over the grand piano. "Recognized the music." She picked up a cushion from a couch and dropped it, touched a restored amphora, stopped at the windows. "Wild view."

She turned, long legs in a model's stance. "You're still gorgeous, of course. Cool as a cucumber in this heat. You haven't changed."

Was it a question? Her pale eyes were intent, unreadable. Almost. She wanted something. Lisa, like all the others, coming to plead and take, angry when they found only a woman and not an oracle. Ariadne had learned to be wary of people's needs.

"Please sit down. We can start to… catch up." She gestured toward the couch, moving numbly in the routines of her father's hostess. "Would you like a drink before dinner? I've sent someone to ask your companion to join us."

Lisa stiffened, the mask cracking. "He's not—"

The door had swung open again, to Ariadne's relief. Marta was ushering someone in, her face still set in disapproval, though the stranger was at least dressed decently in shirt and slacks. He gave the maid a nod of thanks, one eyebrow quirked as he stepped into the room.

Lisa scowled. "He's *not* my—"

"Nope. Just the hired help." The man shot a look at Lisa and grinned, then turned toward Ariadne. "But thanks for the invita—"

He froze. His gaze flew to her crystal pendant and back to her face and he took a step forward, hands raising, face flushing.

Ariadne, beyond surprise, met the stare riveted on hers. Hazel-colored eyes. They'd looked darker in the sunlight by the sea, but now they matched the wavy chestnut hair. That afternoon at the cove, she'd thought he was one of the Greek recruits—straight-cut features and sturdy sun-bronzed figure emerging from the waves—until he'd spoken.

Lisa was glaring at him. He stood with his hands half-raised, just as Ariadne had left him at the spring, after he'd insisted she take the fish he'd caught. Her lips twitched with suppressed laughter.

The stranger cleared his throat and dropped his hands. He shrugged then, a humorous tilt to his brows. "Peter Mitchell here. *Chairete, Despoina* Demodaki." He added in Greek, "Thank you for the dinner invitation."

"We will be eating fish," she answered in Greek, without thinking.

He looked surprised, then laughed, and somehow she found herself chuckling, too, Lisa looking back and forth between them with a puzzled, then peevish, expression.

"Lisa, forgive me." She collected herself, reverting to English. "It seems Mr. Mitchell and I have already met, when he offered us a fresh pompano the cook is now preparing for our meal."

The pale eyes narrowed, shooting daggers at the man, but he hadn't taken his eyes from Ariadne.

She avoided his insistent stare, orchestrating seats and drinks and polite questions, but somehow slow and awkward, her rusty English stilted. She longed for the near-invisibility of her childhood self, wishing she could melt into a shadow beneath the piano.

She turned. "Please, Lis—Leeza, help yourself."

Leeza jerked out a hand to refill her glass, eyes glinting angrily, though her voice came out flat and bored. "So you've never caught my show. Thought they got it even in the boonies. I've got some on chip, you want to check it out."

"I've got an old one she'd like. *Hot Kitten*—"

Leeza turned on him, hissing, "Cram it, Mitchell!"

He held up his hands. "Kidding." He grinned, launching into a humorous tale about the Piraeus taverna where apparently Leeza had hired him to bring her here, but his gaze kept following Ariadne.

And she'd actually enjoyed the encounter with the stranger at the cove that afternoon, a reminder that life was more than threats and urgency. Something elemental in the way he'd risen from the sea, the rush of time halted for a moment and distilled to the essence of sunlight, white stone, blue water, wet brown skin, and the simple pleasure of laughter. And now all she wanted was to escape both of these intruders—the flippant smuggler, and this brittle, cynical Leeza. Ariadne looked out through the open shutters, the last purple glow on the horizon almost visibly shimmering with geomagnetic turbulence. She needed to finish her plans for escape.

"...but I have to admit the joke's on me today." Mitchell was raising his glass in a mock salute. "I throw myself on your mercy, *Despoina*—"

A blinding flash split the darkness beyond the windows, shattering the calm night. Pounding on the heels of the glare, a percussive boom. The floor shook, rattling glasses on the table. Past the terrace, another bomb exploded.

16

THE NIGHT ROARED, SHAKING the house, shattering glass.

Peter shot to his feet, moving before the flash faded. Leeza was struggling upright with a strangled cry, Ariadne Demodakis stepping toward her.

"Get down!" He pulled them both behind the couch. "Keep your heads down." He squirmed across the floor to a window as another explosion ripped the night, shivering the foundations. He could smell smoke. The lights flickered and died. "Damn!"

He raised his head to peer over the sill. "Air attack, I can't make out...." Darker movement, out in the twilight. "There. I think ultralights, maybe shielded, probably came in low so your radar didn't catch them with the ash—"

A deeper, muffled roar cut him off.

The *Despoinis* was climbing to her feet, pulling Leeza after her. "That last was one of our guns. Quickly, this way."

"My boat's down there! I've gotta—"

The door crashed against the wall and a dim clot of Med League soldiers burst into the room. A voice shouted in Greek, "Air attack! Into the shelter!"

One grabbed Ariadne's arm and pulled her free of the clinging Leeza. Two more ran past Peter to crank down an armored shield across the broken windows. Leeza stood gawking as another flare shattered the dark behind the half-lowered barrier. A pop and a hiss, tendrils of black cloud snaking over the terrace in the flash of light.

"Jesus—chemicals!" Peter lunged toward the men, jerking at the lowering shield as the others levered. It snapped down into place.

The soldiers were dragging Ariadne away. Leeza stood frozen. Peter scooped her up and hauled her along, stumbling through darkness and booming echoes.

Dim halls, doors, stairways down. Lights flickered on. The soldiers led them from the basement down a stone passage into a natural rock cavern. Fluorescent lights, air filters humming. The honcho from the quay—a brother of the *Tyrannos*, he'd learned—cut them off, hustling from another rock tunnel.

He stopped, hand on the gun at his hip, breathing hard, stare glinting from Leeza and Peter to the *Despoinis*.

"Well, Ariadne? Take a look at our soldiers hit by these bastard Sons of the Prophet! Turks!" He spat. "Maybe you'll start caring about security now. These are no mercenaries after your healing secrets. These people have one purpose—to kill you, and die."

Peter blinked, grappling the torrent of Greek, staring baffled at that tawny-skinned glorious vision from the cove who'd somehow transmuted into this stony-faced Ariadne Demodakis.

"Uncle Stefano—"

But the man strode toward a group of soldiers in bubble suits coming down another passage. Helmets unsealed, they carried two stretchers. Stefanos Demodakis paused, then moved on as Ariadne stepped toward the men. Peter followed. Somewhere beneath the hum of air filters, overloaded machinery squealed.

"How bad?" She reached for the sheet over the first stretcher.

A soldier, face streaked with grime, shook his head. "He's gone."

She lifted one corner.

Mangled mass of flesh, bone, and pooled blood in the chest cavity. Twisted face and empty eyes.

The sheet dropped over the corpse. Ariadne Demodakis moved woodenly to the next stretcher, the shrill squealing louder now. Peter looked down and saw what it was. The man's teeth clenched in a grimace, a choked scream wrenching his throat to knotted cords. His hands gripped the stretcher bars as he strained blindly upwards.

Peter was locked there, staring, like it was all just yesterday. Now, then, all the same. The man's burned eyelids couldn't close over bulging eyes covered with a milky film.

"The chemical bombs." The soldier's voice echoed out of some dim remorseless replay. "We killed the filthy dog, knocked him from the sky. But by Christos, poor Yannis—" The voice broke. "He was slow with his helmet. We tried to rinse his eyes with water, but it only burned. I gave him as much morphine as I dared...."

Peter cleared his throat. "Dragon's Breath."

Beside him, Ariadne Demodakis made a startled, arrested movement.

He raised his head, saw her watching him with a face blank as a marble statue. Peter jerked his chin at the wounded man. "That's what they called it—Dragon's Breath. Solvents just make things worse. Attacks the cornea, slowly dissolves it. Only thing to do is operate fast, transplant a new cornea later." He paused. The shrill scream kept on. "Don't suppose you've got a surgeon handy?"

"Doctor Kouris is at the village," she answered slowly, "and we have only a medic here in the complex." She was looking past Peter, off into space. For no reason, he shivered.

He shook it off. Nobody—no Father, no frigging Saint—was going to pull that holy flimflam on Peter Mitchell again. "Well, Saint Ariadne? What are you waiting for? Lay on your hands."

Her gaze shunted onto him, boring into him. She turned abruptly to the soldiers, switching to Greek. "Bring him to my laboratory. Hurry." She strode off down the tunnel, past Leeza's white face and fixed stare, then broke into a run.

Peter followed the stretcher down the rock passage and through a doorway into the glare of a small lab outfitted with some equipment he didn't recognize. The *Despoinis* swept a counter bare with one arm, knocking papers to the floor as everyone crowded in.

"Here." She gestured to a soldier. "Clamp his head in that vise. Tie him down." She ripped open a first-aid cabinet, pulled on a paper mask, hesitated as she touched various vials and syringes. A new arrival pushed past Peter to her side. "Pello! Thank goodness. We must...."

Peter couldn't follow the rest, but the medic had selected a syringe and injected the soldier, whose face and white-knuckled grip relaxed as his thin wail eased off.

"You." She was thrusting another mask and an oxygen cannula into Peter's hands. "You won't faint? Set it on demand. Positive pressure if he stops breathing. We don't dare sedate him too deeply."

The medic taped Yanni's eyes open. The *Despoinis* bent low over the straining face, touching the man's wrist, and whispered into his ear.

Directed by the medic, Peter clamped the oxygen cannula into position on the lab table, plastic extension tight over the soldier's mouth and nose. He opened the valve to a low hiss.

"Hold him absolutely steady now." She was moving a bulky device into position over his eye, powering up a console. A thin red target beam aligned the tube. Laser. "First we map the contours." Her finger moved toward the power trigger.

The lab lights flickered. Peter's gaze jumped to the console indicators wavering. They steadied. A drop of sweat rolled down Ariadne Demodakis's marble-smooth brow and into her paper mask. She triggered the laser, and a contour grid appeared on the console monitor.

The device tracked slowly then, red guide beam leading the laser's invisible tightening spiral, burning poisoned tissue to smoke as suction vacuumed it. Done. The oxygen cannula hissed its slow rhythm. It faltered, the soldier's chest beneath the thin cover going still, but then it shuddered and rose again. The medic's gloved hands moved steadily, bathing the occluded eye with sterile saline, packing it with gel, taping a bandage.

She repositioned the laser and reprogrammed the console. After a pause, she pressed the trigger and the beam energized.

A deep, bone-shaking shudder in the caverns. Another bomb? The lab lights flickered, flared, dimmed. Peter wrenched around to the console readouts. Power plummeting.

Ariadne Demodakis jerked back as the power failed, releasing the trigger, her hands shaking. The lights flickered again, shadow rippling over her carved features and purple-blue eyes staring blindly.

17

ARIADNE STOOD BRACED BEFORE the laser, trembling as she waited for the backup power to engage. If it would engage. Her gaze wavered in the dim battery lighting to Yanni's livid face, the horrible poison still eating his unbandaged eye. She shuddered, then forced deep, slow breaths. Only another specimen trial, only another injured animal. She felt the weight of her crystal pendant rising and falling over her breast. Stone. She must be stone, cool and steady. She couldn't afford to feel Yanni's pain and terror.

She took another deep breath, visualizing the three differently-hued crystals in the laser's triad array. *Disparity merging to a timeless white fusion of blended light….*

A click, and the backup shunt finally engaged, instruments powering up again. *Healing white light, rippling, pouring from her hands.* She triggered the reset laser, and it completed its tracking. Done.

Ariadne closed her eyes and sagged back against the lab counter as the medic bandaged the second eye. Peter Mitchell was examining the power panel, the retracted laser. "This little baby doesn't draw much voltage. What've you got, some kind of souped-up transformer or—"

"Shock!" Pello exclaimed. "We're losing him!" He leaned over Yanni's chest, gesturing to Mitchell and the oxygen mask, and the cannula hissed into positive pressure. Yanni had gone blue, locked in stiff tautness as the medic started chest compressions. He paused, listened with his stethoscope, shook his head and started more compressions. "He won't make it, *Despoina.*"

Ariadne ripped off her gloves to pick up Yanni's wrist and close her palm against it. She shivered at the touch of his clammy, cool skin. Obeying an unthinking surety, her other hand found the quartz prism of her pendant. She summoned its serene order, breathing deeply and evenly. A high, pure tone rang in her ears. As the medic stepped back, shaking his head, she held her grip on Yanni's wrist, empty of a pulse. She leaned close to the soldier's ear. The world had gone dim around her, enclosed within planes of stone, clarity narrowed to a dark tunnel and the inward spiral of blue-tinged flesh. She summoned the blended white light once more, let it flow into the wounded soldier.

"Yanni." She breathed against the tunnel of his ear, in and out, whispering the rhythm, the vibrant silent hum, sending it into his cold stillness. There. A faint flutter, a shallow pulse like wounded bird wings. It strengthened, steadied, began to beat in rhythm with her own. *Calm. Harmony. Deep at the heart of a stone maze.*

Her voice was a soft breeze. "You've done well, Yanni. Sleep now, let your body heal itself. I will give you tonic water to teach your own fluids how to heal. Sleep."

She straightened, steadying herself against the counter as dizziness darkened her vision. She blinked, saw that the blue-tinged rigidity had drained from Yanni's face. His chest rose and fell evenly as someone's hands pulled the hissing cannula away. The livid skin had regained a ruddy flush.

Ariadne turned numbly to the vat of mineral water she had activated, experimenting at the spring with her laser-calibrated quartz rod—was it only that afternoon?—and wearily drew off a liter. The tonic water was more heresy rejected by the medical establishment. And the people preferred "miracles." She sighed and turned with the bottle.

They all stood motionless, watching her. Peter Mitchell with a speculating look. Leeza's pale eyes glinting avidly. Pello and the other soldiers stiffly at attention, faces wearing the look of awe Ariadne had come to dread.

She moved briskly, breaking the tableau. "He must drink a small glassful four times daily. Pello, have the men bring him to the infirmary. We must arrange his transport to the mainland for replacement surgery. Gently now, he must not be shaken."

Pello saluted smartly, touching his crucifix as he turned to direct the transfer to the stretcher. The soldiers furtively crossed themselves before obeying. Ariadne followed them to the door, wanting only to sink into a chair. But Leeza and Peter Mitchell were still standing there.

Leeza broke away from the wall. "Maximal!" She strode to the laser, touched it, ran a finger across the console, walked over to Ariadne and took the bottle from her hands, peering into it. "So what's this? Saint Ariadne's holy water? You did a number on that guy all right, really thought he was flatlined. We have to talk, Ariadne. This lab, it's fantastic. And those animals in there with the electrodes on them." She jabbed a bright fingernail toward the glass door to the adjoining lab where Ariadne kept the injured animals undergoing bioelectric therapy. "Pure nuclear. What do you—"

"Enough." She took the bottle, flinching at the touch of Leeza's hot, jittery fingers. "I must see if there are more wounded. I will ask if it is safe for you to return to the house."

Leeza pried herself away from the lab. Ariadne waited by the door as Mitchell turned from a last scrutiny of the laser. She locked the door and led quickly down the rock tunnel, ignoring Leeza's chatter and the questions in Peter Mitchell's eyes.

18

PETER CURSED METHODICALLY, SWEAT stinging his eyes as he pried at the shrapnel-cracked radar housing and nicked his thumb with the screwdriver. He sucked the cut, pried some more, pulled the broken piece off and inspected the innards. Grunting, he traced the coaxial cable, shredded halfway up the mount.

He wiped his damp forehead on his arm, clipped the damaged coax, and snaked free a replacement length.

"Sonuvabitching mess...." He wrestled with the springy coils, wire-wrapping them straight down the mount. "*Nereid*, gal, how we gonna dance our way out of this one?" Finally the new cable was connected, housing patched—three cheers for duct tape. He pulled off his drenched T-shirt and mopped his face and back. He'd fix her up prettier when he had the time.

If he had time. It was still unclear what Stephanos Demodakis was going to do with him, but he'd told Peter to go ahead and repair his "spy boat." A wrist flex activated his watch readout. 1637. Would have been done by now if he hadn't spent the morning helping the fishermen haul out a couple of *caiques* partly sunk by one of the suicide Prophet boys dropping old-fashioned grenades along with the chemical canisters. About all the weight the radar-shielded ultralights could handle. Half-assed attack all around, but then the fanatics didn't figure odds on making it back.

Peter did. He climbed down into the wheelhouse and flicked the radar on. "All right." No major damage. They'd just have to live with the shrapnel dings in the aluminum hull. She was a tough old gal.

For luck, he patted the flaking painted mermaid giving him her come-hither over the console. "Take more than some Arab shrapnel to slow you down, baby." He winked. She kept smiling.

He ducked out the side door, headed aft, and vaulted down the ladder into the hold. He eyed for the Nth puzzled time his new cargo. He'd been thrown for a loop that morning when the soldiers had finally let him check *Nereid* over, and more boys in blue had come marching down the quay bearing gifts. From the *Despoinis*, for repairs.

He hadn't pointed out that the fancy microprocessor didn't resemble anything on the boat that could have been damaged. Or that she'd also sent down a crate with the compact laser unit she'd used the night before on the injured soldier.

Peter figured Saint A. would enlighten him when the spirit moved her. He didn't want to wonder what was going on—the "gifts," the angry uncle, the laser setup in the cavern lab that didn't jibe with the Miracle Healer. What about that soldier, looking like a goner until she whispered in his ear? What was going on behind that stiff mask she wore, those sea-deep eyes? He was in over his head, but something in him just wanted to keep swimming.

Brushing past the crate, he cranked open the engine room door and ducked inside to check the stuffing box on the port shaft, see about that persistent leak. Straightening, he wiped his greasy hands on his cutoffs.

"Now where'd that wrench go?" He scrambled up onto the deck, found it. Whistling, he patted the bulwarks. "No problemo. Sweetie, you're built like a brick shit-house."

"A brick—?"

He spun around, stubbing his bare toe on a cleat. "Christ!" He squinted into the sun, a dark silhouette on the quay splitting light rays.

"I didn't mean to startle you." Voice low-pitched and even, a resonance to it that went clear through his bones.

"Damn." He flexed his throbbing foot.

The saint Herself. She was peering curiously over the rail, gaze sweeping from the cabin to the open cargo hatch. "I hope the... replacement parts were satisfactory." A smile, twitching her mouth?

No. She was watching him with her sober, attentive look—scientist waiting for the white rat to exhibit an interesting behavior pattern. And all he wanted to do was touch her mouth that was a little too wide but somehow perfect, feel the curves of her lips warm to his.

He turned abruptly to lean on the rail. "We need to talk."

"Yes. May I come aboard?"

He made a mocking bow and offered his hand to help her over the rail. She swung up easily, skirt flaring in a pretty swirl.

"Just a minute." He ducked into the cabin, grabbed a towel to wipe off his face and chest, threw a wrinkled but reasonably clean shirt into a plastic deck bucket along with a couple of beer bulbs from the cooler (working again). He paused in the doorway.

Fierce sunlight glared off the concrete, the cliff, and the sea. *Nereid* rocked gently, her deck hot beneath his flip flops. His visitor stood at the rail, looking out across the cove toward the rocky shingle where the fishermen and sponge divers were still working on the beached wooden boats. A couple of baggy-trousered duffers were hauling off the carcass of a goat caught in the crossfire, and some young boys from the nearest village were up on the taverna's verandah roof, reweaving damaged thatch. But Ariadne Demodakis didn't seem to be looking at the activity, just staring at the cove.

A visceral hum buzzed the aluminum deck, intensifying to a noisy thresh as a helicopter shot up from behind the cliffs, then veered to sweep down toward the cove. Peter tensed. Only a Demodakis chopper. The racket of the blades echoed off the rocks as it dropped low in a reckless curve over the water. "Cowboys."

The wind they'd kicked up ruffled the clear aqua and tugged wisps from Ariadne's braided bun. Her crystal pendant glinted as she turned with that dancer's grace, tilting her head to follow the chopper. The gust caught her dress, whipping its folds against her curves. She smoothed the skirt as the chopper's buzz faded around the cape.

Peter cleared his throat, tilting his head toward the breakwater and open sea beyond. "They keeping an eye on that boat out there, circling the island? I'd guess a high-speed hydrofoil, not one of your father's."

"Mercenaries. They seem to be keeping a... watch."

"Surveillance? You mean for the Sons of the Prophet?"

"No." She paused to nod at a sleepy-looking soldier walking the deck of the cutter farther up the quay. She continued in a low voice, her English a little slow and stilted, "We believe the mercenaries are employed by a pharmaceutical consortium. They wish to obtain the rights to my experimental healing techniques. They consider me a threat to their monopoly."

"Are you?"

A piercing look, then she turned back to the cove. "I don't know, Mr. Mitchell. But I will not allow them, or the cult followers, to suppress my work."

Despite her healthy glow, she sounded tired. Probably up all night with the wounded soldiers. *"Despoina* Demodaki, it looks to me like—"

He broke off as a young boy came running down the quay toward *Nereid.* He stopped, stared at Peter, and blurted something about "the village."

Ariadne leaned over the rail and touched his shoulder. "Tell them I will bring the water soon."

The boy pelted off down the quay. Ariadne watched him go, a line of worry creasing her brow.

Peter cleared his throat. "All work and no play. Here." He took the beers from the bucket and handed her one. *"Chairete, Despoina."*

She gave the plastic bulb a bemused look. Peter showed her how to pop the nozzle, and she surprised him with a quick gleam of teeth as she touched her bulb to his, meeting his eyes.

Deep, drowning purple-blue. He jerked his gaze away, taking a swallow.

She sipped, then examined the bulb. "This container—is it special for...." She frowned. "To do with boats?"

"Nautical?"

"That's it." She was serious.

"No, just handy. They've been big in Athens only about five years now."

"I see." She looked at the cove. "I rarely leave the island.... I want to thank you for your help last night, Mr. Mitchell, and this morning with the boats."

"No sweat. How's Yanni doing?"

"He is resting well. The helicopter will take him to a mainland hospital today."

"That's some bedside manner you've got."

The little frown again, working it out.

"Means you got him believing you'd pull him through. That's what the whispering was about, right?" He shrugged. "There's a Cherokee saying from my old stomping grounds. 'If it works, it's good medicine.'"

She gave him a surprised look.

"But that laser setup of yours, that's really something. You're a gem-cutter? I still can't figure how—"

"I hope you were not delayed too long in your boat repairs, Mr. Mitchell."

"I.... What?"

"Your vessel. It will be operational by tonight?"

He blinked. "Sure. But I'd still like to know—"

"It would be best to finish your work today."

"Okay. Fine. Does your uncle want me to take it somewhere? You know he's...recruited me?"

"You will be under way tonight."

"Oh.... I still don't get the picture here. I mean—"

"If you need more diesel fuel, I will have it delivered. Is your boat fit to handle rough weather?" Her gaze worked slowly over the battered, stained hull, casual as a weld flaw exam.

He finally got the message. "All right! I follow orders. But first you answer some questions. Like what the hell that equipment's for, sitting in my cargo hold. You want me to transport it for you? Or just draw those mercenaries off your neck? I'm tired of all this cat-and-mousing!"

She fixed her stare on him, like he was some kind of lower life form she couldn't quite fathom.

How could any Peter Mitchell come off, under those X-ray eyes? He was pissed-off, and awkward, standing there ripe in his sweat. He realized he'd been sucking his gut in. Christ. He stalked to the stern, threw the deck bucket on its line over the side, hauling up seawater and dousing himself with salty cool. He shook it off, raked fingers through his matted wet hair, rubbed his stubble, and was perversely glad he hadn't shaved. He yanked the shirt on, leaving it unbuttoned.

"I've got my work cut out. So talk."

She frowned, then lifted her shoulders and palms in a fluid gesture. "I want to hire you and your boat to take me through the islands."

He broke out laughing. She waited. He shook his head. "You've got cutters, choppers, God knows what geared up with the latest fire power. And you want to hire me."

"Yes."

She wasn't kidding. He glanced over at the cutter deck, the watch down at the far end. "Do I have to remind you I'm under your uncle's orders? That he'll have me shot if I don't play nice? So who's in charge here?"

She looked up past the clear shimmer of cove to the house on the cliff. "I should return soon before my uncle becomes suspicious. You see, my father has not allowed me to leave this island for several years."

Voice low and even, her English picking up steam, "They are protecting me. From the mercenaries. From the terrorist Muslims who misunderstand my work. From the Corybant warrior women, who have made an attempt to kidnap me." She might have been reading a grocery list. "To complete my research, I must visit Tinos and Crete. We will need to leave tonight—while my uncle is still occupied with the terrorist threat. Before my father returns."

A pelican crash-landed in the cove, then surfaced gulping. Peter cleared his throat. "That's it?"

"My work is urgent, Mr. Mitchell. This is why I am forced to turn to you. I will pay more than your customary fee, considering the dangers involved."

He shook his head. "Research?" It was the first thing that popped into his mind. "And that laser? What are you trying to do? Don't play games with me."

"This is no time for games!" Her face flushed, eyes sparking. "We must have an agreement—how you pilot your boat is not my business, and my work is not yours. When my research is done, I will share it. There is a desperate need for this healing."

"So you're saying it's true? You really can heal RP-Hansen's?" He shook his head. "I don't get it. That laser. The holy water. Which is it?"

She ignored his question. "Will you take the job?"

"Damn it!" He paced the deck. "That's the Demodakis way? Buy or kill whoever you want? Saint, or *Tyrannos?*"

"How dare you accuse me!" she burst out in Greek, eyes flashing, voice spilling pent-up passion. "Who are you, a man with no loyalties, to come here like the others—always invading our islands, for centuries! Bringing violence and sickness, and now the world itself is crying out in pain, and still you men with your weapons and greed steal the life from the earth. Still you use, and destroy, and take—"

She gasped, hand raising to cover her mouth. Her eyes blazed at Peter. Then she took a deep breath and her face went eerily blank, like a stone statue.

She turned to fix her gaze on the cove. Finally, voice level and controlled, she continued, "If you agree, we will leave after 2300 hours, when the guards change. Some of the men are loyal to me. I assume payment in gold certificates would be acceptable?"

"Jesus Christ!" He paced the deck. "How the hell do we get free of the patrols? What about your uncle and those mercenaries, not to mention assorted religious maniacs, hot on our tail? Thanks, but no thanks." But he knew damn idiot well he was going to say yes.

"As you see, I have my own secure account through the Athens branch of Global Trust." She held out an embossed hologram card with the familiar logo in gold, tilting it to reveal the display, and his eyes widened at the figures. "I will advance you one hundred thousand in gold certificates now, and transfer to your account two hundred thousand more when you bring me to the mainland after stopping on Tinos and Crete."

He swallowed. "Everyone has his price?"

"Is it not your business?" She lowered the account card, took a deep breath, and met his eyes. "Please, Mr. Mitchell. People are dying. You can help me make a difference."

Peter gave her a sharp look. Her eyes held steady on his, unnervingly clear. Crazy as a loon? But he wanted to believe her. Damn. He'd believed his daddy Reverend, until it was too late. Toss the son onto the sacrificial pyre....

He sighed. "All right. I'll do it."

"Thank you."

He held up a hand, palm out. "But we need to be clear—we'll both be in the cross-hairs, escapees from the Med League. There'll be no turning back, definitely not for me."

"Nor for me. My father is planning to imprison me in his new fortress." She squared her shoulders. "So. There will be a storm tonight, and—"

"Wait a minute. Radio reception's still iffy, but I caught a weather report. No storm-fronts."

"My... sensors are more accurate than the news service." Her voice was taut, control slipping. "There will be a storm. Rough seas. The mercenaries will be forced to withdraw to shelter, and our patrol boats will be secured to weather it."

He started to argue, then dropped it. "Okay, say we make a break. What about my defensives? Your soldiers took the missiles and my assault rifles."

She glanced at a sailor pacing the cutter deck, and lowered her voice. "They will be returned when the watch changes tonight. The soldiers will allow us to 'escape.'"

"Great. Into this hypothetical storm of yours. What about the big gun up top?" He jerked his chin at the cliff, the emplacement above the bay.

"There will be a distraction. An explosion in my lab." She took a deep breath, chin lifting. "Be ready. When the watch changes, Spanos will help you reload your weapons. He is the one with the stockings that are bright even in the dark."

"Those day-glo disco socks? What if he changes them?"

A glimmer of humor as her lips twitched. "He owns four pairs." She turned and climbed in an easy swing over the rail onto the quay.

"One thing." Peter vaulted after her.

She paused.

"No ditzy blonde along, or no deal."

"Lis—Leeza? You would leave her?"

"Your uncle can send her back to Athens. No way does she come along."

Score one for Peter. She hesitated, gnawing her lip, and he wondered what was between them—some kind of bad vibes there. Maybe Lizard Conreid had something on Her Holiness. What a laugh. But somehow it wasn't funny.

She raised her gaze from a scrutiny of her sapphire ring. "Perhaps after all that would be best." That steady, appraising look on him. He didn't like what she was seeing.

A swirl of skirts and she was gone, leaving Peter under the burning lens of the sun. He swore, threw off his sticky shirt, and dove into the cool blue shadows beneath *Nereid*.

19

DUST. SUN GLARING THROUGH the ash haze. Heat. Sweat.

All going on chip. Leeza paused, reaching a hand to steady herself against the cliff face, and the stone burned her palm. *"Chinga tu madre!"* She cradled her hand as she turned to suck in a searing lungful and look down over the villa to the cove far below.

The water shimmered cool clear aqua, tantalizing. She swallowed, throat dry and dust-coated, savoring it. She swung her face carefully: blue seascape, stark rock headlands. Maximal.

She was wearing her new goggle-camera setup, Linked in to the portable neuro/aud/vid recorder strapped to her hip, like all the freelancers used now for rough field work. Resolution wasn't as fine as her bigger unit, but no way was she lugging all that gear up this goddamn goat track. Besides, the gritty look was part of the image, the in-the-thick-of-it. She scrubbed her damp, grimy forehead with the back of a hand. She was paying her dues.

She fanned her face with her hat, replaced it, and chugged on up the trail, pacing herself a little slower. Thing was, she was starting to get it. Like the heat and dust and killer climb were what made the view worth it. Like maybe the drones could plug into it later, get the thirst and the aching lungs, but maybe not get It.

She shook her head and shrugged irritably. Couldn't follow that thread, where would that take Leeza in the Link? Got to keep it together, keep her focus. Her art. Link was where it was all at, give you anything, everything, way past the Meat.

She cracked a grin. So the Meat, the neuroporn, had gotten her into it, so what? Let'em laugh now.

She paused to pull the sweaty shirt free of her back and tug long sleeves down to protect her skin. Ariadne's ring flashed sharp blue on her finger. She frowned, twisting it, tempted for a crazy second to tear it off and throw it down the fucking mountainside. Miss-Princess-Saint-Ariadne-Demodakis too busy to give her the time of day, let alone an interview.

Leeza clenched her hand on the bulky ring and stared down over the sun-scorched switchbacks of the goat trail. Blue ice, those Ariadne eyes. But just see if Leeza can't break through the freeze, she has moves Ariadne's never seen. The ring was her ticket.

Had it been only a bribe, shut little Lisa up and let Ariadne exit clean?

The sapphire was top quality, a dealer back in California had offered what had been a small fortune to Lisa at the time, but she hadn't sold it. That was the low point, after she'd dropped out of the university. But she'd gone ahead, flung it in the faces of those snide sorority bitches, one of their sisters turning up on posters plastered all over. *Kitten—Watch Her Claws!* What a laugh. She'd been hot, though, neuroporn was just taking off then, and it paid the bills. She'd learned the production end that way, trading favors with the guys for time on their recorders. So what if they snickered.

Leeza scowled, wiped her face again, and pushed on around another switchback.

"Ah! Oh Christ—!"

She stumbled back, rocks clattering, teetered on the sheer edge and almost lost it but fell to her knees and scrambled back onto the trail, shock screaming through her. She stared.

The dead eyes stared back, dulled over with dust.

The corpse was hanging upside down on a crude stick cross jammed into the rocks at the edge of the trail. Naked, skin blackened along one side, cracked and oozing, broken ribs and gore poking through. A dark hand, tattooed with the Sons of the Prophet crescent moon, dragged in the dirt. Legs sprawled, lashed with ropes to the cross-piece, dried blood everywhere. They've cut off his balls.

Leeza doubled over, hot gorge rising, and she spewed it on the trail. Gasping, she staggered to her feet, started to back down, but couldn't tear her eyes from the grisly display. Panting, she stood staring.

She's seen—felt—worse, in the Link. This is just Meat. She's past that.

Somehow her feet are moving her closer, effortless, like she's zooming in Virtual Reality, and from far focus she sees/feels her hand move slowly forward. She has to touch it. Him. The dead meat.

Her fingers touch skin, not cold, no, baking in the heat and the blood's still sticky Jesus the smell hits her and she hears them now, black clots of buzzing flies and the smell *Madre de Dios* it's flooding her, filling her death rot inside. Somewhere someone is screaming and Stop! won't the bitch stop she's trying to throw up again but she can't and the screams chase her all the way up the trail into that burning blue empty sky.

Leeza stumbled over the crest of the trail and fell into the dirt, coughing and gasping. "Shit. Shit." She sat, head down, as the dark dizziness ebbed. Was this It? Nothing but meat.

She pulled herself to her feet and staggered on. Around chunky boulders. Over a dry streambed. Still recording it all, refusing to think. She'll find another way down.

She suddenly came up short as scattered pieces of stone columns and ruined walls swam into focus. Some kind of funky old old chapel. She caught a quick breath and wiped her shaking hands on her pants. Reflexes kicking in, she strode forward.

A quick pan of the front, crumbling rock and low doorway. Scattered column pieces, carved marble in exquisite fluting and left lying around like junk. She ducked under the lintel into dimness. She let her eyes adjust, dim candlelight flickering over her. Switching on the goggle headlight, she scanned the curved leaking ceiling, faded faces of those weird Byzantine saints with the huge eyes staring down, accusing. The old original-sin-and-hellfire whammy.

Leeza shook her head. She stepped over to the wooden altar covered with a cloth, the candles guttering, tossing shadows across a bunch of stuff: miniature painted versions of those frowning saints with halos, bottles of oil, crosses, tin strips with body parts stamped in, dried flowers and seeds. Her headlight kindled a blue flame.

"Subliminal!"

Leeza reached out to pick up the dusty sapphire crystal, wiping it clean until the facets gleamed. Water and fire in her hands. And there were tiny pictures carved into it, between spiral lines—horns, crescent moon, a winged serpent.

The lines, like a maze winding into the depths of the stone. What was that old myth? Ariadne, daughter of the ancient Cretan king what's-his-name. Minos. He had that bullheaded monster guarding some treasure at the heart of his stone labyrinth, and it was Ariadne who gave somebody, some stupid hero, the thread to find the way in and out. Ariadne, the priestess of the secrets. The old lost magic.

She swore she could feel it, stirring here, all those layers of history shot through with it. Maybe the cult rockheads had something, and this was one of those power spots. A Link.

Leeza stared into the clear facets, cool deathless perfection. Her hands closed around the beautiful crystal, light winking out. *Eternal and Unyielding Stone*. It's Ariadne. She has to have it. For Ariadne. Rekindle the magic?

Just for Ariadne. Leeza jerked around, clutching the crystal, and strode from the chapel.

20

"YIA SAS!" PETER RAISED his beer.

"'Sas." Josef clinked his ouzo shot against Peter's bottle. His contorted fingers painstakingly spilled the traditional good luck drop onto the taverna's packed earth floor. He tossed off the shot and smacked his glass on the plank table, lamplight and shadow etching the creases of his leathery face.

Peter twisted in his chair, looking for another round. An arm in a sling pushed through the curtained back doorway and the owner followed with a tray, casting a gloomy eye over the empty blue-painted tables in the whitewashed concrete cube of a room.

"Kyrie Mavroyenni." Peter gestured at Josef's glass. *"Parakalo."*

The man moved heavily, setting the tray on the table and mopping up around Josef's glass with the end of the apron straining across his belly. He grunted, awkwardly refilling the shot glass with his left hand.

The old man cackled and nudged the owner's paunch with his elbow. "Wound of war, eh?" He winked at Peter. "They say Mavroyennis leapt like a goat as the roof came crashing down on him last night." He jerked his chin toward the verandah, almost repaired. "They all moved quick enough to run from the Turks! And where do they hide tonight, eh? Home, with the women? Cowards." He slapped his thigh, stirring a gust of body stink and dust, then tossed off another jibe, the local patter too fast for Peter—something about David somebody and his big wife, obscene gesture for a punchline.

"You love the sound of your own voice." The owner sniffed, collecting glasses from an emptied table, oil lamps throwing his doubled shadow over the wall. He pulled wooden shutters closed over the two glassless rectangles in the quayside wall, shutting out a rising evening wind, shutting them in with a fitful Athens radio station crackling snippets of the international news hour.

"*…unprecedented step of cancelling their legislative session… the quarantine… World Health Organization declaring states of emergency in….*"

Peter massaged the tense knots in his neck as Josef's arthritic fingers fumbled the shot glass. The old sponge was at least a distraction. Peter could have gone for a stiff belt himself, but he was nursing his beer. Work tonight.

Maybe Her Holiness was right—there was a storm taste in the wind. The mercenary hydrofoil out there would have to head for cover, and the Demodakis boats were already snugged down. His trawler was built for rough seas, as long as it didn't get too dicey. Weather patterns gone as crazy as everything else.

"'*Sas!*" Josef was holding up the glass.

Peter dribbled his beer dregs over the floor in his own libation, and ordered himself an ouzo along with Josef's refill. He tossed it back in a jolt of licorice fire. What the hell, maybe it really hadn't happened that afternoon:

∞

Blazing sun easing lower, wind rising, swirling dust up the trail. Peter's talking to the boys at Supplies—maybe laying in some extra diesel isn't a bad idea, after all.

Behind the corrugated-metal warehouse, the chopper's perched on its landing pad, mechanics busy. The stretcher with the wounded soldier is still waiting for his trip to a mainland hospital.

Peter wanders over to see how he's doing. The medic's worried, scowling at the lowering sun and the rising wind pushing puffs of cloud. The Despoinis is off on a mercy mission to one of the villages, and she'll be royally pissed the soldier's not already on his way. They'll have to swing wide to avoid the cindercone ash, more delay. Could Kyrie Mitchell help him check the bandages, the gel-pack? The Despoinis told him Mitchell had seen these cases before.

Peter blinks in surprise, then crouches by the stretcher. "Hey, Yanni. Doing okay?"

Drugged, he mumbles vaguely.

Peter remembers you have to keep the bandages moist, eye bathed with the gel pack. Yannis still has a chance, the ones that got corneal implants right away got their sight back. The others.... He can still see those blind, milky eyes, the tissues shriveling. Corneas won't heal and regrow after the Dragon's Breath.

Peter helps the medic move Yannis into the building out of the wind, and rigs a light. They lift the first bandage to squirt in more of the moistening gel. "Holy Christ!"

The center of the eye is still cloudy white. But around the rim of the iris, it's come clear again, bright red new vessels growing, glowing against the brown iris. The goddamn cornea is spontaneously regenerating.

The medic just crosses himself and measures out the next dose of Saint Ariadne's holy water....

∞

Peter ordered another shot from the taverna owner.

Josef was still rehashing his glory days as a sponge diver, before the bends got him. "Pah! I said to Georgios no puny storm will stop *me*...."

The old fossil reminded Peter of Gramps. His tall tales of the Bayou, gator wrestling and running moonshine past the Revenuers, naturally the Reverend couldn't abide him but Petey always found a way to sneak off and tag along. Damn—Peter never even found out when he died until years after. Both of them just erased off the family tree in that fucking gilt-edged Bible. Even Ginnie, after everything that went down, even his adoring little sis hadn't had the decency to write....

"...and a man does not crawl beneath the skirts of women when trouble comes!" Josef waved a contemptuous arm at the empty taverna, jabbed a finger toward the battered icon on the back wall lit with a string of antique colored Christmas bulbs. "A man does not go whining to the saints." He slammed the empty glass onto the table. "This—" he smacked his lips—"is finer than holy water. A man will not beg in line for a drop from the *Despoinis* in her father's rich house. Pah! The wine she drinks is made from grapes." He spat over his shoulder. "*Magdalena.*"

Peter blinked. "The *Despoinis*?" The old guy's dialect was pretty thick, but if Peter had it straight, *Magdalena* meant "whore." He shook his head. "I thought she was your saint."

Josef snorted. "The fools say she need not come to chapel because the holy spirit dwells already within her. *Poh-poh-poh!* My goats and I, we know, we see her. We're the true masters of this island. The rocks and sky belong to us! There's no slope too steep—"

"Right, I can see that. What do you mean, you and your goats saw her?" An uncomfortable prickle goaded Peter.

The old man puckered his lips. "You, too? On fire to know her?"

Peter wanted to tell him to shut up. Instead, he waved the owner over.

"*...another shoot-out at the survivalist compound in—*"

Mavroyennis snapped off the radio static. He gave them a weary look, but came over to refill Josef's raised glass.

"My goats and I, we see everything on this island. Oh ho, the fine lady was so kind! Always bringing her holy water to the wife of Michael Vendemis, sickly after birthing her sixth. Stillborn, like the one before. Puny little girl-children she gave him, always, never a son he could be proud of. Ha! But I saw. It was more than water she brought to the house of Michael Vendemis." Josef tossed off the drink. "Blue-eyed *Magdalena.*"

Peter frowned. "That's enough." He scooted back his chair, stupidly jealous of this Michael Vendemis. He dug in his pocket for drachmas to pay up.

One of Josef's goats peered in through the verandah doorway, black splotches over the pointed white face, fixing its satyr's eye on Peter. Beard and wattles shaking, it trotted over to its master, butting him half off the chair.

"Young upstart! So you think you can take me?" Josef roared with laughter and kicked the goat away. Mavroyennis came flapping his apron to shoo it back outside.

The old man hauled himself out of his chair, straightening with a grimace, teetering like one of the island's wind-twisted olive trees. "Josef Andrianopoulos will live forever. Still potent as the devil!" He drew himself up and gave Peter a fierce look. "Seize life, boy! Grip it like a sponge and wring it dry! Fear is for women and—" He broke off into a coughing fit.

Peter waited.

Josef smacked himself on the chest with a shaking hand and proclaimed, "I spit at death! I spit at God and the devil!" He hawked and spat on the floor as the owner threw his arms up. A brown hand gripped Peter's shoulder as the old man leaned close to give him a significant look. "*Toh tharos!*" *Courage.* He seized his carved staff and shuffled out into the night, stiff but upright in his baggy tattered pants and cracked boots, calling for his dog, calling for his goats.

Peter grinned and laid some bills on the table.

"*Mierda!* You'd think they'd keep those goats fenced up." Leeza Conreid gripped the door post and scraped the sole of her hiking boot over the lintel. She made a disgusted face.

Peter mirrored it.

"Nice to feel welcome. You gonna buy me an ouzo?" She sauntered over in a pseudo-expedition outfit, all khaki and flaps, and plopped herself into the chair Josef had abdicated. She panned her camera goggles slowly across the bare walls, the rickety tables, the barrels at the back, the Christmas bulbs and the icon. Pulling them off, she shrugged out of her shirt to show off pale gleaming shoulders, breasts molded by a skintight tank top.

Peter sighed and signaled the owner.

He stood frozen, giving the near-naked breasts a look of mingled shock and appreciation.

"Another shot for me, too, *Kyrie* Mavroyenni." Then in English, "Looks like I'll need it."

"Lighten up, Mitchell. So anal-re." She pursed her lips. "Watch this." She flashed a blinding smile at the Greek as he served her. Mavroyennis, stare jumping from her face to her breasts, nearly dropped the glasses. He retreated in confusion.

Leeza grinned and plucked free the neural leads from the small of her back. Then she winced, rubbing her face. "*Madre,* I could use a drink." She set her gear on the table, hands trembling. She yanked them onto her lap.

"I've been all over that dusty mountain today."

"Didn't get enough blood and guts last night?"

Her face snapped up, eyes narrowing. "Give me a break. This on-location biz ain't easy." She sagged in the chair, raking a hand through her limp blond spikes.

She looked prettier this way. Almost human. Peter raised his ouzo glass to her. "*I si yia.*"

She straightened and raised her glass. "Smooth sailing."

"What?"

"Don't bother. Ariadne wouldn't take me along to the villages to pass out her holy water, but I ran into her on the way back. She let the cat out of the bag, Mitchell."

Damn. He flicked a look at Mavroyennis and growled, "I don't think he understands English, but don't push it."

She tossed off the shot, spun the glass on the table, and smacked it down bottom-up. "I'm coming along."

"Like hell!" Peter slammed his glass down. He saw Mavroyennis watching openly now and hissed, "I told her that wasn't part of the deal."

Leeza shrugged and gave him her nasty smirk. "Tough luck, Mitchell, you don't get her all to yourself."

"I got you here. End of contract."

She yawned. "What do I have to do to get a refill around here?" When Peter didn't respond, she turned to Mavroyennis, giving him a pouty little smile, tilting a shoulder back to thrust out her breasts.

He jerked forward, galvanized, clutching the ouzo bottle. His stare locked on the visible dark points of her nipples as he poured, the glass overflowing.

"Hey. Nicht-so-schnell!" She laughed as he hastily mopped the spill and retreated. "Grosero...." She leaned over the table to suck off the top layer in the glass, sprawled back and ruffled her hair again, pale eyes glinting at Peter.

He stood, dropping more bills onto the table. "Demodakis will give you a free trip back to Athens. Now I recommend you head back up the hill before the shit hits." He called out thanks to the hovering owner and headed for the door.

"Don't fuck with me, Mitchell!" She grabbed her glass and tossed off the drink, scrambling for her gear.

He was striding down the dark quay, blinking at the dim flurries the wind was stirring over the cove, when she grabbed his arm from behind. "Nobody walks out on me, dreck!" She spat it. "I'm coming along, or I blow the whistle right now."

He whirled and grabbed her wrist without really thinking, twisting her arm up behind her.

"Ow! Get your hands off.... *Alto*, you—" She gasped and stopped fighting.

He spoke slowly and clearly. "I'm walking you up to the house right now and have our saintly hostess lock you up somewhere they won't find you until we're gone. And don't open your mouth on the way or I'll break your arm. It might help if you smile for the boys."

She started struggling again. He cut it off with a little more pressure. He caught a glimpse of her pale, furious face in the dimness as he turned them around and started back down the quay. A crescent moon was climbing above the mountain, and he could just make out the two soldiers at the foot of the steep trail, darker shadows in the gloom. He pulled her closer against his side. "That's it, nice and cozy, romantic moonlit stroll."

She hissed, "Better think again, Mitchell. You can't shut me up forever. Once I get back to Athens, I'll put your face all over the Link, free advertising—your illustrious smuggling career, not to mention AWOL and stealing the Navy boat. Greeks might decide to dust off that extradition agreement with the Feds, score some brownie points with Uncle Sam."

He halted, his grip on her arm tightening, and she caught a sharp breath. He walked her forward again. "Bullshit. That's history, nobody in Athens cares."

"I've got contacts, Mitchell. How do you think I got the dope on you in the first place? Even if they don't ship you back to rot in some charming lockup, don't you think they'd jump at the chance to confiscate your crummy hulk over there?" She jerked her head toward shadowed *Nereid*.

He stopped and swore. Finally he turned her loose.

She wrenched away, eyes glittering pale in the night as she rubbed her arm. "Looking forward to it, Mitchell—watching you strike out with her."

21

LIGHTNING SPLIT THE NIGHT sky. Thunder crashed and echoed off the cliffs, a tremor quivering the ground in response. Ariadne could feel the building forces, and she understood the old myths of Zeus with his sky-bolts and Poseidon the earth-shaker. They were just as real as the instruments she'd left behind in her lab, digital data scrolling field intensities, turbulence, air pressure.

The rising wind whipped strands from her braid, chased clouds over the mountain and across the waxing moon. Ariadne pulled Leeza deeper into the shadowed switchback of the trail as the moon sailed free. She checked her watch. 2240.

She tightened her grip on the restless Leeza. "Wait for the clouds to cover the moon again." Darkness swept over them, and they hurried, panting with Leeza's heavy gear bags, down the last stretch. The wind shrieked, waves tossing the lashed *caiques*. They scurried into the deeper shadows behind the taverna at the head of the quay.

Leeza paced the wall longlegged in black tights, black cap hiding her hair. Her disturbing camera goggles tracked the agitated cove with nightscope. She'd promised not to capture Ariadne on camera.

Leeza whispered, "Nothing shaking yet, Chica. I can make two soldiers just standing out there by your daddy's big boat. No sign of the dickhead."

Ariadne's gaze flinched from Leeza's goggles, the waistpack with the recorder jacked into her neural leads. Was it all just a game for her? She was clearly addicted to the neural network, more insidious than her drugs, reducing the world to "image bites" and the nervous rush of sensation.

A shadowy premonition shivered through Ariadne. But she couldn't leave her old friend here—*abandon her again*, Leeza had accused. She obviously didn't believe Ariadne about the confiscated letters. What rang true in all of this was her anger and grief over her cousin Kenny, whom Ariadne vaguely remembered meeting once. She didn't know if money for early treatments might saved him, but she wished the messages had come through and she could have helped. One more loss to lay at the feet of the *Tyrannos*.

Lightning crackled, thunder booming closer now.

"They're coming!" Leeza hissed.

Ariadne hunkered in the shadows with her as soldiers marched past down the quay, leaning into the wind. The watch, changing just on time.

They waited. Ariadne could feel Leeza's nervous tremor beside her. She closed her eyes, pulse racing, shadowy waves shivering through her, building with the force of the storm, as the timer ticked away in her lab. The explosion should at least confuse pursuit. The old miner had clearly enjoyed placing the dynamite for her to trick the *Tyrannos*.

She hadn't managed to harden her heart and leave the animals to die convincingly, so she'd set them free. She had appropriated the goat carcass hauled off the beach after the Sons of the Prophet attack, and had left some of Leeza's and her own clothes with it in the lab, to be scattered in the blast.

Thankfully, many of the island soldiers seemed to revere—or fear?—her and were willing to risk helping her "sacred mission." The two guards at the cave's emergency exit gate had quietly closed their eyes and turned away so they could truthfully report that they had seen nothing as Ariadne used her key to pass through.

Voices, nearly stolen by the wind. The retiring watch stamped past, eager to get to the barracks. "Better Spanos than me, drowned rat in the storm!"

"Or puking his guts out in the boat!" They were gone up the trail.

"*Despoina Demodaki!*" A curly dark head thrust past the taverna wall.

Leeza bit off a scream.

The young soldier grinned, hiking up his pant leg to reveal a shimmer of flamingo pink, his favorite disco socks.

Ariadne touched Leeza's arm."It's all right. Only Spanos."

"We must hurry now, *Despoina*."

"Yes. Thank you, Spano."

He helped them with the bags as they struggled down the quay, waves splashing over the concrete, wind shoving them. Peter Mitchell and another soldier, Xavier Kakoyannis, were wrestling a bulky object over the side of the heaving *Nereid*.

"Christ, watch it! She's slipping—"

Spanos leaped forward to help them secure the missile in its compartment along the bulwark. White teeth flashing in his handsome face, he insisted on helping Leeza with her gear bags, handing her aboard, taking her arm to guide her into the cabin.

Peter vaulted back onto the quay beside Ariadne. "All squared away." He turned to peer across the choppy cove, whitewater churning through the breakwater entrance below the high cliff. "We've got to get out fast. If the storm kicks up any harder, we'll never make it past the turbulence at the point."

The boat heaved, foam splashing, engines rumbling. The soldiers climbed back onto the quay beside them.

"Thanks, men." Mitchell shook hands with them.

Ariadne took a deep breath. "*Efcharisto*, Spanos, Xavier. I'm sorry to place you in this position."

Xavier touched his breast and gave her a salute.

Spanos laughed. "Don't worry, *Despoina!* We'll spin a good story about that pirate Peter Mitchell ambushing us, escaping. God and the Virgin be with you." They headed back up the quay to watch the trailhead.

"Come on. Let's go." Mitchell tugged Ariadne's arm.

She stood staring through the storm to the dark cliff, unable to see the house atop it. She suddenly felt weak and foolish. Her hands clenched, the family ring digging into her fingers. Was she mad to do this?

"Ariadne! We have to go."

She shuddered. The forces were still building, winds screaming. Lightning flared behind them, illuminating the mountain. No sign of movement up there. No sound but the wind and waves, the rumbling thunder.

"We need to wait. For the explosion. They must be distracted, or they will fire from the gun emplacement up there."

"I'm still getting a clear window now and then on the radio. Once we clear the breakwater, I could let them know you're onboard. They wouldn't fire then."

"No! They must believe I was in the lab. The mercenaries, too, if they are monitoring."

"We'll never make it if we wait! If we get more electronic interference, my radar might cut out, and we won't make it through the mine field. Your diversion isn't going to happen, *Despoina*. Dynamite was probably some fisherman's old stash, won't go off 'til the Second Coming. We've got to make a run for it. Now."

She laid a hand on his arm. "Wait. There *will* be an explosion." She stared through the dark clouds, toward the lab inside the mountain. Her fists clenched tight, tighter. Clashing fields of air, sea, and earth wailed to a high-pitched frenzy.

A jagged bolt scissored the sky, a direct strike on the mountain. Thunder slammed and echoed. Then a second bursting roar, light flashing up on the cliff as the dynamite exploded.

Mitchell grabbed Ariadne's arm and flung her into the bucking boat. "That bolt had to zap their systems. We're out of here!"

Rain stung her face as she groped forward over the heaving deck and staggered into the cabin. Mitchell hurried into the wheelhouse. Engines roaring, they leaped forward into the storm.

22

ERRATIC GUSTS BURST IN through the harbor entrance, over the high rock cape to the east. Cat's-paws whirled over the cove, lashing the front screen with rain and froth. Peter took it fast, curving out and to port for a straight shot.

"You got something to pray to, do it now. Get anything loose stowed or lashed down." His sweat-damp hands clenched on the wheel. He was praying the radar would hang in through the static.

Lightning flared the scene:

Boiling black clouds and wind-whipped spray. Wet cliffs looming close, jagged rock teeth in the waves. The narrow cut out all whitewater churning, froth spewing, waves surging in at them. Beyond in the storm, dark crashing seas.

Thunder. The black curtain dropped back over the brief glimpse. Rain lashed harder.

"Holy shit." He took a deep breath. "Hang on!" They were in the thick of it now, southeast wind whipping down off the cliffs. *Nereid* rolled and bucked, water breaking over the bow.

"*Chinga—!*" A scream from Leeza as they swerved in a big wave hitting starboard, rolling then veering sharp back as Peter gunned the port throttle. A crash behind him, glass breaking.

"For Chrisssake strap in back there!" He squinted through the splatters of rain and spray, couldn't see shit. Then another lightning bolt ripped, and he wasn't thrilled with the glimpse. Waves still building, breaking over black rock reef off to port. Over the darkness he tried to place a map: scattered islets out in front of the harbor entrance, straggling off to west, along with shallow rock reef and the tricky winding channel between the mines. Off east, into the teeth of the wind, deeper open seas.

He blinked and decided to risk the forward spotlight, maneuvering tight, turbos howling into a churning clash of waves. He glanced at the radar, the mines glowing green dots like a vidgame maze.

"Slowly." A hand fell onto his shoulder.

He jumped. "Jesus! Don't do that."

"I'm sorry." Ariadne, rumpled, hair coming loose, dragged herself up beside him and braced herself in the wheelhouse. "Mr. Mitchell, I can guide you out. We must go slowly."

"No way, we can't wallow around broadside in this shit! Gotta get clear, hope my scanner doesn't get scrambled. I got your chart, deep water out that way, east. We'll circle back once we're clear and head northwest for that steep little island, shelter behind it." He gunned it, surging forward with the waves, into the maze, following the little green blips.

Another flare of lightning over the chop past the rainstreaked shield. The radar screen shimmered, flared, went black.

"Shit!" His hand jerked the throttle back and they were foundering, tossed in the darkness. Peter closed his eyes, ice gripping his gut, feeling the mines close in.

Squat, seaweed-coated, warty monsters lurk in the shadows. Just a brush, that's all. The dull, final thud and that split-second of clarity before everything explodes. Bursting metal in the roar of the submarine's alarms and fire and water spraying as they plunge deeper into the black swallowing sea—

"Peter!" She gripped his arm, *Nereid* wallowing in the turbulence. "Take us to port. Now!"

"Sir!" Reflexes obeyed as he goosed the throttle, tugging the wheel. They rolled through the chop, the following seas slamming them side to side. He tapped the radar screen, hit reset. Nothing. "Got to turn back," he shouted over the roaring of wind, engines.

"No! We must keep on." She ran a shaky hand over her face, raking the dark tendrils back. "I can guide you through the safe channel."

"What? In the dark?"

Nereid's spotlight speared futilely through whipped rain, glimpses of foam-capped waves, dark rocks off to starboard.

"I know these waters, Mr. Mitchell. I know the channel. Ahead, off to port, another reef coming. Immediately after it, swerve starboard, and I will guide you. There, see it?"

They were toast if he tried to turn back blind, maybe capsize broadside anyway. He had to trust her.

"Now. Starboard. Just so." Her voice was eerily calm in the midst of the howling storm, and Peter was busy just keeping *Nereid* from broaching, the following seas building and tossing the boat like a toy. The wind howled, pushing them toward the rock fangs, and everything in him was focused tight, hands jumping from throttle to wheel to other throttle in tight correcting bursts as she dictated turns, sweat pouring off him and he had to trust her. Damn if she wasn't right, though, they were finally looping between two islets toward deeper water, and she must have had some bloody sixth sense, radar in her bones. One more turn and that was it, they were out into deeper water, beyond the mines.

Beside him, she sagged and let out a gusting breath.

"We're not out of it yet. Hang on, got to run for it."

Out of the sheltering lee of the island now, the storm winds hit full force. Pushing big waves, twelve to fifteen footers and building. Green water broke over the rail and sluiced the windows as they slid wildly to port.

"Mitchell! You dreck! You're gonna kill us out here. Take us back!" Leeza was screaming from below.

"So swim back!" he shouted over his shoulder.

He tried to head due north, but couldn't hold it with that wild following sea off the stern quarter, had to veer more west, hoping to hell he could find that island. The boat broached. Again. And again, waves bursting over them, superstructure screaming in the wind, turbos howling below. Hands blurring from throttle to wheel to throttle, gunning and slowing the engines, if he just once lost that fine edge of control over the monster waves trying to surf them, swamp them....

Peter skated the razor edge, nerves and muscles screaming.

"Is there anything I can do to help?" She was still there, hanging on, flinching as another big one broke over them and shuddered the hull. He couldn't spare her a glance.

"Pray, Saint Ariadne. Pray."

23

"MITCHELL, YOU DRECK! THIS is fucking crazy! Take us back—" Leeza loses her grip as the boat slews crazily. She smacks her hip against the table and falls. "Shit!"

The storm bellows, mocking. Lightning strobes. She's zinging with the hot spinal surge of fear, adrenaline, the onset of the second upper she'd popped. She bares her teeth, gums tingling, biting the sharp tang of the high.

The boat bucks and heaves, waves breaking over the windows. Leeza's plugged into her backpack unit, trying to catch some visuals on nightscope. The boat shudders sideways and she scrabbles for a grip, loses it, slides across the floor in a clutter of plastic dishes. Alarm flames, the rush exploding through her nerves into panic as beyond the rain-smeared window a mountain of churning water rears up raging monster *Madre de Dios* black abyss beneath it sucking them down.

"Oh, my God!" She dives under the table, huddling, eyes squinched shut and hanging on as the boat tips, rolls way over, shudders and shakes and finally plunges upright again, climbing another wave. Wind bellows, engines shrieking in her ears.

"Damn it, that's it!" Terrorized, and pissed-OFF, she crawls out, slithers and gropes her way to the wheel where Ariadne and the asshole are shouting over the noise. Ariadne's waving a hand, they're totally ignoring Leeza and all she can see is black out there, rain lashing streaming over the windshield.

"Mitchell, you bastard!" she screams. "You'll get us killed! Take us back!"

They don't even look at her, Mitchell leaning over the wheel, one hand reaching for the throttle.

"Stop it! I said, take me back! I'm out, get it?" She grabs his arm.

"Christ!" He jumps, then shakes her violently off, and she bangs her elbow on something. "Keep her off me!" he yells at Ariadne as the boat slews crazily over again and he's like a madman on the wheel, swearing, foaming whitewater breaking against the side windows.

"Asshole!" Leeza lunges for him. "Don't you dare—"

"Lisa!" Ariadne grabs her arm and pulls her back, Leeza fighting but Ariadne's like a rock, shit she's strong.

Another bellow in the night, flash of lightning and a breaker foaming, spilling over them, they're tipping under it.

"No! Help!" Leeza screams and clutches at Ariadne but they're falling, nothing under her feet and then Wham! Pain bursts through her head. Darkness....

"Lisa."

Voice far off beyond the roaring, heaving, and the pain throbbing her head. "Lisa. Leeza. Can you hear me?"

And then the touch. That magic touch. Cool water in a desert, gentle mother-love, a bed of blossoms, sparkling sun on soft seas and the laughing dolphins. Fingers lightly stroke her head, voice murmuring, "Let the pain go, Leeza." That touch tingles down her spine, the pain of her cracked head washing away in the waves to a distant ache. "It's all right. We're through the worst."

Warm arms hold her as the boat crashes and shudders through the storm, the murmur of Ariadne's heart near her ear. Lisa's come home.

∞

"Wow." She wakes up alive the next morning, sunlit blue sea past the bunk porthole, rolling by in smooth innocent swells now. The engines droning steady-Eddie. Just to make sure, Leeza Links in and pulls on the monitoring headset.

*** *"Madre de Dios!"* Raging monster black seas heave and hurl Leeza into the maw of the storm.

"Holy shit!" She's plugged IN! It's the ultimate Link, nerves flayed on the razor edge between blind gibbering chaos and the transcendent art of terror. A scream sings electric down her spine.

That giant fist of foaming whitewater grabs her, hurls her against the hull, and her head cracks in a blossom of pain and then darkness....

"Lisa." Warm whisper in her ear. And bringing her home, Ariadne's arms hold her safe***

"Yes!" Leeza exited, humming. That storm—pure gold stored on chip. *"Blast me to the heart of your fire...."* she sang, watching jagged black islets swell closer up ahead.

She cautiously touched her head where she'd cracked it the night before and conked out. Still a little sore, but there wasn't even a goose-egg. Leeza grinned. Even better—now she could add her own experience of "Saint Ariadne's healing touch." She glanced over at the other bunk and saw she was still sleeping, turned toward the hull.

Leeza gathered her gear and crawled up the ladder to the cabin. Resetting to Record, she raised the camera to her eye, a tune dancing at her fingertips. She panned the trashed kitchen alcove, scattered food and dishes, and stealthily zoomed in on the wheelhouse, Mitchell busy at the controls.

He turned to the side to check something, and she caught his face, looking ragged-out. He sipped from a coffee bulb—clueless, turning down her offer of uppers. Bouncing sun and wave lights played up creases around his eyes. Leeza tightened focus. Face square and blunt-edged, dark stubble of beard coming on, wavy hair rumpled. Sweat-stained sleeveless T-shirt showing off biceps.

Female audience would go for the low-life macho appeal. Welcome to it. Leeza made a face and took her gear back down below to the forward bunks. The foc'sle, Captain Bligh called it.

Ariadne had turned, sleeping face half-hidden by her upflung arm. The strong hand lay palm up, fingers relaxed, cupping something invisible.

Choice. Leeza hummed, zooming in. She was buzzing along on a nice even keel, jagged bummer of the night before melted away into the warmth she could still feel of Ariadne holding her close. Fingers soothing away the pain of her bashed head.

Ariadne stirred, blanket dragging down over her cheesy cotton dress. Where did she dig up those dumpy good-Hejab sacks she wore? Could have closets full of designer originals. Ariadne took a deep, sighing breath, her perfect profile serene as a statue.

Warmth rippled down Leeza's spine as the camera lingered on Ariadne's face. She panned to the lax fingers she could still feel stroking her head, calming her. That old magic touch she remembered from those massages back at the sorority. Pulling back to wide angle, she drew in the harsh aluminum angle of the hull, good contrast to soft skin, cloud of loose hair.

The story kept expanding on Leeza. She was stretching, trying to capture all the angles—the facets?—but she could almost taste the overall concept. What a rollercoaster ride, from the crucified Son of the Prophet, and the wounded Med League soldier Ariadne had miraculously saved, to the raw speeding jolt of last night, to this peaceful bubble out of time. Not that distant Saint Ariadne, but the flesh and blood woman, vulnerable.

Right, Chiquita, stick to the plan, she reminded herself. *Get close enough to stick in the knife. Don't forget, Kenny died because she wouldn't send some lousy funds she wouldn't even notice, bunch of bullshit excuses she didn't get my messages. Right. Now I'm gonna make sure <u>she</u> loses what matters most....*

She took a deep breath. What *did* matter to Ariadne? It had been Leeza, once. She closed her eyes. Maybe it could be again. That would change things, wouldn't it? Maybe they were both here, together, for a bigger reason. Put the word out about this mission Ariadne was on?

A pang at the thought of sharing her this way with all the world, but this was Art. If they could see the true Ariadne through Leeza's eyes, feel her bone-deep through Leeza's honed senses—

"Knock it off." A hand thrust over the lens, pushing the camera aside.

Leeza, jolted out of her vision of synthesis, saw Mitchell's bleary mug glaring down at her. She yanked the camera back. "If you touch my gear one more time...." She flushed with rage.

"Then put it away." He moved between the bunks, crossing his arms. "You agreed not to record her." He leaned over to awkwardly pull the blanket up over Ariadne's shoulder.

"Don't make me puke, Mitchell." Leeza plucked the leads free of her spinal insert. "You her big hero now?"

He scowled. "Look, whatever you're up to, save it 'til you're off my boat. And that might be right quick, like over the rail, if you pull another stupid stunt like last night. When I'm at the wheel, you stay clear and obey orders. Get it?" He turned to go.

"Hey, Mitchell, I'll give you some free advice, you're so clueless. You might as well save the effort. Not that Ariadne would bother with a loser like you anyway, but she doesn't go for men. Get it?"

He turned sharply, gave Leeza a look, then shook his head. "I get it all right." His nostrils flared. "*You* should save the effort. Josef at the taverna told me all about her lover on the island—some guy named Michael Vendemis. So I doubt she'd be interested in your reptile charms."

"You're lying. She gave me her ring, told me we'd be together again—"

"Jesus." He stepped back, looking stunned. He glanced at Ariadne and swallowed. "That sapphire ring."

Another time Leeza would have laughed at the look on his face, but she felt sick. Ariadne, letting some gross hairy peasant fuck her? No, Mitchell was lying. She pulled her lips back in a sneer, flashing her ring at him. "Ariadne gave it to me when we were in college together, back in the States. We were lovers."

He spun around and headed for the ladder up. He turned back, jaw clenched. "I don't have time for this shit. I need you up top, help me spot reefs. *Now*. We're... taking a shortcut."

"Great." Leeza made a face, but peeled herself off the bunk to follow him up. "You're the one full of goatshit, Mitchell. You and your pal Josef." She stepped into the cabin, waggling the flashy blue stone again.

"Maybe not." He gave her an ugly leer. "I've been around Greeks awhile, and they think about some things different than you do. Like the young girls are watched pretty close around guys, but they're real touchy-feely with other girls. It's okay if they experiment a little. You know, nothing they take seriously."

24

WHITE LIGHT SHIMMERS IN Ariadne's hands, flowing from the stones of the earth, all colors blended to one smooth wave, ringing that pure ethereal tone. The world rings like a tapped crystal.

She cups the glowing white light in her hands. But the saints are frowning on the cracked ceiling of the chapel, climbing down to surround her, their dark stares stabbing, accusing—

Her eyes snapped open. She stared, disoriented, at the metal cubicle enclosing her. A coffin?

She bolted upright in the bunk and saw the bow wake slapping gently past the porthole. Letting out a shaky breath, she lay back again and closed her eyes.

Maze lines—*electrical schematics, crystalline lattice matrix*—glimmered afterimages behind her eyelids. She could still feel the forces pulsing through her, feel her hands funneling a laserlike light to guide Yanni back to life.

Had she gone too far? She'd finally had to accept what Dr. Singh had pointed out—she held some unexplained ability to affect the bioelectric fields of those wounded or ill, to help them heal. She respected the scientific method, and if she was indeed "the variable," there had to be an explanation. But she was treading perilously close to some undefined boundary, losing grasp of the delineations of reality. What was happening to her? Was she becoming a divining-rod to minute electromagnetic, bioelectric field variations? She could feel them in her bones.

She raised her hands and pressed trembling fingertips against her aching skull. All she knew was the great need. She could feel the imbalance in the earth itself, in the sky. If she was mad, so be it. The old realities were obsolete.

She sat up, taking a deep breath, one hand raised in habit to the soothing planes of her crystal pendant. All she could do now was to wait until they arrived at Tinos.

Clang. A sudden blow against the metal hull. The jolt threw Ariadne against the side. *Nereid* shuddered and swung around, jolting again. *Clang*. The engines cut back, boat wallowing side to side.

Ariadne pulled herself upright and hurried up on deck, blinking in a bright, acrid haze.

"Damn it! I told you to watch off to port. Sonuvabitch!" Peter Mitchell was clambering down off the flying bridge to confront Leeza. "What are you on this time?"

"Fuck you, dickhead!" She shoved past him from the bow.

"What's wrong?" Ariadne rubbed her eyes.

Leeza scowled. "Why don't you ask Captain Bligh?" She slammed into the cabin.

Mitchell was up in the bow, leaning over the side. "Great! Just terrific."

Ariadne peered under her hand over the sea. "Where are we?"

Craggy black outcrops pocked the waters. Two larger fragments of an islet, curving around them, formed a cauldron of jagged cliffs, streaked in irregular bands of color—pinkish, brown, purple   cut by flows of steaming black, solidifying lava. They closed in on both sides of the boat, passage narrowing ahead. Drifting with the breeze, a haze of ash, steam, and smoke. Over the low swells, all around the boat, washed a bobbing flotsam of pumice, carved in fantastic shapes.

"What is this? You're taking us through the eruption zone?" Ariadne moved to the rail and leaned over. The channel shimmered an unhealthy acid-green color, steaming. Now and then a bubbling boil rose from the depths, bursting in bitter fumes. She straightened, staring at Mitchell, who'd come up beside her.

He wiped his sweaty face. "Caught a report, said that little eruption yesterday took the pressure off. I was trying to shave some time, cut through the channel where nobody would look for us and maybe make Tinos by nightfall. Hole up while everyone's busy cleaning up after the storm." He rubbed reddened eyes. "Radio cleared for a while—interference kicking up again now—but I caught something from Radio Med. You were killed in an explosion during the storm."

Ariadne caught a quick breath.

"Could be your uncle just putting that out for the mercenaries, and the Sons. Hope they bite." He blew out a breath. "But I picked up a fisherman's distress call south of here, too. He was trying to hail a hydrofoil he'd spotted, maybe that mercenary boat. So we have to stay sharp."

She nodded. "What happened here? Is the boat damaged? No one uses this passage now, with the renewed volcanic activity."

He raked a hand through his hair. "Miss Congeniality was supposed to be spotting for shallow reef. One nailed us. I wasn't going fast, so the hull just got dinged. But it looks like the port prop got bent, too, so I'll have to compensate. We might not make Tinos before dark."

Ariadne stared over the seething surface, the shifting chunks of pumice and wafting steam. She shuddered with foreboding.

"What a scene! Prime material." Leeza, emerging from the cabin with her recording gear, shot them both a defiant look. She stalked to the bow and strapped on her camera goggles, facing the sea and the scorched cliffs closing in. "Subliminal."

Mitchell rolled his eyes. "Better get underway." He started for the bridge.

"Wait!" Ariadne's hand shot out to stop him. "I...." She shook her head and pulled her hand back.

"What is it, *Despoina*?" His voice was surprisingly gentle.

She met his gaze, and cleared her throat. "I... have a bad feeling about this place. Can we go back, go around the cindercone instead?"

"It's farther back now, through the volcanic junk, than ahead. Better to push on. No safe place to anchor around here, come nightfall."

"Yes. Of course." Her gaze was drawn to the lifeless rock, gray ash dusting ragged ridges in the smoky haze. The sea heaved its grotesque carpet of floating pumice, bubbles splatting on the surface. She shuddered. "It looks like the end of the world."

"Lighten up!" Leeza sauntered over, recorder at her hip, camera goggles like insect eyes. "It's primeval." She struck a pose and sang, "*New world, planet vibes, it's the evo-LU-tion....*"

Peter Mitchell snorted. "Either way, we're all dinosaurs." He climbed onto the bridge and started the engines. They roared, then settled to a lower pitch as the boat eased forward. The hull vibrated jarringly with the damaged prop.

"Up in the bow, you two!" Mitchell shouted down. "Fend off the bigger chunks with those boathooks. Sing out if you see any shallow reef."

Ariadne started forward, but stopped short as uneasiness shivered through her again. Her ears were ringing. She closed her eyes, gripping her crystal pendant.

With a jolt, she felt it clearly now. That disturbance, the dread shuddering her bones. Pressure building on a quake fault. Close. Building to the critical point.

"Mr. Mitchell!" She hurried up beside him. "Hurry! We must get through that channel, into open water."

"Look, I'm doing the best I—"

"You don't understand. There's a quake coming. Soon."

"Quake? You've got to be kidding."

"It's coming. An earthquake. I can feel it."

Clearly exasperated, he started to snap at her, then took a deep breath and looked into her eyes. He finally stepped back, lifted his palms, and groaned. "Okay, an earthquake. That could mean a tsunami, too. You know what a wave like that would do to us in here?" He jabbed a hand at the tight channel ahead, the floating pumice chunks. "What am I supposed to do now?"

"Hurry, Mr. Mitchell." She turned to climb down, but couldn't resist returning his gibe during the storm: "And pray."

25

"COME ON, *NEREID*. HANG in there." Peter, at the wheel, muttered through the bandanna tied over his nose and mouth against the ash and fumes. "Get us through here, I'll pray to old Poseidon himself."

The engines roared and rattled in response, dinged-up prop vibrating to the point of damage, but he had to push her. They were entering the channel, skirting a fresh lava flow. The pumice chunks formed a thick carpet now, undulating on their wake. Even working the poles, the gals couldn't fend them all off. "Damn!"

A muffled call. Ariadne, gray wraith in the bow, Peter's spare shades dusted with ash, turned to gesture to port.

He nodded and swung wide around the floating wreckage of a fishing boat. The smashed timbers were festooned with plastic bags, a rusted bucket, seagull carcass, rumpled wad of cloth.

"Wait!" Ariadne shouted up at him, pointing at the wreckage.

"Fuck! Gross!" Leeza, covered head to toe in some kind of hazmat jumpsuit, pulled down the filter mask she'd produced from her bags. "Keep going, Mitchell! It's a body, who knows what germs!" She slapped the mask back on and pushed the pole at some pumice.

He blinked and saw the bundle of rags was a bloated corpse. For once Conreid was talking sense. He edged the throttles up to the tooth-rattling point, just below the rpm's that really triggered the hammering hull tremors. His ears were ringing with the engine noise. They had to get through the channel.

"Mr. Mitchell!" A hand tugged on his arm.

"Shit, don't do that!"

Ariadne was pointing at the corpse. "We must bring the body in."

"No way!" He turned back to the wheel. "No time. What about that quake?"

She winced and rubbed her temples. "I can't sense the pressure now. Perhaps I was—"

He caught her arm, eyes widening as he looked past her.

She blinked, turning to look at the narrowing rock walls of the channel. The shivering flotsam of pumice, burned lumber, fishing nets, oil drum was slowly subsiding. The seawater level was sinking down the walls.

Ariadne turned and stared into his eyes. Recognition and shock echoed between them.

She gasped and hustled down the ladder to grab her pole. "Hurry, Peter! We may have only minutes!"

He didn't need her to tell him. Subsidence. Front trough of a tsunami wave train. They had to get through the channel into deeper water.

He shoved both the throttles forward. *Nereid* surged ahead erratically, turbos screaming, hull shuddering deep in the guts, trying to tear herself apart. They plowed through the floating chunks, crashing and clanging off the bow.

"Motherfucker!" Leeza, dropping her pole, stumbled and went sliding back, catching the rail. She shot him the bird and kicked the pole aside, huffing off to the stern.

Gripping the wheel, arms shaking with the tremors of the laboring boat, Peter wrestled her around another floating mass of tangled boards and lines and bleached bones. He rammed on through more debris, muttering half-forgotten prayers they didn't catch a piece of net wrapping the shaft or they'd all be corpses. Ariadne, in the bow, gripped with one hand and still gamely tried to fend off floating pumice with the pole.

"Let it go! Get aft and tie yourselves onto storm lines!" The sea level was still dropping down the channel walls. Up ahead, open sea. Close. Not close enough.

Jostling, shivering, the flotsam had stopped sinking.

"Shit!" He pushed *Nereid* for a final spurt. The damaged prop churned up flailing foam, roar of the engines deafening, boat pitching, all wrong forcing her, but he could feel the seas gathering, sucking the water in like a giant breath, all those tons and tons gathering to come crashing down. He muscled through a last clot of pumice and debris panicky voice shrieking in his ears Hurry Hurry rank sweat cold plastering itchy grit down his back—

Finally! They roared past the cut and Out.

He shuddered, gasping, easing off the throttles. Somewhere hot metal stink and oil burning. Christ, he was going to have a mess on his hands down in the engine room. If the shaft bearing went she was fucked, but they just needed to get a little farther out into deep water. He checked the chart readouts and matched the dropping bottom contours until they were past the point where a crest would break. He sagged and dropped her back to a steady chug.

"Sorry, *Nereid*, old gal. You did it." He patted the rail.

As if nodding, the bow rose and slowly dipped over a smooth rolling hummock of ocean swell passing under the boat.

He pulled off the bandanna and wiped his face, turning to call back below. "That was the wavefront passing. We're okay."

"What? You've got to be kidding!" Leeza flung down her storm line, unzipped her jumpsuit, and pulled off her camera goggles. She threw back her head and laughed. "Fucking-A! Really had us going, Captain Dreck! What a joke." Kicking away the jumpsuit, she snorted and gestured at the smooth seas rolling past.

Peter grabbed his binoculars and scanned back over their heads. The first tsunami crest was hitting the shallows now, rearing up and up into raging whitewater, unreal against the distant stark ashy islands. His ears were still ringing. He caught a sharp breath as the monster wave smashed into the mouth of the channel, flinging foam high up the walls, churning the channel full of debris. He could feel the second wave front passing smoothly beneath them.

Ariadne was peering over the stern rail. She shuddered and turned to look up at Peter, her face gone pale. She slid down to sit on the deck, head in her hands.

"Hey, Conreid, bring your gear up here. Got a good zoom on that camera?" He suppressed a grin and waved her up.

She shrugged, but climbed up. He gestured back toward the channel.

Rolling her eyes, she raised the goggles to her face again. The second wave was just hitting the channel.

She jerked back against him, and he steadied her.

"What?" She gasped, then whispered, *"Madre...."* She went white and slumped back limp into Peter's arms.

26

BOBBING LAVA PIECES, TWISTED *into gargoyles leering.* Jodas! *She's trying to run, jumping from bobbing chunk to chunk as they sink beneath her. Ariadne, her face like one of those frowning Byzantine saints, looms huge overhead, filling the sky. "The quake. Hurry. It's coming."*

Leeza can't even scream. Tsunami! Killer wave foaming over her—

"Uhn!" She jerked upright and smacked her head in the bunk, stars flaring. *"Chinga tu madre!"* She rubbed her head and scowled. Big deal. So the banged-up propellor slowed them down and it was all her fault. They'd made it out to open sea okay, hadn't they?

She shook her head, rumpled her hair, did a quick series of face and jaw exercises, ending with a grimace. Sitting up on the bunk, she called, "Ariadne?"

No answer. The boat rocked slow on its anchor lines. Leeza tugged a silk tunic over her head and stepped gingerly onto the metal decking, toes curling at the damp grittiness. The open skylight funneled a fresh breeze and stars. She climbed up, out to the stern deck, blinking at the night. She hadn't gotten two winks the night before, once they'd finally crept up on the island after dusk. Too wired. Now she'd slept the day away.

Above her, Ariadne sat on the flying bridge, gazing out at the black water of the cove shimmering faint silver reflections. Leeza tilted her head back to see more stars winking on as black patches of ragged cloud swept off toward the blacker horizon. Folded sheets of pale green and magenta auroras hung from the dark heavens, twisting like worms.

"Maximal." People freaked over the displays, used-to-be only in high latitudes, before the geomag shakeup. Called them signs of the Apocalypse. For a second, fear clutched Leeza. What if they were right, what if none of it meant shit because they were all dying? Like dinosaurs.

"Bull-*mierda*," she whispered. "It's a free light show." She bared her teeth in a grin and turned back to the bridge. "Ariadne?"

She didn't move, just staring at the water as the boat rocked slow like a cradle. Leeza started to raise her voice, then caught a quick breath, glanced around, and darted back down below.

It might be her only chance. She'd seen the chips in with Ariadne's stuff. If they were compatible with her own system.... She yanked open the cabinet under the bunk, rifling through Ariadne's bag. Her fingers closed over a microchip in its envelope. She was sure she'd seen another one, but she couldn't find it. She pulled out her own recorder. Ariadne's chip was lower density than Leeza used, but it read anyway, her fingers tapping a crazy tattoo as the damn thing blinked its Wait light and it was taking freaking forever—

Movement tipped the boat. "*Carajo!*" Leeza thrust the chip into Ariadne's bag, started to stuff it back in the cabinet.

"Leeza?" Ariadne was peering down from the ladder.

Leeza produced a grin and lifted her recorder. "Oh. Morning. I mean night. I was just looking for a fresh chip, thought I'd run some copy on the auroras up there." She risked a glance at Ariadne. "Can't find my extra gear bag."

"Your equipment is in the other compartment."

"Oh. Right. Still half asleep." Leeza latched Ariadne's cabinet, opening the one on the other side to rummage through her own bag. "Here it is. Don't want to miss that color." She slung camera and recorder over her shoulder and hustled up the ladder, avoiding Ariadne's eyes.

She made a show of Linking in on deck, raising the camera, and it was good stuff, sheets of rippling aurora lights against dark sky, cool breeze off the water, rhythmic sway of the boat. "I'm getting some super material." Transmission and reception were still blocked by turbulence, but she could record to chip. "You want to Link into my files, check out a replay of that storm? It's a rush."

"No." Voice emphatic.

Leeza lowered the camera. "Not you, too! Don't tell me you're afraid of the NeuroLink."

"Have you thought about what it could be doing to you? It's addicting, Leeza. Have you read the studies raising questions of longterm nerve and cognitive damage? And there may be a higher incidence of RP-Hansen's among Link users."

"NeoLuddite buzz crushers! I'm telling you, the Link's a mind-blower."

"Maybe literally!" Ariadne touched her arm. "Leeza, what about taking a break from it? And the drugs? Use this trip to slow down, see how you feel without this constant overstimulation."

Leeza wrenched back from the pity, that old goddamn arrogance. "Save it for your adoring peasants, Saint A." Jaw clamping, she jerked the camera to her eye and turned it on the shimmering auroras.

"Leeza...."

Bitch. She locked into the Link. Switching over to Scan, she checked out what she'd scored down below from Ariadne's chip.

Most of the files security coded, she'd have to get the techno geeks back home to work on that. A couple of open files were copies of scientific papers. Scrolling through, she couldn't get much except they were results of some Russian studies connecting geomagnetism and dowsing. She didn't know what good that would do her, wasn't even sure what dowsing was. Walking around with a forked stick looking for water?

Leeza shut it down and jacked out. She shot a half-guilty, half-gloating look at Ariadne, back up on the bridge and brooding over the dark sea. Her own fault—she was so uptight. Refusing to discuss the healing stories, refusing to be recorded, refusing to come down off Mount Olympus.

Leeza sighed. *Don't blow it, Chiquita.*

"Ariadne?" She stowed her gear, climbed up the ladder, and eased onto the bench beside her. "Hey. Take Two?" She looked over the cove, dark curve of cliffs enclosing it, shush of waves lapping. "Does the water always keep moving like this?" She made a rocking cradle with her hands.

"It's caused by the earthquake and tsunami. Sometimes it lasts a few days—like water settling in a washtub."

"And we're the rubber duckies. So where's the big hero?"

Ariadne dropped her hand from the glinting facets of her pendant. "Mr. Mitchell took the dinghy around the island to town." She rubbed her eyes. "He needed parts for repairs. And with radio reception still blocked by electromagnetic interference, he wanted to see if there was any news in town. Anyone searching for us."

"Oh." Leeza shrugged off a prickle of alarm. "Maybe we'll get lucky and he'll spend the night. Miracle we got here at all with that clown in charge."

"He's done a good job."

"He's a loser." Leeza waggled a dismissing hand, lounging back on the bench and curling her legs up catlike. She arched against the thin silk of her tunic, exposing a nice stretch of hip and thigh. Propping her chin on her cupped palm, she gave Ariadne an unblinking straight-on.

Deep blue eyes held on hers, unreadable in the dimness. Then Ariadne turned back to the cove, sighing.

"You need to relax, Ri. You'll burn out." She lifted her hands to Ariadne's shoulders and kneaded, then glided her palms down the firm arms.

Ariadne edged away, shaking her head. "I need to think."

A pouty smile up at that grave, shadowed face. "So serious! Forgot how to have fun? Let it go 'til morning." She ran a fingertip over Ariadne's hand. "I can help...."

She pulled her hand away.

"Hey!" Leeza sat up. "You can talk to me. Remember?"

"That was a long time ago." Her silhouette had gone stiff. "I told you, if you came along, you could not expect—"

"Damn it!" Leeza caught her wrist. "I'm not asking you for anything! But we were friends, Ariadne. Lovers."

Ariadne pulled loose from Leeza's grip. "I'm sorry if you were hurt, Lisa. But you need to move on."

"Oh, right!" She snorted. "You can't pretend with me, act like you don't need anybody. I'm the one who knows you best."

"You don't know me." Voice flat. "Neither of us is the same person she was eight years ago, and—"

"I'm not good enough for you? Sounds like the same old story." Her voice shook. "Ariadne Demodakis can't lower herself to keep promises to a lowly muck-raking journalist?"

"No promises, Leeza." She shook her head. "There were never any—"

"No, of course not. Bet you got the shock of your life when I showed up with your precious ring." Leeza thrust her face close to Ariadne's. "Well, you can lay off the purity routine, stop pretending you're not down here in the dirt with the rest of us. Fucking some grubby goat-herder, that's real class."

Silence. Swish of waves. Then her voice, still infuriatingly slow and measured, "What are you saying?"

"Mitchell told me. He was digging around, found out you were sleeping with this Michael somebody on the island." She sucked in a quick breath, mind racing. "Too bad you didn't see him. Licking his lips while you were sleeping, saying what a juicy piece of ass you'd be once you shed the Saintly act."

She went on, picking up steam, "They're all like that! They don't know how to tune in with a woman, can't connect the way we can. We *had* it, Ariadne. You really want some gross prick?"

"Enough!" Ariadne stood abruptly, boat dipping as she climbed down the ladder.

A buzz swelled over the cove, shadows spitting out the inflated dinghy and its whiny little electric motor. Mitchell called, "Ho, *Nereid*. Just me." The motor cut off and the dinghy bumped up against the boat. "You two get some sleep?"

When neither of them answered, he raised his voice. "I could use a hand here. Got the stuff I needed in town, lucky thing the waves didn't hit the other side of the island. Just a little quake and storm damage. So I taverna-hopped around the harbor to check things out. Radios are still out, no news." His dim shape hoisted a bulging sack. "Told them I was a trader, blown off course by the winds, laying up for repairs offshore. They're busy cleaning up the town, nobody will be bothering us here." He paused, his shadowed face tilted up to the silent deck. "What? Something happen here?"

Ariadne looked down, silhouette rigid. "Nothing." She spun on her heel and strode into the cabin.

Mitchell looked up at Leeza on the bridge. "What—?"

She threw back her head and laughed.

27

LATER IT WOULD BE hot. But this early, the sky was still a cool, cloudless blue, the sun just rising above the hills.

Ariadne drank in the breeze with its taste of the sea and the dusty earth. She lengthened her stride, moving easily along the goat path through jagged rocks and thorn, savoring the solitude.

The path turned sharply. She climbed over a steep jumble of boulders, rough surfaces gripping like sandpaper. The raw landscape showed no sign of the storm's passage, until she came up onto a ridge crest to look out over the sea and the cove below. Against the far walls, flotsam dipped and rose against the rocks—smashed planks, a red plastic basin, the carcass of a dog already attended by hungry gulls. Closer, *Nereid* bobbed like a toy, anchor lines threading clear azure. A curly dark head emerged from the cabin, and Ariadne backed quickly from the brink.

She turned, putting behind her Leeza's sulking face and Peter's exasperated protest against this solo foray ashore. She hurried down the trail.

Descending turns took her into the next ravine. She tried to recover the simple pleasure of the breeze sliding over her face and her bare legs beneath the skirt, the flush of exertion after her confinement on the boat. But all she could feel now was an irritable sensation of urgency goading her along. At the same time, palpable waves of pressure pushed against her, as if she were breasting an incoming surf.

Thick silence closed in. No chatter of small birds. Within these clashing geomagnetic fields, they could become disoriented, lose their way....

It was a physical effort to concentrate. She took a deep breath and strode faster down the trail, rounding a switchback past a bluff cutting off the view of the sea. She stopped short. The trail broke away in a gap of raw earth and tumbled rocks where a fresh fault ran through the bluff, dropping the ground level beyond it. Pressure beat inside her head, breaking into jarring eddies. She edged along the remaining stone lip, glancing uneasily up the fault line.

Her ears were ringing again. The earth was a cracked bell, clanging with the reverberations that could last for days after a quake. No one else seemed to hear them, but now they screamed inside her, demanding... *what*, she didn't know. She had no choice but to obey. Fear slithered through her, but it didn't matter. She tightened the straps of the knapsack holding her magnetometer, a portable model used by mining scouts to locate mineral seams. She scrambled down shifting rocks to the chopped-off trail, using the tall sensor rod as a steadying staff. She glanced at the data readout clipped to the knapsack belt, adjusted the rod's orientation, and hurried on without pausing to shake the pebbles from her sandals.

Another switchback brought her back toward the cove, into a rising breeze. The restless itch down her spine intensified, driving her on as the trail ended in untracked rock. She climbed up another weathered bluff and looked over into a cleft running toward a dropoff above the sea.

In the heart of the parched ravine, a patch of green glowed jewel-like. A scatter of wild crimson poppies bobbed in the breeze.

Ariadne climbed down. As she did, the insistent thrumming fell away into a muffled sensation, an underwater gliding as she stepped onto the shelf of green grass and blossoms. She suddenly *knew* it: this was the place, the calm heart of the maelstrom.

She shrugged off the knapsack and set it down, initiated the data analysis of the magnetometer measurements of the wavering fields, although she already knew it would confirm the anomalies Arun Singh and Teresa Esposito had charted. Then she closed her eyes and took a deep breath, arms dropping to her sides. Slowly she sank to her knees, pulled toward the cool earth where the sun had not yet penetrated. She reached out to touch a translucent blossom.

Helen Vendemis had loved the poppies Ariadne would bring, beautiful and frail as Helen herself after that last tortured childbirth. Tears stung Ariadne's eyes. She pressed them tightly shut, suddenly furious at Leeza and Peter Mitchell for prying at her life, her memories.

The shivering silence of the place beat against her ears. It was Helen who'd been the strong one, even in her physical pain and weakness, the one who'd challenged Ariadne to face the growing attraction to Helen's husband Michael. She'd begged Ariadne to relieve her of the burden of "wifely duty," the agony of further pregnancies.

Ariadne had flung aside caution all too readily. She'd willfully lost herself, with Michael, in the blind mazes of the body's delight.

Helen had known she was dying, had gone serene in the belief that Ariadne would marry Michael and take care of the family. Then he started making demands. Ariadne had made another mistake—the traditions in the islands were too strong, and she had no intention of becoming a Greek wife, a man's property. Retreating in alarm, she'd guiltily established a trust fund, dowries for Helen's daughters. And she'd been relieved when Michael found a new wife on another island, moving his family there.

Perhaps Leeza was right—all men were the same in their need to control and possess. She should have learned that from her father. But were women only different in their methods?

Ariadne wondered if she were incapable of the surrender that true friendship, intimacy, seemed to demand. The trust. And even if she had wanted to let down her guard now, it was too dangerous, impossible with so much at stake. Her loneliness simply didn't matter.

She opened stinging eyes and touched the blossom again, careful not to loosen its tenuous hold on the rocky soil. Helen would have reminded her that the first poppies meant rebirth for the islands, the blood-red cups a sign of the coming Easter season.

Smiling through her tears, Ariadne nodded, rose to her feet, and lifted her chin. Raising her arms in a smooth sweep—*bird wings, lifting, circling*—she stepped slowly, ceremoniously, dipping and rising in a peasant dance. She flung back her head, crying out to the sky as she spun, twirling. Her feet were light over the grass, feathered, as she danced the silent music ringing up from the earth.

Finally she dropped onto the grass, blood pulsing in her ears. She pressed her flattened palms over the soil and felt the forces whirl around this center, pulling her inward. Into the comforting, frightening velvet darkness at the heart of mother earth. A tense fullness poured into her, welling up like the underground spring flowing beneath her, through fissures in the ancient vein of quartz, itself a frozen river of stone. She could see it.

She blinked. It was only common sense telling her, as any island goatherd would know, that beneath this green oasis ran an underground spring. Of course it would find its course along a mineral seam. The instrument readings would verify her hypothesis.

As if mocking logic, her fingers reflexively found the polished crystal of her pendant, though its cool serenity eluded her today. *Why do you play this game?* some inner voice was accusing. *You feel it. You know.*

She *could* feel it, a strange effervescence fizzing along her nerve pathways, something like the energy of the activated mineral water she used for her healing experiments. But this was more intense, ebbing and flowing with jarring eddies. Rising to her feet, she closed her eyes, obeying an impulse to open her arms, sweep her downturned palms in a slow circle as she cut through the shivering waves like a rolling wheel. She had to push against resistance until she was aligned, arms parallel to the flow.

She opened her eyes, saw that her right hand was pointing through the hill, in the direction of the town and sanctuary of the Tioniotissa, where the healing waters of the sacred spring bubbled out of the ground to fill Her sacred well.

Turning abruptly, Ariadne paced down the ravine. The drop above the narrow end of the cove stopped her, as she stared unfocused over the water. A dark glimmer caught her eye, and she leaned out to peer over the cliff, squinting through the reflections of rising sun over stirring sea. To her left, the cliff plunged straight into the cove. Farther, in a narrow cleft she hadn't noticed from the water, the cliff was undercut, and a cave sucked in and spewed out a swirl of restless waves. Eddies clashed and foamed, fighting the regular beat of the surge, swirling like the waves of pressure assailing Ariadne.

The whirlpool sucks her into its chaotic depths. Blackness spinning inward to a blind tunnel—

She wrenched back from the ledge, turning to face a dazzle of sunlight spilling over the bluff into the ravine. Blinded, she raised a shielding hand. She strode over to the magnetometer to check its analysis, dimensions and orientation playing across the display. The data confirmed a substantial quartz seam, laced with ore veins, its diamagnetic charge aligned as expected in the opposite direction of the predominant ambient field. The seam ran directly beneath her in the exact orientation she had found with her outstretched arms, cutting through the steep hills toward Tinos town on the other side, and behind her toward the cove. Arrowing straight to the submerged black cave entrance and its whirlpool of subterranean forces calling her, pulling her.

Ariadne shivered in the warm sun. She hastily packed up her instruments, hurrying through the red splashes of poppy petals to the trail.

28

"NO WAY." PETER TOSSED his coffee dregs over the side. They splashed beside the dinghy where Ariadne sat looking stubborn as a mule.

She tied off the inflatable to the stern transom and climbed up on deck to face him. "But—"

"Too dangerous with that turbulence. Anyway, it's probably flooded inside, if the cave goes anywhere at all."

She lowered her knapsack to the deck, taking a deep breath. Ready to lay down the law to the hired help. Since yesterday, she hadn't bestowed so much as a thank-you-Mr.-Mitchell-for-saving-our-butts-in-the-storm.

Peter turned to scowl over the cove, raking a hand through his hair. Between Her Holiness and the Lizard they'd drive him nuts, unless the *Tyrannos* or the mercenaries got him first. And now she wanted him to take her scuba-diving into a flooded cave.

He was already in too deep, his allergic reaction kicking in—people expecting, demanding things of him. Only this time he more than half wanted to pledge allegiance to Saint Ariadne Demodakis of the ocean-clear eyes. Fanatic's eyes?

"Where is Leeza?" Her low voice made him jump.

He turned back to her with a stiff shrug. "Down below, messing with her media gear. Transmission wavelengths still screwed up, otherwise she'd be sending out one of her nifty newsstims on you."

"She gave me her word not to transmit or record without my permission."

"And you trust her." He shook his head. "Ask her what she was doing while you were asleep underway."

"What *she* was—?" She bit it off, jaw clenching.

He lifted an eyebrow. "Time to cast off, now you have the measurements. I got the prop replaced, so we need to keep moving. I doubt your father bought your 'accident' in the lab, and the mercenaries won't trust it. We need to make ourselves scarce."

"Scarce?"

"Vamoose. Make waves."

Ariadne touched her crystal pendant in that habit he was getting to know. "I need a crystal from that quartz vein." She pointed toward the cleft at the base of the cliff. "We have time. You said no one was suspicious at the harbor."

"Too busy cleaning up the damage. But a sponge diver pulled into port after the storm, got to talking at the taverna and said he'd seen a fancy hydrofoil in the islands south of here. Could be the mercenaries."

"Mr. Mitchell, I appreciate your concerns. But I have not completed my experiment. That *is* why we are here."

"All right." He threw out his hands. "I'll get back into my diving gear and take a look inside that cave, get you a crystal if there really are any. Then we take off."

"I must go myself."

"You've done any scuba diving?"

"No." She steadily met his gaze. "But I am an excellent swimmer."

He paced the deck. "Look, that wouldn't be an easy dive, even for an experienced diver. Current. Cave penetration. Could be an undertow. Forget it. Tell me what to look for."

She looked out across the glinting bright blue of the cove, toward the cliff and the undercut black seam of shadow where the surge broke against the rocks into swirling foam. She made an odd little shaking-off motion. "I must go myself, Mr.—Peter. Truly, you would not recognize what I am looking for. Show me please how to use the equipment. As quickly I start, quickly we will leave."

"The sooner."

"I beg your pardon?"

"The sooner you start, the sooner...." He raised his palms. Out of his goddamn mind. "All right. I've got gear for two. Let's suit up."

29

THE INFLATABLE DINGHY BOBBED restlessly beside Ariadne as she floated face down on the cool sea. She was grateful for the warmth of the short wetsuit. Below, through wavering blue shadows, Peter was looping the anchor line around a boulder. A trail of air bubbles rose to the surface. She tightened her lips around the rubber grips and took in a slow, deep breath as he'd instructed her. The echoing sound was strange, but the steady, calming rhythm was something she didn't need to practice.

A school of fish darted in a synchronized cloud below, filtered sun shimmering over silver scales. They scattered in a burst of bubbles as Peter surfaced through them.

He activated her vest inflator, floating her shoulders and head out of the water. Pulling out his mouthpiece, he asked, "Okay?"

She started to nod, then remembered the signals he'd shown her and raised her hand, index finger joined to thumb in a circle.

He grinned. "Good." Reaching into the dinghy, he pulled down a coil of thin line, knotting one end to the anchor tether. "We'll pull this line along, in case there's an undertow inside. Keep a hand on it and stick close to me. I'll adjust your vest for you, just remember to clear your ears, and keep breathing out, especially on the way back up or you could rupture your lungs. Got it?"

She nodded, shivering as the sea foamed out from under the ledge behind him, swirling around her legs with the charged ripples of agitated energy she'd felt above on the ridge. It was stronger here, somehow threatening.

He touched her shoulder. She jerked her face to his, blinking through mist inside her mask.

"Sure you want to do this?"

She nodded, clearing her throat. "Yes. You have the tools? You will be very careful making an extraction?"

"You just point out the spot. Better clear your mask again, then we'll head down." He waited while she removed the mask, spat in it, and rinsed the glass. "Here we go." He handed her back the mouthpiece on its hose, then winked and sank below the surface, pulling the cord to release air from her vest.

A moment of disorientation as the water closed over her and she rolled, weightless. He touched her shoulder from behind and guided her slowly down. He turned her to face him and they hovered near the anchor line, surge tugging them toward the rocks and then pushing them away. She looked toward the gleaming, restless ceiling above and glimpsed a sleek shape darting. She made the OK sign. He reached over to snap on the light he'd strapped to her wrist, then gestured her after him.

His fins moved him slowly toward the submerged contours of rocky cliff. She followed closely, fighting the urge to flail against the surge tugging her off-balance. She clutched tighter to the line he pulled. He moved in close to the wall, his light sweeping back and forth. He gestured her closer, jabbing his thumb quickly up and then sideways, pointing at the boil of agitated water in the cave entrance. Before she could respond, he shot ahead, dragging her along on the line.

Hiss of air in her ears. Black rocks. Shadowed water pulling and tossing her back. Her leg slammed against a boulder, sea tumbling her, and she lost any sense of up or down in the maelstrom. Her breath caught in her throat, the suit and vest choking her, squeezing her lungs. She flailed, fighting the frightening force of the water, her fingers loosening on the line.

It suddenly jerked. Her hand tightened on it just in time to be tugged in the split-second pause between crashing surges through a narrow rushing gap and into a dark, open place. The water boiled, sucking back at her, but the line yanked her forward until she was free of the current. She remembered to let out the air trapped in her lungs, and a spill of bubbles escaped.

A light flashed over her face, then flicked away to highlight his hand in the *OK?* query. She took a careful breath, easing the tightness in her chest, and answered him. He squeezed her shoulder and adjusted her flotation valve, then his light was gesturing, the line pulling her deeper into blackness.

She was still off-balance, disoriented in the buoyant dark, but she flashed her light to catch her air bubbles as he'd told her. Their rising established up and down. She followed the glow of his light, shining her own through the inky water.

She saw only sweeping glimpses out of the darkness: His fins. A low, jagged rock ceiling overhead. A wall of featureless gray stone. She bobbed closer beside Peter and flattened her hand on the wall, closing her eyes. The air feed hissed to the restless energy jittering through her. She could no longer deny her link with the energy fields. The source was close, strong here.

Peter touched her shoulder. She opened her eyes to a diffused glow off the rock, his shrugged question.

She held up her hand, gesturing him back. She moved slowly down the wall, probing with the light, the back of her neck prickling with tension swirled by the trapped water. As she pulled herself across the rock wall, her light caught something that sparkled and gleamed.

She jerked back, throwing herself off-balance. Peter caught her arm and steadied her. She barely noticed. Her heart was pounding furiously, air hissing, skin crawling with the lapping waves of charge. She fought to keep her breaths deep and steady.

The quartz seam was exposed to the sea here, shining white in the dimness, glinting with metallic veins and crystalline flecks. She touched her flattened palm to it, an electric shock running up her arm. She gasped, held there by the jolt of it, the crystalline structure magnetized in opposition to the dominant ambient field. But there were also jarringly disruptive eddies, swirling in serpentine coils that pulled at her.

The dark waves throbbed through her. She could feel the hidden crystal, had to have it to understand… what? She couldn't think. Peter Mitchell's hand touched her shoulder again, but she shook it off. She moved closer to the wall, sliding her hand over the rough surface—no, as if her hand were being pulled, sucked like a magnet to the right spot.

There. She could feel it beneath the stone's rough surface. *Waves pulsing, pulling—*

With an effort, she tore herself away. She jabbed her hand at the spot, gesturing emphatically to Peter, pushing herself back and blinking in surprise that he could be calmly hovering, feeling nothing of the chaos swarming in the dark cave. Jerky swerves of her light beam revealed him pulling out a sealed compression drill. She watched in agitation as he drilled around the sample, then worked agonizingly slowly with a chisel. Chips of rock drifted free, glinting.

Her nerves jittered. *Hurry. Careful.*

Finally put the tool away and turned in the trembling sweeps of light to hold out a rough oblong of opaque white quartz. Along one side, where the matrix had broken away, the smooth gleam of a buried facet.

Her hands closed around it, and darkness opened its jaws to swallow her.

A crackling surge. Jolting, sucking her into the rock vein. Racing her downward into the earth out of control. Out of her self. Where was she? Was she? Blackness.

She could grasp only a vague identity—*Ariadne*—but it was ripped out of a body. *Flowing along planes and facets of the crystalline deposits. Perceptions flattened, shaped by the weight of stone crushing flesh.* Somewhere a silent scream. Then even her terror was ripped away. *Identity pressed, heated. Refined. Spread into an alien geometry of pattern and order within the heart of the earth. Its strange imperatives insinuating, replacing human will as the last tatters of alarm shrieked—*

A wrenching shift, and the panic fell away. Nothing—no, white silence, humming with vibrant force.

Fear left behind with her body, she could hear now a distant music. The eerie tones swept closer along the glowing branches and veins, the filaments of her distilled self spread infinitely thin. The music deepened, pulsed in silver waves, and somehow in a place beyond thinking she knew there was a harmony to it, if she could find the key.

A black, roaring wave slammed into her, shattering the music, pounding in a burst of pain. *Blind whirlpool spinning, sucking her downward into the darkness of disruption. Crashing chaos. Nowhere. Nothingness. The surge ripping her apart—*

Ariadne fought. She kicked and clawed to escape the dark churning. The stones of the cave were closing over her, crushing her chest. She lost the last of her precious air.

A terrible roaring filled her ears, pain hammering her head and chest. She was heavy, cold as the black stone pulling her down. Shadowy hands tugged, trying to rip her arms from their sockets. They dragged her deeper, into the lapping heat at the core of the world, the molten lava to melt away her flesh and remake her.

Hard fists slammed into her chest, forcing out a last gush of her human fluids. The roar of chaos gave way to crazy gibbering, "All right, damn you God! Give her back, you bastard. Please." Wracking nausea, but she had no air, no lungs.

Another jarring shake. Then startling warmth. Soft pressure against her lips, and a gust of air forcing her lungs to expand. The air rushed out. Lips pressed again onto her mouth bringing air, bringing life, the warm flesh a shock of connection.

Ariadne jerked upright, fighting free of the blackness. Her eyes snapped open, and she doubled over the hot rubber side of the dinghy, choking and retching. She gasped. She pulled herself around to stare at her white-knuckled fist still clutching the rough oblong of stone. Her fingers loosened and the stone slid to the bottom of the dinghy. She raised her eyes to meet Peter's.

"Thank God—" His face was stricken, pale beneath the tan.

He blew out a breath then and shook his head, making a wry face. "You know how long it's been since I prayed?" His eyes, sharp gold-brown in the sun, belied the joke.

Ariadne coughed again and managed, "Thank you."

"Had some fight left in you, anyway." He grinned and displayed a darkening bruise down one muscular thigh.

"I'm sorry."

"It's nothing, just lie back, take it easy." He leaned over the side of the dinghy, grunting as he pulled up a tank with flotation vest attached, the little boat dipping and bobbing. He snapped the oars into place. "I hope that rock was worth it." He shot her a look, then started pulling on the oars.

Ariadne looked numbly at the gleaming white stone. The exposed crystal facet glittered in the sunlight.

30

"ALL SYSTEMS GO." PETER climbed up from the aft cargo compartment after checking the port shaft seals again, wiped his greasy hands on a rag, then lowered the hatch cover back into place. He straightened his back, working out the kinks. "We'll be ready to take off at dawn."

No response. Leeza was hunched over her media gear up on the flying bridge, silhouetted against the lowering sunlight that laid a shimmering copper trail across the calm surface of the cove. Plugged in, eyes obscured by her viewing goggles, she was oblivious to the world. Peter rolled his eyes and turned toward the stern where Ariadne, equally absorbed, was polishing the crystal she'd worked all afternoon to free from its opaque matrix. After nearly drowning, she'd refused to take a rest before tackling the job. Now, her guard down, she looked exhausted, and he noted with a pang that her hands trembled as she turned the big crystal to catch the last of the sunlight.

"*Despoina?*" He cleared his throat. "Ariadne?"

She jerked, then straightened on her stool, gripping the crystal as she looked up at him. As she raised her chin, her features firmed into their usual seamless calm, the sunset gilding her face to the likeness of a bronze Amazon warrior, indomitable. Except that now he could see the chinks in her armor.

"So… was it?" He tilted his head toward the new crystal.

She blinked. "Was it…?"

"Worth it." He smiled gently. "The crystal. Is it what you wanted?"

Those generous lips curved into an answering smile, and he could feel them again as he'd fought to give her air, the salty sweetness of that brief vital connection. For a moment, now, she held his gaze. *Contact.*

Then she caught a quick breath and broke away, face closing over like some goddamn override switch. "Yes. It should help with one more… piece of the puzzle. Thank you for your help, Mr. Mitchell."

"Right." He shrugged. "No problem. Be ready to leave at dawn."

"Yes. I have just one more task to finish before then." She rose from the stool, but stumbled and swayed back against it.

"Here." He moved quickly to catch her arm, steady her shoulders. "You had a close call down there today, in that cave. You need to rest, eat something. Let that go for now." He tapped the crystal she was still gripping.

She flinched, drawing her shoulders straight and stepping away from him. "Truly, I'm fine. I'm really not hungry—"

"No arguments. I'll heat up that lamb souvlaki I got in town." He kept his voice light. "I've got my reputation on the line here, you know. I always deliver my cargo intact."

"Yeah, good old Captain Mitchell, cut-rate but dependable when he's sober." It was Leeza, dropping down from the ladder behind him, snapping a wad of chewing gum in his face as he swung around. "That's a quote."

"You—" His fist clenched. "I've had it with your crap."

She started to flinch back, then stuck out her chin, defiant. New image today—she changed identities like outfits. Now the hairdo was a pale, short tousle, face scrubbed clean of paint, wearing worn cutoffs and a plain T-shirt. A colty look, like a wannabe-tough young boy, somehow disarming.

"So, hey! Let's see the big deal here!" She danced around Peter to Ariadne's side, reaching out for the glinting crystal.

Ariadne pulled back from her, slipping the quartz into the pocket of her peasant skirt. She blinked, swaying again.

"Oh, *Chica.*" Leeza took her arm and tugged her toward the cabin. "No arguments. You need to eat." She bent proprietarily over Ariadne, arm around her shoulders and their heads close, the pale and the dark.

Peter shook off a stupid bite of jealousy and followed them in to the galley. He pulled the wrapped souvlaki from the fridge and stuck the packet in the microwave to heat, then uncorked a bottle of retsina, pouring three glasses. "Here, this'll clear your sinuses at least. *Chairete.*"

Ariadne, sitting with Leeza at the table, raised her glass. "*Chairete.*" She sipped.

Leeza made a face. "Great. Like drinking turpentine."

"It's an acquired taste. Try some olives with it." He set down a bowlful of the glistening black ones along with some feta, laid out plates and utensils, and brought the heated lamb and rice over. "Dig in, ladies."

Leeza picked at her food and pushed the retsina aside, but Peter was relieved to see Ariadne put away a decent amount, her healthy glow returning.

"Leeza, have more," Ariadne suggested.

"I'm good." She hesitated, then turned to Peter. "Thanks."

"You're welcome." He grinned. "And thanks for volunteering for cleanup duty."

"I didn't—" She blew out a breath. "Right." She stood to gather the plates. "Big happy family."

Ariadne rose and pulled a dark scarf from the coat pegs, tying it over her hair peasant-style. "Yes, thank you, Peter. Now I have one last task before we leave Tinos. I will need to take the dinghy ashore."

"Wait." Peter jerked to his feet. "Where do you think you're going in the dark?" He waved toward the sea beyond the windows, deep velvet shimmering with purple streamers of twilight.

She pulled the strap of a woven carryall over her shoulder and placed the new crystal in it, along with some plastic vials. "I must visit the shrine of the Tiniotissa to get samples of the springwater."

"You mean that spring at the church? No way, that's too dangerous." Peter shook his head. "Somebody could recognize you, I saw some Med League uniforms in town."

The radio he'd left tuned to the crackling static of Radio Cyclades suddenly spat out a weak burst of music.

"Wait." He fiddled with the tuner. "Reception's clearing, maybe there's some news."

A whine from the radio, then scratchy Greek: "...bulletin repeat. Ariadne Demodakis has been kidnapped. A search is underway for—" Static crackle and a squeal. The voice continued faintly, "...disguised as a fishing trawler, aluminum hull...." More static. "...reward for information...." It faded out.

"Son of a bitch!" Peter cruised channels, got nothing more, left it on scan. He pushed past Ariadne, pacing the cabin. "Sitting ducks here...." He raked a hand over his face. "I hate risking it in the dark, with all the shallow rocks and my depth scanner still iffy with the geomag interference. But it might be safer than waiting. They'll all be watching out for us now."

Ariadne was staring at the radio. "Why would they say I was kidnapped? My father had already announced my death."

"Papa *Tyrannos* playing the odds? His very own Saint Ariadne's worth more in P.R. value alive than dead. Fastest way to get you back is offer a big reward, hope it's more than the mercenaries will dangle."

"But the Sons of the Prophet, too, will know I'm still alive, and they would only scorn a reward. They want my death."

"Yep, and they're *all* out for my blood."

"Terrific!" Leeza thrust her head between them. "So what do we do, sit here waiting for those Sons to blow us up?"

"I'm sorry. I've put you both at terrible risk." Ariadne straightened. "From this point, it's best that I go on alone. Take me to shore, Mr. Mitchell, then leave the island with Leeza."

"Now just a blasted minute!" Peter scrubbed his sweaty forehead on his T-shirt sleeve. "We're talking this one over."

"There is nothing to discuss. You must leave, save yourselves." She started for the cabin door.

"I'm sick of you high-handing me! You agreed I was captain on this job, remember?" Peter stepped in front of the door, blocking her. She stood her ground, face closed over with that seamless sheen that only pissed him off more. "You ever hear of teamwork?"

Her face was looking strained again, but she didn't waver. "I have heard men talk about team work. It seems to mean that the women do what they want, or what they force us to do."

"Don't give me that dodge! That's not what I—"

"Sure, Mitchell." Leeza jumped in, azure eyes glittering. "That's exactly what you big hombres want. Flex the muscles. Women know how to cooperate."

He snorted. "Who elected you Miss Congeniality?"

"You are such a crock of—"

"Wait." Ariadne put up a hand. "Leeza, let us listen to what Mr.—what Peter has to say. He has more experience, after all." She turned back to him. "Please."

He about said forget it, but she was giving him the Look. "Okay, so I don't know what went on—your father locking you up on that island and all. But that's not what I'm talking about. I mean...." He waved vaguely. "All right, take the war. I was in a submarine, coastal patrol, nobody there by choice exactly but when you're in the thick of it you're a team. Take Anastasio, he wasn't normally my cup of tea, but he was hell on sonar, pick up stuff I'd never tumble to. I was a better pilot. When it came down to it, I was happy it was him on the sonar, trust him more than me there. So we all ended up getting something from each other, you know?"

"Quite the hero, Mitchell!" Leeza sneered. "Don't forget I scanned your records. So why don't you tell her what happened to your pal Anastasio, and whose big brave ass you saved in the end? That what your macho teamwork comes down to? Look out for Number One?"

"Fuck you!" He grabbed her shoulders, thrusting his face close to hers. "You dig any more in my life, you snake, you'll be—"

As his fingers tightened, a smug little smile twisted her lips.

"Shit." He dropped his hands and jerked away from them both to stare out the window at the purple-bruised sky.

"Enough." A world of weariness in that voice. Ariadne headed out the door. "I thank you for your help in getting me to this point. I must complete my healing experiments, and if I'm captured, so be it. Please take care and find a safe port for Leeza."

He followed her out to the aft deck. "That's it? You don't think we can find a middle ground here? If it's that important, then I could go along, I've got some sidearms."

"I'll go, too! I've got a stun-gun." Leeza jittered after them.

"Right, you'll blend right in." Peter cast a sardonic eye over the platinum hair and long pale legs.

Ariadne turned and gave them a real smile, beaming a surprising warmth that caught Peter in the gut. "Thank you both for your courage, but I must go alone." She smoothed down her rumpled skirt and drew back her shoulders. "I will be only another... pilgrim coming to the shrine." An odd expression rippled over her face in the dimness.

"But—"

"Truly, Peter. Leeza. You would only draw attention if you came with me. But if you must have a compromise, you could remain here until midnight, which should give me more than enough time to take the overland trail to town and back. If I do not return by then, you must agree to leave. I do not want your blood on my hands."

"How about this? If you don't get back by midnight, we'll make for Amorgos. I'll take a wide swing east, avoid the usual route, then circle back south. I've laid in there for repairs before, I know a guy might hide us in his boathouse. We can check out the news, try to reconnect if you don't get picked up by your father's men."

She blinked. "Excellent. My uncle Demetrios had a trading route some years ago, and would also put in there. If I can make my way to the island, I will leave a message for you at Aegialis, the Taverna Poseidon."

Leeza pushed forward to give her a clinging embrace. "Be careful, Ri."

Ariadne stroked her head and gently eased her back, then turned toward the stern, climbing down to the inflatable.

Peter vaulted after her to row her ashore. He took one look at her face in the dusk and gave up on trying to talk her out of it. He sighed, pulling on the oars, the sea rippling purple and black around them.

The rubber prow crunched onto the stony shingle. He jumped out and pulled it higher, took a deep breath, and made one more try. "I could walk over the hill with you, wait outside town."

She shook her head.

"Has to be your show? Then keep your eyes and ears peeled. Be careful."

"I will. If I do not return by midnight, you must leave without me."

"All right. Stick to the plan."

"Peter. I do…appreciate all you have done." She surprised him by briefly touching his hand, then she ducked her head, hurrying through the gloom to a goat track up the rocky slope. When she reached the crest, she was silhouetted for a moment against the smudged twilight. He thought she turned and looked down at him. She was gone.

31

ARIADNE FOLLOWED THE DIRT ROAD winding dimly down toward a cluster of whitewashed huts gleaming beneath the rising half moon. The breeze carried a clink of dishes, a voice calling, the plaintive notes of reed pipes. Skirting the village, Ariadne slipped through terraces of young olive trees and lemon groves in the scent of blossoms and dust. Leaves shimmered, touched by moonlight and a cool breeze spinning the arms of an old stone windmill.

She paused above the road on a final terrace of mature olives, silver light and leaf shadow trembling over her. She could still see Peter's shadowed face looking up at her from the beach. Could feel the shock of his warm mouth touching her sea-chilled lips as he'd pulled her from the drowning darkness.

She shook her head and ducked beneath a bough, dropped over a rock ledge to the road, hurried on. Collecting the springwater samples, like her sensor readings verifying the local geomagnetic anomalies, was only an excuse for this visit to the shrine. A voice that she couldn't deny insisted she return to the ancient site she'd visited as a girl with her uncle Demetrios. The holy water hadn't healed the pain of her mother's death and her father's coldness. Would it help her now?

Her fingers touched the new crystal in her bag. Its silicon quartz structure of gleaming planes and angles held a template of the geomagnetic currents between the dark cavern and the emerging spring. The smooth waves and the jarring disruptions echoed within it, and somehow she knew it was a key. To what?

Bring it home, a silvery voice sang. *Help me bring the light.* It was the voice of the Tiniotissa, the voice of the ethereal music she'd heard in the flooded cavern before the dark whirlpool caught her. She could still feel the seething energy fields, the crystalline lattice imprinted in the circuits of her nerves. Her hands tingled with waves of electric sensation and irrational surety, seeking the disruptive currents of illness in the bodies of living creatures, and now the larger body of the earth.

Tingling with the power to heal, as Saint Ariadne?

She shook her head in refusal. But something was happening to her, setting her footsteps on an unmarked path. As she strode down a last hill toward the lights of town and the gleam of the harbor, she was afraid.

∞

Ariadne made her way silently through the twisting maze of stone-cobbled streets. Glimmers of light escaped the shutters of outlying houses as ghosts beckoned from shadowed yards, morphing into laundry hung on lines. Piles of broken roof tiles and storm-ripped branches lined the road. Fresh plaster glowed in white veins on dark walls, tracing earthquake cracks.

As the houses crowded closer, Ariadne recognized sights from that visit years before on Uncle Dmitri's trading boat. Above the rooftops, pale against the night sky, the church tower loomed. Near it was the smaller sanctuary chapel of the Tiniotissa, the miraculous icon of the healing Virgin, built over the ancient site of a sacred spring.

Her uncle's comfortable deep rumble: "You know the ancients found these springs first, my little Kri-Kri. Maybe the gods got tired later and gave them over to the Virgin's care....Remember the stories about Apollo and Artemis? He ruled the sun, and she the moon. But they were twins, man and woman, and only together could they make up a sky complete. When he looked into the sacred pool, there was her reflection looking back at him...."

Ariadne smiled at the memory. Making her way closer to the harbor, she passed an open-air taverna filled with laughter, shouts, the slap of dominoes. Bouzouki music whined and twanged. Glimpsing the Med League insignia on a blue shirt, she moved hastily on, past a *kafenion* where a cluster of men drank from tiny coffee cups and listened to a scratchy radio.

She stopped short, alarm crackling like the static still breaking up reception.

Peter was right. She was in danger here. Edging back toward the terrace, keeping to the deeper darkness along the wall, she strained to hear more news from the radio.

"Late to be out, *Despoina*. Are you lost?"

Ariadne spun around, biting back a cry, to see an old man with a laden donkey. She ducked her head in the scarf, passing him quickly. She dodged an electric car, hurrying between apartment buildings over storefronts. Finally she passed through the gateway into the open stone-paved square she remembered.

A whitewashed gallery ran along the far side, broken by dark wood doors and dimly lit by paraffin lamps. Behind its wall, a higher building stretched toward the tower of the big church. Closer, newly-leaved trees rustled in the night, and a carved stone stairway flowed in a frozen wave from the entrance to the sanctuary. Its open doors spilled flickering candlelight and the distant surge of an evening service. Incense wafted through the night.

A murmur rose from the dark courtyard—a ceaseless lament of moans, coughs, sobs, shuffling feet, and muttering voices, punctuated by an occasional sharp cry.

The ebb and flow of suffering was a presence more palpable than sound, washing through the dim figures spread across the square. They lay on blankets and rags and stretchers, lit by the wavering glow of olive-oil lamps. Some lay prostrate, some tossing from side to side, some twisted in motionless postures of pain, some rocking slowly to the rhythm of the common lament. So many supplicants, with the Assumption of the Virgin and Her summer healing pilgrimage still months away. The sick waited through the night for their turn to be carried into the chapel, to make an offering to the miraculous icon.

A baby cried, its healthy wail cutting through the murmurs of suffering.

Ariadne steeled herself to walk through them. Even in the dim lamplight she could see the sores of radiation burns, cancerous lesions, mutation-caused deformities of the younger supplicants among the older victims of arthritis and gout. She had healed radiation-induced illnesses with her ionized water. But there were so many here, and even more, she knew, at the quarantined encampment for the RPH "plague" victims. She ached to help them, but didn't dare risk revealing herself with so much at stake. As she passed through the stricken, each gaze raised to hers carried a mute accusation. Or worse, dull resignation.

Finally she was through, moans and cries lapping at her back.

She fled along the gallery toward the smaller courtyard at the back of the chapel. She remembered the sacred spring emerging into a stone-lined basin in a little garden there. But now she was accosted by vendors spotting a last customer moving into the light of their paraffin lamps.

A middle-aged man in a fisherman's cap— "Dried fish, to give you strength in your vigil." A toothless crone grasping her arm, waving ribbons and thin candles— "Offering for the Virgin, cheap." Two heavyset young women sitting beside baskets of dried fruit and olives, wrapped chunks of goat cheese, dusty bottles of retsina—"Wine to keep you warm in the night." Three children running after her with cheap painted figurines of the Virgin— "Souvenir? Pretty like the Tiniotissa!"

As Ariadne stooped to give the ragged children some coins, a young man passed, shooting her a curious look. He stopped by the two women vendors. There was a low murmur of conversation as he helped them pack up their wares.

"Saint Ariadne!"

She froze, the children dancing before her with outstretched hands.

"*Poh-poh-poh!*" The woman went on in a loud, scornful voice. "I'm already tired of hearing about the kidnapping."

"Anything new? Who did it?" the other one asked eagerly.

"Who knows? Turks?" The man spat casually. "Fancy foreign boat sighted around Naxos, maybe the Sons on a purge."

The first woman shook out her skirt. "I say she called it upon herself in her pride. We've got the Tiniotissa here, She's saint enough."

Ariadne thrust some coins at the children. They squealed in delight as she pushed past another trinket vendor and hurried around the plain white walls of the chapel, her heart pounding. She finally reached the end of the wall and stopped short.

The garden of the sacred spring had been fenced in.

Beside the shut gate stood a closed kiosk with a painted sign: *Entrance offering, 400 drach. Water cup, 200 drach.* Ariadne moved numbly to the low wooden gate. It was chained and locked.

"Damn them!" Irrational, elemental rage filled her. "They have no right!"

The healing water was for everyone. No priests could own it or charge the poor for its blessing. Ariadne shook the gate, rattling the chain. Suddenly it was barring more than one small garden. Anger blazed through her, hands grasping to rip the gate from its hinges and fling it aside, free the healing water, let the sufferers in.

"They would steal even the soul from the earth—"

She came up short at the sound of her own raving. From the moonlit garden, only a rustle of leaves, the quiet gurgle of the spring upwelling into its basin. Muffled chanting inside the chapel walls.

Ariadne blew out a breath, then hiked up her skirt and pulled herself quickly over the gate to slip along a shadowed hedge. A glance behind her, and she darted across the garden to kneel in the shadows beside the spring.

Budding cyclamens nodded over the mossy-rocked pool, and a fresh mist cooled her face. She closed her eyes and listened to the splash of the water, the lulling voice of the spring. She could feel it now, its tingling energy. She touched her palm to the shivering dark surface, the tingle intensifying to an effervescence like the boiling surge inside the cave.

Suspended in the surreality of moonlight and shadow, Ariadne pulled the new, double-terminated crystal from her bag and gazed into the winking facets.

Like a gate springing open, her fears and denials fell away. She held the crystal and felt herself attune to its lattice. Its perfect order. Touching it to the surface of the water, she knew once more the electric thrill of the contact from the cavern. *Her essence funnelled through the lattice, flowing into the vital waters of the spring. Rushing downward over the buried quartz seam. Awareness pouring into the pulse of white light, the crystal's pattern flowing outward through her nerve pathways with the silver singing voice: "Blessed One, you have returned to us. Join us in the light, leave the dark evil behind. Drink and ascend!"*

The voice was pure and clear as the silver moonlight shimmering in the springwater, rippling through her, compelling beyond beauty. It sang a siren song, luring her into its cool passionless harmony. An order—beyond flesh and blood and pain, beyond life and betrayal and death—hauntingly flawless. Transcendent peace. Benevolence. All she had to do was pour herself into it, become one with it.

A loosening, a last tether snapping, and she was flowing, draining away to join the mesmerizing pulse of moonlit water….

A jarring drumbeat broke the spell—her heart, lurching in alarm. She jerked back from the lip of the spring. Her arms had plunged deeply into it, wetting her bodice, submerging her face. She sat back, heart pounding, shadows and moonlight swirling dizzily. She stared at the glimmering crystal still clutched in her hands.

She took a deep breath. There was more than light beneath the surface here. Like a basso rumbling counter to the silvery soprano, a deep presence sent jarring stabs to disrupt the smooth waves. Deep in the coils, a black seething reached to snatch and rend, kill and devour.

"The Serpent. Turn away, child, do not listen," the silvery voice called faintly, and Ariadne wanted to obey its surety of goodness.

Yet there was more she needed to do. She could feel it somewhere, deep in the layers of primitive awareness at her core, calling her to her place, her… home. She shook her head. She had no home. No place. No family.

Somewhere a guttural voice laughed, mocking. *"Claim yourself. Your power."*

She shook her head, pushed past her weakness and fear to grip the crystal firmly, staring into its winking facets as she lowered it into the water again, this time bracing herself on the rocky lip of the pool. Now she could hear both voices, the silver and the ebony, could feel the jarring interface of their clashing. The flow was blocked, disrupted not only by the earthquake eddies and shifting ambient fields. Clogging the natural currents were thick, muddy gray clots of interference that pulsed and crackled with random charges. Dense and heavy, they jolted her as her awareness probed, generating static shocks and strobing images that lanced painfully behind her eyes: microwave towers emitting deadly frequencies as factories spewed smoke and poisons, supersonic jets booming through the airways once owned by the birds, toxic radiation pulsing on the seafloor, the roar of motors and pounding oil drills and explosions weaving through shattered silence like searchlights ripping the velvet night. The pollution choked her, jostled its noxious clots to seal off the sacred spring and trap her in the muck without air.

Ariadne fought to stay afloat, pushing through the drowning heaviness, using the crystal's light to pierce the gray cacophony, peel it back to free the silvery moonlit song of the springwaters. But how to keep it free?

The crystal, magnetized in opposition to the dominant geomagnetic field, held the key. If she could let the flow circle through her, return to the source through the cleansing light of the crystal, the cycle would be purged, the snarled strands of energy released to flow freely.

As she opened herself to the currents, a last vestige of logic screamed in protest of this madness, but it didn't matter. This was what she was meant to do. And with her fading strength, she held herself open to the buffeting waves swirling through her, funneling into the crystal and beyond. *Yes. Help us purify the song. Banish the Serpent who has led mankind astray in creating this pollution.*

Wave after wave swept through her, the light and the dark, surged on toward the source and back. The crystal lattice helped her guide them into their proper channels—the light above, and the dark pulsing deep below the buried rock layers. But her strength was fading, *she* was fading—the effort of pushing the ebony voice safely distant had drained her strength, and now she couldn't let go as it sucked her deeper. The dark basso voice sang its force, thrumming in her bones: *Power. Power. Claim it.* She needed air, but there was only water, and the deep veins of stone, pulling her down into the crushing black depths. *Here is your power. Power. Power….*

With the last of her will, Ariadne turned into the next dark wave, released her grip on the crystal, and let the forces slam into her, throwing her free into the night and oblivion.

32

A PALE HALF-MOON floated over the velvet sky. There was a silvery face in it, lovely profile gazing down on Ariadne where she lay on soft grass in the scent of moisture and leaves.

"Mother?" She blinked, and the face was gone. She thought about sitting up, but she was so relaxed, her limbs so heavy and tired, it was too much trouble. Singsong chants swelled and ebbed behind the chapel walls near the garden, soothing, beckoning her back to sleep....

She wrenched herself up to a sitting position, head spinning. The garden was still deserted. Taking a deep breath, she pushed through her lassitude and touched the water. The "voices" were safely purged and separated in their channels now, the currents rippling smoothly. She started to reach into her bag for the sample vials, then let it go. She didn't need to test the waters. On her knees, she leaned over the pool. An amorphous moonlit reflection stared up from the ebony mirror. She dipped her cupped hands and drank deeply, the cool blessing of the water flowing down her parched throat.

Rising exhausted to her feet, she moved on shaky legs to the gate and started to climb over it.

"No need for that. I've got fresh well water from my farm, guaranteed safe to drink. And a lot cheaper than the priests charge here."

With a jolt, Ariadne dropped from the gate and spun around, lightheaded.

A sturdy peasant woman, balancing a jug on a padded coil atop her head, grinned beneath a scarf tied low over her forehead, moonlight picking out a shadowed gap in her front teeth. "Got a nerve, though. You know what they say about this spring, don't you? The Virgin owns it during the day, but at night the Old Ones reclaim it. You can see them around town—the crazy folk had their wits stolen by the water nymphs. There's dark powers here, waiting to grab you."

Ariadne flattened her damp palms on her skirt and tried to calm her racing heart. "You sell your water to the pilgrims?"

The woman shrugged, easily balancing the thick jug. "They get thirsty, and it brings in a little extra. Fifty drachma each liter."

Ariadne reached into her bag. "I'll pay you two thousand to do a job for me."

The woman gave her a skeptical look. "I don't want trouble with the priests."

"No trouble for you. Leave me your jug and wait around the corner of the chapel." She handed over the money.

The woman stuffed the bills inside her bodice and lowered the jug with a practiced twist. "Careful, it's heavy." She moved off around the building.

Ariadne hefted the earthenware jug and poured it along the fence, into the hedge. Climbing over the gate once more, she hurried back to the pool and plunged in the jug, heaving it out brimming. Still weak from her struggle, she grunted with effort as she lifted the jug over the gate and carefully lowered it.

The woman was waiting. She gave a resigned shrug and accepted Ariadne's instructions, starting to turn away.

"Wait. Do you know what time it is?"

The woman gestured toward the chapel. "About one. They're just finishing the midnight service."

Ariadne closed her eyes for a moment as the woman moved ahead of her. She must have lain unconscious a long time by the pool. Too late now to return to the boat.

The collective murmur of suffering lapped over her as she followed the peasant woman back to the courtyard and the sleepless supplicants. She watched from the shadows as the thick figure with the jug stopped at the first pallet and poured out a measure. The woman moved on to the next blanket, repeating dutifully, "Healing water from the Tiniotissa."

Ariadne leaned against the shadowed wall, her strength drained, her options narrowing around her, the pursuit closing in. She rubbed her throbbing head. Incense from the open doors of the chapel wrapped suffocating tendrils about her as across the courtyard, the water bearer made her way among the flickering oil lamps.

In silence now.

Ariadne leaned forward from the shadows, ears ringing, the night gone quiet. The moaning, sobbing, coughing chorus had faded away as the supplicants waited mutely, faces raised to the woman with the water.

"It's a sign, dearie. Go on in and ask Her. The Virgin will take pity on you, too."

Ariadne startled and turned to face a bent old woman in black, hunched under the weight of a woven basket on her back.

The woman carefully lowered the basket to the ground, fumbling with arthritis-twisted fingers. "If you need an offering, I ask only what you can give." She indicated her freight of tin votive strips glinting dully in the moonlight, stamped out with shapes for appeals to the healing Virgin. A foot. An arm. A head. A staring eye.

"Don't be shy, now." The aged face tilted to give Ariadne a look of motherly concern.

Tears welled and spilled as Ariadne reached impulsively to take the woman's contorted hands between hers, squeezing them and smiling into her seamed and sunbaked face. The warmth of the sun in the poppies, the cool moonlit song of the spring flowed through her.

The woman gasped and pulled her hands free. She stared at them as she slowly flexed her fingers. Made a tight fist and opened it. Wriggled her fingers.

Her eyes were glinting wetly now, widening as she peered up at Ariadne's shadowed face. "By the blessed Virgin...." She crossed herself hastily, then bent to her basket to pull out an offering foil, pressing it into Ariadne's hands. Tears streaming down her face, she ducked her head and hurried with her basket into the night.

Ariadne looked down at the stamped design in the shape of a heart. She gazed blankly at it. She turned numbly and walked up the stone steps into the chapel, into the candlelight and incense and chanting, into the claustrophobic church where the pious narrow faces of the Byzantine saints stared from the walls.

Someone handed her a candle and she moved forward to join the shabby congregation singing responses to the bearded priest in his black robes and tall hat. The walls were lined with offerings—Bibles with jewel-studded covers, gold and silver plate, rich figured silks, painstaking embroideries. Silver and tin-foil strips stamped with their afflicted body-shapes were gummed everywhere to the pillars with wax, along with shreds of infected clothing. Silver candelabra molded from past offerings ringed the chapel in flickering light.

It lapped gleaming over the famous icon in its guarded corner, so encrusted with jewels that the figure of the kneeling Tiniotissa was barely visible. In the dome overhead, a painted image of the Virgin's elongated features and pale broad forehead seemed to float out of the darkness, distilled into fleshless abstraction, enormous eyes gazing down in remote pity.

Ariadne pressed her offering, the image of a human heart, into the soft wax on the nearest pillar, muttering an incoherent petition, garbled with words from childhood prayers. "Grant me Grace. Clarity. Let me see with your dispassionate eyes. Let me transcend this weakness the flesh is heir to."

Finally she stumbled from the church, breast aching with the unanswered plea.

∞

Somehow she made her way through the sleeping petitioners in the courtyard, but once past the gateway she hesitated, unsure where to go, trembling with weariness.

"Come with us." A hand grasped Ariadne's arm from behind.

She spun around, alarm flaring through her exhaustion, legs tensing to run.

No Med League soldier, but a woman in a dark dress and scarf, her surprisingly strong grip pinioning Ariadne's arm. Another woman stepped up close, smiling in the dimness of the cobbled lane as she raised her hands to push her scarf back. She was young, with a pretty but stern face. A black sash held back her short-cropped hair, the strip embroidered with a white spiral enclosing a staring eye.

Corybant. The women warrior cult.

Ariadne jerked back, too weakened to break free of the woman holding her arm. "Tell them no. I won't join you."

The young woman studied her, ignoring her protest. "We hoped the power would draw you here. Those pigs of priests haven't stolen it all." The spiral eye flickered in the shadows. "We must stop them. Join us now, freely, before you have no choice."

Ariadne shook her head. "No. I have important work to do—"

"Now you'll work with us. Why do you think you were called here? We must destroy the machines of the patriarchy polluting the earth, restore the true power of Gaea." She jerked her head at the other woman and started to lead the way down the street. Ariadne didn't dare call out. Who would respond, but worse captors?

The silent woman warrior prodded Ariadne with a knife as she stumbled along, trying to delay, trying to think.

"Here, now, old mother." The Corybant in the lead had paused as a hunched old woman, limping with a cane, tottered out of an alley in front of them, stumbled, and dropped her mesh string bag. A cabbage rolled out. "Let me help."

As the Corybant leaned over to assist her, the old woman suddenly straightened in a swirl of ragged skirts, bringing the cane up in a sharp crack against the warrior's head. She dropped to the cobbles as the woman holding Ariadne cried out in surprise, loosening her grip.

Ariadne ripped free, pulling away from the knife as the stranger, now oddly tall, jostled her aside to confront the Corybant.

"Peter?" Ariadne gasped as a scarf slipped off his head. "Careful, she has a knife!"

"Sit on the other gal!" He dodged a sweep from the glinting dagger, knocked it aside with the cane, then the woman was pulling out another knife and was on him. They struggled, stumbling over the cobbles as Ariadne dropped onto the downed leader, making sure she was still unconscious. A grunt, a muffled oath from Peter, and then a snapping crackle. The Corybant went stiff, then limp, and fell beside her comrade.

"Peter?" Ariadne was still staring in disbelief at this apparition in a peasant skirt and shawl, holding a small black device with metal prongs.

He grinned in the dimness and stuck it in a pocket of the skirt, picked up the fallen scarf, and tied it back around his head. "Better keep the disguise 'til we're out of town. Come on, let's get a move on."

"But…." She caught her breath as he pulled her to her feet, urging her along. "But you promised to leave."

"I lied."

33

DIGITALS PULSED ON THE console, blurring to meaningless hieroglyphs.

Peter rubbed his eyes and raised a bleary gaze to the breeze-whipped sea. He scrubbed his face with his hand, tilted back in the captain's chair, and drained the last of the cooled coffee bulb.

The monitor beeper on the radio scanner started up, and he swivelled to turn up the volume. More static and the low-frequency reverbs he'd been picking up all morning, then a hiss and faint phrases: "...in southern Italy.... variable magnitude. The continuing seismic disturbances have triggered volcanic.... irregularity of geomagnetic phases.... thunderstorms passing over West Africa with more devastating hailstones...." A sharp squeal and it was lost.

He thumbed the volume down and turned back to the endless swells *Nereid*'s bow was slicing.

Since leaving Tinos in the pre-dawn, he'd monitored the fragmentary news. There was still a "significant geomagnetic phase shift" going on, though the local Aegean field was holding pretty steady. Farther west, and south, they were still getting strong nodes of disturbance. *Nereid* was cruising through the calm eye of an electromagnetic hurricane.

And just a break from other kinds of storms. The local news was full of it—the "kidnapping" of Ariadne Demodakis and the Med League rescue mobilization, more death threats from the Sons of the Prophet, incursions of an unidentified high-speed hydrofoil—spicing up the routine end-of-the-world stuff. Like the "ever-rapider" rate of new Rapid-Proliferating Hansen's cases they were starting to call the New Plague, more guerilla insurgencies in hungry Africa and South America, more anti-tech terrorist bombings, more louder bloodier Doomsday cult activities: pick a, b, c, or all of the above.

Peter rubbed his eyes, drowsiness lapping through him with the dip and rise over the swells. Another day running on zero sleep, but no time to cop a nap now. He had to keep scanning radar on the boat traffic, no way to ID individual vessels, especially with radio reception still so iffy, but he could watch patterns. One radar blip troubled him. Fast-moving. Heading their way? It was moving along a regular trade route, so he'd just have to watch it.

He blew out a breath and swivelled one-eighty to peer aft at the galley.

Whoever designed the Lizard's electric-blue leotard must have won the ecology prize for fabric conservation. She was jacked into her Link, face blank behind the goggles, going through a calisthenic routine. Peter's eyes glazed over as her bare body levered up and down, pale sinewy arms pumping pushups to a silent beat. He pulled himself to his feet and shuffled back to tap her on the shoulder.

"What?" She startled and sat hard, pulling off the goggles and reaching for her recorder controls. "*Jodas*, Mitchell! *Now* what's wrong?"

He swallowed a sluggish reflex sarcasm. She'd done all right the night before when he'd decided to go after Ariadne, lending him her stun-gun and paying attention when he showed her how to use his pistol. He'd found her and her gear a hidey-hole up in the cliff above the cove, in case any hostiles came after the boat, and she'd actually given him a salute as he'd set out for town: "Aye, aye, Captain. Just let those fuckers try anything."

Now he cleared his throat. "Look, I was wondering if I could take you up on your offer. Coffee's not cutting it any more." He made a face and tossed the empty bulb in the compactor. He'd checked his medical kit and discovered he must have used up his backup speed tabs on another trip. "Maybe some of whatever's got you plugged in."

"Ha ha." She pulled off her leads and rubbed her terry wristband over her glistening face. "Looks like you could use something." She grinned, then jumped to her feet. "But no way could you handle Leeza's working mood juice, baby. Guarantee you wouldn't need this tub for locomotion, you'd be the original rocket man."

She bent over storklegged to rummage in a bag, pert butt thrust up at him, smooth white cheeks divided by the token strip of bright blue fabric. Peter shook his head, shaking off the memory of his hands on that taut flesh as she mounted him, blood-red lips parted in a mocking smile. Now he could see the faint outline of her spinal implant beneath the thin fabric.

"You want'em or not?" Leeza perched on the edge of the table, pulling on a short-cropped purple T-shirt, holding out her fist and unclenching it to offer four little criss-cross tabs. "They're only appetizers, but they should keep you from nodding off at the wheel."

"Thanks." He swallowed one dry, stuck the rest in his pocket for later, and moved forward to the wheel.

She followed. "So what's the scoop?" She ran a restless finger over the console, tapping lacquered fingernails and peering ahead at the sea. "What's the plan now? I'm picking up some news hits on the Link—you heard Papa *Tyrannos* just upped the reward? Guess he's still trying to top what the Sons are offering for her body." She shuddered and glanced over at the ladder down to the bunks, where he hoped Ariadne was still sleeping. "Should we tell her?"

Peter sighed. "Yeah, she's the boss. Just hope she's getting some rest, whatever she was up to in town just about did her in." And she'd declined to discuss it, as usual.

Leeza bit her lip. "Link's full of chatter—what I can grab that's not breaking up. People saying 'Saint Ariadne' descended from the sky and cured a bunch of sick pilgrims. Now they've got a mob scene back at the Tinos RIP-Hansen's camp, the ones that can still walk or crawl trying to break out and get to some sacred well she supposedly turned into her 'holy water.' What the fuck is going on?"

He scrubbed his face with his hands. "Great. I didn't hear that bit. Turning up the heat." He checked the radar again. "We're making as good time as we can. Still scanning boat traffic, mostly looks normal."

"So why are we headed east? I thought Ariadne wanted to go south to Crete."

"Look, I've got to plot some courses here." He rubbed his eyes again. "You want to help, go hydrate one of those juice packets back there and bring me some."

Her eyes narrowed, and she stalked aft. At least he'd punched her Off button.

He stared at the radar screen, shifting pattern of blips on long-range. The radiating circles and quadrant lines glowed, etching a brighter, sharper resolution as the hit of speed took effect. His thoughts moved in sharper circuits, too, foggy gray indecision burning off. He pulled out the charts and spread them over the console.

By the time Leeza had come forward to the wheelhouse again, surprising him with a glass of juice, he'd scoped out some alternate routes. Just in case.

"Thanks." He took a long swallow.

She perched on the edge of the console with her own glass, hand trembling just visibly with whatever she was on. "We're heading to Crete, right?"

He nodded at the spread charts. "South coast. We're swinging wide east to stay out of the inter-island traffic and muddy our tracks." He smoothed a hand over worn paper folds, fingertips finching despite himself across the inked-in Hot Zones from the war, crimson X's over the blue. "Might have to take a little detour."

She peered at the charts and scowled. "Like that last detour—through a goddamn volcano?"

"I wish." He spread a larger-scale chart. "Just a backup plan."

She squinted again at the charts, gave it up. "So what then? After Crete?"

He gave her an exasperated look. "Go interview the boss, maybe she'll talk to *you*." Then he shrugged. "Egypt? Draw a line from Tinos through the center of Crete and that's where you end up." He traced a finger over the big Mediterranean chart, skirting those glaring red X's.

"Egypt! Maximal." She snapped her fingers, kinked her arms ninety degrees, and tried to look 2-D.

"Look, do you mind?" He slid the extra charts toward the space she was taking up.

She went stiff and pushed away from the console, face closing over.

"Hey." He cleared his throat. "Thanks for the tabs."

"Yeah."

∞

"—sighted off the coast." The wheelhouse radio finally cut in, crackling static and broken phrases.

"Huh." Peter jerked in his seat, swiveling to adjust the tuner.

"...limited resolution... appears to be a flotilla of small sailboats and dories... coastal patrol attempting to stop their... stated they must reach Saint Ariadne's healing water on Tinos.... Conflicting witness reports—" More static, then a briefly clear voice, "Just received: The ecoterrorist Corybantes are claiming that Ariadne Demodakis has joined their forces. Sources are attempting to...." Hissing swallowed the rest.

The intermittent radio bursts kept him from nodding off at the wheel. More of the same. The wave of pilgrims converging on Tinos might be a good thing, muddy their tracks. His gaze shifted from sonar to the still-schizoid navigation readout to the gray-black cinders of the islets swelling ahead. He could almost see those crimson X's inked over them.

He gripped the wheel, caught somewhere between sleep-deprivation and the relentless gritty drive of the second hit of speed, nerves firing the gut response to cut sharp to port, swing wide and run far. But not fast enough.

That troublesome high-speed boat on radar had veered off the regular route and was surging east. Right toward *Nereid*.

He had some choices, if it was the pharmco's mercenary hydrofoil out for Ariadne's healing "formula." He doubted it was Med League, or they'd have tried to hail him. He could keep on his eastern swing around the long east-west band of the Zone—nuke-blasted islands, contaminated ship wreckage, spilled nuclear fuel still hot as a pistol. Use his missile if they attacked. A nasty little voice whispered he could give Ariadne up if it looked hopeless, and hopeless was the operative term. The mercs might keep the exotic blonde to sell for a sex slave, but Peter Mitchell? He'd be toast.

Or he could use the bolt-hole he'd plotted as a last resort—through the Hot Zone. Speaking of toasted....

Closing his eyes, he could see the fuel facility at the Navy training center, that deep tank where they stored the spent rods waiting to be processed. Through the shielding water, you could see the Cherenkov's radiation. The unnatural deep blue of the luminescence had an unearthly beauty, pulsating, the color not really in the water but his own eyes, sizzling bursts of rods and cones. Like those sapphire eyes of hers. X-ray vision.

"Damn." He glanced over his shoulder. Should he tell them?

Leeza was Linked in, goggles on, fingers twitching on the control spindle. Ariadne sat at the galley table, her face just as zoned-out as she stared down at that big double-pointed crystal from the Tinos cave. Whatever she'd done on that little excursion to town had clearly exhausted her.

He swivelled around, rubbing his eyes. Bottom line, he knew damn-all about this Ariadne Demodakis. Maybe her father was right, keeping her locked up. Maybe she was crazy. Sure as hell Peter was nuts, dodging the Med League, the mercenaries, the suicide fanatics. For some gold standard he'd most likely never see. He didn't need this.

He could try to call in some Med League air support right now, turn their Saint over. Take a vacation. Nice long stretch in the home islands off the Pelopponese, laze around swimming and fishing, take it one day at a time. Who needed Judgment Day and Papa Reverend's voice whispering guilt and duty?

Peter shook his head. Up ahead, the contaminated islets were looming closer. Better tell them now, though he didn't relish another Conreid panic attack. That boat on sonar was getting closer, definitely heading their way.

"Damn!" His fist pounded the armrest. Sweat broke out on his back, hand reaching for the fifth-liter in its slot.

"Mr. Mitchell?" Radiant blue gaze on him.

He blew out a breath and gestured at the view outside. "We might have to take a detour. Through the periphery."

"I don't understand." Beside him, she leaned over the console, bringing a tantalizing aroma of skin and some kind of fresh herbal scent. "Is that...?"

"That's right." He rubbed his face.

"But... why?"

"What? What's going on?" Leeza was crowding into the wheelhouse, too, jostling behind Peter.

Ariadne gave Peter her considering look. She was back in her Scientist mode, and right now he was glad of it. She turned to Leeza. "It's a Hot Zone. Tactical nuclear weapons were used against ships in this area."

"Hot Zone!" Leeza grabbed Peter's chair and spun it to face her. "What kind of bullshit detour is this, Mitchell? Now you want to fry us? I told Ri you were clueless, but this is just plain—"

"Can it." He turned back to the radar display. "You're the boss, *Despoina*. I headed this way to throw off pursuit, thought we'd circle east around the Zone, but it looks like a fast-moving boat is closing in on us. I think it's the mercenaries. They'll be sure to outgun us. Radio's erratic, but I could try to hail your father's forces to bail us out. Or I could try running through the fringes. Most people are too freaked to even come near the Zone. They might turn back."

"Are you out of your mind? I did some research on this area, Captain Shit-for-brains! People were dropping like flies, anyone who came near this place!"

"That was right after the attack, lots of particulates still stirred up, and the short half-life stuff hadn't decayed. There's still contaminated wrecks and windblown dust, of course, but the spilled fuel's the major—"

"No way! Ariadne, you're not going to let him—"

"Wait." She grasped Leeza's shoulder. "Please don't call my father's troops. Are there alternatives?"

"We can't outrun them. We could fight it out. They wouldn't want to kill you, if they're after your healing secrets, but...."

"They might decide to simply eliminate the competition. And they would not hesitate to kill you or Leeza if we were captured. Go in *now*, Peter. Straight south through the middle of the Zone."

"What—?"

"Are you out of your freaking mind?" Leeza grabbed Ariadne's arms.

"Give it up, call up the troops! Haven't you seen what those fry-babies look like? Even the ones who survive. Cell damage, skin ulcers, immune systems shot, all their hair falls out and—"

"Leeza!" Ariadne pulled her arms free and grasped Leeza's shoulders. "Yes, I've seen them. I've healed many of them."

She turned to Peter. "People here call these Satan's Islands. The fear is so strong I think no one would follow us."

"Locals aren't the only ones afraid." He shot another look at the radar, the blip closing in. Hands clenching on the wheel, he curved in closer to the islets, roaring in full throttle as long as he dared before he'd have to slow down to weave his way in. He tossed back at her, "Look, I'm not cutting through the heart of it, no way. I've plotted a course along the periphery."

"*Madre de Dios!* I don't believe this shit!" Leeza spun around, tore through the cabin gathering up her gear, and disappeared down below.

"You don't understand, Peter. We can go through the heart of the Zone. If we're exposed, I can cure us. Even with significant dosage, and especially in acute versus chronic cases, my experiments with activated mineral water have demonstrated clear reversal of damage in—"

"Jesus!" Peter jerked the wheel, swerving around a barely-submerged rock reef. He had to cut back the throttles and check the chart. "Look, *Despoina.*" He glanced at her, bracing himself against the lure of her eyes, clear blue with those purple glimmering depths, or was that just in his own cycs, like the Cherenkov's? "Maybe you're a genius or a saint or maybe we're all out of our minds, but I don't care if you can make the dead rise, I'm not taking us into the heart of this Hot Zone."

He swerved again, *Nereid* bucking over the waves, taking them past the first charred islet and in. One last glimpse on radar before the islets blocked behind them. "Shit!" The pursuing boat had picked up even more speed, closing in fast.

"Please, Mr. Mitchell—"

"—*boat bearing Ariadne Demodakis*—" The radio scanner locked in on a fragmented burst as they cleared the first islet. It cut out, then crackled in again, "—*last warning.... out of the Zone and prepare to be boarded*—"

"Fat chance!" Peter cut the wheel again, taking *Nereid* behind another islet, curving around it. He pointed at the channel running ahead between reefs toward a larger island, burned and lifeless. "Can you handle the boat, keep her on this course while I get the missile launcher set up? Good, go on up to the bridge, take the wheel up there."

He waited until she was up there, then he hustled back to the deck to pull the fishing net and tarp off the launcher. He hefted a wire-guided missile into position, activated the guidance scope. Panting, he raced back into the wheelhouse to grab the chart and one of the assault rifles. No sign of Conreid, probably cowering below.

He scrambled up onto the bridge, thrust the chart at Ariadne, took the wheel. "Here. Keep us on that pencilled-in course, help me spot for reef."

"Firing in sixty seconds. Turn around now and—" The radio sputtered through the shriek of the turbos.

Peter kept on, weaving around another jagged little islet as *Nereid* heeled hard starboard and spray lashed and he tried not to think about the contaminated dust swirling off the rocks in the breeze. Ahead, the bigger island swelled on them. They'd have to skirt it to the outside, couldn't risk going in deeper around the other side. There were only a few of the smaller islets sheltering them from the open sea before his course would take them in a little deeper again, past the edge of the island.

"Damn!" He could see the hydrofoil now, closing in but still staying out beyond the Zone. "Hold on!" He shoved the throttles full forward, praying the chart was right, *Nereid* leaping ahead as Ariadne grabbed the sprayshield for balance.

"Peter!" She clutched his shoulder, pointed back.

The mercenaries were launching a missile. Peter punched the button to release a floating electronic decoy, hoping to hell the geomag static would screw it up less than it would their attacker's missile guidance system as he cut the starboard throttle, spun the wheel and nearly broached taking her sharp around and back past a reef in a foaming whitewater loop as the missile corrected, started to re-seek, and exploded in a roar on the reef.

Peter pulled Ariadne down, ducking as rock fragments sprayed past, then he popped back up to grab the wheel and ride out the churning chop.

"Take the wheel! Back on course toward that channel. You okay?"

She nodded tersely, face set as she grasped the wheel, and he was dropping onto the deck, running back to guide the missile while he still had an open shot at the hydrofoil.

"Christ!" They were closing in. "Come on, come on...." His hands were shaking with the adrenaline rush. He couldn't fix on the target dancing in the scope sights. *Nereid* jouncing up and down on the chop, the hydrofoil jittering along, but then he had the target locked and was about to trigger Fire when the blank gray of another islet blocked his view.

"Damn!" That was the weak point with wire-guided—hitting a moving target from a moving target.

Whoomph. Another short-range from their attackers exploded behind *Nereid* under the surface, throwing up a gout of spray, soaking Peter and surging them forward. Merc's tracking systems had to be off from the electromag interference—the weakness of non-wire-guided these days. He took a deep breath, steadying the target scope, waiting for the hydrofoil to reappear from behind the islet.

"You said they wouldn't follow us in!"

He jerked his head up, saw Leeza in her hazmat jumpsuit and stocking cap, cowering by the rail, portable camera-goggles on over the filter mask. She shrilled in a shaky voice, "You said they wouldn't attack Ariadne!"

"So write your Congressor!" He reached over to snap open the launch control for the defensive mines. "Here." He tugged her closer. "If I give you the word, hit this button a couple times, releases a mine each time. Got it?"

Her goggles fixed onto the control pad. Clutching the rail with gloved hands, she nodded jerkily.

"Good. Stay down here behind the gunwale. Safer." He shot a look ahead, then back to see the hydrofoil behind them now. "Bloody hell." They were following *Nereid* in. Gut knotting, he swiveled the mounting, focused on them jiggling in the sights. "Keep her steady!" he shouted up to Ariadne as he clung to the scope.

He touched the trigger. With a jolt and a gout of vapor, the missile launched. He stayed with it, had to keep the target in his sights, guiding with the unspooling control wire until it hit, just a few seconds.

Back in the distance, the hydrofoil veered, and he followed it in the scope, grip slippery with sweat on the controls as *Nereid* bounced over some chop, he still had the hydrofoil in his sights, had to be close, but then it veered again. His missile ripped past their stern and into the sea. A muffled explosion and white foam sprayed the hydrofoil as it slewed sideways but kept after them.

"Damn it. Damn!" Peter raced up the deck, onto the bridge, grabbed the wheel and took them into a lurching evasive course. The hydrofoil was closing the distance between them.

"Conreid! Now! Conreid!" Nothing. "Ariadne! Yell back to her, dump those fucking mines *now*!" He gave the wheel another hard pull, goosing the throttles to pull them off to starboard.

"Peter, look out!" Ariadne grabbed his arm, jabbing a hand at an approaching reef. She staggered back to shout down at Leeza. "Release the mines!"

Peter never saw if she did. He was wrestling the wheel, barely missed the reef, closing in on the end of the big island and the blasted hydrofoil still on his tail. Ariadne groped forward beside him again, hair whipping, shouting as she pointed off to starboard. "That way! We will be safe then. They will not follow us that far in!"

He started to shake his head, no way was he taking them into the hot heart of it, but then he looked back and the mercenaries were launching another missile, all he could do was dump his last decoy, it was now or never as they shot past the end of the big island and he hit the port throttle, cut the wheel hard starboard, roared into the narrow cut taking them straight into the Hot Zone.

Their missile held on his old course, exploded on the decoy. Peter shoved the chart at Ariadne. "Start navigating!" He shot a look back. The hydrofoil was looping back, around to the cut. It slowed. Stopped.

Nereid flew on into the angled passage, island blocking off his view of the hydrofoil, taking them out of radar range. He cut speed, looked back again. Waited.

"Phew." Dicey little skirmish. And he hadn't even winged the hydrofoil. Would the *Despoinis* cough up for expenses on top? Re-arming on the black market would be pricey.... Just better hope they didn't run into any more action before they made Crete.

"They are no longer following." Ariadne had straightened, raking the hair off her face to peer back over the stern.

"They'll be waiting for us to turn back." He swallowed and gestured with his chin.

She turned to look. "Oh."

The narrow cut between islands opened out into a natural harbor sheltered by the high cliffs now blasted into a lifeless moonscape. Twisted, blackened masses—most unrecognizable as former pieces of ships and a nuclear sub—were scattered over the rock slopes. A jagged thirty-foot length of twisted metal was imbedded in the cliff face to starboard. Sharp spires and melted blobs hulked out of the water, making the bay into a bizarre obstacle course. Gray ash drifted in the breeze off the lifeless islands.

"Here. Cover your nose and mouth." Peter handed Ariadne his bandanna, then pulled up his T-shirt to cover his own lower face. He cut the engines way back, edging cautiously forward to grope out a passage.

Through the crystal-clear water as they passed over some shallows and more sunken wreckage, he could see them etched sharply: scattered, broken fuel rods. The sea shimmered a harsh radiant blue.

"Hellfire and damnation...." he whispered.

Beside him, Ariadne stirred, then laid her hand on his bare arm. He turned to look into the steady, deep blue of her eyes. The color wasn't at all like that sizzling virulent Cherenkov's.

"Holy shit!" Leeza scrambled up from her huddled crouch on the deck, camera-goggles craning back and forth. She stepped forward, jerked back, hesitated, finally scurried forward to the rail. She aimed the goggles over the side, into the shimmering blue glow of radiation. "Subliminal...."

34

RIPPLES OF DYING LIGHT washed over the sea, weaving a shimmering copper net that melted and reformed with the waves.

"Perfect." Leeza, up on the flying bridge, held her camera on the red-gold sunset, a mellow buzz finally easing her overwired nerves. The soundtrack, Kiri Menoth's "Ectoplasmic Wavelengths" through the ear buds, and she was soaking in the scene, electric sparks racing through her nerves and down the leads, gold stored in her chip. Magic—like she could dissolve into it, become pure energy. Humming, she rode the waves of light and sound, reflections fading into deep sapphire blue.

She lowered the camera to the bench, twisting the Demodakis ring on her finger to frown into the gem's facets. The color was changeable, like Ariadne's eyes—untouchable cool, but catch her off-guard and they'd go Cherenkov's, sizzling heart-of-a-star blue.

She shuddered, but couldn't resist Linking in to scan the recording once more: The Hot Zone.

> ***Desolation. Pulverized rock crags dusted with white ash, deadly glowing waters lapping, the only sound. Like some weird lifeless planet. No, post-life. Anti-life.
>
> Leeza flashes on a memory byte: surrealistic painting, clock faces dripping impossibly fluid over sharp stone edges. Here in the nuked bay, pieces of once-rigid ships, melted into impossible contortions, massive metal flung and twisted ribbonlike and fused into the stone cliffs. And that sparkly radiant glow of the nuked sea. Hypnotic. Luring her closer deeper so totally drop-dead gorgeous....
>
> "Ugh!" She jerks back from the rail, swallows, then carefully leans forward to follow the startling movement in the shallows. Fins wriggle awkwardly, dragging the fish along. It turns, flashes a glimpse of misshapen tail fin and grotesque pinkish blobs of mutated flesh where streamlined gill slits should have been. The shimmering hot blue closes over it ***

Leeza shivered and resisted the sick urge to scan once more her data on ionizing radiation, RADs, REMs, somatic effects, cancer deaths per million organ-REMs, chromosomal damage....

CUT. That track was definitely a no-win. Time to get back to the homework, run some file compilations, now she had a buzz going. Couldn't let this trip turn into a writeoff.

Leeza found the right library chip, keyed Cult references, and found the Gaea Speaks subfile. She danced through the branching directory, sampling snippets: the bedsheet-robed rockheads holding up their crystals to be blessed at a shrine with a garlanded portrait from that old boarding-school photo of Ariadne. *Jump*. News copy of an Israeli nuclear fuel facility exploding in flames, soldiers grappling a furiously-spitting Corybant warrior as one of them backhands her face and her staring-eyed headband drops to the dust. *Jump*. Subfile, Greek history refs. Cruising "alpha index," she found "Healers."

There was some stuff she'd scanned before:

Old Asclepius and the caduceus staff with the serpents wound around it, symbol of healing. Maybe related to that Kundalini sexual/enlightenment Yoga biz, energy rising up through your spine. Leeza had always wondered, thought someday she'd try it, new rush maybe she could work it in the Link. Amplify, supercharge. But snakes gave her the creeps. And the caduceus image was morphing into the double-helix DNA diagram, taking her right back to RADs and REMs and mutations—

JUMP.

More history snippets, miracle shrines to saints and Virgins, healing springs, but something buzzing at the back of her head kept her pushing into branching subfiles—

> ***Artemis. And she's staring at Ariadne's distant eyes and etched profile in stone. Fierce goddess, guardian of wilderness. The statue rotates, empty gaze fixing on and through Leeza, face beautiful and powerful and forever untouchable***

Leeza swears and jumps to:

> ***Funky Victorian line drawing of a tamer plump goddess in draped tunic with bow and arrow and friendly animals, crescent moon behind her. Brit voice clipping syllables: "...twin sister to Apollo the sun god, the two representing the intertwining balance of male and female, of heaven's opposing forces. The healing power he later claimed was first attributed to sister moon-goddess Artemis and her wand—"***

Leeza jacked straight out of the Link, blinking and disoriented. Stupid stunt. But looking into the ageless eyes of that statue, she'd suddenly *felt* through the Link those cold marble hands raise to touch her hot skin, soaking up the fever and the tightness, magic touch draining her pain and filling her with cool moonlight....

Bullshit. Nerves. Maybe she'd got a bad hit, Certified Pure meant diddly half the time.

Leeza thrust the camera and recorder into their case and took a deep breath. She picked at her flaking burnt-sienna nail polish, scowling. The situation sucked. She needed to talk to Ariadne.

Right, like Saint A. was going to talk. Just when she looked like she'd thaw, *Cut!* Back to the deep freeze.

Leeza had gotten maybe two words out of her since they'd finally made it through the Hot Zone. Ariadne had insisted on dosing them all with her holy-water, and some "treatment" that involved touching them with that big crystal. Was she a rockhead, after all? And then she'd rolled up her eyes and conked out.

Leeze had nearly freaked then, thinking it was the radiation zapping her, zapping them all.

So she'd been scared. Hadn't released the bloody mines like Mitchell said to, got a little wigged-out about the radiation dose. Where did that prick get off, dissing her like he was somebody? And Ariadne just lying there in the bunk for a whole day, staring hypnotized into that crystal the dreck had almost drowned her to get. The scene was definitely getting out of hand. And what about Leeza's story?

She chipped off another shiny polish flake. She had to get off this tin can before *she* went certifiable.

Leeza stared at her pale outstretched arms and hands washed by the fading sunset to a livid hue, shuddering with a mixture of dread and fascination at the memory of that blue glow in the sea. The Cherenkov's.

The Link. The Meat. Reality not Virtual at all. She was losing it, losing the delineations. Nausea burned at the thought of that real-time radiation eating into her smooth skin. Pitting her flawless complexion with those hideous ulcers, perfect face and body melting in the mirror into monstrosity. She yanked her arms back—*Madre all she needed was to get herself tripping out on a bummer*—hugging herself and refusing to think about it. Ariadne had promised the doses of her special water, like she'd given that soldier, would cure any potential cell damage. Ariadne promised. Ariadne promised.

Leeza jerked to her feet, dragged her gear down to the deck, and stalked into the cabin, up to the wheelhouse where Ariadne and Captain Blighted were poring over a chart. Like he really had to lean that close to her.

She clenched her fists. "Are we there yet?"

35

COPPERY SUNSET SLANTED OVER the boxy whitewashed houses perched above the steep shoreline. Indigo sea pawed at the base of the cliffs as stark mountains and secret green gorges slid past like the wake off *Nereid*'s bow.

Ariadne traced the coves on the spread chart, where she'd jotted readings from her magnetometer as they'd worked their way west along Crete's rugged southern shoreline. Now she was trying to match contours to her memories. The boat rose and dipped beneath her feet, and she gripped the console edge, resisting the persistent dizziness. She felt weakened again, after using the Tinos crystal's pathways to cleanse their bioelectric fields and combat the radiation effects. Taking a steadying breath, she closed her eyes as the sea rocked her gently....

Clear purple-blue swells, rocking Uncle Demetrios's battered old trader. Little Ariadne stood stiffly gripping the rail as they headed for the Petrides' sheltered cove, refusing the prick of curiosity, the wild lure of the rugged south coast of Crete. She knew it was all a plan of her uncle's, to make her forget her mother's death. But she'd never forget. Never.

"My little Kri-Kri!" His rough hand tousled her braids. "Meet Mistress Kriti. She's a wild, glorious witch—the Big Island. You'll see, she'll enchant you, too."

She turned to him, unsmiling and armored, looking up at those dancing dark eyes always teasing. She frowned, sticking out her chin. "You're just making up stories again."

He grinned and spread his arms to the sea and rocky mountains and endless sky. "Making up! When the stories here are bursting all over, blossoming like flowers out of the stones and spring rains? What about Homer and the fabulous ninety-nine cities of the Minoans? Those crazy girls and boys dancing with the sacred bulls. Even old Zeus was born up in those mountains!" He jabbed a hand.

"And your great-great-great-grandmother Ariadne. She was the priestess of the labyrinth her father built. There's a lesson in that. Watch out for those scoundrel gods. Old Minos, now, he thought he could dodge them, outshine them. Hubris. Crafty Zeus, that philanderer, showed him up, came down as a giant bull in all his glory—charmed Minos's wife right out of her skirts. When a god comes bearing gifts, now what's a poor mortal to do but bow down and take it? And what a visitation that was, all the power of his magic rod!"

He shot Ariadne a look and sobered, stroking his long black mustache. "But those gifts of the gods—always a price, eh? She bore Minos a godgiven monster child. The minotaur, half man and half bull. So old Minos locked him at the heart of the labyrinth to guard the treasure. Only daughter Ariadne brave enough to hold the key to it. But then she had the power, the ancient serpent magic from the original matriarch Gaea herself...."

Despite her stubborn stiffness, Ariadne broke into a grin. "Uncle Dmitri!"

Remembering, she blinked away tears and smiled. That pirate Demetrios and his outrageous tales. Was he still here, living up in those mountains? She'd been allowed no word of him, since he'd defied her father's orders to join the new Med League.

"Are we there yet?" Leeza's voice broke in on her.

Peter was rubbing his eyes. "Maybe." He pointed at the shoreline and handed Ariadne his binoculars set on nightscope. "How about that one?"

Blurred images resolved into grainy monotone cliffs, a shadowed black cove beyond a narrow cut of foaming waves. Inside, a darker, tilted bulk. "Yes, I think that's it."

"The grounded freighter you were talking about?"

She lowered the binoculars and nodded. "When I first came here as a girl on my uncle Demetrios's trading boat, Georgios Petrides said the ship had been damaged in a Meltemi storm from North Africa. It must have tried to shelter in the cove, but it was too shallow. He used the abandoned wreck for his fishing base."

"Hope he remembers you."

"The villagers would not forget my uncle." Ariadne, lightheaded again, reached out to steady herself on the rail.

"You okay?"

She nodded.

Leeza stared, eyes dilated, trembling with some kind of drug again. "Hey!" Her voice shrilled. "You sure it's not radiation sickness?"

Ariadne managed a smile. "Don't worry, Leeza. We are in no danger from the radiation exposure."

She gnawed her lip. "So how does that holy water work, then? If you expect us to just—"

"Conreid," Peter broke in, impatient. "Lay off her. I'm taking *Nereid* in. I want you on deck to watch for rocks."

"Why do *I* always have to—"

"I didn't invite you along, remember?"

Ariadne took a deep breath, stepping out the door. "I will watch."

Leeza followed. "Jeez, I was just—"

"Okay, both of you," Peter called after them, climbing up to the flying bridge. "Sing out if we get too close going through that gap. And get ready to run out the white flag. There's somebody on the wreck in there."

In the bow, Ariadne took a deep breath of cool salt air. Stars sparkled overhead.

Leeza glanced apprehensively toward shore as they eased closer.

"Don't worry, Leeza. We will be welcome here."

Silver and black ripples fanned out as they glided into the cut. Watching the jagged boulders where the surge foamed, Ariadne called, "To starboard, there are shallow rocks." The boat veered, and they were through.

Enclosing cliffs rose around them. Across the cove, the tilted wrecked freighter was a darker bulk in the dusk. Ariadne peered and saw movement, a shadowed figure on deck, rifle pointed at *Nereid*.

"*Jodas!*" Leeza jerked back. "He's got a gun."

Ariadne waved an arm overhead. She called, "Georgio Petride?" *Nereid* rocked, gliding to a halt with engines idling, as Peter came down with his assault rifle.

Silence for a few seconds, then a grudging, "*Neh*," from the wreck. The man's rifle was still trained on them.

Ariadne identified herself.

More silence, then a challenge, the rifle waving.

Leeza clutched Ariadne's arm. "Now what? He going to shoot?"

Peter's grip tightened on his weapon. "What's wrong?"

"He thinks you're a kidnapper. They've heard the reports."

More exhausting arguments back and forth across the dark water. She reminded the old fisherman of Demetrios, their visit years ago. "May I come ashore to talk?"

Finally the blocky figure thrust his rifle up at the air, called out a grudging, "*Neh, neh!*" He jumped into a dinghy, started its motor with a roar, and shot toward the boat, rifle still gripped and pointed toward them.

"*Mierda,* not again! He said *no,* Ariadne. I'm not sticking around to get shot at!" Leeza spun around, diving for the wheelhouse.

"Leeza, wait." Despite her weariness, Ariadne couldn't help chuckling. "*Neh* means yes."

36

"*CHORIA POLI!*" PETER RAISED his glass into the lamplight.

The old fisherman scratched under his flat cap and reached for his own chipped glass, giving Conreid a wink from his one good eye, the other one covered by a stained leather patch. "To the blond *Magdalena.*"

Leeza sat stiffly, staring at Georgios. Good thing she didn't know Greek.

Peter nudged her, indicating her handleless crockery cup. "Join the party."

She took a token sip, wrinkling her nose at the retsina. "Where do they get this turpentine? Look at him, swilling it down."

Peter said in Greek, "She's afraid she won't be able to resist you if she drinks any more."

Georgios roared with laughter, slapping Peter on the back. A gap-toothed leer on his wind-seamed face, he scratched his chest under the layers of motheaten sweaters.

Leeza shuddered. "He's probably got lice."

"Lighten up, he's an okay guy."

"Then ask him when I can see Ariadne. I need to talk to her."

"Look, I already told you—"

"Just ask him." She gritted her teeth.

He shrugged, laying it on thick for the geezer.

Georgios eyed Leeza, spat out a stream of Greek, chopped his hand in the air, and tilted his glass again.

Peter turned back to her. "Like I said, they're sticking out their necks here, what with the word out on Ariadne being kidnapped, and the Med League boys nosing around. Not to mention the Sons of the Prophet—made a raid last week up on the north side near Iraklion, killed a priest. And now some stranger through day before yesterday asking questions...."

Georgios had told them the foreigner claimed to be from the World Health Organization managing the RPH quarantine camp down the coast. Apparently gathering information about some local sanctified mineral spring that was drawing more "plague" victims to try for a miracle cure—sort of a small-scale version of the Tinos well Ariadne had insisted on visiting. The guy had left contact info, said to report any strangers so they could control the "contagion." But Georgios didn't trust him, said his eyes were shifty.

Peter blew out a breath. All they needed was more attention on their hideout—especially since the *Tyrannos* had upped the reward for information leading to Ariadne's safe return. "Look, we've got to keep a low profile. We're nothing but bad news here, you know some of these villagers could hold you and me accountable for the next quake or mutated baby. Evil eye— easier to just off you. So you should be making grateful noises they let us in at all."

"I don't trust the old prick. How do we know Ariadne's even up there in his daughter's house?" Leeza jerked her head toward the cabin doorway, the steep hill above the cove's beach. "So what's the scoop, Mitchell? I mean, did we get zapped with bad stuff in that Hot Zone, or what? We just trust this holy water of hers?"

He spread his hands. "She's got a reputation for curing some bad cases. And you saw that soldier back on her island." He didn't want to think about it. He'd scrubbed *Nereid* after the Hot Zone to wash off any radioactive particulates, had to hope for the best. "We'll probably make it 'til Doomsday, anyway."

"Well, I plan on being around awhile! Where does she get off, sticking us here under house arrest?" Her chin thrust out defensively. "I mean, we were friends! Lovers. What am I now, her doormat?"

For once, she wasn't acting. He shrugged. "It's her trip, she's paying the tab. I guess we're just some kind of minor annoyance at this point."

He lifted his glass. "Might as well enjoy the ride." He nudged her cup at her. "Bottoms up."

She looked at it and chewed her lip. "Hey, I...."

Abruptly, she pushed back her chair. "Man, this fun-house is making me dizzy enough." She waved a hand at the cockeyed freighter cabin, rusty metal walls flaking drab paint scabs, one narrow window tilted toward the sunset and the opposite one toward its reflection in the cove, boards nailed in to make a second, level floor meeting the original walls at all the wrong angles. "I need some fresh air." Leeza skirted the table, ducking as she moved under the downslanting ceiling and through the foreshortened doorway.

Georgios barked out a warning. Peter translated, "Stay on board."

"I think I've got the idea. Give the cyclops my share of that poison."

Peter pushed her cup at Georgios and raised his own glass. "To the *Despoinis*. Is she feeling better now?"

"It's no good, the way she spends all day working at that infernal computer of hers, or else staring into that crystal. But my daughter Marta finally put her to bed, to rest. I sent word by a goatherd to her uncle Demetrios." He tilted his head toward the mountains.

Peter frowned. "I thought the uncle was a trader."

"Not in many years. But yes, he brought his boat to our village in the old days. The pirate!" He laughed, thumping down the cup. "One time he brought with him the girl. Kri-Kri he called her, and she was a shy, wild young thing. Climbing with the goats all over the mountain. But a beauty, even then." He nodded sagely. "Demetrios knew our glorious Kriti would cure her of the grief."

"Grief?"

"Of her mother's death." He splashed more in his cup. "Better she'd stayed here. That father of hers...." He turned, wobbly in his chair, and spat.

"So you won't turn her over to the *Tyrannos*?"

Georgios scowled, shoving his face close to Peter's and gripping his arm hard. "You're talking to a Cretan, boy!" He leaned back, pounding his chest with a fist. "I, Georgio Petride, owe a blood-debt to Demetrios. I will guard his Kri-Kri until he comes." He fumbled for the rifle leaning against his chair. He missed it, blinking and looking surprised as it clattered to the floor.

"Good. Tha's...." Peter frowned, trying to clear his throat. His tongue was suddenly too thick in his mouth. He stared at Georgios, gone fuzzy around the edges. The crazy-angled walls were spinning.

"Wha—?" He groped for the table, but it was falling up at him, his hand going out in slow-motion to knock over a glass.

Somewhere a voice was cursing. A crash. Blackness.

37

BRACING HERSELF AGAINST THE outside of the cabin, Leeza worked her way through the junk piled along the slanting side deck, pausing to check out the fading pink and purple clouds over the darkening cliff. She was going stir-crazy. She pulled herself along the rusted and bent rail, past the layers of fish nets they'd strung for camouflage from the tilted high side of the freighter over *Nereid* tucked between it and the cliff.

She didn't like being so close to Mitchell's boat. What if it was still radioactive?

Working her way around the broken crane and piles of baskets and nets on the back deck of the freighter, she looked for something to sit on. The nets reeked and everything else was rusted or dusty. She leaned on the downside rail, careful not to get her jumpsuit dirty, and stared out at the cove. Her eyes slid out of focus as the soft reflections of sunset color shimmered and dissolved into night. Out beyond the cove's bottleneck, glimmering lights of the village fishermen dipped and bobbed. A fresh breeze ruffled the cove.

She took a deep breath and sighed, foot tapping an impatient rhythm on the deck.

Reaching into the pouch hung around her hips, she pulled out the sapphire crystal, holding it into a glimmer of lamplight from the cabin window. She could feel, more than see, the designs etched into it.

She couldn't give it to Ariadne, couldn't believe she'd been so stupid. Ariadne would know it came from that cheesy chapel on her island. But she couldn't make herself throw it away, somehow the cool facets felt good in her hand and wanted to stay. She could see the look Ariadne would give her if she knew, and the whole situation just pissed Leeza off.

Her fist clenched around the stone. She started to raise it to throw, then shoved it back into the pouch, in with her little stun-gun, and stalked back down the deck.

She peered into the downtilted cabin window, smiled, and ducked through the doorway. Mitchell and Georgios were snoring on the floor, beside the overturned table.

She stared, fascinated by the sheer wreckage of the old fisherman, bulky in layers of dirty, smelly, wornout shirts and sweaters, hands scarred and callused and stained into blunt paws, gray stubble and high-beaked nose under the greasy cap, and the frayed leather eye-patch hiding God knew what disgusting mess. The thing was she could almost see the vanished beautiful boy inside all that, like those pretty young men strutting around Athens or Ariadne's island. All heading for this? She started to shudder, but turned it into a shrug.

"Sleep tight, boys." Leeza dumped the rest of the retsina bottle with the dissolved 'ludes over the side, grabbed her portable recording gear, and popped a purple-striped capsule, expectancy humming through her. Up and running. "Showtime."

∞

"*Sto plaz! Sto plaz!*" Leeza was laughing, the boys were laughing, and she never wanted to stop, peaking on the Purple Flash sizzling through her veins, beat-up electric car packed to the max, whole goddamn Crete merchant marine on leave and she'd hardly got her thumb out when they'd peeled over in a cloud of dust, crazy hot wind blowing, antique boombox on the floorboards blasting out some ancient disco crap but it was loud enough it didn't matter, boys chattering and she didn't understand, but what the hell she'd learned, "*Sto plaz!*"

To the beach! She wanted to go skinny-dipping.

The boys just laughed as the car careened drunken along the dark cliffs and the hot wind blew through the glassless windows. She was coughing on the dust, jostled on top of knees and shoulders, somebody's flat cap pulled low over her eyes, somebody else copping a feel. She slapped randomly, clutching the camera goggles and laughing, jacked in to the leads and riding flying swooping down out of the hills to the spark of town lights below.

Leeza went a little fuzzy on how they'd gotten out of the car, but somehow they were all stumbling along winding cobbled alleys.

Dizzy sweeps of closed storefronts, a tethered donkey, terraced houses above on a steep hill glowing dim white in the dark beneath the stars and the slow writhing serpents of colored auroras. Somebody caught her as the hill spun and tumbled down on her through the camera goggles. More jerky glimpses of frowning women in black hurrying past, cobblestones snaking away, harbor at the end of the side street, boats bobbing under lamplight.

"*Sto plaz!*" She spun around, tucking the goggles away, tugging free of their arms. "*Sto plaz.* Come on, you troglodytes, I wanna go swimming!"

The boys in their caps and imitation American jeans—the beautiful, carved-statue boys with their perfect profiles and big dark eyes and incredible eyelashes, *Madre* it wasn't fair to waste those on men—the boys just laughed and took her arms and jostled her along, chanting, "*Sto taverna! Sto taverna!*"

She decided after all maybe she could go for some beer—none of that retsina swill—she could feel the buzz leveling out and the thirst setting in. So she let them sweep her along toward the harbor. People were eating under diner awnings in the lamplight, one old man dancing slow by himself to that whiny string-music farther on, then a flash of sputtering pink neon spelling out *Space Cafet ia*.

"Let's go in." Leeza dug in her heels. "I want a drink in the Space Cafeteria."

Arms kept dragging her along. "*Ohi, ohi.* Eleni's." They stumbled toward a low, cement-block building on the edge of the harbor. Music pulsed out the door to nab them and float them on in.

An enormous greasy man swathed in a stained apron pushed through some dancers to smack a tray of glasses and a pitcher of wine on their table. Leeza blinked up, grinning. "Hola, amigo. I mean, ciao Eleni. I need beer." She winked.

The boys roared and the waiter looked pained, but a bottle of warm beer appeared on the table. She gulped it thirstily. Little plates started passing around, weird things like soggy leaves wrapped around mush, big raw peas, and sausage-like appetizers stuffed into chewy skins, which tasted okay until she gathered from a real hilarious pantomime that they were made from some kind of animal guts.

Music pounded through dim lights. Time to dance. Two or three sailors at a time gyrated and twirled her, strutting and rubbing their crotches up against her with soulful looks. Some other macho cut in, max-fusto in open shirt and gold chains, tight pants. Leeza laughed and stumbled against the table, a glass crashing to the floor. Like some kind of signal, everybody went nuts, jumping up and hooting and flinging plates and glasses onto the floor, dancing wild in the shards.

"Maximal!" Leeza flung another plate, dancing, pounding to the music until she couldn't feel her feet.

"Whoa, boys, Leeza's gotta take a break." She pushed back the next sailor lurching with a grin toward her, and slumped into a chair.

"Best you slow it down, girl."

Leeza's head seemed to turn very slowly through the smoky dimness as she tracked the source of the husky, Caribbean-tinged drawl. Expecting to see a man, she fuzzily changed gears. It was a woman sitting next to her at the table, and as her eyes slowly focused, she wondered how she'd missed her earlier. Definitely eye-catching. Shiny black skin, and hair in those long skinny corn-rows all beaded and bangled that Leeza had always liked, smooth face too strongly bony to be pretty but more like pretty was irrelevant, dramatic heavy eye makeup, and some kind of tattoo—no, bumpy scars in a spiral design on her forehead. She was wearing a shimmering, sleeveless long dress in bronze and black stripes. Copper bracelets above and below the elbows accentuated the muscle definition of her shapely arms.

Leeza got a hot little twinge in her gut. "Hey. You're Jamaican? Bob Marleyville?"

"Ha. You like de Mon?" The woman turned her head. "Back off, Jack." The sailor who'd been tugging at her arm lurched away. "Trouble with these clowns, they think you foreign, you free for the taking."

Leeza found her beer bottle in the clutter and took a long, warm swallow. "You worried about it?"

A deep, throaty laugh. "Puny pretty-boys?" She lifted her glass. There was another scar slicing across her upper arm beneath the bracelet, and this one hadn't been designed.

Leeza's tongue darted nervously to moisten dry lips. "So what are you doing over here? Sightseeing?" Or one of the Rasta-man drug runners?

The woman drained her glass and turned finally toward Leeza, giving her a slow appraisal. Long sinewy fingers, so dark in the neon and fluorescent spill from the bar they gleamed purple-black, caressed the curve of the glass. "Enlightenment."

"What?" Leeza blinked in the smoke haze.

"Wake up, sweet heart. En-light-en-ment. These islands where it at. Ancient wisdom and power, all that jazz."

Leeza focused blurrily on the strings of tiny beads around the woman's neck, seeing there was a big crystal pendant among them. "You one of those rock heads?"

She only lifted one narrow-plucked eyebrow. "So what you doing over here, Miss Media Conreid? You got a big story in this dive?"

Leeza could feel her mouth dropping open at her name, but the room was starting to do strange things, spinning dizzily around her. She always forgot what a bummer the crash could be off the Purple Haze.

"You don't look so good. Where you staying?"

Leeza pressed her hands against her eyes and took a deep breath. "Just thirsty. Order me another beer?"

Things went a little fuzzy, then she was gripping a fresh bottle, gulping greedily. Her stomach calmed down, and she could catch her breath. "Thanks. Guess I'll call it a night." She groped for her camera goggles and recorder pouch, looking vaguely around the taverna. The music had gone quieter, some kind of innocuous pap. Two of the sailors were back, and one of them grabbed her arm, babbling something.

"You with these boys?" The woman tilted her head scornfully.

"No. I mean—no. I gotta get back." She clutched the pouch. The sailor was tugging harder at her arm.

"Look like you getting nowhere you want to go, with they." She stood, and Leeza blinked at her height. "Party over, boys. Damiana taking she home."

But the Greeks didn't seem to get the message, and there was a scuffle, the fat bartender shouting something, table crashing over, and Leeza trying to butt her way through, hunched over and laughing helplessly inside despite it all. *Damiana!* Too perfect. Then the flash of a knife, cool smile playing over the woman's face, she knew how to handle it all right, the boys were backing off, and the two of them were out in the street, Leeza giggling even as her stomach did hip-hops of fear and excitement. That elusive ultimate rush.

She shivered, savoring it. The woman swung away from the door, stepping back, lines of the dress swaying around her, tiger stripes. Yes. She moved like a tiger.

Leeza took a deep breath as the gleam of the knife disappeared in the flowing folds. "Thanks."

A shrug, glint of eyes in the shadow of the building. "They nothing. I be hearing Sons of the Prophet sniffing 'round though, now word has it they be some bad worth thinking on."

Damiana stepped closer out of the shadows, peering down, as Leeza froze in alarm. *Sons of the Prophet.*

A shapely arm came around her shoulders, guiding her along the dark cobblestones. "No fear, Ms. Newslady Conreid, no bogey-man get you tonight. Where you staying? You got a crew with you?" Her hip brushed against Leeza. "So what worth recording in this dusty dump?"

The fresh air was helping, but a vaguely remembered warning tightened Leeza's gut again. What? *A stranger asking questions....* She shook her head dully. "Can't remember."

The arm steered her around a turn, down another narrow street. "Can't remember? You big story?" Low voice mocking.

"Story...." Leeza bit her lip, mind racing. "My camera! Where's my camera?" She pretended to panic, groping.

"Gear right in you pouch here." Throaty laughter.

"Oh." She kept leaning against the woman's support, half covering her confusion, half drawn to the tantalizing smoky musk of the body draped by the flowing dress. "Can't lose recorder... got great stuff. Old tourist places. Then and Now. You been to the Acropolis? Statues before the Athens acid smog ate'em...." She swayed.

Damiana stopped, turning Leeza around and looking down into her face, dark eyes studying. "You come back with I, sleep it off." A slow, insinuating smile, gleam of teeth.

Leeza sucked in a quick breath. She had to get back, how the hell she didn't know, she had to warn Ariadne. *Sons of the Prophet. Strangers asking questions.*

Screw it. Saint Ariadne and good ol' Mitchell weren't exactly going out of their way for Leeza. Think about it in the morning. Her hand was reaching up to touch the planes of the face gleaming like dark burnished metal in the shadowed alley. Her fingertips skittered nervously, soaking up the smooth texture, the heat glowing beneath the skin.

Long black fingers reached out to slowly stroke the curve of Leeza's jaw, tracing a deliberate path across her throat. The invisible line burned on her skin as they walked on, arms linked.

38

PITCH BLACK—THE DARKNESS found only deep inside caves. Ariadne shivered in the damp cold. The twisting passage took her deeper and deeper, feet pounding to a heavy rhythm echoing through her bones, hand trailing along the rough stone passage.

She had followed the wild goat back to her secret childhood mountain grotto. He waited out there, at the entrance to the cave, yellow eyes staring beside the empty gaze of the carved temple guardian. But Ariadne was lost in the maze. The pounding rhythm filled her, stone thrumming beneath her hand—no, her body was the drum, reverberating to the summons. Deeper. To the core of the earth. Blackness engulfed her as the voices called.

Ariadne. Another voice—faint and almost swallowed by the dark—was calling her back. But she had to go deeper.

Ariadne. It was the goat whispering. No, the minotaur with his thick curved horns, staring from the carved facets of little Kri-Kri's magic blue gem, and she was lost inside its shadowed turnings. That voice—it was Peter, in the molten sunlight of the cove, pulling her out of the drowning depths, pressing his warm sea-salty lips to hers.

"Ariadne."

"Uhn." She jerked upright in bed, heart pounding. Fingers of light pried through the wooden shutters. She rubbed her eyes, the heaviness of the dream receding slowly.

"Ariadne? Are you awake?"

She swung her legs off the bed and pushed the shutters open. "What is it? What are you doing here?"

He was a dark silhouette against the dawn. "I had to tell you—"

"*Despoina.*" Another dim figure loomed—Georgios. "It's the little whore. She's gone."

"Wait. Let me get dressed." Her fingers shook as she pulled the shutter to. Closing her eyes, she felt her hand rise of its own volition toward her crystal pendant. She dropped her hand and pulled on her dress in the darkness, feet groping for sandals.

Outside, the sky was brightening over the sea, wind swirling drifts of dust. The two men stood stiffly in the dirt yard, the family hound sprawled at their feet. Peter's face was set, lips pressed tight. Georgios looked shamed and angry.

The old man burst out, "The *Magdalena*, I tell you not to trust her, no? Now she's gone. Poof, vanished."

"Did you search around the cove?"

He pulled himself straight, chest out, gripping his rifle as the dog sat up on its haunches against his legs, suddenly alert. "Of course we searched. I tell you it's good for her I don't get my hands on her now—"

"No fault of yours, Georgios." Peter spread his palms. He turned toward Ariadne, voice picking up an edge. "It was the wine. She...." He dropped back into English. "I think she slipped us a whammy in the retsina. Something from her drug stash."

Ariadne clenched her fists until the thick ring dug into her fingers. "Where would she go? The village?"

The hound gave a baying cry, lunged out the gate, and bounded up the path behind the house. More barking. A bitten-off scream. Georgios cursed, running with his rifle after the beast, plunging through a flurry of wings and feathers as chickens burst from their roosts around the shed.

"*Alto!*" Shrill voice up the hillside. "Call him off! Don't—Ariadne!" Barks, ending in an injured yelp.

Ariadne swung around to see Peter still standing in the yard, staring blearily at her. She started past him to the gate, but his hand shot out to grasp her arm. She looked down at his fingers on her bare skin, then back at his expressionless face. It seemed they stood that way for a long time.

He dropped his hand. "Don't. Just rile up the dog. Here they come." He jerked his head toward the path.

Leeza stumbled around the curve of the stone fence, Georgios dragging her roughly by the arm in a swirl of dust, the hound yapping excitedly. Georgios gave it a kick and it yelped again, whining and skulking after them as Georgios pushed Leeza through the gate. Chickens scattered. Leeza skidded and fell at Ariadne's feet.

"Ariadne! That prick—he...." She coughed on windblown dust.

"Georgiou. No need for this." She bent down to help Leeza to her feet.

Georgios spat and leaned against the rock wall. Marta hurried out of the house, pulling a shawl over her nightdress. Her teenaged son Nikos followed with his rifle. Leeza braced herself on her feet and brushed shakily at her rumpled, stained jumpsuit.

Peter strode over and grasped her arm. "What the hell are you trying to prove? And don't go pitiful on us, Georgios and I just happen to have these doozy headaches and we're not in the mood for more of your crap."

Leeza grinned feebly, face pallid beneath smeared makeup.

He gripped her tighter. "Where did you go? Don't you realize, you stupid twit, you've blown our cover here?"

"Enough." Ariadne pulled his hand away, peering into Leeza's exhausted face. "Leeza, look at me." The bloodshot eyes slowly focused. "We must know where you went last night. Who saw you? Were you followed?"

Leeza blinked, lifting a foot and wincing. "Don't you come down on me, too! Bloody miles I walked, trying to get back here. Didn't realize it was so far, had to ditch those stupid sailors, just started walking. On the way back, I mean. I needed a break, you keeping me locked up on that stupid boat, won't even let me come ashore. I thought we were friends, Ariadne. All right, so big deal, I hitched a ride to a town and went dancing. I wasn't the only one, there were other... other tourists around."

She took a sharp breath. "Nobody paid any attention to me, except those pushy sailors. And I got a lift with the vegetables in some crummy donkey cart."

A short bark of laughter as she tugged a garlic bulb from her pocket. "Old crone thought I was a vampire I guess, mumbling and crossing herself, wanted me to eat it."

Ariadne ignored Leeza's feeble grin. "Which way? Did you go along the coast, or inland?"

She waggled fingers toward the shoreline. "A ways. But it was more like a little town, not one of those dinky villages."

Ariadne turned toward Georgios, still leaning against the rock fence with his arms crossed, glaring as she translated. "Could she have gone as far as Skaloti?"

He scowled. "Wherever that one goes, she'll draw the wrong notice. Bad luck for everyone."

Peter broke in, "He's right. We should leave now. They'll be after us."

Ariadne shook her head. "One more day. I need to—"

"If you're talking about me, you could do it in English."

"Just be glad all we're doing is talking, you—"

"Enough!" Ariadne held up a halting hand to him, then turned to Leeza. "Why, Leeza? Why put us all in danger?"

No answer.

Ariadne looked out over the sea, sun rising into a hazy pink band. She took a deep breath and grasped Leeza's shoulders, forcing her to meet her gaze. "This is not a game! If I allow you to stay in the house here with me, you must promise to stay inside, out of sight."

A smile twitched Leeza's mouth as she shot a triumphant look at Peter. "Okay. Now I've really gotta crash, Ri."

Ariadne bit back an angry retort. What was the use? Her hand groped for her crystal pendant, seeking its solidity, its reassuring order.... She needed just a little more time to verify the local site she'd now calculated from the magnetometer readings, send the data from Tinos and this new anomalous geomagnetic field to Teresa Espinoza and Arun Singh, once she'd had a chance to check the healing spring nearby and see if she could duplicate her earlier results. Even two sites was not enough for proof, but it would give her researchers something to work with.

The deep, mocking voice from her dreams laughed silently. *"Yes, cloak it all in your pseudo-science!* You *are the answer—claim your power!"*

Reason was dissolving around her. What power? Even her physical strength was draining away each time she experimented with the crystals. Or was it being funneled somewhere else? Someplace far beyond this dusty yard and her body moving numbly through abstracted motions. Ariadne seemed to watch from a great distance as her arm reached out to support Leeza and guide her into the house.

Peter lunged to cut them off. "You're swallowing her bullshit? Listen, you may be so wrapped up in your five-star Quest you don't care, but it just so happens she—and you—are putting everybody in danger. With your father's reward upping the ante, don't you think the villagers would be tempted? And even if they kept silent, they might be threatened by the pharmco mercenaries. If you won't protect yourself, what about Marta and Nikos here?"

Ariadne met his furious glare. "If the mercenaries come before I finish my test here, I will give myself up to them. They want only me."

"What if they shoot first and ask questions later? And what about the Sons of the Prophet? They're still on our trail, too."

A gasp. Leeza spun around to stare at Peter. She started to say something, then snapped her mouth shut. Her face had gone colorless.

"What is it?" Ariadne's arm tightened around her shoulders. "Marta," she called to Georgios's daughter staring confused from the doorway. "Please help."

Leeza's eyes were closed. "Don't feel so hot."

Marta silently took Leeza's other arm, and they helped her toward the house. Ariadne looked back to see Peter stalking out the gate with Georgios. "One more day," she called to him. "Then we can go."

He didn't look back, just threw out his hands and strode on with the angrily gesturing fisherman. The hound circled them in agitated lunges.

39

"NOW THAT'S WHAT THE doctor ordered."

Ariadne sighed, looking up from her tablet computer and the maps she'd spread over Marta's table.

A splash, as Leeza tilted her head back, eyes closed, and squeezed the sea sponge over her face and shoulders. Drops spattered onto the tiles around the metal washtub. Leeza's long limbs were folded into the tub, firelight from the hearth sheeting with the water over her glistening white skin. She opened her eyes and smiled across the room at Ariadne, holding out the sponge. "Scrub my back?"

Ariadne looked down at the report she was preparing to send to Teresa and Arun, wondering if they would dismiss it all as madness. She'd included the magnetometer readings and her speculations about her increasing attunement to the bioelectric and geomagnetic fields, but none of it explained what had happened on Tinos. She needed to go to the sacred spring near the road to Skaloti, to the shrine that was becoming another pilgrimage site for RP-Hansen's victims. According to her magnetometer readings that confirmed her researchers' aerial report, it was roughly the locus of the anomalous fields. And, as on Tinos, when she put aside the instruments and used her own senses, she was clearly pointed down that road.

But adding to her confusion was a sense of deep disturbance beneath the surface here, jittering tremors of small earthquakes and aftershocks. She could feel the upheavals intensifying, blocked forces building beneath the mountains, shaking her with their trapped tensions. Mounting.

She groaned and shook her head.

"Ariadne? You okay?" Leeza had lowered the sponge to her lap.

Ariadne dropped her pencil onto the maps, rose, and stepped over to the hearth.

Leeza leaned forward, humming, as Ariadne sat on the wooden stool and squeezed the coarse sponge over her back. "Mmmm... still do those magic neck rubs? I've got this kink." She pointed over her shoulder.

Ariadne smiled ironically at the old tactic. But she started massaging, the familiar motions of her fingers against Leeza's firm warmth somehow comforting to her, too, as Leeza sighed and leaned back against her knees.

Ariadne's gaze travelled absently. Licking flames and a nodding blond-slicked head. Marta's prized painted crockery on a plank shelf against the whitewashed wall of the kitchen. Wooden shutters closed against the dust haze prematurely darkening the afternoon. Hanging clusters of garlic and onions, copper pans gleaming in the shadows. If she could capture this moment and remain cupped in its simplicity....

A bough snapped in the fireplace, scattering sparks. Ariadne stood abruptly.

"Don't stop," Leeza whispered. Arching against the tub, firelight sheening wet skin and her small breasts thrusting, she reached a languid arm. Catching Ariadne's hand, she smiled, and—almost—they were back in their college sorority as Leeza's lips brushed her fingers.

She fought a sudden fierce longing for human warmth and comfort. How long since she'd been able to trust anyone?

She reclaimed her hand. "I need to finish the report to my researchers. Peter is right, we can't stay here much longer."

"Right. Peter." Leeza jerked away to face the flames. She mocked, "Peter says we're in danger. Peter says leave your old friend out in the cold. Peter's peter wants in, doesn't it?"

"Stop it, Leeza."

"Look, I know what that dreck's after, and—"

"We've all had enough!" Ariadne snapped. "You seem to think this is all about you and your story. Don't you realize what's at stake? And the danger? It's not just an adventure to record for your entertainment media." She took a shaky breath. "Leeza, I simply don't have energy to spare. Please don't push Peter too far. I need his help."

Leeza snorted. "He'll help himself—to anything he can get."

She took a deep breath, gripping the sides of the tub. "He didn't tell you about... how he took all my money for his lousy boat ride to find you, then threatened to dump me off on some godforsaken rock if I didn't put out for him.... Might as well call it rape. That's right. Now he just wants me out of the way so he can move in on you. He's a real gem, your precious Peter." She jerked upright, streaming water, and grabbed the towel.

"Lisa!" Ariadne shook her head. "I can't believe—"

"Go ahead," muffled in the folds of the towel, "ask him about our glorious one-night stand." She yanked the towel tight around her and faced Ariadne, shaking with outrage. "The reason he hates me is I told him exactly how thrilling I found his pitiful dick. I don't want him using you, too."

Ariadne closed her eyes. The weight of the Tinos crystal pulled in her skirt pocket, drawing her fingers to touch its facets, the light-gathering structure holding firm against dark chaos. Erratic individual molecules bonded into powerful unity. She could feel its insistent whisper, calling her away from these petty human confusions and pains and deceptions, calling her deeper into the mystery of the stones.

She took a shuddering breath. "Lisa, you need to stop this." It didn't matter if she was lying to Ariadne, or to herself. But Ariadne did owe her the truth. "It was a different time and place when we were together. I came to love you as a special sister, my little *ouno*. I'm sorry if it meant something more to you, something I could never give you." She added with a lift of the palms, "You and I are... 'wired' differently."

"No! That's just your patriarchal programming!"

Shaking her head, Ariadne turned back to her computer. "I need to get back to work." Her fingers tightened around the crystal in her pocket as she tried to focus on the data display.

Leeza strode over and grasped Ariadne's wrist, yanking her hand with the crystal from her pocket. She snorted, pulling the crystal from Ariadne's startled fingers and slamming it onto the table. "This is it? Your important work? And you keep talking about science! Bad as those cult flakes, you're starting to believe what they're saying about you. Look, I can understand—I mean locked up on that island, half the people there nut-cases already if you ask me, you just got too cut off. I'm the one trying to tell you there's a world out there, Ariadne!"

Leeza grabbed her recorder from a chair and thrust it at Ariadne. "That's my work—what's going on in the world. You think it's just a game for me? I've got stories in here that people have to see. Information is power, Ariadne. We're all fed up with the pricks in charge stuffing their bullshit down our throats. How do we even know this RPH plague is really that bad? It's just what they tell us to keep us in line."

"Leeza, that's not—"

"No good sticking your head in a hole in the ground!" She poked a sharp fingernail at the crystal. "*Power*. You want to find out about power, why don't you check out my newsstims and see what the crazies are doing back in the States? If you really wanted to do something, you could come back with me and give the cults some leadership. People would follow you, Ariadne! Maybe you could get some changes going that would make a difference, like regulating those power transmissions that have you all worried. Like maybe getting equal health care and food for everyone, stop the government hoarding. Helping people—that's what you want, isn't it?"

Her azure eyes glittered. "I could help you. I've got connections. I know how to work through channels." The words tumbled faster, urgent. "I'm giving you a chance to get free and break out of these stone-age macho islands. Let's go, before I—before you get hurt, before it's too late. Don't waste yourself on this hocus-pocus crap."

Ariadne's gaze dropped from Leeza's intent face, drawn to the polished quartz facets glimmering on the table. She was shocked by how badly she wanted to reach out and grasp the crystal, let its weight, its whisper pull her down and away.

She raised her face to Leeza's. "You don't understand. I don't *want* that power."

"*Despoina*." Marta stepped into the room from the hall doorway, glancing at Leeza and quickly away. "Excuse. Here are clothes for the foreigner." She set her armful of folded dark garments on the stool by the hearth and moved over to the kitchen shelves, pulling down a bowl and glass jars, a knife.

"*Efcharisto*, Marta." Ariadne turned back to Leeza, gesturing wearily at the clothing. "Your disguise. Best to cover your hair with a scarf, in case someone passes by the house."

Leeza raised her hands, then dropped them and stalked over to the hearth, muttering, "Hell with it all. Jesus, don't they wear anything but black? Catch me mourning some jerk for five years...."

Marta suddenly turned from her cutting board, stepping over to the table and bracing her shoulders. "*Despoina?*"

"What is it, Marta?" Ariadne looked up into the lined and worn face beneath the dark head-scarf. She had to remind herself that this woman was only a few years older than she was. She reached out to touch the roughened fingers nervously pleating folds of black skirt. "Thank you for all you've done."

Marta dropped into a crouch and bent over Ariadne's hand, clutching it. "Please, *Despoina Sancti*, would you come to the shrine and the sacred spring with me tonight? My aunt and the others from the village, they're so ill with the heaviness in the lungs, and the dust from the windstorms makes them suffer more. The medicines of the doctor from Spili did no good. And many of the plague victims have come, too, camping at the shrine. We're afraid they've infected my niece Pelagia, she has the rash now." Her words tumbled faster. "They're all praying to you since they heard the news from Tinos on the radio. They know a miracle brought you back from the dead to us, after those accursed Turks killed you. Will you come to them, give them your holy water?"

Ariadne stiffened, biting her lip. She gently pulled her hand free and grasped Marta's shoulders to raise her up.

"Marta, try to understand. Please. What my father's people are saying, it's all lies. I'm no saint, I wasn't killed and resurrected. I have no holy water. I'm only a woman experimenting with purifying the mineral springs to give relief to the pilgrims."

She had to lie to Marta. There wasn't enough of her, and they all wanted pieces. If she went to the village, she would be swamped. They would all expect her to try to heal them, and even if she succeeded with a few, she would be too exhausted to test her interaction with the mineral spring and balance the currents. She was only now recovering her strength, after countering the effects of their radiation exposure in the Hot Zone. She had to ration herself so that she could learn how to control this... attunement. But Marta was hurting. They were all hurting—Leeza and Peter and the stones of the world itself crying inside her.

"I'm so sorry. I can't heal them, Marta."

The older woman stepped back hastily, ducking her head, but not before Ariadne saw the secret reproach, the dying hope too familiar in the faces of the island mothers.

Marta turned away, then came up short. "Ah!"

A stranger stood in the shadowed doorway to the porch, loose worn trousers tucked into high herder boots, plain vest over a faded blouson, black fringed headcloth tied at a rakish angle over dark hair, unshaven face staring grimly across the room at Ariadne as he gripped a long rifle.

Marta gave a nervous little laugh. "*Kyrie* Mitchell! I didn't recognize my own husband's clothes."

His shadowed gaze flicked over Ariadne, then he ducked under the low lintel into the room. "Sorry, Marta. Georgios and I decided—you and Nikos are taking the fish boat down the coast. Visit your sister."

"But... I must cook for Father." She picked up her knife, started chopping onions.

His hand covered hers. "Now, Marta. Get ready."

"Yes, that would be best." Ariadne stepped around the table. "I should have thought of that."

His dark gaze raked her again, still angry.

Clapping echoed off the bare walls. Leeza waited for them to turn toward the hearth before her lips twisted in a mocking grin. "The outfit's *you*, Mitchell. Finally found your level? Dung collector." She stood like a pale wraith in Marta's loose-hanging black garments.

Peter eyed her and burst out with a harsh laugh. "Afraid I can't return the compliment. Marta could put you to work scaring off crows."

Leeza, lips pressed tight, grabbed her recording gear and stalked down the hall to the bedrooms.

Ariadne swung around to Peter, opening her mouth.

He leaned over her, jabbing a finger. "And don't you start." Nodding curtly at Marta, he strode out to the yard.

40

⑤⑤⑤⑤

*** "GO WITH GOOD CHEER. Remember me. You know how I've cherished you...."

Harp music, the splash of water, soft hands stroking Leeza's breasts, parting her thighs***

Leeza hit Kill, and the clear alto recitation broke off, blanking the viscerals and image of an ancient urn painted with the dark profile of a young woman playing her stringed lyre. Sappho, love-poet of Lesbos.

She ripped off the goggles and started to pull free the leads, then stopped. Shadows swooped over whitewashed walls, oil lamp guttering. Ariadne was asleep on her bed, face serene and distant as that long-dead poet's.

Leeza gnawed her lip, caught by a longing so sharp she could taste it—just to stroke that tawny face, smooth the mussed dark strands and see Ariadne wake up to smile into her eyes. That link, nothing else, time or any of this shit—*Mitchell her story Damiana this freaking Quest*—between them. Hadn't it been that way?

Doubts, itching down her spine, tightened her fingers on the leads. Rage at the whole bloody mess blazed through her.

Her hands clenched to fists, and she hissed, eyes narrowing. She jumped up to move the recorder closer to Ariadne's bed. Whipped out her extra set of leads, the needle electrodes. Checked her own spinal connections. Tapped in a new program.

She tore off her gauzy tunic, stood naked panting feet braced apart staring down at million-miles-away Ariadne, black and white leads swinging, needles glinting sparks in the lamplight. She's had plenty of connected sex with NeuroLinked partners before, but never someone inexperienced or unaware they were Linking.

But nobody treats Leeza Conreid this way, like some servant yes-ma'am-no-*Despoina* keep your mouth shut behave I'll throw you a bone maybe. And lost in those crystals she's losing her grip maybe she *needs* Leeza to jolt her clear. Shock treatment.

She took a deep breath. Humming high-pitched an antique tune Lizard King breaking on through, Leeza plunged the interface needles into Ariadne's spine.

***Contact!

Sharp, flaying her/them open. Knives. Dagger-sharp-pointed crystals lancing the nerves, pinning them together to a screaming dive into deep purple-blue –

Leeza's plunging. Swimming down into clear blue seas. Ariadne's eyes, snapping open in shock. No, swimming in light-sparkling blue facets, inside that stolen sapphire crystal from the shrine, spinning down the etched coils and from the inside out Leeza can see the designs shimmering into life—fish leaping, moon glowing, sharp bull's horns pricking her No the shape is a womb she sees that now and she's swimming inside, caught. No, not stupid guilt, they need this—

No thinking now, Leeza/Ariadne melting, fingers breasts thighs slippery, throbbing to the hot beat, jolting live wires coiling around them.... Black-and-white strands of their hair plaited together.... Serpents hissing hot—

Madre the power! Too much ripping her/them into crazy whirl out of it What's she tapped? fucking volcano flaming up their spines what a rush too much No NO! but she can't stop it.

Out of control the orgasm jolts on and on and on and someone's screaming***

41

DARKNESS, SPINNING TO A heavy drumbeat. Ariadne falls, whirling down its blind spiral.

Fire and pain sizzle through her, the bite of twin winged serpents—one white, one black—bursting out of the darkness to dig their fangs into the base of her spine and coil themselves about her. The shock of their life force, twining about her. A galvanizing jolt runs up her spine to explode out her head in a flower of crimson light.

Drums pound. Her body throbs. Dark fingers probe, tug, split her open and pour an alien presence into her.

The serpents twist their coils tighter, the stream of spinal light igniting to a sexual surge. The alien presence is merging with her. Ariadne screams voicelessly, lost in the fiery waves, pulsing, rolling through her, flaming upward from her solar plexus. Image/sensation/sound exploding outward too fast to grasp. She's falling, clutching in panic at emptiness.

Terror. And a horrible twisted arousal, pulsing hot, fire consuming her as the tunnel walls melt and crisp away—

A scream tore Ariadne's throat as she fought the invasion. Her arms flailed at the invisible coils of the serpents, and she ripped free in a burst of pain.

Sharp stars flared in her eyes. Gasping, she tasted a familiar tang of dust. She slumped, blinded, curled into fetal agony. Finally the pain receded. She blinked, rubbed her throbbing forehead, and slowly sat up.

The low flame of an oil lamp on the floor cast wavering light and shadow over the bare whitewashed walls of the bedroom. Leeza's cot was empty. Ariadne was sitting among snarled blankets in bed, Leeza stretched naked beside her.

She blinked again, her head heavy and aching, an odd itch subsiding down her spine. Alarm jolted as she saw Leeza's blank, unfocused stare. She leaned forward to touch the pale face. Leeza was breathing, but slowly, lost in a stupor. Drugged? Her body gleamed with a sheen of sweat, pale veined marble in the lamplight.

A thud behind her in the shadows as Ariadne stared mesmerized at Leeza's sprawled white limbs. A louder thump, lamplight guttering wildly as a gust of wind banged the loosened shutter against the wall. She started to turn, then jerked back as she saw Leeza's NeuroLink recorder on the floor beside the bed, indicators glowing, one set of black-and-white leads snaking over the mattress into her spinal insert. Another pair stretched over the bed.

Ariadne sat up straighter, head spinning, fingers groping over her own naked lower back. One neural lead had been knocked loose. She grasped the one still clinging to her spine, ripping the electrode free with a sharp sting, pulling it around to stare numbly at the tiny needled interface.

A scuffling noise outside the window. A shocked exclamation.

She seemed to turn very slowly, still holding the interface lead. Her dazed eyes met Peter's frozen stare through the window. The ringing in her ears was a silent scream, shrilling in the air between them.

His arm shot out to slam the shutters closed.

Ariadne was hardly aware of dropping the neural leads, groping for dress and sandals, stumbling from the room. She wasn't sure how she came to be sitting out on the rocky hillside, Georgios's hound whining under her hands as she stared out at the dark, wind-driven sea. Her fists clenched, fighting the urge to howl at the green and purple auroras writhing like worms beneath the indifferent stars.

She took a deep, shaky breath, fingers groping for the coolness of her crystal pendant. The old, inconsolable grief fell over her, and she could feel her childish fingers gripping Uncle Dmitri's magic blue crystal, feel its archaic etched figures. *The moon. The winged serpent. The bull.*

Ariadne suddenly straightened, blinking. She would send Leeza and Peter away, and go to the mountain village where Demetrios had retired.

She couldn't stay here any longer, putting everyone in danger, struggling futilely to make sense of what was happening to her. She didn't need to test the second mineral spring, to justify her findings to send to her researchers. Demetrios had told her, so long ago, to study the antique carved sapphire. Maybe there was a forgotten key in the ancient amulets made in this land of the Earth-Shaker god.

"What are you doing out here?"

Ariadne startled to her feet, the hound leaping over to the dark figure picking its way through the boulders. She turned without answering to face the sea, wind whipping her hair. Peter stopped a pace away, cradling Nikos's rifle.

He muttered something and started to walk away, then said shortly, "You shouldn't be out here. Too risky. Better get some sleep."

She turned but couldn't see his expression in the night. "I will leave tomorrow."

"Good." Voice grudging. "We need to get off this island."

"No, you don't understand. I must consult with my uncle Demetrios in the mountains. You will take Leeza in the boat west along the coast and north to Souda port. If you are willing to continue taking the risk, you could wait for me there." When he didn't respond, she stepped closer, peering into his shadowed face. "You were right. It's too dangerous for you to stay here."

"Right!" He swung around, exploding, "As if you give a damn about any of us! Sounds good, though, doesn't it? Great excuse for your big experiment, your noble work for posterity. All hail Saint Ariadne!" He snorted. "Maybe you've forgotten you're still human. I heard Marta ask you to help the villagers, but you were too good to lower yourself. Look, I don't give a damn about your holy water, but they really believe in you, and it might have made them feel better. Like maybe somebody cared."

He threw the rifle over his shoulder and strode up the hill, kicking away a loose rock to clatter over the slope.

The wind howled, pushing high clouds to obscure the stars and the lurid auroral filaments. Heat lightning flared, thunder booming distantly, a false promise of rain in the parched air of the drought.

Ariadne stood stiff, hands clenched, fury surging with the wind and the swirling force fields clashing in the sky. If only they'd leave her alone. She couldn't let herself feel all the suffering, let them all drain her for healing.

She had to save her strength for the larger work. Couldn't he see that? She didn't want the believers, their adoration, their wounds, their pain and their demands....

"Maybe you've forgotten you're still human."

She clenched her fists tighter, hating Peter Mitchell.

∞

In the end, she came to the church. Ariadne hadn't realized that the sacred spring emerged in the village well, in the courtyard fronting the chapel. But it hardly mattered. By the time she'd made her way in the fitful dry-lightning bursts down the dirt road to the sleeping village, and past the impromptu encampment of the desperate RP-Hansen sufferers, she was numb to reasons and doubts. Guided by two children from the camp and followed by more pleading stragglers as they limped or were carried along, she threaded dark lanes between stone fences and crumbling masonry walls, waking a swelling chorus of hounds and cocks and finally reaching the stone basin pooling the upwelling artesian spring.

Another strobe split the night, thunder rolling. She took a deep breath, grasped the polished Tinos crystal in both hands, and plunged her arms into the shadowed spring.

No knowing how long she knelt on the coping of the well, reaching down into the spring, letting the cool waters and the liquid voices of its deep source lap up and through her, swirling her down.

Darkness, and light, and the singing, the two voices jarring and buffeting, tugging at her. She anchored herself with the crystalline lattice as it unpeeled the facets of her self, and she let herself flow into its calling.

"Our daughter," sang the pure high tones of light. "Come to us. Ascend." The silvery voice of the Tiniotissa lifted her up a moonbeam, and she launched free of the exhausted husk of her body, unfurling diamond-bright wings to fly in the exaltation of freedom toward the stars. She soared as the music swelled, spreading those glorious wings as her heart opened and the taut wariness dropped away, the song filling her with joy as she dipped and plunged and spun among the spinning planets. She was the song, filled with its grace, its purity, its benevolence to shed upon the poor groveling humans below in the muck and mire.

Ariadne, enraptured, flew higher into that distillation of pure light, free of confusion, free of pain, free of longing and caring—

"Ha! That's how they trick you!" A deep voice caught her, pulled her down from the heights into a velvet black cavern where swirling warm water caressed her naked limbs. "Down here in that muck is where you'll find your real power. Come with me." A strong hand gripped hers, pulled her floating through tunnels of fizzing hot water, glowing magma that pulsed with the heartbeat of the earth, to emerge on the lip of a black volcanic crater overlooking a lake of molten lava.

Ariadne's heart pulsed with the flowing currents, power rippling through her as she swept her arms and the lava surged at her command, the forces tingling through her as every cell in her body sang — Alive! Alive! — with the compelling dark voice.

"Yes! Stay with me, and I will give you dominion over the earth and all its creatures. All you need to do is plunge in with me." Beside her, gripping her hand, stood a dark stranger, carved in ebony male beauty, the god Vulcan come to life. He smiled, eyes glowing coals, as he drew Ariadne into his muscular embrace. She gasped in arousal as his hardness pressed against her and she wanted nothing more than to melt into his heat and be reforged into his dark queen.

She looked up into his face as his warm hands stroked her breast, and it was the face of Michael Vendemis smiling down at her, dark eyes kindling with passion as she raised her face to his, and then it was Peter Mitchell leaning closer, his warm, sea-salty lips claiming hers, offering her earthly delights, offering her all the power she wished, to help or brush aside the sickness as she chose, and she longed for him, longed to be rid of the weariness and doubts and sink into the pulsing heat melting her....

"Ohi! No!"

Ariadne ripped herself free of the embrace, tumbling dizzily through the buffeting waves of the light and dark battling for her. "I have not forgotten I am human," she whispered as she groped to find her hand, still gripping the Tinos crystal submerged in the springwater.

She ignored the tempting voices, gathered herself, aligned herself with the lattice, and poured herself into its orientation to recreate the flow and return of the healing waters, realign the buffeting force fields so they would slide smoothly past each other with the life-giving water. Now smooth waves pulsed from her fingers, through the crystal, to ease the remaining sharp jitters of misalignment shivering up from the earth.

Far away, much deeper, a building tension of blocked subterranean forces boomed against the smoothed currents, but for now they were held back. Ariadne and the spring and her own music floated in a sparkling crystal lattice. *Singing its glowing pattern....*

A cock crowed. Ariadne blinked. The well's stone ledge was digging into her knees and arms. She shivered in the gray prelude to dawn as she withdrew her arms from the water. The storm had passed, dropping no rain.

Ariadne stood slowly and turned. The courtyard had filled with people watching her, shifting and murmuring. Old women in black. Men in shabby trousers, caps gripped nervously in their hands. Young women with sleepy children. And the RPH victims to one side, lying or sitting on the cobbles. All of them waiting.

"The water." She cleared her throat and gestured heavily toward the well. "It will help. I hope the purification will hold...."

She saw the old priest in his faded black robe standing above the others on the steps to the chapel, a shadowy phantom against the pale walls. She blinked, bracing herself against everything the Church had come to mean to her—sin and judgment, restriction and abandonment.

The priest finally raised a hand, touching his long gray beard and the rosary tangled in its strands. He walked slowly and carefully down the few steps, reaching out a hand to steady himself on the shoulder of a young boy. He and the boy moved through the others as they stepped back. He stopped before Ariadne, straightening his bent shoulders to look into her face.

Eyes shadowed in wrinkles studied her. "Come into the chapel, my child." The voice from the ancient face was surprisingly firm and resonant. "Too windy out here for the ill to wait." He gestured to the RPH victims to one side of the courtyard where the villagers were avoiding them. "Bring them in as well."

Some of the men moved to obey, helping those who couldn't walk.

Ariadne hardly noticed. Exhausted and numb, she was led into the chapel, into the musty presence of incense and candlelight flickering over the narrow faces and distant eyes of the few poor icons. Far-away voices howled with sardonic laughter as the saints mutely watched and a long-ago voice teased: *"Those gifts of the gods... always a price, eh?"* But Ariadne was beyond caring, and soon there was not even herself, only the pulsing colored auras of pain and illness, the crystalline lattice pouring out blended healing light until the source was drained.

Hands touched her, touched the husk of her as she hovered in the shadows looking down on it all. She watched them guide her stumbling footsteps out into the courtyard as prone figures on their pallets slept, chests rising and falling smoothly now. Seated men and women were touching their disfigured faces as scaly flakes peeled away to reveal smooth skin. A young girl raised her hands, wiggling her fingers and shouting, "Mother, I can feel them again!" Faces crowded close, mouths and eyes brimming gratitude, fingers moving in blessing, hands offering food, bottles, flowers. Voices repeating, "*Ariadne Sancti. Efcharisto.*"

Ariadne was spent. She had only the ebbing strength to hold her body upright as it moved woodenly through the crowd, feet carrying her away to the road.

42

"CHRIST ON A STICK...." Someone had ripped open her skull and poured Clorox down her spine. "Where...? *Madre*, my head." Leeza pressed her hands hard against her throbbing forehead. Pain sparks subsided to colored pulses. She took a deep breath and cracked her gummy eyelids open.

White glare lanced in. She squeezed her eyes tight again, wincing. Cautiously peering through her eyelashes, she focused. The glare resolved into daylight behind loose shutters, leaking between slats and splashing off harsh white walls.

A hospital—? She panicked, then recognized the shabby room. The bed. Raw aftertaste of a drug cocktail as she painfully swallowed. Must have been a lulu. Sluggish, all she could remember was black hot darkness and a driving synthesized beat, riding out on the rhythm, flying high, every cell in her body lit up in a sexual rush—no, more than her body, like a spiritual orgasm. Too much power, overpowering, and then plummeting into a black horrifying space filled with things she didn't even want to think about as a cold hand slapped her away and pain seared her nerves, short circuit ripping across the Link....

"Oh, shit." *Ariadne.* Groping in the snarled sheets, she found the leads still jacked into her lower back. She managed to sit up and pull them loose as her head spun and something cold and heavy settled in her gut.

A scraping sound. Leeza jerked her face up to see her standing in the doorway. Ariadne. Giving her that marble statue stare.

"Oh god, I'm sorry!" Leeza scrambled up from the bed, gasping at the flaring pain but pushing through it, stumbling dizzily to grasp her hand. It was cool in her feverish grip. "I didn't know what I was doing. Just wanted it to be like before—open between us. Not all this static. Must have been crazy—I'll throw out the drug stash, I promise. You know I'd never do anything to hurt you, it was just I had to show you. You don't realize where you could go with me, with the Link—" She choked, tasting bile.

Ariadne didn't move, didn't blink, didn't pull away the hand that lay like a rock in Leeza's. Face blank, eyes looking through Leeza like she wasn't there. "Leave me."

Leeza shivered, all her desperate arguments falling away. Nothing to appeal to in that chiseled face. The cold was spreading out from her belly in sickening ripples, and she could only stand there watching Ariadne move heavily past her to drop onto the rickety chair and stare at the closed shutters.

Rage—pure, sourceless, objectless—flared through Leeza then, searing away the numbness, and if she could have pushed a button to blow up the bloody world itself she would have jumped for it. Galvanized, she whipped around and snatched up her bag and her recorder with the trailing leads, stalking naked from the room. "Fuck everything!"

The kitchen was empty and dim, fireplace cold. Goosebumps shivered down her arms and back. She set the recorder on the table, hands shaking. Ripping into her clothes bag, she yanked out a knit pullover. The door swung open to spill morning light over her.

She spun around and scowled as Mitchell ducked through the doorway and came up short. "You ever knock, prick?"

"You ever wear clothes?"

"Fuck you."

He slammed the door in puffs of windborne dust. "Ariadne just came in? I thought she was in bed all this time. Where was she?"

Leeza only sneered, jerking one shoulder into a shrug.

He scowled, gaze flicking over her bare bod. "Not that I give a damn, but Georgios already thinks you're a whore."

"Fuck Georgios, too." She jerked the tunic over her head and took a deep breath, trying to get a grip on her furious shaking. "Nobody tells me what to do." She yanked on a pair of leggings and turned to face him, clenching her jaw tight so she wouldn't scream.

He was planted by the door in his grubby goatherder outfit, face stubbled and streaked with grime. "Yeah, I forgot—the world revolves around Little Miss Leeza." His glare raked her gear on the table. He muttered, "Christ, how could she...."

He shook his head and strode over to grip her arm. "Now listen." His fingers tightened, hurting. "Go fuck yourself forever in that thing for all I care." He jabbed a finger at her recorder. "But leave Ariadne alone, she needs to rest."

He turned away, rubbing his face. "Got to catch a couple hours myself, then I'm taking her out of here. So stay out of our way." He headed down the hall to the kid's bedroom.

Leeza stood gripping the back of a chair, still shaking with unvoiceable rage. The bastard. So that was it. He'd talked Ariadne into leaving her. Here in this godforsaken flea-bitten dive with the Cyclops. Well screw them all. She still had some moves.

Taking a deep breath, she groped in the bottom of the bag. She took out her stun-gun and studied the twin prongs on its tip.

∞

The hardest part was making herself wait until she was sure Ariadne and Mitchell were asleep. Didn't take long to pack up her gear. She peered out through the shutters and saw the old fisherman slouching along the cliff edge with his rifle. No sign of the dog, but it had to be around.

She found the smelly meat scraps Marta had left for it, and dusted them from some 'lude capsules. She wasn't sure how much. She remembered the ugly thing lunging at her, drool flecking her as it howled, and she dumped another capsule in.

The dog, nosing around the chicken shed now, spotted her when she edged out onto the porch. She smacked down the dish and bolted back inside, watching through the crack of the door as it wolfed the food. The dog wandered off.

She made herself wait some more, mesmerized by the rhythmic aching down the back of her neck. She shook her head and moved for the door. She paused, turned, and pulled Marta's hideous black skirt over her leggings, pinning the extra folds. She tied the black scarf over her head and hurried out the door.

The wind had died down, sun cooking already. Wincing under the glare, head still pounding, Leeza crossed the dusty yard and passed through the open gap in the stone fence. She didn't see Georgios, but the dog had curled up against the sun-warmed stones. It made a sleepy attempt to get up as she neared, then lowered its head again. She skirted it, making her way carefully over the rocky, thorny slope toward the cliff, loose stones sliding under her sandals.

The cove shimmered turquoise-blue in the sunlight, so clear she could have drawn the rocky bottom contours. Past the jagged pale stones of the headland, the darker sea stretched flat and empty. At the foot of the cliff, below her, the wrecked freighter still spread its nets over shrouded *Nereid*, but there was nobody on its tilted decks. She turned back toward the blocky shape of the house and saw Georgios making his way down the hill above it.

She waved and started back for the dirt track, her other hand nervously gripping the stun-gun in the skirt pocket. Sweat broke out under the layers of clothes.

Georgios came around a goat path behind the sheds, on the opposite side of the house from the dog, so he hadn't seen it yet. She hurried down the track to cut him off beside the back gate into the yard.

He stopped and scowled at her, gripping the gun, barking a question, all Greek to Leeza.

She shrugged and moved cautiously closer, gestured toward the house. "Ariadne. Needs to talk to you." She waved Georgios past her toward the house, her other hand slipping out of her pocket, activating the stun-gun. Then, as he was moving by, she faked a gasp, eyes widening, staring over his shoulder. "Oh, my God!"

Georgios made a startled noise and lumbered around, swinging the rifle up.

Leeza jerked forward, jabbing the activated prongs against the back of his neck and feeling the jolt of the shock hit him. He cried out. It was choked off in a gargling sound as his body convulsed backwards against

Leeza, knocking the gun spinning from her hand. She hit the shed wall and managed to stumble out of the way as he crashed to the ground, arms and legs thrashing and then going limp. He lay with the dust settling over his blank face, and for a second something wrenched sickeningly in Leeza's gut as she thought he wasn't breathing. But his chest finally shuddered and rose slowly.

She crouched trembling against the shed wall, ears straining. No sound from the house. Hands shaking even worse than before, she found the stun-gun and deactivated it. She grimaced, disgusted, as she picked up one of the limp heavy arms and tried to drag him into the shed. He didn't budge.

"Shit. Shit." She caught a ragged breath and moved around behind his head, forcing her hands under his armpits and heaving. Staggering, nearly falling backwards as his shirt ripped, she caught a better hold and managed to drag him in a series of wrenching lunges into the filthy shed.

She stood panting, sweating, mind spinning but refusing to engage. She took another deep breath, trying to think what they did in action vids. His belt. She dragged it off him and hooked it around his ankles, looping them behind him to his hands tied together with some twine she found on a dim pile of rotted straw and manure. She ripped off more of his shirt to tie a gag over his mouth.

The smell of his lolling body and the stifling shed was making her sick, but she made herself lean down close to make sure he was still breathing.

She stood, lightheaded, ripping off Marta's heavy skirt and cramming it under his head. Reeling out into the sunlight, she leaned over, gasping. Moving toward the house, she found herself tiptoeing, and even though it was ridiculous she couldn't make herself stop.

Inside, she had to wait again to let the pounding recede in her head. No sound from the back bedrooms. She started to move toward Ariadne's room, just to check on her. She stopped short, lips pressed tight. Grabbing her gear, she staggered down the track toward the road.

43

"WHAT?" PETER WOKE ALL of a piece, wrenched upright in bed from heavy, dreamless sleep.

He groped hastily and found the rifle where he'd leaned it against the wall by the bed, then sagged back in relief. Why hadn't Georgios gotten him up? He'd slept too long. Hadn't slept long enough. He groaned, rubbing his eyes and bristly chin. He squinted at his watch—barely past noon.

"Huh?" He frowned, listening. There it was again, somebody knocking—no, kicking—at the door. But it sounded too far away.

"Sonuva...." He staggered into his pants, grabbed the rifle, and padded barefoot down the narrow hall, pausing for a second outside Ariadne's shut door. He shook his head. The muffled thumping came again, insistent.

Peter took a deep breath and cocked the rifle, sprinting across the dim kitchen and peering through the shutters. He couldn't see back through the angle to the door, but there was nobody in the yard. The dog wasn't barking.

He edged toward the door and flung it open, stepping back in the same movement into a half-crouch and bringing the rifle around to bear. Nobody there.

He straightened, edging to the doorway and throwing a quick look out. Nothing.

More pounding then, louder but still distant. The back shed. Squinting scan through the afternoon glare, and he darted around the corner of the house.

Georgios's rifle was lying in the dirt beside the open back gate. Peter shot another look over the deserted yard and shimmering rock slopes, leaned over to pick up the rifle, and jerked his hand back from the searing barrel. More pounding erupted inside the low shed.

Swinging his own rifle around, Peter moved to the side of the building, counted ten, and peered low through the doorway. He blew out a breath and straightened.

Georgios glared up at him over a filthy cloth gag, body arched back in the straw and dung, arms straining behind him against a tangle of twine as his boots poised to kick backwards against the splintered wood manger. An old black billy goat stood over him, eyeing Peter and then lowering its head again to nibble at Georgios's cap.

"Mmrrmph!" Georgios jerked his head, and his tethered feet dropped behind him. The goat stepped back half a pace, looking expectantly from the old man to Peter.

Peter wiped off the start of a grin as he met the single glaring eye. He crouched quickly to untie the gag.

Georgios spat it out, swearing in a cracked voice. "The *Magdalena!*" He cleared his throat, spat again. "That little whore, I swear I'll kill her this time!" He twisted, jerking at his fetters.

"Leeza—? Here, wait, easy." He unhooked the belt twisted around the old man's ankles and fished out his pocketknife to cut the twine. "You all right?"

Georgios bit back a cry as he straightened his legs and started to climb to his feet. Pressing his lips tight, he fell back into the manure, beating at his arms and legs.

"How long were you here? Wait, first rub the blood back in."

Georgios batted his hands away. "You fuss like a woman. All I need is to get my hands on that whore."

Peter stood back as Georgios rose painfully, clutching the manger, swearing and kicking the goat away. "Filthy beast! Out of my way, fine help you are." He lumbered out into the yard, legs still bent, straightening with a visible effort. He leaned over to pick up his rifle baking in the sun.

"Wait—"

Georgios dropped it, shaking his hand and raging, "Sacred Christos! The devil take her." He picked up the butt end, jerked around, glared over the hillside and yard. "And where is that worthless hound when I need him, eh?" He stalked stiffly through the front yard to the dirt track, still swearing.

Peter gave him a lead, then followed the hobbling, dirt and straw-encrusted figure across the yard. Georgios came up short outside the gate, breaking off mid-oath.

"If she goes to town now, it could be real trouble—" Peter came up beside Georgios and saw what he was staring at.

The dog had tried to crawl through the dust, before falling on its side against the stone wall. Its eyes were closed, nose dusty, head stretched stiffly at an uncomfortable-looking angle. Georgios dropped heavily to his knees to touch the motionless ribcage.

"Christ, man, I'm sorry." Peter had fallen back into English. "She must have—"

The old man jerked up his head, turning his one fierce eye on Peter to shut him up like a door slamming. He turned back to the dog.

Peter took a deep breath and backed into the yard.

"What is it? What's happened?"

He swung around to see Ariadne swaying in the same rumpled dress from the night before, face drained to a sallow hue.

He pressed his lips tight, stepping back and jerking his chin toward the open gateway. "See for yourself what your darling Leeza's done now. She's gone again."

Ariadne hurried past him toward Georgios. She gasped, put out a groping hand for the rock wall and missed. She swung around, staring blinded through Peter, still groping with her hand. He just stood there while she sank onto the ground, spattering the dust with her tears.

44

NO SAILORS ON THE road today.

Leeza lugged her gear past the turnoff to the village below, noting automatically the way the slanted morning light defined building-block houses and the rounded double lozenge of the church with its bell arch at one end, but past caring enough to pull out her camera. She rested for a minute, counting the aching beats in her head. She wiped the dust off her shades and shifted the recorder strap on her shoulder. Dragging the canvas carryall with her clothes now, she trudged up and down the twists of the dirt road snaking into a ravine, over a stone-arched bridge across a stream threading a pocket of greenery and coolness, then out into dust and heat again, around the rocky flank dropping to the sea.

A buzzing electric motor swelled behind her. The boy wasn't pretty, face like a potato and flab straining a synthetic shirt in eye-piercing scarlet and blue zigzags, but he looked like Prince Valiant offering a perch on the back of his shiny red scooter.

When he twisted around to grin back at her, she saw he did have those prizewinning long lashes. He shouted out something and gestured with one arm as they accelerated, zipping around the next curve inches from the dropoff, scooter wobbling overloaded and unbalanced with the bag crammed in behind Leeza. She closed her eyes and clutched tighter around his paunch.

The kid was philosophical when she waved him a firm goodbye at the harbor.

It looked smaller in daylight, storefronts and open-air cafes seedier. Everything—tables, scraggly shade trees, cloth awnings, ambling old people in black—dusty and faded, except the garishly painted wooden boats tied to the cement piers. Leeza blinked at the glare off paint and ripples, shouldered her bags, and turned up the nearest cobbled lane. Damiana's hotel—closest thing to it in town, anyway—had been a couple streets back from the harbor.

She thought. Somehow the narrow alleys kept curling back on themselves, and the square stucco buildings all looked the same, with their wooden shutters or metal grillwork. She tried to ask some of the women carrying shopping baskets, the ones who didn't shy fast enough around her and take off with nasty sideways looks, but nobody spoke English or admitted it.

"*Caramba.*" She stopped, panting, in a strip of shade next to a wall, about to head back to the waterfront for a drink. A hand dropped onto her shoulder.

She whipped around, stumbling over the bag at her feet. A man in khaki pants and a muscle-crammed T-shirt was running an appraising eye over her.

"Not another one." It came out a dry croak. She glared and cleared her parched throat. "Look, I'm not interested, so bug off, okay?"

A grin split his face. "Hey, I'm shaking. Heard you were asking around about Damiana, but if you don't want me to take you there...." He shrugged and turned away.

"Wait. All right. Who the hell are you, anyway?"

His gaze slid over Leeza's. "You coming?" He started to turn again.

She waited, staring pointedly at the canvas bag. He swore but hoisted it onto his shoulder in an easy flex, striding off down the alley. She hurried after.

∞

Damiana was eating at an inside table, under a slowly revolving fan in one of the harbor cafes. Leeza must have walked right past it. Her shiny black braids tossed back with a click of beads as the man brought Leeza over to the table. Damiana looked up, fork poised above a salad.

"Here she is, Wilson."

She tilted her head, light gleaming over black skin. "So formal, Freddy." Low voice mocking.

He shrugged. "Damiana."

"Baker back yet?"

He made a noncommittal movement.

"Go check."

Freddy nodded, his look sliding over Leeza as he left.

Damiana's dark gaze shifted lazily to Leeza's face. "You come back for more? You mama not teach you manners, girl?" The words lilted with her Jamaican rhythms. "Not polite when you sleeping over, leave without saying thank you." She speared a tomato slice and slipped it between her white teeth, laid down the fork, lifted her wine glass.

Leeza stood mesmerized by the smooth movements of her arms, the play of filtered light over silky dark skin. Today she was all one tone, V-neck black sleeveless top and tight black jeans so she'd blend in the shadows to an almost naked silhouette, the knit top hugging firm round breasts that were too full for her lean frame—implants, Leeza had learned the other night from the tiny scars, but perfect jobs, a provocative contrast to her narrow hips.

She blinked, dropping into a chair. "I need a drink."

"Just bet you do." Damiana waved over a nervous young waiter. "When you eat last?" She laid some awkward-sounding Greek on the kid, pointing at her own salad and a chunk of casserole, slippery-looking shapes in an oily red sauce. "Here. Drink this." She pushed her wine glass at Leeza, spearing a crumble of feta cheese and a glistening black olive.

Leeza didn't want the wine, wanted a cold beer, but Damiana pushed the glass at her again, so she chugged it. The resinated bite brought tears to her eyes but somehow dissolved the dry tightness in her throat and head, fumigating her sinuses.

Damiana spat the olive pit into her palm and tore a hunk off a loaf of bread, tossing it to Leeza. Her strong teeth ripped into another hunk, and she grinned around the mouthful as Leeza stared queasily at the casserole the waiter was setting in front of her. She pushed it slowly away. The kid beat a hasty retreat, and Leeza noticed then that the place was deserted except for their table. Silence beat over the room.

Damiana refilled glasses for both of them. "So what happen?" She'd dropped the singsong drawl. "Saint Ariadne dump on you?"

Leeza coughed, choking on the wine. She managed a weak, "What? What are you talking about?"

"Game up, Ms. Conreid. You know what I and I after here. No secrets now."

Leeza stared at her.

She leaned back in her tilted chair, pulling a flat case from the pocket of the jacket draped over its back, extracting a filterless cigarette and lighting it. A bluish smoke pall settled heavily over the table. She passed the cigarette to Leeza, who numbly registered it wasn't a cigarette. "Go on. You got to loosen up, girl, you going to snap."

She took a pull, tasting the sweet, thick hashish lacing, trying not to cough again. She reached it across the table, but Damiana nudged it back to her.

"One more."

The smoke flowed down Leeza's body to the tips of her toes, smoothing her jangled nerves, settling her deeper into the chair and buoying her up at the same time. She passed the spliff back to Damiana, but somehow it was in her hand again, and now she could relate to the retsina wine. It was perfect for cutting the hash taste.

Damiana's face swam forward through the haze. She eased the spliff from Leeza's hand, long dark fingers touching for a moment her own pale slender ones. Light and dark, braided.

"Nice."

"Right, that nice. You feeling easy now?" Her voice was a low, soothing hum again. "Listen, let I tell you the score. You folks running off half-cocked, that just crazy. That Ariadne Demo-da-kis now, what I hear she be one different lady, hmm? I and I don't mean she harm, just talking about the real world here, right?"

Leeza rocked forward out of her heavy slump. "I told her. Real world...."

"Right. Now fact is she can't go messing up the order, I and I just here to keep things straight. She all confuse right now, and she scared. She not seeing the best way to help everybody is let the medical people in on this secret she got. That way every body get healed, right?"

Leeza nodded on the waves of Damiana's rising and falling voice.

"Looking like she so confuse right now she need some help getting she head back straight. Boys and I just want to help out everybody, no harm. Fact is, I don't find she, those Sons of Prophet sniffing around might do, and you know what they got in mind. I know she hereabout. You smooth things along now, make it nice and easy, you just take I and I there and introduce she all polite."

Leeza shook her head slowly against a great soft weight. "She told me to leave. She's going."

"Going?" Damiana's gleaming face pressed closer. "When?" Then the sudden sharpness in her voice eased away as Leeza blinked, confused, wondering vaguely if there'd been something else lacing the spliff. "Easy, little Lee-za. She been treating you bad. I know. You laying it on the line for you story, too, and she letting you down. You stick with Damiana, you get you story, and a bonus to set you up afterward. That gal not thinking about you thrown out in the cold. She not thinking right *at* all, attack people when they just trying to help."

"No. They were shooting a missile at us, they were—"

"Hush, now don't you remember? She shooting at they first, and they get scared, too. She hurt you, too, and maybe she heading to hurt more people, hurt sheself. I got to know where she hiding, so I keep she safe." Damiana rose and moved cat-smooth behind Leeza, strong fingers rubbing her forehead, easing the dull ache, lingering over her neck and shoulders.

Damiana was right, Ariadne was hurting her, hurting herself. She was crazy, off-kilter. Leeza closed her eyes, easing into the rhythm of the stroking fingers. Crazy. Wasn't that what she'd tried to tell Ariadne about her mumbo-jumbo Quest?

Some stubborn part of Leeza believed it, though, that power she could see in Ariadne's eyes, feel in her touch. She knew in that part of her that Ariadne was the most truly sane person around. But that was the part of herself Leeza couldn't trust.

"That right." Damiana's deep voice purred against her ear, hot breath kissing her skin. "Damiana treating you right, child. Now you tell I where's Ariadne hiding. You and I got to go save she."

Leeza closed her eyes, sliding into the caressing rhythm of Damiana's fingers. "I'll take you."

45

"NEREID, YOU'RE A GOOD old gal. *You* won't let me down." Peter patted the console, checking instruments. Geomagnetic interference was kicking up again, radio reception screwy. But they were fueled, cargo squared away, ready to go. Just had to pry Her Highness loose.

Ms. Conreid was sure to blow their cover this time. They had to at least slip around the island and lay up somewhere else. Not wait here like sitting ducks.

Dropping into the pilot seat, he scratched under his whiskers and ran his hands through matted hair. He stared blankly out the forward window at the tangled pattern of fishing nets, light, and shadow. Beyond the boat's camouflage shroud, the cove lapped at the foot of the cliff. Deep blue, almost the color of her eyes.

"To hell with that." But he stared, hypnotized by the lulling rhythm. He could still see her tears dropping into the dust, first sign she was a woman and not one of their painted icons, and what was it for? Because the double-crossing little shit had run off on her? He hadn't waited around to hear about it. If she wasn't getting her gear packed up and ready to go, the hired hand was cutting loose.

Watery reflections flickered over the cliff face, weaving strands of shadow like the neural leads linking the two naked women in the night. He wanted to rip and rend those shadowy connections. But he could still see the exquisite curve of her bare shoulders and back through the wind-flung shutters, golden sheen of her skin, lovely lift and sway of full breasts as she turned to face him, lamplight and shadow flowing over her. Sweep of jaw and brows and those deep-sea-indigo eyes seeing all the way into him.

A pang that wasn't so much desire as a paralyzing tenderness clutched him. He wanted to wrap up the memory of that glimpse and store it forever in his heart. He knew perfectly well he was out of his mind, there was no way, he should hate her for screwing around with his life, and of all people he had to pick a possibly genuine nut-case. Christ, now he knew why they called it hopeless.

Say it, Mitchell, he told himself, gritting his teeth and deliberately rubbing salt in it. *You're hopelessly in love with this Ariadne Demodakis, and she could care less.*

He slammed his fists against the armrests, wrenching himself from his funk. Pissing and moaning when all their butts could be in a sling. Wouldn't he love to get his hands on the Lizard right now, though. He didn't care what Georgios found out in the village, it was time to move.

He was heading out of the wheelhouse when the red light winked on over the radio scanner. Local channel.

He turned up the volume. Hiss of static, a few garbled words. More static. Then, in Greek, "...the coast road." He frowned as it crackled again, making out, "...the blond foreigner."

"Hell." Twiddling the tuner, he caught a little more. "...fishing boats, the hydrofoil leaving... guns. The others... landrover up the coast road... the woman with them."

"Fuck!" He grabbed his binoculars and scrambled over the deck, fighting his way out from under the heavy, stinking camouflage nets and heaving himself up the tilted side of the wrecked freighter, over its rail. Vaulting onto the wheelhouse, he clattered up the cabin roof, metal baking his borrowed boot-soles.

Binoculars to his face, panting, he sighted over the lower east arm of the cove, scanning the sea. Bright sun dazzles. Hazy horizon sweeping dizzily. Some distant darker blotches. He reset for maximum, and the blurred bow of a fishing *caique* leaped up in the lenses. He held his breath, trying to steady the field of focus, easing over the sheeted glare of the sea to pick out another fishing boat, then a third. Vague figures on deck stood motionless.

He scanned past them and froze.

The image was jumping in the lenses, too far to focus, a dark streamlined shape closing in on the fishermen. Moving fast. It swelled in the field, skittering, glint of spray obscuring the image. He lost it, picked it up again. Moving that fast, it had to be a hydrofoil. The mercenaries, moving up the coast.

He swore and skidded off the cabin and onto the tilted deck, started running. He stopped short, spinning gears. Stood panting in the sun, shirt sweat-plastered to his back, staring through the nets at *Nereid*.

"Blazing son of a bitch!"

They'd be at the cove within twenty minutes. No time to run up the hill, grab Ariadne, get back here and get the boat out. But he could write it all off, take *Nereid* out right now, get free and let the Demodakis mess take care of itself. She was just using him. Time to cut his losses.

He grabbed the edge of the netting and flung it back off the flying bridge, dropped down and into the wheelhouse, started to crank the engines.

"Shit." He couldn't do it. "Mitchell, you idiot, don't get yourself screwed over again...."

But he was already bringing up his systems microprocessor, cueing security access, triggering a systems dump. That would keep anyone from taking the boat out, at least for a while.

The screen blinked patiently: *All systems? (Your code)*

He took a deep breath and punched in the code. Too late to cut free now. He was committed. "Christ."

He tore into his stateroom, groped under a cabinet for his secret stash—pistol, client book, meager hoard of cash—threw it in a duffel with some of his stuff, grabbed his automatic from its cupboard and headed out through the wheelhouse.

He stopped, staring at the flaking painted mermaid on the console. Still smiling.

He paused at the top of the switchbacks from the cove, huffing, shaking sweat from his eyes to scan the sea. Hydrofoil clear now, leaving the fishing boats behind, flying on twin wings of spray up the coast toward the cove. Peter ran for the house.

"Petro!" Georgios was toiling up the track from the village, waving his rifle.

Peter waited as the fisherman panted up to him. "Georgios, we have to go!" He hustled him on toward the house.

"Yes." Georgios puffed alongside. "The village fishermen heard news.

Philip Tsouranis has a radio, and finally she works again. The foreigners with their guns, the whore has joined them, and they—"

"I know. Got to get Ariadne out of here. Too late by sea." They pounded through the gap in the stone fence.

"I know a hidden path through the ravines to the mountains. They will never find it." Georgios hurried into the dirt yard. "*Despoina* Demodaki!"

Peter paused by the open gate. The dog's body was gone. He scanned the sea once more, then raised the binoculars up over the cliffs to what twists he could see of the road running east. No sign of a vehicle yet. Lowering the lenses, he squinted into the fierce glare over rocky ridges running into trackless mountains to the west. Bare expanses, deceptive. When you set off on what looked like a straight course for a landmark, you always ended up lost in mazes of hidden ravines, turned back by the murderous thorn thickets. Georgios was right, the mercenaries would never find them up there.

He gripped the duffel bag and ran into the house. "Let's move it. They're coming after you."

No answer. She sat slumped in the gloom at the table, wearing the same rumpled dusty dress, staring blankly, one hand gripping her crystal pendant.

"For crying out loud." Peter strode forward and grasped her shoulder, shaking her. "Snap out of it! The mercenaries are closing in, and guess who's bringing them straight here?"

She only blinked, looking puzzled.

"Leeza hooked up with them somehow. They're coming after you! Get it?"

Her hand dropped and she shook her head slowly, frowning. She pulled something out of her skirt pocket. Opening her fingers, she stared down at the big polished crystal she'd taken from the flooded cave on Tinos. She whispered in Greek, "It was my fault. I shouldn't have gone, but there was such need...." A sigh as her hand tightened on the crystal. "It's gone now. The connection."

Peter touched her forehead. It was hot, feverish. He shook her more gently. "*Despoina*, we've got to move. Georgios is taking us up into the hills."

Still no response. Swearing, he grabbed her arms and pulled her upright. She didn't resist, but didn't help, either, standing there swaying, gaze unfocused.

Georgios moved in to support her.

Peter swept her maps and tablet computer into the duffel bag, flung it over his shoulder along with his automatic on its sling, and took her other side. "Let's go." They moved her toward the door.

A commotion out in the yard, chickens squawking from their shed, rough voices shouting, "*Georgiou! Georgiou, i Despoinis!*"

Peter swore. "What *now*?"

46

TINY FIGURES, FAR AWAY, crowded the dirt yard as Ariadne blinked in dizzy confusion, tugged along by Peter. Men from the village in fisherman's caps and worn sweaters, baggy dark trousers, and herder's boots were pushing from the track through the gateway. Gray-haired men. A few teenagers. Some of the men gripped rifles, and the rest nervously held scythes or grappling hooks. One boy clutched a leather sling.

Ariadne drifted in a disorienting haze, spinning above it all, the porch and her feet impossibly distant. She could vaguely feel her body being propelled by Peter's and Georgios's inexplicable urgency.

She couldn't make it focus. She was burning up, exhausted. A gap-toothed man with a straggly mustache stepped forward. He pointed his rifle in her direction, and the swirling suddenly focused.

"*We* will protect Ariadne *Sanctis* from the filthy Turks!" The man spat, gripping the weapon. "This is our place. They can't come here."

The others murmured, nodding, putting on determined looks.

Beside her, Peter put up a hand. "Wait. The foreigners, you can't fight them." He muttered in English, "Great. Scythes against automatics. And those rifles should be in a museum."

Ariadne swayed and raised a hand to her brow.

Peter stepped forward into the yard. "You don't understand. Best thing to do is go back to the village and act du— Trick them. We'll take her away and you tell them you saw her leaving in Georgios's boat." He turned to Georgios. "Tell them."

But the men wouldn't listen. Voices rose in agitation, arms gesturing, weapons shaking at the sky. Georgios was shouting at them. They were shouting back.

"No Turks will invade our land again! We protect Ariadne *Sanctis!*"

She blinked. *She* was the object of all this confusion. She shook her head slowly.

"For crying out loud!" Peter threw up his hands and turned back to her. He took her arm and pulled her into the yard.

A babble of protest. It faded as the men fell back, shuffling their feet. Some ducked their heads, crossing themselves. Ariadne stumbled as Peter tightened his hold, hurrying her toward the gate. Another angry murmur swelled. The men closed together in front of them.

"Walk, damn it. Tell them you've got to get out of here."

She blinked, her focus blurring dizzily again. She tried to clear her parched throat.

"Georgiou!" Peter craned his neck. "Tell them! They're putting her in danger. We have to get her out!"

"No! We won't let you take her!" A man with a rifle stepped forward, scowling.

Another voice shouted, "She must stay here! She belongs to this place now. We will defend her."

"God damn it!" Suddenly Peter was bellowing, pushing like a mad bull into the crowd. He shoved a man aside, dragging Ariadne along, hurtling them through. A loud protest as a man grabbed his arm and another tugged at Ariadne.

She shuddered, flinching back as Peter roared, shaking himself free. He swung around, punching a man, kicking to send another one crashing back into the villagers behind him. Peter lunged for Ariadne again as she hunched away from the bewildering violence.

Blackness clouding her vision, she could only gasp for dusty air in the commotion as he lifted her toward the gate and the men were closing in again, one of the rifles swinging up. Peter's hand was going to a black pistol stuck in his waistband, lips pulling back from his teeth as he shouted, "Damn it, you apes—"

"*Arketos!*" A deep voice rang out over the uproar.

The villagers fell back, milling, turning toward the stone fence. They stepped aside.

The frail, gray-bearded priest stood in his dusty black robes at the gate, one shaky hand raised in a calming gesture, the other gripping a donkey's lead-rope.

"The American is right, my children. Ariadne must flee with them into the wilderness. Do as he asks. We must send the invaders astray."

The gnarled hand beckoned Ariadne. Georgios pushed to her side, picking up a bag someone had dropped in the dust. He took Ariadne's arm, urging her toward the gate. She stumbled to a stop before the priest.

He touched her downturned face. "My child. Blessed one."

Her eyes flooded with tears. In desperation, she clutched the priest's robe. "Please, *Papa*. My strength is gone. I'm afraid. What's happening to me?" She swayed, dizziness washing through her, and she would have fallen but for someone's hands catching her from behind. Peter, steadying her.

The old priest took her hands and pressed them between his own, then with a strangely reverent gesture lowered his face over them. He released her hands and made the blessing over her. "I will pray. But you must find the way. Remember the saints, facing their demons in the wilderness. Their trials gave them strength through God."

He gestured Georgios toward the donkey waiting with its head lowered, eyes half-closed in the sun. "Quickly now. Let the beast carry her."

Peter was already lifting Ariadne onto the cloth-covered saddle. "Hang on now. Hear me?"

She could only nod, her hand moving to grip the pommel.

He lashed the bag on behind her and took the lead rope from the priest. "*Efcharisto.*"

"We will say she has gone in the *caique*. Protect her well, my son. Now go with God." The priest led the muttering villagers down the track.

Georgios slapped the donkey's dusty flank and strode ahead. "Hurry. This way."

The donkey started to balk as Peter tugged on the lead. He swung around to bark out in English, "And don't you start on me!" The beast twitched its long ears and jerked into a trot after him.

47

THE SUN WAS STUCK overhead, a blinding smear in the washed-out sky, blazing into ravines to bake back from the stone. Peter stumbled again in the loose scrabble, cursing the worn soles of Marta's dead husband's boots. But they kept the thorn bushes from ripping his legs to shreds.

Rocks and thorns, that was about it, the odd twisted olive somehow finding a roothold in the blasted landscape. He stopped to let the donkey blow, both of them sucking in lungfuls of the searing air, Ariadne still slumped in the saddle, eyes closed. He mopped his sweat-slicked face and squinted up the steep ravine, Georgios clambering on ahead. Goddamn old goat. Peter tugged the unenthusiastic donkey through a narrow squeeze of white jagged rock, the ends of the duffel bag brushing the walls.

Georgios had stopped where the gap widened, by one of the little shrines that sprouted like mushrooms in the most unlikely spots. He crossed himself and climbed on quickly. Peter tugged the lead rope, glancing aside at the battered metal case holding a faded icon, wilting flowers, a bottle of oil, and a lighted glass lamp.

Up another steep chute onto an almost level slope, and here in the middle of nowhere a short graded stretch of ancient finely-cobbled Roman road. Then rough rocks again as they cut up and rounded a tight switchback. Stones skidded out from under the donkey's hooves, Peter steadying it and pushing.

Ariadne stirred, blinking, looking around her with a frown. "What?"

"Here, we're taking a break." They caught up to Georgios on an open ledge dropping away to the craggy shelves above the sea. Peter pried Ariadne's grip from the pommel and lifted her off the panting donkey.

She took a deep breath, drawing herself up and moving stiffly to where Georgios sat in a thin strip of shade against a boulder. Her legs were shaking as she lowered herself to the ground and closed her eyes.

Peter pulled out his binoculars to scan the white dazzle below, the long sweep of one steep headland after another down the coast. He zeroed in on Georgios's cove and zoomed the lenses. He could almost taste the cool, rippling blue in his parched throat. The tilted freighter was a dark shape against the white cliff. Anchored next to it, the sleek lines of the hydrofoil.

"Bastards," he muttered. Clenching his teeth, he scanned in blurry jerks up to the blocky shape of the house and sheds. Too far to pick up much. He was pretty sure the mercenaries couldn't follow. He just hoped those villagers had enough sense to play it cool. He scanned the shimmering rock landscape below him, but couldn't pick out any movement. The binoculars strayed back to the cove.

"Son of a bitch." He swung around, rage swelling. "Hope you're happy, *Despoina*. If you'd listened to me, we'd have been out of there, we'd still have *Nereid*, and we'd still have your laser."

Georgios, holding a waterskin to her lips and urging her to drink, glared up at Peter. "You." He spat to the side. "You do not use such a voice to the *Despoinis*. You, who come to our home with that whore and you make only trouble for everyone."

"*I* make--?" He shook his head, muttering, "That's great, that's just perfect."

Ariadne swallowed and pushed the waterskin weakly away. "Peter." Her eyes were fixed somewhere past him. "It doesn't matter. I don't need it any more, or the magnetometer." She closed her eyes and finished in a strained whisper, "Must go to the mountains. Whatever payment you want, later. I will replace the boat, but now it's not important."

"Not important!" He stood over her, fury cresting as she refused to meet his eyes. "Nothing's important to you except your precious experiment and playing the great Saint Ariadne. Well, I'm not one of your peasants bowing and scraping. Ready to die for you, and you don't even notice, don't even bother thanking that pathetic old priest, gives you his donkey, probably the only thing he's got."

His hands fisted. "*Nereid*'s all I had. But that's your answer to everything, isn't it? Just buy it off."

She didn't move, slumped against the rock with her eyes closed, one hand touching that goddamn crystal pendant of hers.

Georgios lurched to his feet, gripping his rifle, stepping close to Peter to fix him with a fierce glare. "You're like all the foreigners! You have no respect. I, Georgiou Petride, I have only one eye," he jabbed a finger at his crusty eye patch, "yet I can see. She's gifted with the holy touch. She suffers for it. She knows it will cost her pain, and yet she goes to the village last night and gives herself to heal those stricken with the plague. And you, what do you and that whore do, eh?"

He spat at Peter's feet, raising the rifle. "She needs peace to seek strength from the Father and the Holy Virgin. You, she does not need. Go with the other godless foreigners, you are all Turks!" He stepped back, cocking the rifle.

But Peter was staring at the woman slumped against the rocks, his hands dropping as he let himself see the exhausted lines in her face, the sallow hue swallowing her healthy glow. She really could cure RIP-Hansen's? No, it was just superstitious crap. But those other faint spells she'd had, after going into Tinos town… and then those hysterical radio reports about the miracle cures. And that wounded soldier, the first night on her island. Damn. Was he going nuts, too?

Georgios prodded his side with the rifle, hands shaking but face set in a determined scowl. "I tell you, leave her. I will protect her."

Peter blew out a breath and shoved the rifle barrel aside. "Cut the crap, Georgiou." He shook his head and said in Greek, "We'll both protect her. So let's keep on, eh?" *Etse k'etse.*

Georgios pursed his lips, hands tightening on the rifle. He shrugged, throwing his chest out. "I lead."

"What else?" Peter muttered, "Blind leading the blind." He pulled Ariadne brusquely to her feet and got her into the saddle. "You can hang on okay?" The words forced themselves out, grudging.

She nodded, rousing herself to thank him. He turned away, pretending not to hear, grabbing the lead rope and dragging the donkey on.

They climbed higher to the mountaintops, Peter sweating under the blazing blue sky. Endless tight switchbacks in glaring sunlight and shadow. Dusty heat and silence closed around them, not even a birdcall breaking through. Peter squinted up at the sky, out over the ocean. No sign of wings. Ariadne had said something about them—maybe lost without their geomagnetic navigation.

"Ariadne!" The voice came from up ahead.

Peter swung around to see Georgios coming back down the track with a big Greek in a sheepskin vest, high boots, and a twisted wood staff. The stranger came striding, strong teeth flashing beneath a long steel-gray mustache, arms flinging out. "My little Kri-Kri!"

Ariadne straightened in the saddle, blinking. Her face lit up. "Uncle Dmitri!"

48

PETER DUCKED UNDER THE lintel, carrying the covered soup bowl. Demetrios turned, putting a finger over his lips.

Ariadne was laid out on the narrow bed, straight and still, arms at her sides like a corpse arranged for viewing. But she had some color back, chest rising and falling smoothly beneath the sheet, face serene.

Demetrios took the bowl and set it on a wooden stand at the head of the bed. He touched the big crystal lying on the sheet under her lax fingers, and turned to Peter with an inquiring lift of his bushy brows.

Peter shrugged. "Something to do with her healing experiments. She was delirious on the way up, kept muttering about Uncle Dmitri and his magic crystal...."

Demetrios pursed his lips and turned back to his sleeping niece. "Hmm. The ancient amulets I collect?" He touched the crystal again, murmuring,

"What has my poor Kri-Kri gotten herself into? Waking up the Old Ones? And now all the Furies chasing her...." He turned back to Peter, palms lifting in an expansive shrug as he tilted his head toward the cliffs shimmering in the sun beyond the open shutters. "Sometimes I think the old powers are still alive in the stones of these islands." He stepped around the bed to close the shutters, dimming the room.

Peter studied Ariadne's sleeping face. She'd have time to get over the fever now. Demetrios had gotten word from some coastal villagers that the foreign hydrofoil had been seen heading south towards Africa. So they'd sent Georgios home with the *Papa*'s donkey. And apparently the Med League men who'd been through hadn't managed to bribe the locals—their faith in Saint Ariadne and her miracles stronger than gold.

Demetrios was leaning over her, gently stroking her brow. "We'll let her sleep." He headed for the door. "I won't let her up until she has more color than that bloodless saint *Kyrias* Kousoulas insisted on hanging on the wall." He tilted his head toward one of those sunken-eyed grim icons over the bed.

A dark strand had fallen over Ariadne's brow, and Peter wanted to smooth it into place. He turned and followed Demetrios out.

49

ARIADNE WOKE FROM A dreamless sleep, slowly focusing on the icon watching over the bed where she lay. Turning her head, she gazed out the window at the top branches of a newly-budding Judas tree. Her fingers mechanically traced the smooth planes of the Tinos crystal at her side. She waited, hearing nothing.

Shakily standing, she looked down at the nightdress someone had put on her. The fever was gone. She felt stronger, but oddly lightheaded, an absence inside her. Silence.

She wasn't sensing the hum of geomagnetic currents. She frowned, but couldn't touch them. Her hands reached out reflexively—*fingertips curving over an invisible keyboard to summon rippling chords and ease her into the place where she and the music the magic were one*—but the singing had gone silent. Had she gone deaf?

She took a deep breath and made her way carefully down a bare hall and worn wooden steps.

"Uncle Dmitri?"

She wandered through a low sitting room in dim light filtered through shutters. It was cluttered with faded rugs, brass platters and pitchers and a smelly water pipe, shadowed photos and paintings in mismatched frames, dusty bottles. A chipped but exquisite little statuette of a Minoan goddess watched over these treasures, her bell-like flounced skirt still bearing traces of pigment, ringlets cascading over proud bare breasts as she stared serenely through time, a sacred serpent twined about each arm.

There were more photographs on the mantel above the cold hearth. Ariadne stepped closer to pick up a frame and blow off dust. Her own young face smiled shyly up at her between long braids, thin legs beneath an oversized fisherman's sweater, Demetrios behind her at the rail of his boat, white teeth gleaming.

She smiled and set it down, then picked up an ornate gilt frame lying face down. She rubbed the dust from it. Velvet curtains and a gleaming black concert grand, her mother delicate and graceful in a flowing gown, smile ghosting. Her father stiffly imposing, one hand claiming Ellen's shoulder.

Ariadne closed her eyes, remembering the last time she had seen her father and uncle together, shortly after her summons home from America:

"Our future! A new nation for our people. The Mediterranean League." Constantin Demodakis *swept his arm toward the islands beyond the terrace, chin raised. Dark silhouette against sea and sky, profile from an ancient urn.*

A guard unrolled the blue fabric snapping in the breeze, the white key-wave border undulating. The epigram gleamed: Lithos Athanatos kai Akinetos.

"You never heard of hubris, Constantin? Did you ask the family, ask our ancestors, for their blessing? You blacken the honor of generations of our gem trade, stealing those words for your little kingdom!" Demetrios *gave the flag a scornful glance.* "Tyranno Demodaki! *You've brought me here on a fool's errand."*

Constantin's *face flushed darker.* "Watch whom you call a fool."

Demetrios spat, wiped his mustache with the back of a hand. "Only myself, for listening to you." He shot a look at Ariadne.

She stood frozen, wind fluttering her bright American dress. She stared at the brand-new Med League flag.

Demetrios turned back to Constantin. "You shouldn't have called her home. Not now. You know what they're starting to call these latest 'engagements,' don't you? Gulf War Three. If you want to take advantage of the crisis to secede, don't involve Ariadne. Send her back to that Yankee college, she'll be safe there."

"Her place is here. With her people."

"No. With you. So you can possess her the way you sucked the life from her mother?"

Constantin lunged, ring flashing as his hand shot out to strike his brother across the face.

Demetrios fell back, recovered, wiped blood from his mouth. He straightened, pulled the family ring from his finger, and flung it across the terrace. He strode over to Ariadne, grasped her arms, and peered into her face. "Ariadne. Come with me."

She blinked, flinching back. "You ask me now? Why did you wait all these years to come back?"

"Kri-Kri! Didn't Constantin give you my letters? What lies has he told you?"

"Lies!" Constantin wrenched Ariadne away from Demetrios. "What about your lies? Have you told her how you lusted after your brother's wife?"

"Bastard!" Demetrios sprang at Constantin, grabbing his shirt front. Two soldiers grappled and dragged him back.

Ariadne edged away from the scuffle, gripping the rock parapet, rigid. She stared down at her engraved family ring, so recently replacing the one she'd given Lisa.

Weight of platinum and stone, land and sea. Centuries. Family, duty. Lies. Demands. Power and the resources she needed for her work. She stared into the sapphire, facets glittering, blind maze swallowing the sunlight.

"Kri-Kri?"

Wind snapped the new flag. Demetrios swore and pushed past the soldiers, footsteps fading away. Cold blue fire danced in the stone's facets.

∞

Ariadne shook her head and returned the photo face down. She moved on, around a tight corner and down a step into an oddly-angled addition to the house, a whitewashed, earthen-floored kitchen. Emerging from her uncle's dim lair, she blinked in the afternoon light streaming through open window and door to blaze off white walls and shimmer over the black-clad figure at the table. The village woman who came in to cook sat slicing eggplant for a casserole.

"*Kali spera, Kyria* Kousoula."

The knife paused as she raised a brown face netted with fine lines, giving Ariadne a considering look. "You look better. That's good, Demetrios can stop fussing like an old hen."

"It's you I have to thank for the chicken broth and that wonderful herb tea, *Kyria*. Where is my uncle?"

A shrug as the woman rose heavily from her chair, scraping peelings into a bowl and carrying them to a pail by the door. "Took that American with him, up looking for a missing goat." She gestured past the doorway and dirt yard, toward the steep ravine running up into the mountains. As she leaned over with a grunt to dump the peelings into the pail, an odd amulet swung free from the loose folds of her bodice, a carved blue stone bead and a small embroidered bag.

Kyrias Kousoulas heaved upright, stuffed the amulet beneath her blouse, and straightened a silver chain and crucifix displayed outside it. She turned her back on Ariadne's curious glance, busying herself with the supper preparations.

Ariadne cleared her throat. "Is there a place to bathe?"

"Pitcher and basin in your room not good enough?" She didn't turn from the paraffin stove. "Out back. He put up that silly shelter out there, soap and towels and all."

Ariadne stepped cautiously over the threshold to the back yard, steadying herself against the house as she closed her eyes and raised her face to the sun-flooded warmth. She blinked, ears ringing. Frowning, she glanced over the packed dirt yard, the clutter of pails and sacking, a broken wood staff and bundled straw. A few hens pecked over the litter, but the others were nestled closely in the shade of their coop, unusual during the day. The flowering limbs of the orange and lemon trees on the edge of the ravine were empty. Silent. Where were the birds?

She rubbed her forehead, and the ringing subsided. She made her way across the yard, through the sweet scents of the orchard to a vine-covered trellis.

Afternoon sun warmed the rocky spot, enclosed on three sides by wooden lattice and the fresh green of sprouting vines. The fourth side was a steep rock face. A black plastic pipe snaked down over the cut, a rusty, leaking valve grafted on the end with wire and electrical tape.

Ariadne smiled and twisted the stiff valve handle to a surprising gush of clear water. Her smile broadened as she threw off sandals and nightgown, stepping onto a naturally curved stone basin and letting the flow cascade over her. It was warm from the sunbaked black piping. She scrubbed gratefully with soap and a rough sea-sponge until the shower began to cool. Sinking beneath the stream to sit in the shallow basin overflowing back to the ravine, she gasped as the water turned mountain-chill. She closed her eyes and raised her face into the bracing flood. When she finally closed the valve and climbed out, her body tingled, blood singing.

She slapped drops from her skin, wrung out her hair, and straightened to twist it into a thick knot on her head. She paused, caught by her reflection in a cracked mirror suspended from a coat hanger, firm curves of breasts and hips tawny against the green vines.

Ariadne hastily groped for a towel. Avoiding the mirror, she wrapped the towel around herself. She walked slowly back to the house, breathing deeply of the warm, blossom-scented air.

A pungent tomato and garlic sauce bubbled on the kitchen stove, but *Kyrias* Kousoulas was gone. Ariadne crossed the room to the wooden table, where a bundle of fresh greens had been tossed down. Wild asparagus. She touched the slender soft buds Uncle Demetrios had always favored.

She could still see him, all those years ago, climbing ahead of her up a narrow ravine beside a rain-swollen stream, pushing through thorn thickets to find the new asparagus shoots and tearing his trousers to get the last one: "But I can't resist it! This one is the best, Kri-Kri, just look at it. Tender youthful perfection, the most sublime Platonic ideal of a sprout. Now this is beauty. We will eat it tonight and be strong and beautiful, too." His white teeth flashing beneath the pirate mustache.

Ariadne smiled, then and now, eyes stinging as she pulled the towel snug and turned from the table.

"*Kyria* Kousoula? We brought back greens for—" Peter Mitchell stopped short in the doorway to the sitting-room.

Ariadne moved back a step, gripping tighter to her towel. Blinking, she saw the man metamorphosed from Leeza's flippant American smuggler.

This Peter, wearing a sheepskin vest and new high leather boots, gone lean and sunbaked, a thickening beard darkening his square-cut face, looked like he belonged to these fierce mountains.

"Come, Petro, leave that for *Kyrias* Kousoulas. She'll be—Ariadne! You're up and about." Demetrios pushed past Peter in the doorway, a grin splitting his leathery face. "Are you well? You still look...." His glance darted from Ariadne to Peter and back.

Ariadne took a deep breath and fixed her gaze on the table as she lowered herself into a chair. "It's nothing, just a little dizziness."

Peter stepped abruptly from the doorway, striding across the kitchen. "I'll go check the herd. They're still upset."

Ariadne raised her face to see Demetrios watching him cross the yard. He caught her gaze, and his shaggy gray brows lifted as he rattled his string of antique amber worry beads. They'd appeared in his hand, as always, as if plucked magically from the air.

She turned back to the greens on the table, fingers lightly stroking the soft tips. "Wild asparagus."

His arms lifted in a shrug. "Hmm." He swung another chair beside hers and sat straddling it backwards, flicking the beads rhythmically. "We'll eat them tonight and we'll be strong and beautiful again." A low chuckle. He reached out a work-roughened hand to touch her chin and raise her face to his. "Though you have no need for greens to be beautiful, Niece. Didn't I always say you were a young goddess? You've grown lovely as one, easy to see how you've enchanted your American." Again an inquiring lift of his brows, deep brown eyes steady on hers.

She shook her head. "Not *my* anything, Uncle."

He pursed his lips, shrugged again. He swung off the chair and strode across the room, returning with a shawl he draped over her bare shoulders before sitting again. "Have to keep you warm or I'll catch the rough side of *Kyrias* Kousoulas's tongue. Fussing over you like an old hen she's been, mixing up her magic potions."

Ariadne couldn't help smiling at his version.

"That's better. It's quite a pendant you're wearing." He reached out to lift the polished crystal, leaning closer to scrutinize it. "I see you've learned a thing or two about cutting. Still have that Minoan amulet? Did you study it like I told you?"

"Amulet? You mean the blue carved crystal?" She bit her lip. "I… offered it to the altar a long time ago. For Mother. The magic didn't work."

He patted her hand absently, staring out the doorway, the worry beads back in action. Abruptly, he rose to pace across the kitchen and back. "Too bad, too bad. I should have gone back, spit on that ass Constantin—"

She touched his arm. "I'm sorry, Uncle. He's lied to us all."

He nodded. "Well, now you can take a look at what I'm doing here. I've been studying the ancient gemcutting designs, trying to learn their techniques. And what the patterns meant."

She turned eagerly in the chair. "But that's what I came to ask you about! How did you know?"

He tapped his chest importantly. "I'm a magician, remember?"

"Uncle Dmitri…."

"*Siga, siga.* No illusions for an old man? Very well, it was your friend Petros. A good man, that one, even if he is a Yank…." He eyed her, then went on, "Just what is it you hope to find out?"

Her hand raised to touch the cool planes of her pendant. "I'm not sure. It's hard to explain." She took a deep breath, kept her gaze fixed on the whitewashed wall. "It started when I was using my laser gem-cutter, and I was having… odd sensations. I started to feel illness within people. I wanted to help." As she'd been unable to help her mother. "They were simple experiments, after I'd returned home to the island, using certain laser wavelengths and activated mineral springwater for healing, which some practitioners were already doing. I hired researchers to help me, and we had promising results. But what I didn't expect…."

She took a deep breath. "I was somehow… tuning in to the bioelectric fields of the patients. And the geomagnetic fields of the earth, feeling the null phases, and feeling earthquakes building. To that point, I could stretch science for an explanation. But now…." She shook her head. "It's gone beyond that, Uncle."

"The stories are true, then? You cured the plague victims?"

She nodded. "But this last time nearly killed me, draining my energy. I don't know how I'm doing it, but it's all connected with the ambient energy fields. Somehow I have tapped into them—or they have tapped into me." She shuddered. "I can feel them, interact with them—forces in and around the earth. They should be flowing smoothly, like the old geomagnetic field.

But now they're out of balance, with the global field ebbing, and the unstable reversal zones. And the storms, the earthquakes, the electromagnetic pollution caused by our technology run amok. I've... touched the energy fields, the biological and geological disruptions. I can—I now believe it should be possible to realign the violent collisions of the disordered wavelengths. Restore balance."

Silence, but for the click of his beads.

"The stories I've been hearing...." He shook his head. "Do you remember old Zhao Dieng, the Athens Chinatown antique dealer Constantin and I used to trade with? I wonder if he's still alive. He said something once, like what you're saying—he called them dragon lines. A pattern over the earth. Something about keeping them in harmonic balance." He shrugged. "But that sort of thinking—it's just mythology."

"Perhaps not." Ariadne held his gaze. "Uncle, I didn't choose this, but I can hardly turn my back on it now. If I've been given this power to heal, there must be a reason. I must learn how best to use it."

Demetrios raised his hands, lowered them. "That's a dangerous path you're headed on, Niece. It might kill you. And you're certainly stirring up a hornet's nest, all these factions buzzing after you. They've got deadly stingers."

She lifted her chin. "I'm not afraid."

"Maybe you should be."

"You don't understand! There's so much need—I *must* follow through with this."

He raised his eyebrows. "And you know who you sound like now? Your father. Watch your step, Ariadne. Power and will—they can blind you, too."

"I'm not like him! I want to do good, help people."

"I know that." He reached for her hands, squeezed them between his big warm palms. "I can see you're set on this, but it's also clear you won't have the strength to go on alone. Your father's men are searching for you. Here on Crete, they're trying to bribe the villagers for information. And I just received an 'invitation' to rejoin the family at Constantin's new fortress. The *Tyrannos* wasn't above threatening me if you came here and I harbored you."

He snorted. "You know I'll do what I can for you, Kri-Kri, but I'm just an old goatherder. Petros now, he's solid and smart, too. It's clear enough he's with you on this."

She ignored the dangling question. "Whatever you can show me about the old amulets would help, Uncle. I noticed *Kyrias* Kousoulas was wearing a carved blue stone bead. Did you make it for her?" She adjusted the shawl, undoubtedly the cook's, and raised an eyebrow in imitation of Demetrios.

He threw out his arms and laughed. "So you think I'm courting the widow, Niece?" He shook his head and paced the floor again, gesturing broadly. "Yes, it's true I've been studying the ancient amulets. They used all kinds of engraved stones for protections or petitions—moonstone, coral, amber, carnelian, even gemstones. The superstition in the villages now must be a corruption—you know, those blue beads against the evil eye." He shrugged. "If it makes them feel better...."

Ariadne smiled up at him. "Like those worry beads of yours, Uncle?"

He froze mid-flick, amber loop dangling, and looked down as if seeing it for the first time. He spread his hands. "Maybe there's something to it.... The villagers here had only those cheap, lacquered blue beads. So I've been making them lapis or blue topaz copies of some ancient designs. They say they bring luck."

He sighed. "For the very special ones the ancients used sapphires. At the Delphic oracle they wore carved sapphires for healing, to summon the power of the winged Pytho, the dragon. Called it the 'Serpent's stone.' Didn't you realize, my Kri-Kri, that amulet I gave you was a natural sapphire crystal, incredibly rare? Not to mention the age and the workmanship!" He thrust a hand through his thick hair, leaving it sticking out wildly.

She looked down at her hands. "You didn't tell me. I only knew it was the most precious thing I had to offer."

He stepped over and laid his hands on her shoulders, their warmth soaking into her. "I know, Ariadne. Forgive me." His fingers tightened briefly, then lifted away. "Come see my workshop, and then it's back to bed with you. Here, lean on my arm now, and no arguments."

She accepted his arm as he guided her through the dim, cluttered sitting-room. "Uncle, what is that little bag *Kyrias* Kousoulas wears hanging beside your blue stone?"

"Hah! She thinks I don't see it, hidden under her pious crucifix. They all have them, the women. That old hag Cassandra, the midwife—lives up the ravine in one of those abandoned cave hermitages—she makes them for the women. Talk at the *kafenion* has it the women keep the dried birth cords of their children inside. You might see her around. A crackpot, but harmless. Here, sit down, I'll light the lamp and show you what I've been working on."

In the dimness, Ariadne found a wooden chair. A rasp and spark, the flare of an oil lamp on the table beside her. Light blossomed, blazing colored fire from the facets of carved stones.

She knows them.

The light was like snapping flames enveloping her, images dancing: archaic etched patterns of lines and coils, staring eyes, leaping figures, wild beasts. Bird wings, beating at her face. Flying her up into the searing sun.

Ariadne flinched, her ears ringing shrilly. She was dizzy, blackness descending over her as she swayed and groped for her crystal pendant. The ringing smoothed into a hum, the sparks of colored stones coalescing into waves of blended white light.

She can see it now—the perfect pattern. The lattice. She's inside, and it closes around her, the pattern carved on the clear crystal sides of the tunnel—a coiling serpentine funnel for the power of the light….

"Ariadne! Ariadne, do you hear me?" Hands gripped her shoulders.

She swayed in the chair, head spinning. Fumbling to push away his hands, she turned to the work table and pulled off her pendant. She stared down at the precision laser-cut facets of the optical-quality quartz crystal she'd shaped in calibrated alignment with its molecular matrix. The facets gleamed—blank and perfectly sterile.

"I see the pattern now, Uncle. Show me how to carve it here."

50

FUCKING OVEN. NOT THAT she minded some heat, got the mojo rising, but this was something else. She was shriveling.

Leeza peeled her damp skin from the canvas chair back, leaning forward to let the sweat evaporate from between her shoulder blades, plucking her glass off the dirt floor and taking a long swallow. She fished the last melting sliver of ice from the drink and rubbed it over her face, closing her eyes as she slid it down her neck, over her bare breasts. She skated it lower over her belly. Coolness trickled deliciously between her legs as she popped the last slippery remnant into her mouth and let it melt on her tongue.

The drops were already drying up, desert heat stealing every bit of moisture.

She sighed and sagged in the chair, sprawling her legs wider to get the most out of the thready breeze from the fan. Her hand dropped over the armrest to pick up the hash-oil pipe beside her recorder box on the overturned crate. A tongue of flame licked out of the integrated lighter, and she sucked in the sweet smoke, let it dribble out in heavy swirls.

Her gaze wandered. Grimy mud-brick walls. Dusty wooden storage shelves filled with clay pots. Steep stairs molded against one wall running up from the basement to the living quarters of the house.

She waited to hit equilibrium with the upper she'd popped, smoke sinking through her. First couple of days she'd been able to hang out on the roof under the shade awning, catch a breeze and some local-color chip copy of the street down below—camels and date palms and women in long robes and veils—but now with the bloody sandstorm the only place she could breathe was down here. Anyway Freddy Stone-face was up there waiting for the radio to clear again. And making sure Leeza didn't go anywhere.

She ought to go up naked like she was for some more ice, just see if she couldn't get a rise out of him, see about them thinking they could pull this stonewall crap on Leeza Conreid.

But it was too much trouble and she didn't really care, the hash rolling through her now, smooth swells lapping over the taut humming upper, and she was singing down the interface line in slow-mo jitters of pleasure. She pulled her goggles back on and felt for the spindle.

> ***Sunbaked African desert, cracked yellow earth and sand, sun a white flare in the washed-out sky. The heat crushes down, sand and hot wind flaying her as the rover buzzes and jars over the broken road, images jittering as they top a rocky rise and head down toward the shimmery mirage of brown-cube village and patch of green. A muffled voice beside her, somebody jostling her shoulder, and a sharp command***

The images blacked out, Damiana getting to be a real pain about nobody in the crew on camera. Which day was that she couldn't remember, another false Ariadne lead, just some woman from the coast visiting her cousin. Leeza shrugged as the high pulsed through her, fingertips fumbling after another chip address, memory almost as vivid:

A few nights ago. They'd been up on the rooftop, moonless black sky and stars precise pinpricks past the unnatural writhing shimmer of auroras. The hot desert wind gusted her thin tunic, rattling the palm fronds, the terrace gritty beneath her bare feet.

Damiana's voice behind her, low and husky, "Keep that thing off I now."

Leeza panned down to the dim labyrinth of buildings and ghostly palm-fingers beckoning. Somewhere a dog barked. A wobble as the camera settled on the terrace wall, framing the distant town schematic of dark boxy angles, jagged black fronds slicing in and out of the foreground. Leeza took a deep breath. "Any sign of Ariadne?"

"Same lot of nothing." Hot fingers closed around Leeza's upper arm, not tight enough to hurt, quite. "Boys and Esther, now, they starting to get a little restless, little angry, Lee-za. Say maybe you not straight with I and I."

Leeza started to go stiff, but made herself stay still as the fingers tightened around her arm. "That's crazy. I took you to the cove, didn't I?"

"That right. But they say so what, Damiana? So I get this old trawler, a laser don't work, computer wiped, Demodakis woman gone. Now I running some wild-ass goose chase to Egypt, they say, and maybe little Blondie she just leading Damiana by the nose."

Leeza bit her lip, her arm really hurting now, voice going shrill. "That's not true, you know it! I told you what Mitchell said, about Ariadne heading here for the coast next, he even showed me the line on some chart. How do I know he wasn't jerking me around? That guy's the one you should be after, he's the one egging her on, maybe she'd listen if you got rid of him."

"That right, that better." The whisper gusted in her ear, grip loosening, fingertips sliding up and down her aching arm as the tiny hairs rose prickling between fear and jittery arousal. "That what I tell them, little Leeza not going against her Damiana taking care of she right. You and I just trying to get this Ariadne Demodakis safe, get she home before Sons of Prophet do she bad. That right?"

Leeza nodded quickly. That was right, that was it, they'd keep Ariadne from getting killed. No use listening to the voice accusing Damiana of tricking her. Accusing Leeza. *Jodas* it was all the same, use or be used, Saint Ariadne playing it too don't kid yourself. The camera still framed its night angles, hot breeze whispering as the sharp black fingers of the palm tree caressed the image.

"That right." Damiana's fingers were gliding over her shoulder now, to her breasts. "That what I telling Turner, he the Man for this operation, boys maybe thinking they go over I to he, you know? But I tell he you helping the mission, little Lee-za. He be talking to you soon's he get here in the chopper. Just so you know, child, best he believe you."

Leeza nodded again, quickly, throat gone dry in the dusty wind, sweating palms still gripping the camera focused on the night. And somehow the fear stiffened her nipples, made her ache to lean back into Damiana's strong arms. She was trembling. *Madre* she was learning for real now about that cusp of danger and she wanted to ride it, Damiana's hands burning her skin as they peeled the tunic down.

"Easy now. Turn that camera off, you and I sit back on these cushions and have a little smoke."

But it's Leeza's move now. She takes a deep breath and pulls out the extra set of leads to dangle, needles clicking in the night. "Afraid?" And *caramba* the Link intense no words she's flayed they're burning screaming somewhere wild silent crashing chords and dissonance—reverb tearing her apart and a violent thrusting heave against her for escape but she grabs and rides it. Shows Damiana how and then it's sweat-slicked dark and red and wicked all hard-glinting feinting a fast fierce cat dance off the walls of the Link as the rush takes them and wheels of sharp diamonds spin around them shredding their bodies gone whirling what's left down down hot wind lashing as black fronds rake and dissolve into copper knives slashing the dark.

Leeza gasps, "Damiana. Demon lover."

A hoarse, labored voice: "Demon in you, you put I in that box." And again the convulsive thrust to escape.

But Leeza has her number now, and she rides that burning line of interface straight in, no more cat-and-mousing. She plunges ahead blind and

> ***she's falling—through a tight hoarded knot of scarring into empty black space. No, not empty. Echoing an endless playback loop, an old roaring cry: pain and denial. Refusal.
>
> The force of it—*mierda!* It grips her guts and twists, and Leeza is Damiana, no not quite Damiana... refusing her—no, refusing her Self. But not-herself. "No!" Roaring No at the world. Grabbing the hateful dark and ripping it into shreds, splitting herself apart and squeezing the world in her big black hands to reshape it. Reshape herself.
>
> Now, only ringing echoes***

Leeza—lost, bewildered—gropes for the Link again and finds it, lets it pull her back to the space where she can start to separate herself from Damiana writhing in a tangle of sweaty limbs, moaning, "Shit. Shit, girl," caught in the agony of the frozen jolting crest of it. But now Leeza has a handle on it and she lets go the gate as the Link jolts between them finally finally into orgasm.

As the shudders take her, she's still half inside Damiana, Damiana inside her, explosion rolling through the Link, and Leeza gasps again in shocked dislocation—

Linked, they're two/one, but not fused not the same, Leeza storm-tossed seas, and Damiana a sharp plunging torrent, it doesn't match. What the—?

Then she knows. It's Damiana ejaculating inside him/herself. Plumbing remodeled inside that perfect knife job, she hadn't guessed or had she, and the sheer far-outness of the whole situation catches Leeza up and shakes her again so she cries out. Emptied/filled.

"*Madre....*" She could only lie there, panting weakly.

Beside her, Damiana sprawled stunned. Finally, in the dark, a low chuckle started up, swelled to deep laughter. It echoed over the terrace as Damiana sat up shaking beaded braids, ripped loose the interface leads, and strode off down the stairs.

51

MORNING SUNLIGHT STREAMED THROUGH open shutters. Ariadne had forgotten to close them when she'd finally stumbled up from her uncle's workshop the night before. The branches of the Judas tree stretched into the breezeless heat already baking off the wall. She rose and leaned out the window to blink over the tiled rooftops straggling down steep terraces, clustering around the whitewashed double loaf shape of the church.

Her ears were ringing again. Below, the church bell was ringing, too, echoing through the dead air. She remembered it was Good Friday. The earth lay gasping in the rainless unseasonable heat, groaning under the weight of the shimmering sky. Pressure mounted, shivering waves of tension building below.

Ariadne pulled the shutters closed. Reaching for her crystal pendant, she traced the ancient serpentine caduceus pattern she'd laboriously etched the night before—a double helix, also the modern image of DNA—coiling around the crystalline lattice.

She closed her eyes, but couldn't find the cool clarity of the stone. She was still lightheaded, the ringing in her ears getting louder. Etching the spinning-tunnel pattern into the crystal hadn't eased the tension shrilling through her with the dizzying visions—just the opposite. She could feel the cataclysm looming over them all.

Ariadne threw on a blouse and skirt, slipping the Tinos crystal into her pocket and buckling on sturdy sandals. She needed to get out into the open, climb toward the lingering patches of snow at the mountain peaks, away from the suffocating pressure and heat.

She slipped through the deserted sitting room, peering into the kitchen to see the remnants of breakfast on the table. Relieved, she hurried out to the yard, hoping to avoid questions. But once outside she faltered, wincing in the glaring light. The dizziness attacked again, with the wild ringing in her ears, the very ground shifting beneath her feet as the thick air quivered with the mounting forces of imbalance. Groping for the wall of the house, she strode blindly along it, tripping over hens huddled in a tense cluster against its base. Nearly running now, she made it around the side of the house.

"Ariadne, wait! Damn—" Agitated cackles and a whir of flapping wings. Peter burst around the corner and grasped her arm. "You are one hard person to guard, *Despoina!*" He puffed out a breath. "Where are you going? Demetrios is worried, too. You're still feverish, you should be resting."

She tugged against his grip. "Let me go." The ringing in her ears was driving her mad. She had to get away. She tugged again, and this time he released her arm. She strode down the dirt track, not caring where it took her, fleeing the goading church bell as it echoed off the blazing rocks.

"Ariadne." He kept following.

She hurried ahead past a cottage, a black-clad woman in its yard struggling with a bleating, kicking nanny goat. The woman straightened, clutching a milk bowl the frenzied animal had kicked over, crossing herself as she stared at Ariadne.

Peter caught up. "Things are getting crazy." He rubbed his temples, wincing. "Even the goddamn goats are going nuts on me...." He shook his head. "Ariadne, we need to talk."

"Please. I need to be alone." She pushed past him, fleeing down the path, possessed by an urgency she was beyond explaining. She rounded a terraced switchback to join a wider dirt track winding into the village. But there she was stopped again, blocked by a procession of men coming downhill. They were carrying the traditional straw-stuffed dummy of Judas on their shoulders, to be placed atop the bonfire that would be lit at midnight. A scatter of hounds trailed them, darting back and forth, whining and howling.

One of the men cursed and kicked a dog lunging under his feet. "By the Virgin, what's wrong with them?"

The man next to him shrugged. "Another tremor coming."

"But they've never been so—"

They saw Ariadne. They didn't pause, but cast uneasy glances as they hurried past, crossing themselves.

"Ariadne, damn it! Demetrios says there might be a quake coming." Peter, still following, stopped short to stare after the procession. "What the hell?"

"Don't you recognize yourself, young foreigner?" A cracked voice behind them, and snorting laughter. "It's the scapegoat, all the ills you men and your gods have brought upon us, only you won't name him true any longer. You'll sit him on that big stick between his legs, as if it'll do any good! He'll burn all the same."

The old woman must have followed the procession down the hill. Her uncovered head was a wild gray frizz, face and neck baked brown and deeply lined. She wore a faded red blouse embroidered with designs of flowers and swastikas, snakes and birds and spirals in clashing colored yarns, and a loose skirt cut off raggedly just below the knees to reveal skinny, sinew-corded calves and sandaled feet like gnarled wood. Amulets and a small leather bag hung over her chest, a larger pouch strung around her hips. One veined hand gripped a twisted olive-wood staff.

She gave Ariadne a gap-toothed leer. "Send your man away, we don't need a fool along. I'll take you to the place. She's calling."

Peter towered over the birdlike old woman. "No one's taking her anywhere. She's sick, and she needs to rest."

Ariadne was arrested by snapping eyes in the wreckage of the ancient face. She caught a sharp breath as she saw an embroidered dark cloth tied around the crone's throat—a spiral enclosing a staring eye. Emblem of the Corybantes, the woman warriors.

She licked dry lips. "Who are you?"

Again the gusting laughter. "Doesn't matter. I'm only a vessel. You're the one. You've been looking for the place, haven't you? The heart of the mountains?"

"You're the midwife." Ariadne couldn't seem to look away from the black eyes probing hers.

"No bringing forth without a little pain. But I know the ancient ways to ease it. Come, now—Earth's laboring, She's crying out. Men are all fools, don't listen to them." A clawlike hand grasped Ariadne's wrist, tugging her up the track. "We must hurry."

"Wait a damn minute!" Peter grasped Ariadne's other hand. "You can't just go running off into an earthquake."

"Fool!" The crone turned, rapping Peter across the forearm with her stick. "Can't you hear Her in travail?"

Ariadne turned back to him, raising a hand. "It's all right, Uncle knows her. I must go." She left Peter muttering and shaking his head as she turned with the old woman, following the source of the visceral ringing cry up the track into the mountains.

∞

The first physical tremors started when they were halfway up the ravine. The dirt track had given way to a narrow trail climbing stony switchbacks above the village, then to a steeper goat path.

Following the surprisingly nimble, knotted old legs through an inward fold of the rising mountains, Ariadne looked down to the stream making its way past the broken rock foundations of a ruined settlement. High above it on a craggy bluff, the square tower and blank window slits of a centuries-abandoned Venetian fortress frowned down. On their side of the stream, above the precarious path ledge, natural caves honeycombed the limestone cliffside. Vanished hermit-monks had built plastered walls to seal their entrances, and outside one black-shadowed doorway a few bright scraps of laundry lay spread over the rock. When Ariadne paused to point at the cave—"Your home?"—the crone only nodded and prodded her on with the staff.

The pathway narrowed again as they climbed. They were forced to wade up the stream bed itself, slippery stones shifting under the foaming snowmelt from the peaks. The ravine sealed off all but a thin strip of blue far above, sheer cliffs closing in so tightly Ariadne could touch both sides with her outstretched fingers.

She could taste the urgency in the air. The shrill scream of blocked pressures ripped through her bones. Panting, she followed the midwife through the churning current, slipping over wet stones and nearly going under before she caught the staff the old woman stretched out to her from a steep bank.

Dripping, she climbed onto a narrow ledge. She didn't need Cassandra's guidance now to follow the source of the silent scream. Its eddies pulled at her, jagged waves of energy shivering up her spine from the laboring earth.

The stone path trembled in its throes. It rippled beneath her, and Ariadne nearly fell back into the roaring stream. Cassandra cried out, teetering on the brink. Ariadne caught her wrist and pulled her back against the rock face.

The tremor subsided. They leaned together against the wall, panting.

"It's happening much faster than I thought," the crone managed. "She's worse this time. The pain. It's not right. I can feel the dark force of it, pushing so hard, too hard, ripping and rending...." The hoarse voice trailed off, staring eyes gone flat and blind.

"Come. I must try." Ariadne gently touched her shoulder, somehow in the maelstrom finding the key she'd lost. Her connection to the earth forces—her Link. Its currents crackled through her, spinning her inward to the center of the whirlpool.

Cassandra clutched her staff and glared up at Ariadne. "Oh you *see* now, do you? You may have the touch, but you're still a young fool. Too proud, too proud," she muttered, tracing a looping design with her stick on the rocks. "Listen to me, I'm old as the rocks, and I've seen all of it. I'm nothing. You're nothing. Only a vessel for Her power—the Goddess." Her staff pounded the earth.

"I have to go." Clutching her pendant newly engraved with the twining helix, Ariadne pushed past her.

"Wait, you fool!" A talon hand gripped her wrist. "You don't know anything of the Way! The old ways, the wise ways...."

Cassandra ripped the crystal from Ariadne's grip, peering closely at it, snorting and then releasing the pendant. "It's more than just stones, you know." She waved a hand around them at the rocky ravine, the plunging torrent, the blazing sky, and fixed her fierce eyes on Ariadne. "The Mother's alive. She holds us all, beast and human, to Her breast. You have to taste life to know Her power—the salt, the sweat, the rot. Not this bloodless tinkering." She flicked a finger at the crystal, and Ariadne could feel a cry reverberate down her spine.

Ariadne pushed past her, the agony of the blocked and building quake forces screaming through her, ringing in her ears. She scrambled up the cliff from the stream, panting, climbing toward the last traces of snow in the cool high air. Another tremor shook the earth as she clung to the mountainside. The pangs were coming faster now.

A silent voice called her. *"Come!"*

She peered over the flank of the mountain where a slope dropped into a worn, narrow cleft. A curving shelf where rounded rock flanks closed together led to a gaping cave. Its shadows pulled Ariadne inward.

Even as she shuddered, she was scrambling on hands and feet over the scarred rock face, skidding down the sheer drop in a scatter of loose stones as the mountain shook again and the old woman shouted behind her, "Wait! I must guide you—"

But Ariadne knew the way. The power surged through her, coiling down the crystal's etched double helix to blaze out in a glory of white consuming light. She stumbled blindly into the dark cave, the invisible waves carrying her deeper as she crashed against a wall, fell and crawled forward to come up hard against a column of cool stone. She hugged its thick base and a pillar of fire whirled her down.

52

ANOTHER TREMOR SHOOK THE floor, rattling pans in the kitchen cupboards. This time Peter thought he could hear a deep groaning. The wire basket of eggs *Kyrias* Kousoulas had dyed Easter red shivered on the counter and tipped over. Peter lunged unsteadily to catch an egg dropping off the edge. He stood rolling the crimson egg with its black-painted geometric patterns from palm to palm as the floor's trembling subsided.

He dropped the egg into the basket, heading for the open door. Demetrios and the villagers acted like the tremors were no big deal—used to them by now—but they were giving Peter the heebie-jeebies. Like he was standing under a big boulder compressing the air around him, and any minute it would come smashing down. And that blasted church bell bonging all day didn't help, ringing echoes in his ears.

"Drive us all nuts...." He crossed the yard to check the latch on the chicken coop. Inside, agitated clucking. He turned to see Demetrios haul a protesting goat around the corner of the house, two of his hounds slinking after him, fur ruffed up. "She's not back yet."

"Hmph." Demetrios ordered the whining hounds into the house with a gesture. He straddled the bleating, struggling goat, leaning down to whisper something into its ear and stroke its neck. He squinted up at the haze over the lowering sun. "I thought she'd be back before dark, but maybe she'll stay with the midwife."

"I shouldn't have let her go with that old witch."

"Haven't you learned yet, Petro my friend, to save your breath with my headstrong niece? It will go more smoothly as you come to trust each other, you'll see."

"You've got the wrong idea. I'm only the hired help."

One shaggy eyebrow lifted. "Don't worry. She may have her head in the clouds, but she's always had her feet on the ground. She'll be back." He leaned over to fondle the goat's ears. "But you, my foolish one, you haven't got a bit of sense! Maybe now you think you're a wild kri-kri, you can live in the mountain cliffs. Go rushing back up the ravine and break your leg when the tremors come, is that what you want? No, you stay here with Dmitrios and your friends in the pen. And maybe you can tell us why the world is going crazy, eh? All this shaking, and the animals crying, and *Kyrias* Kousoulas is bound to be in a foul mood again because the laying and the milking will be off. Even the blossoms are coming too early this year—just look at the Judas tree—and tell me when are the rains going to come before everything withers like summer?" He picked up the quieted animal and strode with it across the yard to lock it in the high pen behind the house.

A swirl of hot wind, haze thickening overhead. Peter squinted up, uneasy. He followed Demetrios and reached through the wood slats to pat a spotted nanny. She bleated plaintively, butting up against his hand and then shivering back into the rest of the milling herd. "Kri-Kri. That's what you call Ariadne?"

"Always running into the hills with the wild goats. It used to drive Constantin crazy, the stuffed shirt. Hypocrite!" He spat.

Peter raised an eyebrow. "Her father? Your brother?"

Demetrios scowled. "I have no brother now. He persuaded the others to cut me off for opposing his new Med League. You see a man with no family."

Peter lifted his palms. "Join the club."

Demetrios darted a look from under the bushy brows. "You, too?" He grunted and lowered himself beside the goat pen. "Sit, Petro. It will calm the goats."

Peter shrugged and sat on the low rock wall.

"And what was your crime, then?"

Peter shot him a look, but he was just gazing up at the hills, flicking his worry beads. Somehow the sound was soothing.

He rubbed the back of his neck. "My pa was a preacher, real hellfire and brimstone. And I swallowed it—holy crusade, sign up for the war and all, maybe finally make him proud of me. And the whole time…." He snorted. "Funny thing you mentioned hypocrites."

Demetrios settled his back against the wall, the rhythmic clicks unfaltering.

"Guess it must've been different this side of the world, but back home they had us young bucks jacked up on righteousness, like we owned the oil."

"It was about much more than that."

"Christ, man, I know that. Now."

"You still bear the wounds. Like many men in these islands, but that's the way of it, no? Harder, I think, is to be a man without family." When Peter didn't respond, Demetrios cleared his throat. "Perhaps, in these crazy times, we make our own family, eh? Ariadne, now, she's facing it the second time. So young, losing her mother was a terrible blow, and who could she turn to, that father with a heart like a frozen fist? Constantin cut her off from me, too, when I tried to help. So she made the choice of this important work of hers. Her father's wealth and her mother's trust fund made it possible. How she will find her way now, I don't know, but I think you can help each other, my friend. Be patient, let her find how to open her heart again."

"Now, wait, I told you—"

Demetrios chuckled, shaking his head. "These old eyes can still see what passes between you two when you look at each other. She's a fine woman. You can trust her, Petros."

"Trust?" Peter jerked to his feet, pacing. "You're a dreamer, Dmitri. It's trusting people like Ariadne and her father, and mine, that gets you screwed over. You stand in the way of their grand plans, you're road kill." He flung up his hands and headed for the house.

"Wait."

Cursing himself, Peter stopped and turned back to him.

Demetrios was still leaning against the rocks, but he'd caught up the beads in his fist. His dark eyes held Peter's. "Tell me what your father did."

He shook his head. "It's old history."

"I think maybe not."

"All right." He paced. "It was my little sister Ginnie. Virginia." Despite himself, he smiled. "She'd pummel me if I called her that. Anyway, Ginnie was special, she had a shine to her, and it wasn't just that curly red hair. She was... full of life. And she looked up to me, you know?"

Demetrios nodded.

"So the Reverend, my father, he'd finally got me hammered into shape, born again for the fourth or fifth time, sworn off hanging around with crusty old Gramps and the moonshiners. Christ, I'd even enlisted in the Navy to make the family proud, all that glory like a halo I'm strutting around with." He blew out a breath and shook his head. "That's when I heard them making the deal—the Reverend and that old pervert McEachran. He had the big factory in town, and the wife locked up like it's a secret in some out-of-state nursing home, so he could reel in the ripe teenagers for these little 'parties' of his."

Peter closed his eyes, hands fisting. He took a deep breath. "Make a long story short, my holier-than-thou father sold her, right into the kind of Sodom and Gomorrah scene he was always denouncing from the pulpit. Needed cash for his blessed ministry. Sixteen years old, and he arranges her bogus 'marriage' to that... that...."

Demetrios climbed stiffly to his feet and squeezed Peter's shoulder.

Peter stared up at the hazy hills, ears ringing with the echo of the church bells clanging on and on. "So what do I do? Yeah, our young hero Peter makes a big scene in church, denounces the 'whited sepulchers,' the whole nine yards. Dad's goons had to pull me off McEachran." He swallowed. "Then Ginnie stands up, looks through me like I'm not even there, and holds up this huge diamond glittering on her finger. She tells me to grow up."

He gave a stiff shrug. "They wiped me out of the family Bible to please that oily old pig. Shipped me off to the Navy training center, that's the last I've heard from any of them. Never answered my messages." But that wasn't the worst of it. The worst was Ginnie's face, that last glimpse before they'd hauled him off. The old lech had already put his mark on her. She wasn't Ginnie any more.

Despite himself, Peter shuddered.

The hand on his shoulder tightened briefly, then lifted away. "Come, Petros, my friend, tonight is a night for drinking. The straw man's waiting in the village. We'll join the men at the taverna and toast poor Judas on his way to taste the flames of Hell."

He turned toward the house, glancing one more time up at the darkening ravine where Ariadne had gone.

A flash of heat lightning, dull rumble of thunder. Peter stared at the jagged peaks looming over the valley. His head was squeezed in a vise, ears ringing as the insistent church bell echoed off the rocks. He blew out a breath and followed Demetrios.

53

THE STONE PILLAR BURSTS into flames. A fiery torrent plunges her down into the dark heart of the mountain that swallows the brief blaze of light. Falling, Ariadne spins spreadeagled into the vortex, black cataclysm tossing her like a straw in a meltemi wind. A rock tunnel spins around her, the stones shearing, screaming–

Ariadne screamed soundlessly, falling. A hard beat drove the spinning, faster and faster, as flickering lights sparked the tunnel in an infinite crystalline mandala of shifting facets and colors. She knew there was a pattern, but as she tried to grasp it the colors dissolved into nothingness.

She groped inward for escape, searching vainly for the orderly lattice of light. It was broken, shattered by the collision of clashing forces. Stone walls closed in, squeezing her, bursting her cells into thin streaming filaments, pressing out her blood and memories and distilling them into an alien essence.

Panic shrilled. The stone walls cracked as another roar shook the earth. Ariadne clawed her way through a crevice—upward, outward, anywhere to escape. Somewhere far above she glimpsed the night sky, and she scrambled toward it.

With a desperate thrust, she plunged up against a glassy black membrane, shattering it in a burst of pain. Sharp obsidian fragments spun around her.

No, they were dark filigreed wings, birds swooping and darting in a dense flock. Somewhere a voice was chanting, "The birds, the birds, this is where they were hiding," but she shook her head in confusion, flinching as the lacy wings plunged and beat against her face. They swarmed around her, hundreds of tiny claws gripping her flesh, flying her higher.

The earth spun far below, dwindling away to a dimly glowing, cloudy blue marble. But its gravity, its twisting fetters of auroral fire, its pulsing beats of pain and imbalance still pulled downward at her. She hung taut, stretched and racked between the earth and the distantly glimmering heavens.

Ariadne remembered her crystal then—the serpentine pattern of the double helix she had etched on it. She searched for the sun and summoned its light through the interwoven carved channels. Fire blossomed on her breast, the white and the black winged serpents of her nightmare springing out from the blazing crystal, coiling around her. They writhed like the tormented auroras, twisting, spitting sparks, sharp fangs piercing her in a tangle of white coils fighting black.

"Stop!" She grasped at the burning pendant. Her palms scorched as she damped the flow of light, blocked the etched channel of the black serpent and hurled its negative energy back into darkness. She freed the luminous positive power of the white serpent, and it swelled before her, uncoiling, soaking up the light as it grew.

Just as Ariadne was catching a breath in relief, the white serpent turned on her, still swelling and swelling as it sucked up the light, until it dwarfed her, opening its immense jaws. The cavernous mouth swallowed her whole. Inside, the filigreed birds dipped and plunged. Ariadne staggered, and they were on her—swarming, ripping her flesh with their sharp beaks. They flayed the skin of her arms and legs, clawed her face into bloody shreds.

"Stop! Please...." Their merciless beaks tore open her breast and sliced away at her, tore loose her connections of flesh and bone. Her awareness scrambled in shock to escape, but she was flung down onto the earth, slamming into mud dense with the stink of her own rotted corpse.

Ariadne flailed through scattered leg and rib bones. She came up short, gasping and retching, before her own empty skull.

Curling out of the eye sockets, wraiths of smoke. A sapling sprang up between the grinning jaws, then swelled into a leafy young olive tree as the smoke solidified into the twin winged serpents coiling about it. The tree withered into the crone's wood staff carved with an ancient healing caduceus. It burst into fire, and within the tempering flames a crystal glowed like an ember, fiery etched lines spiralled around its lattice. The double helix.

Ariadne blinked. She was inside the crimson lattice.

Light danced in the facets, and the designs of twining serpents, flying fish, and bull horns came to life. Music shimmered crystal-bright all around her, inside her. No, she was inside the music. Shifting mirrors of lights and tones, looking out through glittering angles, looking out through the magic. And the music telling her how, where. Something sprang open in a rich outpouring flood and she was tracing the secret geometry of dazzling light-gem-music deep inside the crystal, treading its tilting dazzling paths, fearless, into the hidden ways of the maze.

54

THE TAVERNA WAS ONLY a slanting shed roof tacked onto the side of the owner's house, propped on metal poles, with a waist-high wall of concrete bricks. At one end, under a rusted Coca-Cola sign, a wooden counter held some bottles and a barrel of olives. They'd dumped cement over the dirt yard to make an uneven, cracking floor.

Peter felt grateful for the night breeze. Every village man over fourteen had crammed into the taverna or yard, and the heat, cigarette smoke, and ripe body stink had reached the suffocation stage. It didn't help that he and Demetrios had been given the privileged table against the inner wall.

Some of them were singing, eyes closed, squeezing out a tear with the drunken lyrics:

"If the drunkards are condemned, Wrongly they'll be hanged;
I am no drunkard, but I like a drop, Because of two blue eyes.

Why, oh why do you threaten, That somewhere else you'll go—
Go on then, go."

Another crackle of heat lightning strobed outside, thunder rumbling off the mountain. Peter rubbed his ringing ears.

One of the bunch sitting with them, paunchy balding man he thought was the baker but he'd forgotten his name, leaned his elbows on the wobbly table, rattling glasses, sloshing the oil in the lamp as he shouted something at Peter, grinning.

Peter returned an all-purpose shrug and grinned amiably. His island Greek was getting tuned, but a lot of the byplay was too fast and heavily accented to catch. The punchlines didn't seem to matter, anyway, to the general hilarity. He raised his glass he kept trying to turn upside down, but somebody kept righting and filling.

"I si yia." Cheers. The local *raki* burned down his throat like his cousin Zach's bootlegger white lightning, and the lamplight and smoke swirled dizzily. He caught the side of his chair as he teetered sideways.

Exclamations and curses around him. Glass shattering. He wasn't quite that falling-down drunk, it was another tremor heaving the floor, shivering the wall behind him. They were getting stronger. A few men furtively crossed themselves. The others roared with laughter, stumbling over the subsiding wobble of the floor with glasses raised, singing and bumping together in a rough dance. Outside, a bolt of lightning split the darkness.

The skinny guy in the patched jacket next to him leaned down to yell at the hound squirming and whining over their feet under the table. He prodded Peter in the ribs with his elbow, spilling more liquor. "So tell me, what do you think of the Med League inviting Crete to join them?"

Peter kept his face noncommittal, shrugging.

"But you have been travelling with *Despoinis* Demodakis, eh? You have seen these miracles?"

Peter's glass clattered onto the table. "I don't know anything about miracles, pal." Then realizing he'd answered in English, he said curtly, *"Ohi."*

The young kid standing behind the skinny guy leaned over eagerly, touching his saint medallion. "But we heard from Spanos in Loutro, that down the coast in—"

"Look, you're talking to the wrong guy." Peter climbed to his feet, shaking his head. It was pounding with pressure, his ears still ringing, goading him. "I'm only the hired man." He pushed away from the table.

"Petro, my friend, don't run off." Demetrios rose, catching Peter's eye. "Leave the guilt go. You could no more save your sister than I could little Kri-Kri, though I flogged myself, too. But that's what this night is for. We give our sins to Judas!"

He turned to wave an expansive arm over the crowd, shouting above the hubbub, "Time for the straw man to face the flames!"

A roar of approval, glasses raised all around. "To Judas, may he roast in Hell! May the fire burn hot!"

They threw the glasses smashing to the floor, then pushed toward the dark yard, surging around Peter as he swayed, rooted. One of the villagers tugged at his sleeve, urging him outside. "Come, Petro! Cast your sins onto the bonfire with us."

He trailed along. His ears were really ringing now, deafening, or maybe it was only the crowd roaring as they ran ahead with torches. Flames streamed in the hot wind. The women and children were milling in the street too, singing in shrill voices. The *raki* burned sickening in his gut.

Another roar of laughter. Cheers. A knot of young men ran past, straw-stuffed Judas with his painted face bouncing on their shoulders, and Peter was pressed among the crowd in the street before the church, blinking bewildered at the huge pile of branches as the boys climbed to the top and impaled the figure on a stake, grinning cartoon face lolling out of the dark. Lightning flared. Thunder crashed. The crackle and dance of sparks answered it. Flames leapt up through the night.

The church bell was clanging, splitting his head, and suddenly he was doubled over in agony, sweating, pressing his head between his palms as the bells crashed through him and his father's voice hammered out of the dark and the swirling sparks. *"And the unfaithful shall be damned to the fires of hell! The day of Judgment shall come upon thee...."*

He's sinned, he's lusted, he's a coward and a failure, and the Reverend is coming to get him, God is going to damn him to hell. Earth splitting open right now to claim him, he can feel it heaving beneath his feet, devil reaching up to pull him down, and the flames are leaping, cocks crowing wildly in the night. Saint Ariadne. Three times he's denied her, and the cocks are crowing, but that's bullshit, he doesn't believe any more. But his father's face looms out of the dark, and beside him there's Ginnie, eyes blazing with the fire of righteousness, thunder booming, pointed fingers impaling him—

He's thrown upwards. A giant hand slaps him back down and he smashes into the earth.

Gasping, he sees the bonfire writhing impossibly upwards, flying apart in a shower of sparks, church bell clanging off rhythm as dark figures drop their torches and stagger, falling beside him. His fingers grip handfuls of dirt. The world churns like water under him and a terrible rending roars out of it.

Screams, all around him. A shivering starts in the ground, then it's shaking faster and faster as the roar builds far below to an agonizing pitch, pressure building like a flood behind a cracking dam, and he can feel the explosion coming. The mountainside's tearing apart, suspended weight no longer taunting and taunting but flinging free to come smashing down.

55

RED CURRENTS SWEEP HER through subterranean passages and shoot her out of the cavern on a river of blood. Steaming rapids rush her into sunlight, trees shimmering in a breeze along grassy banks. The current flings her toward land, where a sleek brown bull waits on the bank, horns glinting, muscular flanks gleaming like a chestnut in the sun—

The bull lowered his head to pluck Ariadne out of the river and lay her in the grass, licking the blood from her face and naked body. His tongue was rough and warm. Hazel eyes sparked golden glints as he licked her clean, suffusing her with his warmth and energy. She surrendered to the slow, sensual pleasure of the sunlight and fragrant soft grasses and the loving touch of the animal. Heat flowed and gathered in her loins, bursting into a cry of delight. *"Chairete!"* She jumped up, strong and lithe, to run and dance with the beast like the ancient Minoan bull-leapers. She sprang onto his back, and his pounding hooves carried her across the valley toward a dark cave mouth.

The rhythm of his gallop picked up urgency, beating through her. Muscles rippled between her gripping thighs.

The gleaming brown hide was dark with sweat now. She leaned lower over his neck, clinging as he ran faster. Hoarse breaths and pounding hooves, thrusting haunches—her legs tightened around the laboring beast. They shot into the darkness of the cave.

Hooves rang against stone and they hurtled down the dark tunnel. There was a great roaring in her ears as the rock shook beneath them, rending with a violent tremor. Boulders broke loose and crashed behind them. Another heave of the earth, scream of shearing rock faces, and they were spewed from the passage.

Ariadne was thrown to her knees in the dirt. She raised her face to see she had emerged from the womb of a giant stone figure, red rock thighs spread in labor.

The mountain was a monumental carved woman, caught in the travail of the earth, enormous blocky shapes of squatting legs quivering with the earthquakes. Ariadne craned back her head, awed by the sheer mass of the figure, the enormous swollen belly looming above, curving up toward monstrous breasts gushing rivers of milk to flow down into the soil. Far above, clouds veiled a square, impassive face.

But the agony of the Mother—of the earth—trembled up through Ariadne's feet, filling her with pain and compassion. As she raised her hands, the twin serpents uncoiled from her crystal pendant and flowed spiraling up her arms. They swelled and flew to twine around the laboring mountainous figure. Ariadne summoned the blended light, the harmony of the crystalline lattice-song, and this time it flowed from her, through the coiling serpents, into the earth.

The effort cost her more pain, but she kept pushing, forcing herself to hold steady as waves of disorientation assaulted her, the light draining her, images flashing in dizzy glimpses as she swayed on the shaking earth and at the same time looked down on her own pathetic tiny figure far below.

Clenching in agony around the glowing stone, she kept trying to send the healing flow. But it was too much. The chaotic forces in the earth were too strong for her, too deep to be touched. She couldn't impose the order, couldn't hold the balance. She was drained, falling....

A blunt, angry presence buffeted her. It was somehow familiar, a screeching owl. Outstretched talons, glinting dark eyes, bristling feathers. The owl harried her, its beating wings driving her back to her knees. As it flew around her again, shrieking, she saw it gripped in its talons a gleaming chalice of beaten gold. The chalice was empty.

Ariadne blinked in exhausted confusion. The owl screeched once more, flying high to drop the vessel spinning in air to a blurred gold disk. *Empty vessel.* Ariadne frowned, groping, trying to remember. But she was an empty vessel herself. She could do no more.

The owl plunged, its wings assaulting her, pounding echoes in her head, shaking Ariadne loose from her last grasp on control. She was empty, open, falling—

But she wasn't. The sudden gush of blended light came from below, buoying her, surging up through her. Using her as a conduit to channel the turbulence of the power, and

Ariadne is the crystal, the seed of a matrix, the lattice forming outward in a burgeoning domino effect. The violent forces enter and shatter through her facets, realigning to flow smoothly out her rippling arms. They are the waves of the sea, spreading a soothing rhythm outward. Her fingers flow into the reservoirs of water within the rock layers, filling and emptying, shifting them to ease the painful pressures. Cool calmness, flowing down her veins, pumps down the veins of the mountainous stone figure and spreads along the layers of the earth's crust....

Ariadne can feel how the violent quake is being diluted by that flow, spread and diffused to a more gentle release. Her thoughts are moving strangely, very far away, in ponderous, heavy cycles as the tremors subside within her. The black serpent and the white serpent lie finally coiled in balance around the blood-red stone of her body, the violence of the clashing powers mitigated in their joining.

A neutral, waiting state. Time suspended.

Ariadne frowns, groping for her own familiar senses and perceptions. But the slow, thick concepts will not gather into words. Somewhere, vague and distant, she can still sense turmoil seething restively, but it is far away, deep beyond her reach, her realm.

Confused, she tries to shake her head. But she is stone, too heavy and immense to move. The blended light flows through her. She drinks it in, filling up, swelling with it. As the lattice spreads, her body stretches to encompass more and more. Finally she looks down to see she has become the mountainous figure of red stone. She is the wind-carved monstrosity of immense pendulous breasts, vast bulging stomach, massive spread thighs. She swells larger and larger, pregnant with the fertility of the earth, throbbing to its rhythms. Humming, pulsing, being *it—*

"Ohi!" She's trapped in that immensity, the grossness of that body claiming her. Its brute pulse beats through her, demanding. She writhes in revulsion—

Ariadne ripped herself free, thrown out into the dizzy darkness again, lost. From somewhere, a rhythmic beat hammered at her, urgent and commanding. The beat was a bell clanging, calling, and she had to follow its summons.

56

GRIPPING THE DIRT, PETER can feel the mountainside tearing itself apart in the deafening roar, tons of rock flinging free to come smashing down—

Silence.

The sudden absence of noise falls over them like a blessing.

And just that suddenly, impossibly, the hurtling weight was lifted, the rending roar halted. Only a fading whisper echoed off the cliffs. The earth had gone still, listening, as if like Peter it couldn't believe the cataclysm had simply drained away.

He groaned and pushed himself upright. Stars winked on overhead, clouds shredding. His head was clear now, the pressure and the ringing in his ears gone.

Peter climbed to his feet, helped a woman up, held a whimpering little boy while his mother brushed off a girl's dress. He turned to see the scattered branches of the bonfire still smoldering, the villagers picking themselves up and raking the wood back together in numb obedience to routine. Amazingly, nobody seemed to be really hurt. Somebody picked up the singed straw man and threw him back onto the reviving flames. They all watched silently, flames reflecting off dazed faces, as the branches flared and the cloth and straw caught fire, and the sins of the year were consumed.

One by one they shuffled off into the dark. A hand dropped onto Peter's shoulder. Demetrios's deep voice rumbled, then his footsteps faded after the others. Peter was left standing by himself staring at a glowing mound of ash and coals.

A grin spread across his face. "Ashes to ashes, you old bastard." He turned and strode up the hill to the house, light as a feather.

57

"FOOL! SO YOU FINALLY decided to wake up? Silly pigeon—no idea what forces you're playing with. Nearly killed both of us."

"What?" Ariadne blinked and groaned. She was heavy as a block of stone, her body stiff and sore. She squinted through the flickering dimness, coughing in a swirl of incense. She pushed up weakly against the hard surface where she lay.

"Here, now. Just lie back and let old Cassandra fix you up." A head swam into view, weathered crone face ravaged and fierce in the wavering light of a rag-wrapped torch, the shadows of wild locks running snakelike over a stone ceiling dripping with spikes.

Ariadne blinked again, still caught in the visions as she gaped at the high dome of rock fading overhead into shadows, the muted colors of stalagmites and stalactites, stone spires, drapery-like sheets of limestone flowing down the walls, glinting veins of rosy quartz. There was a cool, damp gust on her face, a plink of dripping water. From the farther recesses of darkness, a deep, echoing moan.

"Don't worry, you're back." The old midwife wedged the torch into a crack and crouched beside Ariadne to dab something moist and pungent over her face and sore arms. Ariadne flinched as the woman pushed up her skirt to sponge her scraped knees.

"Never seen anything like it, would have gone through a stone wall. Possessed." The frizzy gray head shook side to side. "Guess the Goddess won't mind if I give you some of her libation. Nurse the newborn." She stepped over Ariadne in a rustle of musty smells to kneel before a rippled stone pillar decorated with shells, feathers, goat horns.

Ariadne caught a quick breath. It was the stone column she'd stumbled onto in the dark. She could still feel it pulsing and alive beneath her palms.

The old woman picked up a metal sheep bell, holding it high to beat on it with a stick. Ariadne flinched as the hollow chime clanged through her aching head.

"Just be thankful I caught you with the beat and pulled you back. You could have gotten trapped in there." Gnarled hands caressed the stone column. The crone lifted a brass cup and poured a trickle of red wine over the pillar. She turned back to Ariadne, holding out the cup in her clawlike hands.

For a jolting moment the frizzy mane was transformed to outspread wings, the hands talons, the cup a gold chalice spinning in the air.

Ariadne pushed herself upright through a wash of dizziness. She took the cup, hesitating as she touched it to her lips, nearly gagging as she smelled for a moment the steaming surge-tide of blood. She closed her eyes and gulped, gasping as wine stung her parched throat. Warmth spread through her.

"That's better. Take some of this." The old healer pulled a bundle from her leather hip pouch, unwrapping a goat cheese and handing Ariadne a ripe hunk, pressing a dried fig into her hands.

She chewed without tasting, taking another swallow of wine, staring at the stone column rippling in torchlight.

"The mother, the Goddess. We're in Her womb. I don't need to tell *you*."

"The earth's womb." Ariadne whispered, "Zeus was born in a cave in these mountains."

The old woman gave her snorting laugh. "Men and their gods! They're all fools, don't you listen to them. The wise-women have guarded the power of the Goddess for longer than men can remember. They thought they were so strong and smart when they brought in their angry gods with their thunderbolts and arrows and swords, always thirsty for blood! But we pulled the wool over their eyes, pulled their great sky god down out of the clouds to be born in the dirt like any mortal man."

She leaned closer, gripping Ariadne's arm, her embroidered neckband glimmering its spiral with a third staring eye. "You've got to learn the secret ways, and guard them safe from the men. They've forgotten they're meant to be consorts for the Goddess, help her keep the earth fertile. They keep trying to kill her. We can't let them."

She released Ariadne's arm, sitting back in a crouch. "Well, now She's chosen you, and there's something big She's bringing forth. But it's going to be a struggle, it's just begun. You've got to—"

"I know." Ariadne pulled herself with an effort from the grip of the daunting visions. "It's the cycle of geomagnetic reversal, putting stress on the earth, but it shouldn't be this violent. We've made it worse, these artificial energy fields clashing—it doesn't have to be this violent. People don't have to die of the plagues. These ancient sites are the key to mitigate the damage. I must get to Delphi now, and try to master this—"

"No! You're not ready. There's no *mastering*, that's more man talk! The Goddess ripped the veil from your eyes, and you still can't see! You've got to *live* the earth power with her, plunge those hands into blood and dirt, birth and death and fucking, 'til you *know* the powers." She jabbed a finger at Ariadne's groin. "Wake up! The Dragon's sleeping. The winged serpent. Let him rise, take him into you. When you get a man's seed in you, you double your power. And they think *they're* in charge!" She cackled.

Then she leaned close, intent. "Stay with me and study the old ways. If you go on blind, you'll bring ruin on us all."

Ariadne touched her engraved crystal pendant and squared her shoulders. "I can't stay. There's no time. We touched only a small part of the disruptions here. I must get to the third geomagnetic anomaly, at Delphi. If I can prove that the energy fields can be reharmonized, I could convince others to help."

"Pride! I told you, didn't I? Too proud, fancy words, just like the fool men. You *can't* tell them—they'll use it against Her, against us!" She clutched at Ariadne, eyes wild. "You've got to learn the Wise Way. Join the sisterhood. We've been the guardians of the portals for eons, and if we stay true to the Way, we can purge the illness. But you must choose which of the roads to follow." She gestured around the cavern, to pots and bottles stacked against one wall. "There are two branches of study—the silver road flies into the air, uses the songs to soothe the storms and the earthquakes, but the ebony road clings to the dirt, helps us heal the illness of humans and animals. My Wise-Mother trained me with the potions and herbs to heal the sick and ease the hard birthings, to travel down into their darkness and see what song they needed, to heal."

She pointed a knobby finger at Ariadne. "You're bound for the silver Way, and it's more dangerous. I can start your training, but then we'll need to take you to Wise-Mother Daphne down the coast." She leaned forward to grip Ariadne's wrists, staring close into her eyes. "I warn you, you're courting disaster, trying to twist the two paths together and work them both, no idea what forces you're playing with. You'll kill yourself. Kill others. You can't do this alone, striding off like an ignorant fool."

She touched the embroidered spiral at her throat, then tore the cloth strip free and whipped it around Ariadne's throat, cinching it tight.

Ariadne, choking, pulled free of the old woman's fingers. "Cassandra." She coughed. "Are you one of them? The Corybantes?"

The old woman gave her a sly look. "Names. They don't matter. We're everywhere—the wise-women. You're one of us. You can't escape."

Ariadne pulled the greasy scrap of cloth from her throat and balled it in her fist. "But they're warriors, destroying. That's not the way."

"Blindness. Folly. You're caught in the web, child. We're all caught in the storm now. You're part of it. You have to stay here. Learn." She clutched at Ariadne.

"Cassandra." Ariadne grasped her wrist. "Listen. I *have* learned something from you, from...." Her gaze was drawn once more to the stone column, lineaments of the grotesque, swollen redrock goddess shimmering palpably around it. And farther, beyond any comprehension or order, the seething forces of chaos.

Ariadne shivered. She looked down at the cup, back into the old woman's fierce eyes. "I'll *be* the empty vessel."

That was why she'd exhausted herself before, with the healings, the alignments— she'd drained her own energy into the wavelengths. Now she could see. The power wasn't meant to come from her, she only had to be the conduit, the crystalline lattice to shape the surging energy pulses the way a laser harmonized random light waves. Reorient the unbalanced energy fields, restore them to a life-nurturing web. And rebalance the currents of illness in the plague victims.

"Cassandra, thank you for your help. Now I must go." She rose stiffly, heading up the rough slope of the cavern toward a faint daylight glow.

"No! You must stay!" Her shriek rang off the rock walls. "I can see only ashes and darkness from this. Come back and serve Her! Turn your back on the ancient ways, and you'll bring forth only pain and ruin!"

Ariadne ducked through the cave entrance and climbed out of the cleft, around a fresh crack across the high stone ridge. She stood blinking and numb in the diffused pink dawn glowing over the mountain. Below, the foothills still lay in shadow, the sea a dark shroud stretching to a haze-obscured horizon.

Still clutching the dirty band with its embroidered eye, she started to drop it. The crone's curses echoed from the cave behind her. She thrust the cloth into her pocket and hurried down the mountain.

58

STATIC, REVERB, AND—

> ***dazzle of sun on brass, blare of trumpets, rattling drums, cold wind on Leeza's face. Colors—gleaming parade uniforms, gold epaulets, spinning wheel of a flung baton, snapping American flag. That everybody's-grandfather face nodding, smiling, as he holds out gloved hands. "This time of trial will bring the people of our great North American Federation closer, united in our cause, with God's help defending the ramparts of freedom and prosperity"***

A whine as the visuals cut out into wavering color bands, retuned—

> ***"Our children are hungry!" A choking burn in the throat, and she gags, eyes streaming. Blur of dark rushing figures. Screams. Angry voices still distantly shout a ragged chant, "Our children are hungry, open the gates, open the gates...." Yellow poison clouds swirl, and the riot police in bubble suits swing their prods, moving out from the locked warehouse gates. Sirens shrill, lights strobe. She's gasping, eyes burning, falling***

"Got that box pushing you buttons again?" A pop in Leeza's ear, Damiana's voice breaking in. "You watch, that thing grow on you."

Leeza jerked, shoved back the goggles, and blinked. Dingy hot basement. Damiana in dusty khaki stood over her, dark eyes cool and assessing.

That pushed some preset rage button. "Fuck you! Don't you ever break in on me like that!"

Damiana snorted. "No time for you games now. Waste enough, searching this fool desert up and down. You don't want to stay here, just you and that box, you get yourself packed up."

"Yes sir, *Damon*."

"That old history. No secret, you to ask the boys. Or Esther." Sardonic smile. "I got no problem with what I be. You?"

Leeza's fingers tightened around the chair's armrests. Damiana had her, more ways than one, and knew it, moving closer to brush her fingertips over Leeza's bare shoulder and breast. They lingered, dexterous black fingers against white skin, as the nipple stiffened under their touch. But Leeza had Damiana, too, had what she wasn't sure except it was raw power captured on chip, hoarded gold, and she was moving toward the essence of a vague something, moving way beyond what she'd imagined. *Madre,* if she could keep it together she could blow out of the water anyone else's stims—

"Hey, chief—uh, Damiana!" Freddy Stone-face calling down the stairway. "Reception's clearing up. Might be able to get Turner again."

Damiana turned away without a glance at Leeza and headed up the steps.

Leeza clenched her teeth, then flopped back into the chair, picked up the hash pipe, and took another hit. She reached through the swirling smoke to reset the recorder monitor, pushing in the ear buds. She'd run a frequency/wavelength scan earlier, on the hydrofoil, and located the mercenaries' usual channels. She activated Seek and leaned back, eyes closed.

Static. Interference whine. Then it cued in:

"...still negative. Pulling the boys back in for you rendezvous—" A shrill squeal cut in, and Leeza winced.

"Cancel that." New voice, biting the words even through the static. "New rendezvous back at Med League headquarters on Naxos. Bring the Conreid bitch. Constantin Demodakis wants to cut a deal."

Leeza caught a quick breath, jitters racing down the lines and up her spine. She jerked forward to kill the monitor, glancing nervously over her shoulder. Pulling out the ear buds, she sagged back against canvas, twisting the heavy platinum ring on her finger and staring into the stone's facets as the fan swirled smoke tatters.

59

THE LAST PLACE PETER figured he'd find himself Easter midnight was in church.

Overhead, a twin-barreled roof, the musty dim chapel flickering with candlelight and glints of gold, silver, and enameled icons, choking with incense. He was pressed against the back wall. Beside him, a long crack the quake had split in the whitewashed mortar. Around him, a crush of village women in their best embroidered skirts and headgear. No sign of Ariadne.

It was hot. The villagers had all launched into the Nth round of singsong chants, his throat felt like sandpaper, and the old people were squeezing past for one more circle of the walls to kneel on the floor and cross themselves and get up painfully slowly to kiss each one of the gilt icon frames and the gold-foil plaque with the crucifixion-resurrection scene.

Now he knew why there were so many Orthodox saints and martyrs—suffering this drill.

He cleared his throat and looked over the bowed heads, strings of wildflowers, and racks of guttering candles to the front of the chapel. Demetrios stood beside the brocaded vestments of the visiting priest, holding a thick book and singing the passages for the crowd to echo, his big voice ringing off the walls. No pews, just a few chairs they'd brought in for a couple of really old geezers and the girl with her broken arm in a sling—the only real injury from the quake. The kid with the swinging censer was coming around again, and Peter's eyes glazed with the suffocating swirls of incense.

He could almost smell another scene:

Fumes of the droning diesel generator, ripe muddy swamp, sweatsoaked powder and lavender toiletwater. Strings of light bulbs flickering over tent walls, and he's in the choir in his white robe. The Reverend's voice thunders hellfire and redemption, and the crowd cries, "Hallelujah, amen!"

Ginnie's beside him, eyes dancing as she pinches his butt under the robe. "Don't let Pa get a whiff of your breath, you yahoo. Out with Gramps again?"

Peter swallowed, and sent off a silent prayer for her.

The flickering candlelights and shadows, heat and incense, singsong chants ebbed and surged around him in dizzy waves. He sputtered and jerked back as water suddenly splashed in his face.

Everybody was getting sprinkled. The priest moved down through the crowd, holding a decorated candle, followed by men in their shabby best suits carrying a miniature gold casket decked with poppies. The villagers clotted into a procession as overhead the bell started clanging again.

Someone pressed an unlit candle into his hand. "Come, you must light your candle from the *Papa*'s for good luck this year."

He jumped at the husky voice in his ear. Ariadne smiled up at him, looking tired but radiant, fresh-scrubbed beautiful in an embroidered peasant blouse, damp tendrils escaping a white scarf. Her eyes, almost indigo in the candlelight, held clear and steady on his.

He started to ask her where she'd been, if she was okay. Instead he just stood there, fingers clutching the wax taper, swimming down like a fool into those deep purple-blue seas.

Demetrios's voice boomed over them, and he nudged them forward to light their candles before the procession moved out the door. "*Chairete*, Niece. You'll tell us all about it, eh?" With a wink at Peter, he strode out into the darkness of bobbing candle flames and bell peals.

Ariadne beckoned Peter toward the doorway to follow the candlelit line snaking around the chapel. A woman in a vest stiff with gilt embroidery cut her off, tugging at her sleeve, ducking her head shyly and crossing herself. She gestured behind them. Some villagers were helping the two old men to their feet as they gripped lit candles in determined hands. The injured girl still sat, face pale, hunching over her splinted arm. The woman went to her, leaned down to whisper, and looked back expectantly at Ariadne.

Beside Peter, she went still, face distant. He thought she would turn and leave, but she took a deep breath, handed Peter her lit candle, and moved over to the girl, crouching beside her chair and murmuring. The girl shook her head and cradled the injured arm, then finally nodded. Ariadne untied the sling, gently unwrapped the bandage and splint. She pressed her hands around the bruised, swollen forearm. The girl gasped, whimpered. Her mother took a step closer. Ariadne murmured again, and the girl started taking deep, slow breaths. They stayed that way for what seemed to Peter a long time, as he stood awkwardly in the doorway and the candles dripped wax.

"Now."

Peter jerked, swearing as hot wax spilled over his hand.

Ariadne was rising, smiling down at the girl. "You see, it isn't broken. Just let it rest, and do what I've shown you."

The girl, face flushed, flexed her wrist. She looked up in amazement. "It doesn't hurt now, Mama."

The woman darted forward to touch her daughter's forearm and gently probe it. Peter blinked. It had to be a trick of the guttering candlelight, but the bruising looked less livid. The mother gasped and fell to her knees, clutching at Ariadne's hand to kiss it.

"Irena, don't be foolish. It was only a sprain. I simply eased it."

The mother shook her head, crossing herself. "I felt the broken ends of the bone moving when she hurt herself. They're joined now. It's a miracle."

"No." Ariadne's voice was curt, authoritative. "You're mistaken, Irena."

The woman stared, confused.

Ariadne grasped her shoulder. "It was not broken."

The woman finally nodded and helped replace the bandage and sling.

Ariadne turned and saw Peter in the doorway. She hurried past him out the door.

He strode after her, spilling more wax as the candle flames guttered in the breeze. "Damn it. What am I supposed to do with these things?"

She took one of the candles. "Shield it and make a circuit of the chapel for luck."

The bell had stopped ringing. A gust grabbed his flame and blew it out before he caught up with Ariadne at the front of the church again. He didn't know if she'd blown hers out, or if the wind had gotten it, too.

"So much for luck. Story of my—"

The sudden scream of a rocket exploded over the village, flare dazzling his eyes.

"Take cover!" Blinded, he lunged to grab her arm.

"Wait. It's only the celebration, Peter—fireworks." She pulled her arm free and headed up the road. "I want to show you something."

She led him uphill through a dark tangle of thorn and boulders, onto a slanting outcrop. Another rocket soared and blossomed in a shower of blue sparks over the rooftops below. In the dark alleys, silver and gold sparklers danced through the night to children's shrill laughter. A muffled pop and whoosh, and a crimson streamer of fire snaked across the sky, burning its afterimage on his eyes.

"Quite a show."

"Uncle ordered special rockets from Athens. He's like a child about fireworks. But come, there's a place I want you to see."

She climbed over the rock and down a steep drop, nimble as one of the wild goats. He stumbled, muttering a curse. She took his hand and led him through a gap between crags. "Dmitrios showed me this place when I was a girl. I thought it was a magic world."

They dropped lower, down a narrow cut, then suddenly out onto an open plateau looking over the distant sea. Peter caught a sharp breath. Before him a white stone maze glimmered under the rising moon—an expanse of twisting curves, convoluted angles, tortuous spirals carved into the rocky earth. A labyrinth of silver and shadow.

He blinked. It was the ruins of an ancient town, broken walls and twisting alleys and fragments of stairways climbing toward the stars, all hacked seemingly of one piece from the white stone.

She led him in silence down the deserted narrow passages between walls, threading the shadowy maze inward. A whisper surged and ebbed in his ears—voice of the sea echoing in an empty spiral shell. Peter was lost, wondering if he'd wander the twisting paths forever.

Ariadne ducked through a dark gap, climbed the stairs carved into the side of a wall, and sat atop it. He sat beside her, looking out from the center over the glimmering stone tracery.

"What is this place?" It came out a whisper.

She lifted her palms. "No one knows. We think one of the ninety-nine fabled cities of the ancient Minoans."

"And Ariadne. Her labyrinth?"

"Who can say? There is power here."

They sat in silence, watching the distant flare and sparkle of fireworks.

She turned to face him as another fireburst reflected in her eyes. "Peter, you were right. We need to talk."

"About what just happened in the church? Saint Ariadne and her miracles?"

"Nonsense." Her voice took on an edge. "My work has nothing to do with churches and miracles."

"It did for that girl and her mother. She was down on her knees to you." Something—maybe the shadowy power of the place urging him to just the opposite—made him goad her. "Why don't you let them worship you?"

"I don't want that."

"Then why did you go down that night and heal those plague victims at the village? That's what Georgios said. You *did*, didn't you?" His voice echoed from the stone walls, angry, and he wasn't sure why. He edged back uneasily to stare at her.

She met his gaze in the dimness. "I am all too human, Peter. As you reminded me that night."

"Now, wait, I—"

"And I must ask you now to make a choice." She sighed, raising a hand in that gesture he'd come to know, to touch the crystal over her breast. Somehow in the shifting moonlight and cloud-shadow the movement was slow and sensual, beckoning him closer—to feel the heat of her skin, inhale the fragrance of her hair flowing over him like dark waves, let his hands ride the full curves of breasts and thighs into sweet oblivion....

He blinked and caught himself leaning closer to her. He pulled back to see she was swaying, eyes closed and lips parted, gripping the necklace.

He shivered. "Ariadne...." His voice came out hoarse.

She lowered her hands and took a deep, shuddering breath. "*Ohi*. Not that way," she whispered in Greek.

A ragged cloud drifted across the moon, and she turned back to him, a trick of shadows and moonlight now seaming her face like the ancient, storm-weathered stones around her. She said abruptly, "Peter. Will you come to Delphi with me, to the last site I need to test? It will be difficult, and dangerous for you—not only danger from the mercenaries or my father's men, but for what you may see. I can't explain, only that it must be done. If you turn back now, I'll be grateful for all the help you've given me. If you come, you must trust me."

The waxing moon sailed free of the clouds as she dropped her gaze to her fingers plaiting themselves in her lap. She bit her lip, looking all at once like that shy young girl in the photo in Demetrios's parlor. "Petro...." Her voice trembled. "As I've learned to trust you."

He reached over to take her hands between his and still their tremor. "Easy, now."

She met his gaze. She looked tired, but holding firm.

He gave her a wry smile, squeezed her hands, and released them. *Etse k'etse.* "I guess we're both crazy. Count me in."

60

THE HYDROFOIL SLUNG ACROSS rough swells, remnants of the storm. Leeza was puking her guts out again.

"Damn...." She pushed herself back from the chemical stink of the head, slumping in the corner of the tiny compartment. Bracing herself against another jolting lurch, she got to her feet and splashed water over her face. She didn't *even* want to look in the mirror.

"Uhhnn." She staggered out the door and across the narrow cabin to her bunk.

Bad scene. Shouldn't have popped that upper earlier, but she'd been completely ragged, now she just wanted to sleep but she couldn't. She pulled out her hash-oil pipe and took a deep drag.

The boat slithered. Leeza grabbed a handhold. "When do we get there? I need to talk to Damiana."

Esther, sitting on a folded rug with her stocky legs braced against the wall, didn't answer, just kept cleaning some piece of the gun she was taking apart. She raised her head to give Leeza a look like she'd flick her out of the way if it wasn't too much bother. Ridiculous, that dark-brown pixie haircut framing her moon face and thick features dotted with moles. Obviously Esther didn't give a hoot. Leeza had tried charming her way out of the cabin earlier, but the mercenary wasn't interested.

The door popped open in a gust of cool spray, Leeza gulping fresh air. A wiry young man swaggered through, the one Freddy called The Arab and the others called Hollywood. She'd gathered he was really from Iraq or Iran, but what difference, the way all the little countries and wars kept changing. None of the crew seemed to have a home now, so why not ex-tinseltown at the bottom of the San Andreas Gulf.

His dark eyes flashed toward Leeza in her bunk. He smoothed his pencil mustache with a finger, toe nudging Esther's foot. "The chief wish to speak with you. She say now we are entering this Cycladic water again, I will lie low inside, so not to disturb these hot-tempered Greeks." He raised his hands, shooting another glance across the cabin. "I will watch the girl."

Esther shrugged and climbed to her feet, rolling the gun parts up in the rug and stowing them, turning with a sour face to the door.

Hollywood laughed. "Just think, we will soon finish this job, and how much they will pay us! You can go visit those children of yours. And me, I will go see Rio. Freddy tells me the girls on the beaches wear only a little bit of string."

Esther snorted and left. Hollywood managed to saunter across the unsteady floor to plant his feet and stare down at Leeza, gaze traveling over her rumpled T-shirt and shorts and lingering on her legs.

Leeza jerked the sheet over herself. "Bug off."

He raised shoulders and hands in an elaborate shrug and lounged into the opposite bunk, smirking.

She turned her back on him, pulling her headset out of the storage pocket, recorder box strapped to the inset loops along the inner wall. She uncoiled the leads and jacked in.

She slotted a chip and scanned, local color: *Whitewashed cubic maze of buildings on a rocky cliff over bright blue water. Salt tang and heat. Sky a vibrant bowl overhead.* But there was no way to capture that ultraviolet intensity of light—*toh phos*—like an energy field crackling around and through you. Maybe if she upped selective stims to give it a knife-edge bite... But it was too much work right now, she couldn't concentrate.

So she switched to receiver scan, local transmissions coming through better since they'd upped the transmission power on the remaining microwave towers. Which she recalled had Ariadne all freaked out about the bio dangers. Leeze shrugged irritably. Maybe she could pick up some news and entertainment stims, maybe something she could use. She was floating, killing time, sliding down the lines so she didn't have to think, just ride the Link:

> ***A news program rushes Leeza through its twisting holographic logo to a brisk British voiceover:
>
> "Eastern Mediterranean Updates for English speakers, with Colin Blackwell. Today we take you on the spot for exclusive coverage of what promises to be a reactionary uprising by the moderate Moslems in Pan-Palestine. On Viewer Link-In, subscribers may take advantage of the opportunity to question correspondent Sofiya Ghiabedes from her bed in Athens Orthopedic, where she is recovering after infiltrating a secret orgiastic ceremony of the ecoterrorist Corybantes. These so-called New Amazons are responsible for the explosions two weeks ago that destroyed a nearly-completed nuclear power facility in Thessaly. Then, drought predictions on the Weather Front, with meteorologist Faruk Kassem. But first, a news chip just in...."***

Static and fuzzy gray broke up the transmission, but then it cleared again:

> ***A gray-haired woman in a lab coat points at readouts dated a couple days earlier. "There is some hope that, contrary to earlier projections, the violent transitional effects of the geomagnetic reversal may be easing. Here we're analyzing some very interesting data just in from the eastern Mediterranean area, where readings indicate the sudden, inexplicable appearance of an isolated and apparently electromagnetically stable zone centered in the Aegean."

A mumbled question offscreen, bad pickup. The woman purses her lips. "We haven't explained it yet, but, yes, we'll be watching to see how stable the zone remains...."

Visuals blank for a few seconds—tacky production values—and then snap onto a talking-head announcer ensconced in a podium with viewer-response readouts across the curved panel enclosing her.

"In related news—" The dark-haired woman glances sideways and back to the camera—"researchers in Chile have announced preliminary studies suggesting a link between usage of NeuroLink technology and RP-Hansen's. The study by El Instituto Bioelectrico at the national university in Santiago has analyzed World Health Organization data on what is now being called the New Plague. Their findings contradict the WHO designation of the syndrome as contagious, and suggest instead that increased exposures to electromagnetic stimulation from nanotechnology and microwave transmissions are impairing immunological function and activating dormant bacteria, including a mutated RPH bacteria."

"Hyper verbose!" A new face, young co-anchor in another podium, sporting the hip AndroiGenus look with the smoothed, noseless features a palette for a multicolored mandala tattoo. S/he consults the viewer response display and gives a thumb's-down to the older announcer. "NeoLuddite buzz-crushers! Laugh me out of the room, they think we're giving up our Links? So, keeping it real, here's the latest Neuro rush from Sadis and the Spankers...."***

Synth vibe, pulsing visuals, and prickly pain-patterns danced through the Link, but Leeza just stared, unseeing, groping for fogged-out connections. She took a deep breath, then ran reverse and replay:

"...the sudden, inexplicable appearance of an isolated and apparently electromagnetically stable zone centered in the Aegean."

Ariadne.

The Egypt trip had been just a smokescreen all along. *Madre de Dios!* She'd really *done* something on Tinos. And Crete...?

Leeza slowly shook her head, not believing it, but knowing it. She reflexively imprinted and ejected a chip copy, jacked out, squirmed around in the bunk to pull herself upright. Damiana would goddamn listen to her now, just wouldn't she.

Hollywood's dark eyes locked onto her as she staggered to her feet. She froze, clicking finally into gear. Screw them all—let them figure it out for themselves.

She jerked around, slammed the door of the head behind her, splashed water on her hot face. She gripped the sides of the sink, leaning closer to the mirror and staring into narrowed eyes.

61

"YOU THINK I'M CRAZY? The canvas is falling apart, and the hull's crying for caulking and paint. No fishing permit, so what does the patrol think about a boat like this? Eh? You're making pleasure trips?" Peter snorted.

The man scowled, flicking his plastic worry beads. He gripped them in his fist. "They would also ask what kind of trip it is *you* make in her."

"True." Peter shrugged. "So it's better no one tips them off."

The man flung out his hands. "You would take the bread from the mouth of my poor mother?" He gestured past the wooden boats in the cove, toward the side of the cinderblock building where early morning light picked out faded letters: *Kafenion Psari. Fish Café.* A woman shrouded in the standard-issue black sat in front at the water's edge, impassively beating an octopus carcass on the rocks.

The boat owner checked Peter out again, gave a big sigh. "Okay. For gold certificate dollars, eight hundred, bottoms." His gaze flicked uneasily over the empty decks of the fishing *caiques.*

"Sold. If you find a new sail by noon, when I get back."

He started to protest, then rubbed a hand over his greasy black curls, raised martyr's eyes heavenward, and nodded.

Peter counted out some bills. "The rest later."

The man bit his lip, examining the illegal tender. He stuck the bills hastily in his pocket. "My cousin Costas, he will have a sail."

"No talking to Costas either."

"Hush hush, okay." He hurried down the beach, bills probably burning a hole in his pocket already. He could get twice the Athens bank value on the black market, but he looked nervous enough to keep quiet for a while.

Peter turned to run an eye over the splintered hulk he was shelling out a sizable chunk of his emergency stash for. Moored next to the *caiques* with their electric motors and bright coats of primary color, the old sailing dinghy looked even more of a derelict. Nothing much but an open hull and a mast. He'd gone over it, should get them to the mainland. He wasn't thrilled with the shallow draft, but it was beamy for its length and the centerboard was weighted for a little more stability. At least, sailing, they'd be relatively sonar silent.

His lips pressed into a bitter line. What had they done with *Nereid*, on the opposite side of the island? What the hell was he doing here?

He climbed the slope of coarse sand into the glare of the rising sun, striding along the dirt track toward town. He'd left Ariadne sleeping in the room he'd decided to rent from an old couple. She'd looked about done in from the hike through the mountains, across Crete to the northwest coast. They'd been sleeping in caves and orchards so nobody would trace them, but he'd finally figured what the hell, there seemed to be some kind of celebration working up in town, people coming in on trucks and busses, and nobody was paying any attention to another poor goatherder and his wife.

He looked down at the baggy trousers and no-longer-shiny boots Demetrios had given him. As long as he didn't talk much, which he hadn't until the boat deal, he could pass.

Hopefully Demetrios was taking some heat off them, obeying the *Tyrannos* brother's "invitation" and heading down the south coast to where he could get passage to the Cyclades. He'd be "leaking" the story along the way about Ariadne gone south to Africa.

Would anybody swallow it? Everything out of control. And Ariadne—half the time she wasn't even there, like she crawled inside those crystals of hers and when she came out she was exhausted. And plastered over with Do Not Enter signs. She wasn't talking about what was going to happen up north on Mount Parnassos, at Delphi—the navel, the center of the ancient world. If they made it there.

Etse k'etse. Way the world was going, his cozy little routine couldn't have lasted much longer, anyway. Might as well go out with a bang as a whimper.

"*Kyrie?*" A tug on his sleeve.

A little girl was smiling shyly up at him, holding out an armful of wildflowers woven into circlets—like the daisy crowns Ginnie used to make when they were kids. Blinking, he registered the town outskirts sprouting up around him, people already hiking in from the countryside with lunch baskets, some of the young women wearing the flowered crowns. He'd asked Ariadne the night before if it was some kind of holiday, but she hadn't known of one.

"*Deca drachs.*" The girl's bright eyes were fixed on his.

He dug out some change and gave it to her, chose a circlet of delicate red poppies threaded with yellow blossoms. He hurried up a side road past shabby block houses, let himself in a side gate and around to the back, and tapped on the unpainted door.

Ariadne was dressed, eyes still glazed with sleep. She stepped back silently to let him into the tiny compartment walled off with thin pressboard from the old couple's livingroom and almost filled by the sagging bed and a rickety nightstand with a cracked mirror, water pitcher, and washbowl.

"You got some sleep? Good. No more of those nightmares?"

She raised her hands and shoulders in a pastel take of a technicolor Demetrios gesture.

He cleared his throat, bringing the flower circlet up from behind his back. "Here. Happy May Day, or close enough."

She smiled, reaching out for the poppies. Her hand checked, face clouding for a moment. Then she gently touched a crimson petal. "*Efcharisto,* Petro."

"Here." He laid it carefully on her head, arranging it over her coiled braids and inhaling her elusive scent, hints of wild herbs and the seashore. She sat still as stone under his hands.

As he turned away, he caught a glimpse of his reflected face in the dresser mirror, a sun-hardened, grim-looking stranger with the fringed Cretan headscarf and thickening dark beard. "*A man with no family.*" Hell, they wouldn't even recognize him.

He said brusquely, "I found a boat. We better get going, while everybody's whooping it up."

She turned to gather her things into the woven bag. "Kyrias Arapanzos tapped on the wall earlier, while I was still in bed, to say they were leaving for the... ceremony, I think she said."

"We'll stop by the market. If they're not sold out already. Boat owner agreed to stock us up on water and dried fish, but we should get some bread and fruit."

Outside, everyone was heading the same direction they were, toward the market and town square. They were sucked into the press of bodies. Flowery May crowns bobbed in the packed street, fluttering ribbons and embroidery catching the sun, more of the blood-red poppies stuck into men's buttonholes. Some kind of spring festival? But all the snatches of conversation Peter could catch seemed to be about "the cursed Turks" and some latest outrage by the Sons of the Prophet. Ariadne had that glazed, drawn-in-on-herself look, so he concentrated on steering them past the locked storefronts and the closed city hall and police station, maneuvering through the crowd toward the vendor stalls around the town square. Music thumped, bad brass and drums.

The square was packed, but he managed to score the last few loaves at one stall and some olives and dried figs at another. As he tucked the packet of figs into his net bag, Peter turned to see a cop by the next stall. He was watching them over the crowding heads.

"Damn!" Peter jerked his face down. He tried to turn casually away, block the cop's view of Ariadne as he raised a hand to tug the scarf lower over her face.

"Petro, what—?"

"Hush. Just move on. We have to get out of here."

But it was impossible to get out of the square. People kept crowding in behind them, pushing them forward toward the center where a space was left open and some kind of rhythmic chant was revving up.

"This is crazy. Let's try to go through instead."

Ariadne didn't seem to hear him. She was gripping his arm and staring into the mob, face gone pale.

"Are you all right?" He gave her a little shake. "Come on!"

She wrenched against his grip. "Peter. This is—"

Loud drums cut her off, more hubbub on the opposite side of the square, and Peter strained over the heads to see what was going on. Men shouted, waving their fists, the women warbling shrill animal-like cries.

Then he saw.

Cops or some kind of local militia in uniform were pulling into the central cleared space two thin, swarthy young men in torn, soiled white tunics someone had painted in crude black brushstrokes with a crescent moon. One of them stumbled, was picked up and shoved after the other into the clearing. They cried out in a language Peter didn't know. The uniforms turned their backs and marched out, the crowd closing in the circle behind them. One of the men in white fell to his knees, prostrating himself on the ground. The other one held out his hands, his pleading drowned out by the rising guttural surge. The crowd pushed forward, tighter around them. Peter saw the pile of rocks at the opposite edge of the clearing.

"Jesus Christ." He was pushing back against the press, pulling Ariadne after him, people cursing as he shoved, and he couldn't get through. A shrill scream. He couldn't seem to help straining to see as the upright man staggered back, blood streaming down his face.

A roar went up.

Shouts echoed in the square. Hands were snatching up rocks, hurling them at the men in the center of the circle. Crimson stained the white cloth. The man on the ground writhed in a huddle. The other one flung up an arm as he fell. Peter caught a last glimpse of his face, covered with blood, then he was down, buried under the rain of stones.

Bile choked Peter as he flung around, hauling Ariadne close, plunging past some women shrieking like Furies, faces gone ugly. He ignored men's curses as he shoved them aside, trampled the ones who wouldn't move, dragged her stumbling through. Everything went blurred, a wild ringing in his ears.

Then somehow they were clear, stumbling through the streets still numbly gripping their bags, roar of the mob fading behind them. Peter stopped, panting. "Jesus, they...."

Staring blankly through him, she raised a hand to pull the skewed flower crown from her head. The red poppies dropped into the dust as she groped past him down the road.

62

"REMEMBER, I DO THE talking and dealing. You answer him yes sir and no sir."

Damiana shrugged. "Nothing to I. *Sir*." She sauntered out of the pilothouse of Turner's hydrofoil to lean on the rail.

Beyond her silhouette, deep blue sea, an island's stark white cliffs, and the Demodakis yacht anchored. Finally, after the *Tyrannos* had changed the meeting-place half a dozen times. Leeza started to follow Damiana out.

Turner's hand clamped onto her shoulder. She flinched as he brought his pale blue eyes and acne-pitted face closer. "And you, Ms. Conreid." He bit the words as his fingers tightened, digging around her shoulder bones. "I hope you have a good memory. We don't want any more fuckups. I'm doing you a favor, telling him you're our hostage, so don't screw it up or I'll leave you here. I hear they still stone whores and traitors on these islands."

He showed her a row of shiny metal teeth, then turned back to his instrument console. Reflected light glinted off the stainless steel socket mounted showily at the base of his bristle-shaved skull. Sitting on the pilot stool, he picked up a computer lead and snapped its plug into his interface.

Crew had a joke—Turner didn't have to jack off, just jack in. For a max gross-out, Leeza pictured Linking interfaces with him. Too sick. She joined Damiana at the rail, watching sunlight sparkle off the chop.

The yacht's launch started over to them. As it pulled alongside, Leeza recognized the gray-haired, hawk-nosed man standing stiff in the middle of the boys in blue with their zigzag Med League insignia. Ariadne's uncle who'd pushed her around on the dock. The big sapphire flashed on his pinkie as he climbed aboard. He drew himself up, glaring tightlipped across the deck at Leeza and Damiana.

"That sure she uncle?"

"Yeah. A real prick."

Damiana nodded at Freddy, who went to get Turner. "He wait here, little insurance things stay cool."

Turner kept them waiting long enough to get irritating. The uncle glared, stubbornly silent, clearly pissed at playing his brother's flunky but knowing he'd fucked up royal losing Ariadne. Leeza gloated. Damiana just watched him with a faint smile.

Turner came out and threw a nod at the uncle, then the three of them took his place in the launch, heading over to the yacht.

Constantin Demodakis kept them waiting on deck—his turn. Turner was steamed, face blank but a mottled flush creeping up under the pockmarks before their escort took them aft to the cabin. Leeza was first through the door. She stopped short before the man standing beside a gleaming wood desk.

Now she knew where Ariadne had gotten that carved-statue look. Here was the same built-in dignity to the stance, face cast from the same gorgeous classic mold, but all hard macho this version. The man wasn't tall, but there was a substance about him that didn't need the uncle's posturing. She felt like she was looking up.

She stood gaping like a bol. Turner shoved her aside and stepped past with his hand extended. "President Demodakis." A smile like he was gritting on ground glass.

"*Tyranno* Demodaki." Marble-statue-man ignored Turner's hand, a regal gesture granting them chair and couch as the uniformed escorts took up positions beside the door. "The times decree a return to a more effective, if perhaps severe, political model." His voice rang with a deep resonance, only a trace of an accent. He could have made a fortune in media—hell on wheels with speeches.

Demodakis moved around behind the desk. His gaze traveled from Turner to Damiana, and his nostrils flared in distaste. He shifted the focus onto Leeza.

Despite herself she flinched as his eyes locked onto hers. They were dark, not like Ariadne's, but in a way they were, looking right through her. With a sick feeling in her gut, she recognized that look—no petty personal concerns would stand in the way.

Then she was out of the spotlight, sagging back on the couch as Turner lowered himself stiffly into the chair. Demodakis seated himself behind his desk, like it was really old Zeus king-of-the-gods' throne.

"All right, then." Turner leaned forward. "Let's get down to business. I've been authorized to—"

"That will not be necessary." Demodakis lifted a hand, his sapphire family ring glinting. "I have communicated with your clients in the pharmaceutical cartel. Preliminary negotiations are concluded, contingent on my approval of your task force. By reputation you are efficient, but in this case, it seems, ineffective. You've underestimated my daughter, Mr. Turner. You will have to do better."

"If you don't want her harmed…." The mottled look was back.

"Your clients are willing to forgo a possible interest in my daughter's healing techniques, in return for my guarantee that she will abandon her experiments." He lifted a hand. "In addition to other inducements for her safe recovery, of course. You will have to negotiate your own adjusted fee."

Turner managed a shrug. "If it's all settled between you, why discuss it with me?"

"I want to make it clear that no harm is to come to my daughter. As you may know, we Greeks have a long tradition of personal revenge. You will regret it if you make a mistake in this regard."

He paused to let it sink in. "It is of no concern to me what happens to Mr. Mitchell, as long as he does not return with my daughter." His gaze flickered over Leeza as she caught a quick breath. "Aside from my natural parental concern, she is important as a symbol to our young nation. As such, she will not threaten your clients' interests. If you appreciate the importance of symbolic actions, you will appreciate the dramatic value of a Mediterranean League rescue of 'Saint Ariadne' from her 'kidnappers.'"

Turner nodded stiffly, waiting.

"Once you locate her—my men have information that will help you—I will send troops separately, to stage a mock battle with your... men. Also, as observers, I will send with you two of my soldiers, to be disguised as your own." He indicated the guards at the door.

The mercenary looked them up and down, then shrugged again. "Okay, but they take orders from me or my second." He nodded toward Damiana.

"Very well." Demodakis stood, the audience over. "You may go now, but I wish to speak with Ms. Conreid alone."

Turner, starting to rise, dropped back into his chair. "That wasn't part of the deal."

Demodakis regarded him like some low-grade insect. "Then I am afraid you must tell your clients the agreement is canceled. Good day."

Turner took a deep breath. "The agreement was you'd see we had her, and she could tell you Ariadne was okay." He turned to Leeza. "So tell him."

Leeza braced herself to meet his intense eyes. "That's right. She got away okay."

He finally switched his laser stare back onto Turner. "That is not sufficient. I must have her assurance under no coercion from your presence."

Turner swore under his breath, shooting Leeza a look, like he had to remind her. *Death by stoning.* He jerked upright and headed for the door. "All right. Five minutes."

Demodakis didn't bother acknowledging as Turner strode out between the guards. Damiana gave Leeza a look, slowly unfolded her long limbs, and sauntered after him. Leeza took a deep breath, pulse racing, and raised her face to the man across the desk.

He stepped unhurriedly around it to stand in front of her. "It is true? Did you last see Ariadne safe?"

It was a shock, hearing him say Ariadne's name to her, but his voice was still cool, eyes remote. Leeza thrust past that last glimpse of Ariadne in the Cretan shack, giving her the deep-freeze stare before she kicked her out. "It's true. I can't remember the name of the place, little fishing village on Crete where she knew an old one-eyed guy—Georgios something. The mercenaries caught me, but Ariadne got away, with that creep Mitchell."

"Show me the ring she gave you."

Leeza pulled it off and handed it over.

He turned it in his fingers, examining the inscription inside. "If you wear it, you should know what it means. *Immortal*—"

"*—and unyielding stone.*"

He gave her a sharp look. Then, shockingly fast, his hand shot out to grasp her chin and pull her face up. "You love my daughter?"

She jerked her face away, clenching her hands, palms damp. Shit. She cleared her throat. "Yes."

He strode across the cabin and back. "I, too, love Ariadne, Ms. Conreid. But I cannot let it be a weakness as it was with her mother. I must think of my people now, of larger plans...."

Leeza got out a strangled snort. "Sounds familiar."

"Then you must see I know what is best for her. My daughter is a brilliant woman, but naïve about the workings of the real world. You, I believe, are more… pragmatic." The flicker of a smile. "Her place is with me, with her people and their struggle to regain their heritage. She needs that meaning. As you do."

Leeza's head snapped up, eyes narrowing. "What do you mean?"

"I have investigated your career. You possess ambition and talent, yet there is little chance you will succeed, with your present reckless habits. Even if these mercenaries decide to release you when your usefulness to them is gone."

She tried not to shiver.

"I offer you a position with us, Ms. Conreid. With my daughter. As a realist, perhaps you can help her to see more clearly. And you would be paid well to use your media skills in our unification cause."

She blinked. "You mean expansion, don't you?"

He ignored that. "You can help us, or you can trust the mercenaries."

"What kind of guarantees would I have?"

"None. It is you who must demonstrate good will."

She closed her eyes, mind racing, spinning like a random data search. What the fuck. "The mercenaries don't have anything—the computer on Mitchell's boat was wiped. But I copied some data from her computer. She's doing more than healing people. It's got something to do with stabilizing the geomagnetic fields, and I think it worked, at least locally on Tinos, maybe Crete."

"You believe in these 'miracles,' then?" His voice mocking.

She held out the data chip. "Check out the updates about these new stable zones in the Aegean and Med."

He shook his head, giving her his glacial smile. "Keep it. But your information will simplify the final negotiation with the cartel. Now, as my observer, you should also be aware of the information I will give Mr. Turner to help him find my daughter."

Clasping his hands behind his back, he paced across the cabin. "Ariadne's computer files were destroyed in the explosion she obviously arranged in her laboratory, but the maid found a note in the pocket of one of her skirts. It contained only scribbled phrases, referring to 'three locus points,' I assume her goals in this madness. There was also an arrow between the two words 'Omalos' and 'omphalos.'

"The third 'locus' she is making for is clearly not in Egypt. My daughter has always indulged a romantic attachment to the ancient places and myths of our homeland, Ms. Conreid. I believe she has become unbalanced, perhaps even believing the superstitious reverence of the peasants for Saint Ariadne, and the cult adoration of a new Gaea. Her second 'locus' was obviously in the Omalos mountain plateau of Crete. She has saved the most dramatic site for last—the omphalos stone, the 'navel of the world' in the ruins of Delphi."

His gaze held her like a rabbit frozen in the high-beams. "Persuade her to give up this nonsense." He tossed the ring into her lap. "And welcome to the fold, Ms. Conreid."

63

"NOTHING WE COULD HAVE done, you know. Except get ourselves hurt."

"I know that." Ariadne was gazing over the side of the sailboat at the smooth swells, like they might have changed in the hours she'd been watching them roll to the horizon. Finally she turned to look at Peter. "I'm bringing you only trouble. When we reach the mainland, you must leave me and go back to your life in Athens."

"We've had this conversation. Let Peter worry about Peter, he's a big boy."

A little frown as she worked it through. "No, Demetrios was right. You are a true *pallikar.*" *Valiant warrior.*

"*Efcharisto, Despoina.*" He inclined his head, not moving from his comfortable slouch against the thwart, bare foot steadying the tiller. He'd spent most of the day beating into a maddening, shifting wind and fighting one of the crosscurrents giving sailors since Odysseus a headache. Now the wind had shifted, an iffy breeze puffing from the east. He shook his head, hoping the creaking forestay and shrouds would hold. The boat's rigging was basic to say the least, so all he could do was keep the single sail out on a broad reach and hope they didn't drift too far west so they'd miss the landmark islands to the north, Kythera and Antikythera. It was going to be a slow trip.

The canvas was luffing again, so he brought her around a bit. Didn't help. He glanced at Ariadne's profile etched against the sea, copper-tinged with the lowering sun. "I learned a word for you, too. *Levendissa.*" *The beautiful and brave one.*

She flushed, shaking her head. "That is only for the great women who have served their people."

He squinted up at the sagging canvas again and gave up on it. "Why do you have to fight it so hard? Maybe they need someone to look up to."

"As they need someone to hate and kill?" She swung around on him, eyes flaring sharp blue. "You just saw what 'my people' can be. I will not belong to them, nor to my father, nor to any—" She pressed her lips tight.

He sat upright to grip the tiller between them. "Look, those villagers, *and* the Sons, they're just as convinced they've got the Truth as you are. So who's right?"

"No matter what they believe, no one deserves to die that way."

"Of course not. But people just do shitty things sometimes. You have to throw out the whole barrel, over a few rotten apples?" He blew out a breath. "Look, I was killing time on *Nereid,* trying to figure out what you were up to, and I read about this *noosphere* idea of Teilhard de Chardin. How there's this sort of global field of energy from all life. And how maybe when people do evil things, it's because they're cut off from it somehow. Like they can't feel or hear the truth any more." He shrugged. "Maybe those Gaea Speaks people aren't such flakes. And what you've been saying, with the electromagnetic pollution so bad now, we're really getting cut off from the natural fields."

Ariadne looked taken-aback. "Peter, that's it!"

"Don't look so surprised. I do read, you know."

She surprised him with a teasing quirk of the lips. "And what is your favorite book, then?"

"Two for one: *The Illiad* and *The Odyssey.* Inhaled them when I was a kid. Maybe that's why I ended up in the Med." He shrugged again. "Bet you can't guess my favorite character."

"Odysseus."

"Guilty."

She laughed in delight, giving herself fully to it as her natural glow broke through the strain, and he remembered with a pang that first day he saw her on the beach. She met his gaze now, sharing the laughter with him, and whether or not that *noosphere* was real, he could feel the connection.

"Thank you, Peter." She sobered. "I wish this journey could bring us both to our homes finally, and peace. But I don't know if there is such a thing any more."

"Hey. One step at a time."

Her hand crept up to touch her crystal pendant, and she turned to gaze over the sea. Beyond her, the swells had taken on an oily look in the slanted sunlight.

"I'm frightened, Peter." Her voice was so low it was almost lost to the hiss of the sea against the hull, the slap of loose canvas. "All these forces battling around me... through me. It's building to a crisis—more earthquakes, more plague victims—and those will be only the start. There's no time to learn the best ways to counter these disasters. I simply must go on with this work, even if it tears me apart." She shuddered. "I don't know who I am any more."

"Maybe it's time to let the old Ariadne go."

She turned back to him, giving him a speculating look.

"Dmitri said more or less the same to me. The way the world's going, we've got to change, step into who we need to be now." He gave a pale imitation of the old trader's Cretan shrug. "But it's got you spooked. What is it you *do* when you go in there, anyway?" He pointed at her crystal pendant. "Why is it eating you up?"

She closed her eyes, let out a breath, hand starting to rise toward the crystal again, then dropping. "Cassandra told me I needed to be an apprentice to learn the proper way to control the power. Maybe she's right.

When it courses through me, I feel I could be a god. No—I *am* one. And it's all so right and righteous, and I'm filled with the light. Do you understand?"

Despite himself, he shuddered, seeing his father's face glowing with that righteous light as the believers—including young Petey—raised their arms and cried out, "Hallelujah!" and gave themselves to his will.

He took a deep breath and stepped over the tiller, ignoring the sail flapping louder now, and touched Ariadne's shoulder. "Easy, *Despoina.*" He squeezed gently. "I'm here. I'll help if I can."

"Thank you, Petro." She touched his hand, her sapphire ring catching a spark of fading light.

He cleared his throat. "So what's with this family ring, anyway?"

She tugged it off and handed it to him. "You see the inscription inside?"

He turned it to make out the Greek letters. "*Lithos athanatos kai akinetos.* Like on the flag."

"Immortal and unyielding stone." She shook her head. "My family's motto. It used to represent our gem trade, but now my father applies it to his regime. He wants to extend his control, keep us all in his grasp...."

He studied her downturned face. "There's one way to get free of the *Tyrannos.*" He tilted his head toward the sea and lifted his eyebrows.

She hesitated, then nodded quickly.

He flung the ring far out over the swells. "There. You're a free agent."

"Peter!" Voice sharp as she grabbed his arm.

"I thought you wanted—"

"Get down!" Her eyes had gone wide, startled, staring past him.

A whoosh of wind. He wrenched around, losing his footing as the boat heaved beneath them and the boom came flying across in a crack and snap of billowing sail. He managed to throw himself sideways, pulling Ariadne out of the way as it crashed past against the shrouds. He scrambled for the lines, cursing as he slipped in a slosh of water, full sail dragging the boat heeling to starboard. He pulled it in, regaining the tiller, straightening her out just in time for another howling gust out of the south. She rode it out, shuddered and skittered over the suddenly churning sea, canvas and rigging straining.

"Christ!" He shot a look over his shoulder to the south. A dark miasma had churned up out of nowhere, gaining on them. To port, the sun dropped into a reddish haze over the rising chop.

"Ariadne!" The wind screamed, stealing his shout, lashing cold spray. "Ariadne!"

Hunched beneath the popping dance of the boom as the boat crashed and plowed through the sea, she bailed with cupped hands. More water gushed over the low gunwale as a furious blast caught them.

Peter fought to bring her back up. "Ariadne! Get forward and secure the supplies. Careful! And get some line to tie us down."

Squinting against the wind, she nodded. She crawled forward over the ribs and open decking, fighting the weight of her drenched skirt and hair. The storm whipped in gusts now, wild eddies. The boat floundered, boom crashing over again as the rigging shrieked and groaned. Peter strained at the tiller. He couldn't let go to try and pull the sail in.

Through the hazy twilight, Ariadne clung like a bit of dark flotsam in the bow. The boat levelled out again, shivered into another skating plunge over a steep swell.

Ariadne reached for the flapping edge of the tarp he'd rigged as a makeshift shelter. It took forever, tiller wrenching his arms, wind flaying him and the stays shrilling. The canvas wouldn't take much more, or maybe the mast would go first. Finally Ariadne was crawling back aft, a coiled thin line between her teeth. She fell once against the mast, but gripped the ribs and hauled herself toward his feet.

"Good! Tie yourself off with some slack to the thwart. That's right." His bellow was sucked away in the howl, but she wrapped the line around her waist and tied it off, fumbling in the drenching spray. "Got to try to reef in some sail. See if you can hold the tiller."

She scrambled up next to him, gripped beside his hands, braced her legs and leaned back against the force. She nodded choppily. He slowly let up his hold, watching her. She gasped as the full weight hit her, then clenched her teeth and held steady, arms quivering.

"Hang on!" He slithered forward to the mast, frantically loosened the halyard, line screaming out burning his palms. He swore and got a wrap on his hand, wrenched back as it leaped up and he bit down on the pain. He cleated off the slack. The sail was going crazy now, flapping and tearing against the grommets. "Christ!" It almost got away from him, but he managed to reef it down. He tied the last knot just as another wild gust caught the canvas and ripped the boom out of his hands.

"Shit!" The boom cracked over to port. He staggered, suspended over empty air. Then he crashed down against it, head ringing, stars dancing. Howling mocking laughter swirled around him in the drenching flood as he rolled slippery and nothing to grab over the side. The sea closed over him, black depths sucking him down—

"Petro!" He couldn't have heard it, but somehow her hand was there, in the water. He grabbed it. She tumbled against the dipping gunwale, pulled over after him, but then her line caught her. A sharp gasp in his ear as she strained, gripping his hand.

He groped, floundering, swallowing seawater. Grabbed the gunwale in his free hand. Kicking against the waves, he got one leg over. He wrenched free of her hold and shoved her back uphill in the tilted boat. "Get the tiller!"

Another wild dip, wind howling, and he was still dragging half submerged. Then under again as the boat broached. He popped up gasping on the slope of a towering crest, the boat canted above him, shit *shit* she was going over on him! The old black horror swam up out of the abyss to spin him drowning down.

He gasped, choking on stinging salt. A sodden dark shape, Ariadne flung herself onto the tiller. Christ, she couldn't do it. Desperate heave, and he was somehow back over the gunwale inside and throwing his weight against hers. They drove the tiller back shuddering in an ominous splintering groan. Jesus if it broke now—

The boat shot upright over the crest and sprang forward, riding the wind.

Ariadne slid down into the puddle at his feet. He dropped to sit against the tiller, holding it now against the reduced force on the reefed-in sail. The wind howled, no sign of letup. All of a sudden it was night, only a suffused glow over the sea, ghostly glimmer of the sail and the wind-chopped crests.

He leaned down to Ariadne's ear. "You all right?"

She nodded in the gloom.

"This is crazy, came out of nowhere."

She mouthed something the wind caught. He leaned close and she repeated, "The African wind."

"Too early!" Those desert storms could whip northward without notice, real widowmakers, but they weren't supposed to kick up until late summer. She was right, though. World gone crazy, rhyme and reason were things of the past.

All they could do was ride it out as the storm drove them where it would. After a while he was past thinking, just a floating speck in the darkness, two numb hands on a tiller as the boat climbed and dropped, climbed and dropped before the wind, cleaving the phosphorous gleam of spume through the canyons of the sea.

64

THE ROLLER-COASTER WAS an old one, creaking and groaning under the wheels of the cart as it clanked around a tight curve and sped into serpentine humps and coils, climbing and dropping, climbing and dropping.

Peter wanted to hang on, but he couldn't let go of the cotton candy and the box of popcorn, wind blowing them away in shreds. He was going faster now, *climbing and dropping*, into darkness. The cart whizzed through a maze of steep canyons—lowering black walls traced with glowing graffiti, spirals, cabalistic signs, but he couldn't stop to trace their meaning, and he was afraid to anyway.

He plunged into a black tunnel, glowing hieroglyphs exploding outward in electric mandala patterns as he arrowed down through the center.

He gasped for air, sucked in bitter seawater, and realized with a jolt of panic where he was.

Sinking, drowning. Heavy inky blackness all around him. Iciness laps through him, pulling him deeper. He wants to scream, but his throat is full of water, and he can only flail in helpless horror as the cold dead fingers of the crew members brush his face in the darkness, catch against his clothing, pull him deeper. There's a fearsome voice down there, calling him with the others to the bottom of the pit, promising some horrible, final revelation—

Peter wrenched upright, sweating, wincing in bright sunlight. Beneath him, the boat bobbed gently over a flat sea. "Damn." He rubbed his face, forehead throbbing. He gathered himself to get up and check the boat.

"Sit still. The current is still carrying us on the course you set after the storm, toward those islands." Ariadne pointed toward darker blue smudges on the horizon. Beside the tiller, she was combing the thick dark hair drifting loose about her shoulders. "I'm sure that island is one of the Ionians. You were right, we were blown far northwest, past the southwest point of the Peloponnese."

He squinted around the boat. He'd have to stitch up that rip in the sail before it went any farther.... He rubbed his pounding head.

"Here. Let me help." She moved to kneel in front of him, studying him with her grave, considering look. She reached out to touch his face.

He winced again as she gently examined the bruise where he'd hit the boom. He slowly relaxed as her fingertips worked around it, smoothing his forehead, lightly kneading his scalp. Warmth spread outward from her hands, somehow tingling with energy but soothing, soaking into him. Sliding down his spine in a fluid ripple as she shifted around to massage the back of his neck. *He was riding a river, flowing to the sea past fields of long grasses that rippled in the sun to a lullaby....*

He blinked. The throbbing ache had ebbed away.

"Bad, the nightmare?"

He started to shrug, but let it go as her hands rested lightly on his shoulders. "Variation on a theme. You'd think after all these years...." He was very conscious of the warmth of her palms through his thin shirt. "Scouting sub I was on in the war hit a mine, broke up. Deep enough I almost didn't make it to the surface. The others didn't."

He made an aborted movement away, but her hands stayed still, steadying him. "Dreams always end up pretty much the same. A voice calling me down into the blackness. Death. But it's not just that, it's horrible but... seductive. Promising some secret if I go." He did shrug then, disguising a shudder. "Then I wake myself up."

Her hands lifted away, leaving a cool vacancy. "Did you never go to find out what the voice promised?"

He twisted around, eyes narrowing. Her gaze met his, open, like she really wanted to know.

"No." He cleared his throat. "That's the creepy part. It's something always there, waiting, but I can't go in there and find out or I'll never come back, sane."

"Someday you will have to go." Her eyes were purple-blue in the sunlight, holding his.

He would have shrugged again, made a joke of it, should have resented her high-handing him, but somehow it wasn't like that. "I'm afraid."

"I know. I'm afraid, too." She dropped her gaze, touching her pendant in that way she had. Then she raised her face to meet his eyes. "Petro...."

Her look stabbed straight through him. His hand shook as he touched her face. Carved lines gone soft and vulnerable, and he'd never seen anything so beautiful.

He'd known how her lips would feel, and taste—honey and sun and sea-salt with that teasing hint of pungent herbs. He held her warm against him, felt her heart beating fast against his, and everything had come straight. Sunlight shimmered around them, rippling over the smooth swells. They moved together without hesitation. And she was the one, the perfect fit, new but familiar like it had all been choreographed eons ago and they'd only forgotten until now.

Breath catching in his throat, he opened his eyes to see her lips trembling on a smile. He kissed her eyelids closed, sailing down with her into the purple depths.

65

"MMM...?" ARIADNE WOKE SLOWLY, floating up through luminous waves to the sunny surface. Finally she focused on the long shadow of the sail on the sea, the solidifying blue shape of an island on the horizon. She lay against the thwarts, a blanket draped over her. Peter, still naked, one leg braced against the mast, was stitching closed a ripped flap in the loosened canvas. Westering sunlight bronzed his tanned arms and paler legs.

She smiled, savoring the lassitude, skin still tingling from his caresses.

He knotted and bit off the thread, looking over his shoulder at her. A white grin split his dark beard. "Just about to wake you up for the sunset. Look, we've got company." He gestured.

"Oh!" Ariadne pushed the blanket off and leaned over the side.

Two dolphins rode the bow wake. In a gleam of arrowing bodies and foaming sea, they dove. Curved dorsals broke the surface as they arched up again to cross before the boat, trails interweaving. They skimmed alongside.

One swam so close Ariadne couldn't resist reaching out a hand. A squeal as the slippery head tossed, brushing her fingertips with a tingle of effervescent glee. A dark eye glimmered up at her.

The dolphin dove under. Then both leaped into the air in a breathtaking living geometry of line and curve, gilded with sunlight. They plunged, and vanished into the depths.

"Ah...." Ariadne strained after them over the side.

"Incredible, aren't they?"

She threw out her arms, laughing up at the sky. "It's a blessing, Petro! Dolphins bring luck."

She sat back on her heels, trailing a hand in the cool sea. "When I was a girl, I was swimming one day and they were all around me, a family of them, leaping in the sun. They were dancing with me. And for those moments, I was a creature of magic, like them. When they left, I wept because I couldn't follow...."

"Sometimes I wish I could be one of them." He smiled down at her as a freshening breeze filled the canvas, and he balanced with the dip and sway of the boat. "But not right now. Don't move, Ariadne. I want to remember you just like that."

She met his eyes and smiled. Her gaze wandered his deeply tanned, straight features and the neatly-trimmed beard, over the light-and-shadow-limned planes of his chest, the line of hair down his belly gone lean and trim over the past weeks, penis nestled in dark curls, sturdy legs braced apart on the deck.

He sobered as she met his gaze again. "You know, when I first saw you in that cove on your island, I thought you were Aphrodite risen from the waves. You're even more beautiful now."

"Petro, don't—"

"Wait. Just let me say it." He raised a hand, and she let go the folds of the skirt she'd started to draw up over her breasts. "I know it's ridiculous, I didn't have a clue who you were, but I knew I was meant to love you. Now wait, don't move...."

He stepped around the mast, behind the sail, and came back holding a dripping fish threaded on a line. With an oddly touching dignity, he knelt in front of her, offering the fish, and they were back on the shore of her sandy cove, the stranger emerging from the sea to stammer, "*Despoina*, don't be afraid. Take the fish, a... gift. Please. Welcome. Thank you."

She took the fish, thanking him with a simple, "*Efcharisto.*"

He held out his empty hands, smile quirking his lips. "Please.... Could I just—?"

She set the fish aside, chin out, drawing back her shoulders in an aloof pose. Then she laughed. "Please do."

But as he lifted her hand to brush his bearded lips across her fingertips, the laughter caught in her throat. She pressed hungrily into his arms, needing to feel her breasts against his chest and taste the saltiness of his skin.

A startled sound from Peter, then his mouth was on hers, and she met him eagerly, as if there would never be enough. She gasped for air as her hands slid down his thighs, and he hardened against her. An almost painful surge in her groin, fires coiling up her spine like the meshing of twin serpents. Their heat was burning away her separate self, and for a moment she was daunted.

"Petro. It's too much—"

"Easy, Kri-Kri." Deep murmur against her ear. "Give and take. As much as you want...."

She opened to embrace him fully, his force merging with hers as he pushed deeper, rocking them down. She pressed hard against him until the barriers of their skin dissolved and she knew his essence in each living cell.

∞

The sunset was fading when Ariadne roused, blinking and then remembering. "Petro?"

He raised himself from their joined warmth to fumble for the tiller. "Okay. Still on course."

He sank back beside her on deck, smoothing her hair and studying her, his face intent, as the boat dipped beneath them. "Ariadne...." He pulled her to him in a fierce embrace. Arms finally loosening, he gently stroked her shoulder and bowed his head to kiss her breast.

Ariadne touched his face, laid her palm flat against his solid chest to feel the deep pumping of his heart. His skin was warm, fragrant, and she drank in the firm contours of his chest and arms beneath her sliding palms. They held each other, making small animal sounds of contentment as the boat carried them into the dusk.

Into sweet night—twinned serpents, the black and the white, coiled about her in a still but vibrant balance. The forces were no longer tugging and tormenting, wrenching at her heart, but joined now, in harmony. Her eyelids fluttered closed.

But then, piercing her peaceful drowsiness, a stab of alarm. Somehow *because* she felt this sated serenity. She struggled upright out of Peter's arms.

She could almost hear the crone Cassandra's warning echo over the night sea. "No idea what forces you're playing with! If you go on blind...."

"Ariadne?" Peter's hand groped to tug her down.

She eased her fingers from his grip. "Rest, Petro." She caught a ragged breath, staring down in the shadows at his blunt profile. He was a stranger once more. And that shining hard core of purpose she'd laboriously shaped to the task like one of her laser crystals? Its light was dimmed and distant.

She groped for her etched quartz pendant, searching out the white blaze of energy she'd felt flinging her down the coiling tunnel to heal the wound in the earth on Crete. *Gone.* She couldn't find it. Scrambling inwardly in desperation, she could find only a gentle, diffuse circling of warmth.

"No." She stumbled forward past the mast, dropping to her knees to grip the gunwale and stare into the black waters streaming past the bow. "Gone. It's gone."

"What is it?" Scuffling behind her. His hand touched her shoulder.

She shook it off. "I need to be alone."

"Oh." He stepped back.

She clutched the gunwale, trying to concentrate, searching for the lost link. But there was such hurt in his one word. She swung around, clenching her fists against screaming. "Peter, it's not you. It's my fault, I should have known.... I can't afford to let go this way, I must hold tight to my purpose."

He loomed over her, face masked by the dusk. "What can it hurt, to let yourself love? Be loved? There's strength in it. The last thing I want is to take anything from you."

"I know that, Petro." She reached out to touch his leg. "But I'm too confused. I must think first of the need.... I must feel a person's pain in order to heal him, and so I must keep feeling the earth's pain. It will guide me to the way to heal it."

"That's crazy! You're only human, you can't keep driving yourself until you burn out!" He shook his head. "You really think by making yourself suffer, you're going to save the world? You really believe what one person can do now is going to make a damn bit of difference to the whole mess?"

"I must. If I don't believe...." She sighed. "Peter. You still can't bring yourself to accept what you've seen with me?"

He turned away, gripping the shroud and staring down into the sea. "Look, this whole faith thing, I've been burned before. I can't.... I just don't know."

The boat dipped beneath them, dark water shimmering with bioluminescence ghosting its passage.

"I'm doing this for you, Ariadne. Not for 'the world.'" His voice was tired. "I'll do my best to get you where you've got to go. Right now we're both ragged out. We'll take shifts making for those islands, I'll stand the first one. Then I'll find us a cove to anchor in tomorrow night so we can get a decent sleep. Looks like we'll need it."

He moved heavily back to the tiller, leaving Ariadne alone in the bow to stare at the sliding black water and trace its cool green fire into the depths.

66

DRY LAND! SHE WANTED to kiss it.

Leeza leaned over to look at the flyspecked garbage baking in the alley, and changed her mind. She gripped the flaking grillwork rail of the rickety balcony, studying the two dusty objects on it—the handle of the broken door-latch, and a thick bleached bone. Found art.

She should break out her gear for a shot of it. And that alley the balcony was ready to fall into. Maybe later. She looked across at slumping, soot-stained walls leaning against each other, along the narrow lane past more unpainted doorways, a rusted-out car minus wheels, and piles of trash to a glimpse of freighters and masts jammed in Athens's Piraeus harbor. She made a mistake and took a deep breath, stomach roiling at the stink.

"*Caramba....*" She turned and shuffled back into the stuffy little room, hands pressed over her belly. She'd thought it was finally settled down after that last jolting hydrofoil ride to the mainland, but she still felt like hell warmed over. Just let them try to get her on another boat.

Flopping down into the sag of shrieking bedsprings, she stared at cracked plaster and the garish saint on last year's calendar.

The earth is utterly broken down, the earth is utterly moved, the earth is staggering exceedingly.

Lines from a newsstim on one of the Doomsday cults kept jingling through her mind to a headachey beat. *And there will be signs in the sun, and moon, and stars; and on earth distress....*

She supposed she should unpack her stuff, make some effort to get cleaned up. Too much trouble. She pulled the little hash-oil pipe out of her pocket and took another drag to soothe her stomach, and then she didn't care.

Somewhere circling in the fog she vaguely realized she had to get her act together, the ol' bod completely flaking out on her—*Leeza is staggering exceedingly.* What with the uppers and zingers and downers, she'd lost track of when she'd had her period last, and she really needed to start eating right. To top it all off, she had this itchy ugly rash on her feet and lower back.

Think about it later. Stay on the surface. Images....

She was settling into the cool coils of the smoke, easing back, fingers slow-mo putting the pipe away, pulling out the blue crystal she'd stolen from that funky shrine on Ariadne's island.

Facets gleamed in the dimness. Sometimes it seemed like the stone had a light of its own, burning cool blue deep inside. She refused to see Ariadne's sapphire eyes gazing reproach. The more she looked at the crystal the more fascinated she got with the way the lights broke around a thousand little mazelike corners inside, and the carved crescent moon design flared into detail, winged serpents and the horned bull leaping into life. In a way it was like the Link, amplifying and shooting the images straight through her neural pathways. She stared, eyes glazing as everything came to a humming tight focus inside it.

Incandescent blue, riding her pathways. Leeza is the light, electric.

67

THE MOON HAD COME up late. Ariadne woke abruptly to see it sailing above the jagged black arm of the rocky cove, a full orb trailing its sparkle over the sea.

The boat nodded on its anchor lines. Moonlight poured over her, sheathing her bare arms in an almost palpable glow that shimmered through the clear shallows, rippling the bottom in ebony and silver. No sound but a rhythmic shush against the crescent of sandy beach. The whisper lapped over her, cool moonlight lapping, too, and she could feel the forces connecting land, sea, and sky. They rose through her, pulsing with the fullness of the moon.

She looked down at her open palms, then at Peter lying motionless on his back, stunned with exhaustion. She took a deep breath and knelt beside him on his mat. He didn't stir as she pushed the blanket down to bare his chest.

Fluid silver glinted in the facets of the Tinos crystal. Ariadne held it, breathing with the sea's rhythm, until it warmed in her hands. She laid it over Peter's heart. He frowned and made a strangled sound, then subsided. She touched her crystal pendant etched with the serpentine caduceus, orienting her focus within the coils, inside the lattice. She leaned forward to place her hands on either side of Peter's face. Closing her eyes, she summoned the connection, rode it down with him into the black spirals.

Dark sea, and they're drowning.

With a sickening jolt, they were plunging. Deeper and deeper, and now she could hear the voice—a pulsing chant drawing them down. Mesmerizing. Seductive. She was caught in the whirlpool of chaos. *Black sea surging in a flooded cave. Crushing weight squeezing her lungs.* Panic flared. She wanted to claw her way to the surface for air. Peter flailed beneath her hands, but she was stone, holding him as they plummeted deeper. Darkness calling—

"Nnn.... No!"

He fought, but she was immoveable—*lithos athanatos kai akinetos, eternal and unyielding stone*—pulling him down with her as the fearsome voice echoed around them, bringing terror and temptation. He shook in her hands, forces vibrating through him until she could feel him splitting open. She poured the glow of the crystal into him then as the darkness chaining him rang and cracked, and then he ripped free, shattering the blackness in a cry of terror as light exploded around him. Ariadne spun out gasping into the moonlit night.

Peter thrashed, sweating and groaning. She touched him again, trying to send steadying energy into him. He wrenched sideways, flinging her hands away, and jerked upright with a scream.

His eyes sprang open. He fell against the side of the boat, panting, the crystal knocked clattering across the planks. "Oh, God...." Tears streamed down his face. He scrubbed his face with his hands, raked them through his hair, and looked wildly around.

He startled back, then lunged across the planks after the gleam of the crystal. He grabbed it, staring down at the facets, at Ariadne.

Fury in his face now. "What the hell are you doing to me?" His voice cracked. He thrust the crystal roughly at her.

"I felt your need, Peter. You told me yourself you needed to go into your fear."

"No. I didn't say you could...." He scrubbed his face again, sucking in a rasping breath. "You don't have the right."

She held the crystal, its cool weight anchoring her. "If your leg was broken, wouldn't you want it healed? I had to help you heal the old wounds."

"Don't cop out with that Saint Ariadne mumbo-jumbo! Look at me, damn it!" He grabbed her arms, and the crystal fell from her grasp. "Maybe you think you own *me* now, but you don't. Just remember how you felt when that snake Leeza linked you up to her machine in your sleep."

She flinched from his eyes. "That wasn't the same."

"Looks like it from here! You can't make those kind of choices for me. It's not part of the deal."

"Yes it is—part of the deal! If you want me, if you want my love, this is part of it. Part of what I am. There is no halfway, Peter! If you cannot face yourself, if you reject what I give you, then you reject me, too."

"That's bullshit! It's always play by your rules, isn't it?" His grip on her arms tightened, hurting her.

"Let me go!" She wrenched away. The surf crashed, drumming in her ears. She was losing her grip, losing the reins to the clashing forces, and the moonlight was liquid fire now, burning her skin. She turned to fling herself over the side, into the beckoning coolness of the sea.

"Ariadne!"

The sound of ripping cloth, and she was falling free of his clutch, gasping as the salty cold closed around her. She knifed through it, flying. But the moonlight was a rippling web around her now. She couldn't escape. The coils only tightened, pulling her up onto the sand, choking her as she stumbled through the lapping shallows.

"Wait!" A splash behind her. Peter broke through the surface.

She ran against the resistance of the waves, stumbling. He caught her from behind.

"Damn it, Ariadne, don't run! Driving us both crazy—"

She tried to wrench free, but only flung herself off-balance in his grip and they both fell in the foaming surge. The fire was a madness in her now, a boiling flood behind a straining dam. She hissed and clawed at him, fighting him even as the forces rolled up through her from the wet sand and the rock below it, sweeping her will before it. Her hands closed on him, pulling him tight against her.

"What in bloody hell is going on?" His eyes were wide and blind in the moonlight.

Then there was only flaring red on blackness as they grappled and writhed between land and sea, his hands ripping the rags of her dress, pressing hot on her breasts as her fingers groped over his slippery skin. They grunted and howled like animals as the net of moonlight pulsed and tightened, binding them together.

She bit and scratched, panting with the heat pouring through her. She gripped him, demanding, and he thrust violently into her. They both cried out.

They're swept down a river of blood, plunging through the rapids and up the bank as her thighs grip the heaving flanks of the bull—

They gallop into the cavern, tremors shaking the earth. It closes around them, laboring and groaning. They are nothing now, only a part of subterranean cataclysms, shuddering as lava surges and bursts free. Then no more awareness, no will, only a devouring something ancient and other, wearing the faces of the redrock monolith, the coal-black master of the magma depths. Blind power claiming its human vessels.

68

BLUE FACETS, GLEAMING AROUND her. Leeza's inside the crystal, shooting down its sapphire tunnel, light glowing through it, splashing around the mazelike corners. Sea waves surge, the etched horny bull lunges, and the flying serpents swirl along. They're alive, growing. Incandescent Cherenkov's blue, electric, hums her nerves on fire and Leeza is the light—

"Shit, girl! You zoned out again." The door slammed, Damiana scowling, fists on hips. "You give I that dope, see if you get with the program."

Leeza jolted upright, scrambling back to huddle against the wall, the etched blue crystal clutched in her fist.

"You give it to I now." Two long strides, and she had Leeza's wrist in her grip, prying her fingers open.

"No, it's mine, ow, give it back!" The blue stone fell into Damiana's palm. She looked down, nostrils flaring as she started to fling it aside.

Leeza pounced and grabbed it, fumbling for the hash pipe and thrusting that at her. "Here, take it. You don't give a rat's ass what happens to me."

Damiana snorted, slipping the pipe into a fold of her drab dashiki. "The vial, too." Husky voice impatient, hand out. She'd taken off her rings and bracelets. A round cap hid the long braids, and she wasn't wearing any makeup.

"Decided to turn into a man again?"

Damiana ignored the taunt. "The vial." Then, as Leeza grudgingly handed it over, "You got any more pills stashed?"

"You went through my stuff already. What's it to you?"

"Nothing to I what you do to yourself later, but now you got to get straight, you going to stay with this show. You want to look at youself—lay here drooling over pretty rocks, too stoned to wash you face."

"What am I supposed to do, you locking me up in this hole and leaving me clueless? I want out of this flophouse, somewhere with a shower where I'm not afraid to walk into the bathroom and get the clap just from breathing. I need some medicine for this rash." She pointed to her bare feet, where little red blisters had started to form. "And I want a decent meal in a restaurant."

"You stay here. Boys and I keep low this time, wait on the Greeks to get back with the score before I and I move out at night. I got a watch on that bank, she got to go in person, she want to access that trust account. But I think big daddy *Tyrannos* right, she heading straight for this Del-phi. So I set a trap for she. Remember, I got to keep you locked in so the Demodakis boys thinking you truly a hostage. No difference to Damiana, you want to fill they in."

Leeza glared, the pleasant hash haze shredded. She didn't dare ask if Demodakis had played fair and given the mercenaries the word to bring her back okay along with Ariadne. Damiana hadn't dropped any clues, but then she wouldn't, the bitch. The *Tyrannos* could be screwing her over royal, and there was nothing she could do. The scene was definitely out of control.

Damiana turned, folds of the dashiki swaying gracefully, to hoist Leeza's recorder bag and plop it on the bed beside her. "So get you head clear, you got work to do for Damiana."

"What work?" She eyed her suspiciously.

White teeth flashed. "We see how smart you be now, Ms. Media Stim Lady. You know enough to set up a data base, scan news reports?"

"Sure. I'm a pro."

"Right. Then you get the straight dope on this new Pan-Palestine uprising, what the Moslem reactionaries doing. Turner, he getting too full of heself, he going to dick around and screw up. So maybe I check out another scene."

Madre, she wished her head would stop throbbing. "What's this got to do with Ariadne?"

"No ting. 'Cept maybe Sons of Prophet too busy now over east to meddle here. Damiana just ready for this one to be over, whole lot of double talk and wasting time, then she done with Turner and heading for where the action at. Sound like it suit I style more."

Leeza shrugged and started unpacking her gear. "Depends on what transmissions I can pick up. I might need to get to a data center, scan some chips."

"You get what you can here."

She rolled her eyes. "Then you've got to bring me some food. And I mean a decent meal, like a real synth New York cut and baked potato, or at least a nice thick burger, not that greasy Greek crap, it's messing me up. *Madre*, could I go for a genuine milkshake!" Ages since she'd had a craving for red meat, real or synth, but the seasick queasiness was gone, and all of a sudden she was ravenous.

"Where you finding that kind of meal?"

Not looking up from her gear, Leeza flicked a dismissing hand. "That's *your* problem."

"So wrong." With one of those catlike moves, Damiana was beside her, plucking her up off the bed and pinioning one arm tight behind her, the other hand glinting a knife up and under Leeza's chin. "You problem, girl, you diss Damiana."

"Shit! Hey...." She choked as the sharp tip pressed the flesh above her adam's apple, and she was straining up on tiptoe away from it.

The knife tilted, flat of it sliding slowly from side to side across her throat, blade just scraping the skin.

"Damiana, don't...." She sobbed, "Please."

The hold on her wrist tightened, tears springing into her eyes, and she gasped, cringing as the blade pivoted, point starting to dig in, flicking and teasing. A sharp sting, then Damiana was thrusting her back onto the bed.

Leeza's hands went to her throat, came away with a tiny stain of blood. "Oh, god...."

"See that? That real, Ms. Conreid. You think on that, you playing this chickenshit make-believe like you some kind of bad. You flake when it come down for real, little Lee-za?"

Leeza scraped the tears angrily from her cheeks, chin thrusting out. "Then why drag me along? Why don't you just do it, get rid of me?" Her heart was slamming wildly against her ribs, but she clamped her jaw.

Damiana looked down, and her husky deep chuckle broke out. "That better." She reached up and pulled off the cap, shaking the beaded braids free with little clicks. "So you got some promise from big *Tyrannos*? But you not knowing how much it worth, you thinking maybe Damiana and the boys give a fuck you live or die. You catching on." She pulled the dashiki off and tossed it on the bed, unfastened the band flattening her breasts under the disguise. They sprang free, a trickle of sweat glistening between them on the shiny dark skin as she turned to pace her restless tiger strides across the room and back.

Leeza watched, fascinated by the play of muscle in dark shoulders and arms as Damiana stretched and turned, the contrast of the perfect firm globes of those fake breasts riding above the narrow hips, the mesh of long, lean thighs and vivid white slash of the scanty thong dividing burnished haunches. She was a living piece of art.

Pale glint of teeth and eyes in the dimness as Damiana shot her a mocking look, still pacing. "*Tyrannos*, he get you confuse, heh, get you a little hot maybe? He looking like the daughter but you not sure it maybe she looking like he—big daddy?"

Leeza's hands clenched in the blanket.

"You like the smell of power, little Leeza? You don' want to see it, but you maybe liking to feel youself in he grip, think about he big rod splitting you open? Who's he they got here—Zeus, that the one, he the big shot throwing that thunderbolt around." Her hand chopped as she strode, taut energy filling the room. "Just you remember they all like that, just want a bigger dick, they big important wars and cause and countries. Don' mean shit, just screw whatever handy, include you. I know. The juice. Just so you know the score, you decide to play." The long legs planted themselves in front of Leeza.

She raised her gaze up the sweat-sheened height to meet dark eyes. "What was all that for?"

Damiana threw back her head and laughed. "Little Lee-za." She brought her face close. "You think twice about you trust he, that all. That family not even trusting they own. Turner just get a message from Demodakis, he say the other brother come from Crete with story Ariadne left to Egypt, but he thinking it bone rap like I figure. Now he keeping he own brother lockup, you think he keep promises to you?" Her eyes narrowed. "So you think about playing Damiana...."

Ice gripped her guts. Leeza managed to keep her eyes on Damiana's, keep herself from flinching. *Jodas!* She knew. But she was giving her a break, why? Turner. Damiana was holding out on Turner. Maybe that would give Leeza an edge, but....

Long fingers reached out to stroke Leeza's throat, dark eyes still holding hers as she tried not to cringe. Shit. *Shit*. And she couldn't help herself, that hot tingle ignited between her legs.

"Remember, girl. I know you, know they. You want to come out of this, you don' cross me." Her eyes waited.

"All right, all right. I told Demodakis you didn't get any data from Mitchell's computer about Ariadne's plans, but he already knew Turner was bluffing him." She caught a sharp, painful breath.

"That Turner problem. What else?"

Leeza started to shake her head, then blew out a gust. "Nothing, really, I mean I didn't think it mattered." She'd been saving it back, just to have something. "The only other thing he told me, I swear, he just happened to mention it when I was leaving, about this Chinese antique dealer in Athens, maybe she'd go there to sell her jewelry if she couldn't get to her account. That's it." She didn't dare tell Damiana now about Ariadne's data she'd copied, maybe it was all bullshit anyway. Fuck, what has she done? *Ariadne*.... How did she get herself into this? *Todo jodido.*

The strong fingers slid casually around her neck, tightening as Damiana leaned closer. "You forget this, then. Right?"

Leeza nodded hastily.

The fingers moved around to her shoulders and pulled her upright off the bed. Beads clicked as Damiana bent her head over Leeza's, tip of a pink tongue darting between parted lips. Leeza shivered at the touch of her mouth, tongue flicking against hers and teeth catching her lower lip, and then the tingle was kindling to a blaze up her spine.

She pulled back, gasping for breath. Her flattened palms slid over the lush curves of those chocolate breasts and she wanted to lick them, bury her face in their musky heat.

Damiana gripped her wrists. "Work first." She pushed her onto the bed beside the recorder gear. "You do a pro-fessional job, then I see." The mocking grin.

"Bitch." Panting, Leeza glared from the bed.

"That so right." Damiana pulled the dashiki over herself and sauntered out, lock clicking shut behind her.

69

IT WAS QUIET IN the cab of the produce truck, just the electric motor whir, now the driver had turned off the loud synth-pop tunes. Skinny little guy with a froglike face, he kept darting his stare from the headlights spearing the night road, across Peter's face, to Ariadne. She was gazing out the side window. Tension hummed, coiling tighter with the windup of the motor as they climbed a rise. The truck veered into a steep switchback down, setting the cloth baubles and miniature icons strung along the top of the windshield to quivering. The plastic suspended saint swung from side to side.

Peter jerked out a hand to stop it.

The driver shot them another look in the glow of the dashlights. "Your man, *Kyria*, he never talks?"

Beside Peter, she took a deep breath. "As I said, we have been to the doctors. They say he must rest his throat."

"So. You say you're not from Missolonghi? But yet you look like I should know you, *Kyria*."

She shook her head and turned back to the window. Peter could almost feel the waves of agitation rippling off her, ringing in his own ears. He was wound up tight as a spring. Like he'd felt on Crete before the earthquake, weight pressing down, only this time it was worse. He was afraid Ariadne, rigid beside him, was going to crack with it.

He reached for her fingers, squeezing them gently. She gripped his hand, hard. Closing her eyes, she leaned toward him to whisper, "*Efcharisto*, Petro."

He gave another little squeeze, murmuring near her ear, "Petros—the rock. That's me all over."

She released his hand and turned back to the window. Peter flexed his fingers and wanted to shake them, shake himself like a wet dog to throw off the dread shivering through them both. Growing, since that night in the cove. What had she done to him with her crystal? What had possessed them, driven them like animals rutting on the beach, everything else ripped aside by that blazing lust? Like it was feeding on them.... He shuddered. They'd both been leery of touching since.

She whispered in his ear, "Petros, I can't ask more of you. My father's men will be searching for me. And the mercenaries. They probably won't harm me, but you are in terrible danger. I'll get out at Amphissa to hike onto Parnassos. You go on with the driver to Athens."

He hissed, "No way!"

The driver was glancing at them again, openly suspicious now. Peter gripped Ariadne's wrist, stilling her. Past the side window, moonlight silvered the steep rock plunges and the breeze-shivered leaves of olive groves below, rippling shadow patterns.

The pitch of the engine changed again. A sign floated up before the headlights, hovering for a vivid second, then gone. *Amphissa 8 Km.*

The driver shot a look at Peter, and his hands shifted nervously on the wheel.

Peter sucked in a sharp breath. "*Stomat!*"

The driver jumped, swearing. "Stop? Here? You said Amphissa."

"Here. Now."

He glanced sideways again, speculation on his rubbery features. The engine wound up higher as the truck gained speed on a straight stretch, and the driver's gaze flicked toward the radio mike.

"Petro...." Ariadne pressed his arm in warning.

"I said let us out here." His ears were ringing, pressure pounding.

The driver, sweat gleaming on the folds of his face, looked Peter up and down. He pulled abruptly to the shoulder.

"Petro, what are you doing?"

He reached across her to unlatch the door, urging her out, pushing their bags to her and jumping down. "*Charisto.*" He slammed the door shut. The driver's gaze flicked toward the radio again, then he jerked the controls into gear. The truck buzzed away.

"Peter, now he knows you're not Greek!"

"I know, but I got a bad feeling about this." He rubbed his pounding head and shrugged irritably. Pushing the cords of her woven bag over her shoulder, he yanked on his knapsack straps and pulled her off the road onto a scrub-treed slope. "We had to get off the road soon, anyway. And I think if we head cross-country that way—" he pointed east toward dim, jagged peaks—"it's a shortcut across the road doubling back south from Amphissa. Just hope he doesn't get on the horn and blow the whistle...."

"The horn?" She stumbled as he hustled her down into the straggly cover. "The radio?" She shook her head, like she was trying to shake off the ringing, too. "I think his radio wouldn't work now. The pressures of colliding fields are building again." She pressed her fingers against her forehead.

Nearby, an owl hooted. Silent wings ghosted past.

Peter shivered, hand going to his waist where he'd thrust the pistol under his belt. "Feel like oil on a hot skillet." He rubbed his face. "Maybe I'm just—"

"No. You feel it, too. We must hurry."

She turned toward the black looming peaks, moonlight glittering over the rough slope, leaves shifting in agitated whispers. The flank of the mountain quivered like a taut drumhead.

70

"CHINGADA!" THE TRUCK JOUNCED over another pothole, throwing Leeza sideways in the dark to slam her shoulder against something sharp-edged in the pile of equipment rattling over the bare metal bed. The tarp tied over side rails flapped as they careened along the twisty road, cold drafts whipping in. Tires squealed as they tore around another switchback, throwing Leeza against Freddy and his lumpy ammo belt.

"Christ on a stick. Why did I have to come along, anyway?"

"Quit your bitching. You think she'd leave you behind to screw things up? If you'd get in here beside me, you wouldn't get thrown around." A hand out of the dark grasped her arm and pulled her roughly against his side, wedged between him and a pile of knapsacks.

She went stiff, then resigned herself to his muscle-bound arm braced around her shoulders. It was easier, steadied against him, so she let herself relax, rubbing her arm and pulling straight the rucked-up legs of the hideous camouflage pants they'd made her wear. "Just don't get any cute ideas."

He snorted. "I like a woman who's a woman."

Chortling from the dim figures sprawled on the other side of the truck bed.

"Ha ha." She sniffed. "And you're such a prize, Freddy, you deserve a real gold-plated pig."

More snorting laughter under the snap of the tarp. "Hear that, Freddy?"

The arm over her shrugged. "I just want to get this dragged-out joke over with."

"Hey, I hear you, man."

"Yeah, when the fuck we gettin' out of this truck, anyway?"

"Thought we'd be there by now." Flash of a lighted watch face. "Got to meet the other truck and the Med League boys, get dug in around this Delphi site."

"Still don't see why we gotta hoof all our gear in at night. Crappy hiking around here, break your leg in those rocks."

"You heard what Turner said. Place used to be some tourist draw—bunch of mostly rubble, stinking with history. Then the earthquakes and landslides got bad and finally closed off the roads. So we gotta hike in over a slide area. And avoid the locals."

"What do you mean? What's *this* shit now?"

"Huh. Maybe this is getting interesting after all."

"Probably nothing." Freddy shifted his legs. "But the Demodakis boys tried sounding out the villagers around, on maybe helping him recover his daughter from us 'kidnappers' and had they seen anything. Locals wouldn't give 'em the time of day. Boys said they were acting funny, like they were scared or hiding something. Just told them stay away from Delphi—and some kind of superstitious shit about 'the Furies' getting them. So stay on your toes."

"Chee-rist! All this just so's we can have us a little pretend skirmish with the Med League? I don't get it."

"You don't have to. Just remember, that's *after* we bag the Demodakis bitch. Turner and me, we got the sedative dart-guns, so nobody opens up until after we got her secured and safe out of it. You got that clear?"

"So okay, we don't hurt her. But what about that guy supposed to be with her, what if he opens up?"

"Only if you got a clear shot, and I mean you be sure on nightscope she's out of it, or your head's gonna roll. Then sure, take him out. Good to have a body, make things look real for the locals."

Leeza went stiff, hands clenching. For a minute she thought she was going to get sick again.

She shook herself. She didn't give a shit about Mitchell. Just another prick, asking for it dragging Ariadne all over hell, and he'd screwed yours-truly over good, now hadn't he? Hadn't he?

She took a deep, shaky breath. "You better be sure you don't hurt her!"

The tarp flapped again. The truck was slowing down, pulling over with one last tooth-rattling jar. It stopped.

Leeza scrambled onto her knees, pulling up the lashing and peering out. All she could see was a shadowed ditch. Up front, doors opened. Footsteps. Leeza was looking into Damiana's face. "Are we there? Why can't I ride up front with you?"

"Quiet." Voice pitched low, taut. She gripped some kind of dull black gun. "You get out now. McIntyre, Lorca—you, too." She moved around to the back.

Leeza crawled over Freddy's legs as he cursed and the tarp was pulled up at the back to let in a breeze carrying the tang of the sea. She scrambled over the tailgate and dropped to the ground. She blinked. Across the road, a sparsely treed slope dropped to the sheen of a moonlit bay. "Hey, I thought this place was supposed to be up in the mountains."

Damiana swung around and gave Leeza a casual cuff that sent her stumbling against the truck. "I tell you keep it down." She turned back to the others crawling with knapsacks and weapons out of the back. "You out too, Freddy."

They huddled, talking in low voices, ignoring Leeza as she edged closer to hear.

"...change of plan, I pick up word from Turner before radio reception go bad again. His contact turn up abandoned boat on the coast, west of here at Messolonghi. It match the one reported stole on north Crete. And he just got a sighting at a truck stop there, could be Demodakis woman and Mitchell."

"So maybe they're catching a ride this way?"

"Could be nothing. But if they coming that way, they got to come through here on the coast road, turn at Itea where I and I just pass through, or they taking inland route to Amphissa crossroad. Could be easy catch before she come to Delphi. Lorca, you and McIntyre, you roll a couple they big rocks onto the road ahead there, so any truck got to stop."

They moved up the road. Freddy nodded. "Okay, so I take this truck and the rest of the guys up by this other crossroad? Maybe have a breakdown blocking the way?"

"That right. You don't see anything coming close to dawn, you come back down and I and I all get up to Delphi with Turner and the Greek boys."

Freddy nodded.

"You remember, the Demodakis woman, she not to be hurt."

He raised the barrel of his weapon. "I got the sedative darts."

Damiana swung around to grasp Leeza's arm and pull her out of the shadow of the truck, raising her gun to point it at Leeza's forehead.

Everything went spinning, heart thudding. Cold sweat broke out.

A gleam of teeth in the night. "And I got bait."

71

ARIADNE HAD LOST HER grip on time. The steep trails winding and turning back on themselves and fading into goat tracks, black peaks bulking closer beneath the sinking moon—all was an endless maze of darkness and pulsing pressure.

A wordless chant rang in her ears, driving her on, pulling her inward to the cave mouth she could feel whispering on the mountainside. The song echoed inside her, ringing off crystalline facets. Ariadne was the crystal. Some part of her still fought it, but her feet were hurrying her on to the insistent beat. She ran, panting, stumbling up the rough slope. Her ankle turned in the shifting scree at the foot of a cliff.

"Ah!" Pain knifed, cutting through her trance. She caught herself against a boulder, heart pounding.

"Hold on." Peter puffed up behind her, taking her arm.

"Petro! Hold onto me." She gasped for breath. "Keep me human, Petro...."

"Here. Easy, now." He gave her a hug. "You keep this up, you're going to kill us both, Kri-Kri or not. Come on, let's sit up there." Where the rockslide ended, there was a dark patch of overhanging foliage. "We'll have a drink."

She nodded, throat parched.

He helped her limp over the short stretch, onto a rock shelf shadowed by drooping branches. "Is it bad?" He passed her his water bottle.

She swallowed gratefully, handing back the bottle and massaging her ankle. "Only twisted a little. It's feeling better already." A breeze shivered the tree's sparse limbs, stirring scents of dust and crushed leaves.

"Well take it a little slower, for chrissake." The lighted face of his watch flared. "It's only two-thirty, we've got the rest of the night to get there."

Ariadne kneaded her throbbing forehead. The demanding drumbeat only intensified. "No, we must hurry." She winced, the pain suddenly knifing her head.

Seconds later, a tremor rocked the cliffside beneath them.

72

"NOT AGAIN!" ADRENALINE BURNED through his edginess as Peter flung himself back from the lip of the rock shelf, falling against Ariadne as the earth shivered and groaned. Pebbles rained over them.

A sickening sliding motion, lifting them up and then suspending them for an impossible eternity. The rock finally dropped, slid down in a weird flowing. They dropped together, jarring onto the hard stone. Peter pulled Ariadne beneath the shield of his body as rocks came crashing from the cliff overhead, bouncing and clattering over them. One punched his shoulder.

Another grinding jolt. Dust settled around them to a last clatter of rocks. Echoing silence.

Peter pushed himself upright with a groan. Ariadne sat up. The thin branches overhead still trembled, dropping a few leaves.

"Are you hurt?" She peered through the shadows.

He worked his shoulder. "Just winged a little."

"That eased the pressure on the fault line. We should go on."

"Just rest, ten minutes."

A vague, impatient movement.

"Take it easy." His hand groped for hers. "You're sure about this cave up here?"

"Can't you feel it?" She coughed, went on hoarsely, "The old legends were right. The cavern of the nymphs. In ancient times there were wild bacchanals on this mountain. Dionysus and his Corybantes...."

He peered, trying to make out her expression. "I thought Delphi was Apollo's place—you know, light and logic."

She answered in a halting whisper, like she was only half there, "But Apollo took over Mount Parnassus from older powers.... He slew the ancient *Pytho*, the sacred dragon, earth serpent. It's said there was a bronze column here, until the Turks stole it hundreds of years ago, of three intertwined serpents. The two serpents rising, many cultures have depicted that, but three...?" She sighed, shaking her head. "Perhaps the meaning is lost."

She glanced at Peter and cleared her throat. "Even before the Delphi temple site was declared the *omphalos*—the navel, the center of the world—this mountain was sacred to the earth goddess. The ancient word *delphis* meant womb, or cave. There are stories, too, of a lost secret passage from the inner caverns up here on the mountainside, leading to the temple site below."

"And this *omphalos*? You think it's inside a cave?"

Her hand tensed beneath his, like she was gripping the rock to hold herself down. "There is power here, Peter. A connection going deep into the earth." A shaky breath. "But now the unbalanced forces are whirling around it, blocked, building until the violence must break loose." She shuddered.

His hand squeezed hers. "You sure you're ready for this... whatever it is you do? Can I help?"

She shook her head. "I must finish what I started. The final locus of the triad."

"And then?" He was suddenly bone-tired. "You said this was some kind of trial just for this region. What if it works, and you get the energy fields balanced here? What about the rest of the world? You going to kill yourself trying to take that on, too? And healing the RPH victims just for icing on the cake?"

Her hand pulled away from his, groping for her etched crystal pendant. "I don't have a choice. I'm only an empty vessel for the power." Her voice seemed far away.

Peter shuddered. "What if we're both going crazy?"

She squared her shoulders. "We need to move on now."

He sighed. "First let me take a look. We'll be exposed on this slope." He scooted to the edge of the rocky lip, peering down, raising the binoculars and setting them for nightscope. "Looks like the tremor broke off part of that ridge down below. Wait, what's—?" He caught a quick breath.

Coming into focus now, just visible beyond the ridge, were two fluted stone columns—no, three—set in a broken-off curve and joined by a thread of crumbling cornice. Silvered by moonlight, the slender shafts looked impossibly delicate and unreal, cupped in the desolation of cliffs and broken rock.

Peter passed her the binoculars.

"Ahh…." She slowly lowered them. "The Tholos of Athena. I visited it long ago… with my mother. A magic place. In the spring it's carpeted with grape hyacinth, tiny lizards scurrying over the rocks. We sat in the shade of the sweet bay trees and listened to the bees. I swore I could see the ancient ones dancing among the ruins." She touched his hand. "Someday, Petro, I would like to walk among those sacred stones in the sunlight with you."

He touched her shoulder. "It's a deal." He took the binoculars back and scanned again. "Thought I saw something…." He swept the lenses to the left.

Tiny figures etched in monotone night-vision moved directly below them on the slope, darting in quick crouches along the jagged ridge. One of them paused before the cut newly opened by the tremor. The figure turned to scan upward as Peter held his breath, the pale blur of face somehow broadcasting fierceness. An arm waved, beckoning the others along.

The focus sharpened: rough belted tunics and leather leggings, glinting spears along with slung rifles, darting synchronized movements as each passed the open spot to melt into the shadows of broken rock. They were women. Holding back their braided or short-cropped or loose long hair, each one wore a knotted dark headband, some kind of white design on it.

"Damn," he whispered. He handed Ariadne the binoculars. "Take a look."

She frowned and swept the lenses. She stiffened and lowered the binoculars. "The eye in the spiral," she whispered. "Corybantes."

73

DESPITE ARIADNE'S URGENT ARGUMENTS, Peter was stubborn as stone: They had to wait after spotting the women warriors. She huddled beside him on the rock ledge, chafing as the moon sank behind the peaks above them and its light faded from the open slope. Serpents of colored auroras writhed over the dark land, filmy streamers twisting across the sky to the pulse of the geomagnetic fields.

The tumult shivered her, crescendoing to a roar in her ears. Voices screamed in the swirling dark, calling her.

Old Cassandra's warning shrilled: *"You must stay, learn the old ways."* But there was no time, and the power was howling through her.

"I must go!" She wrenched away from Peter's grip, scrambling heedless over the ledge and loose rocks in the dark. She caught herself and lurched onto the nearly-invisible trail. The forces caught her, and she ran blindly up the rough slope.

"Ariadne!" His cry was swallowed by the wind.

No knowing how many times she stumbled and fell, catching herself on the sharp stones and scrambling mindlessly on, panting for breath and only vaguely aware of the pain in her bleeding hands. Once she heard Peter's voice as he nearly caught up, calling, "Ariadne, wait!" But the surging forces rang louder, insistent, as the pressure built and built and the mountainside groaned beneath her.

Finally she staggered over a crest, into the deeper darkness at the foot of another ridge. She fell to her knees, sobbing for air, before a black slash in the overhanging cliff. The earth groaned again. Cold air gusted over her, then ebbed back, into the cave mouth. Thrusting herself numbly to her feet, she clambered up the rocky debris toward the entrance.

"Are you out of your mind!" He grabbed her from behind. A curse as they were both staggered by another tremor. "You can't go in there!" Peter panted, clutching her arm.

The voices were calling. She fought to break free from him.

"There's a quake ready to cut loose and cave it in on you! We'll get up onto that solid outcrop, ride it out."

"It will be too late." She wrenched against his grip. "I must go now!"

A sharp crack echoed up the mountainside. They both froze. Then a percussive explosion—gunshots, far below.

"What next?" He swung around, dragging her back from the cleft. "We've got to get out of here."

"No!" The power roared inside, and a frenzied strength possessed her. She flung sideways, kicking out to knock him back from her. He fell with a startled cry. She didn't care if he was hurt. The voices, the seething powers owned her, and she had to get inside the cavern to join them.

Again she attacked the slope of loose rock, scrambling up and through the narrow gap. Inside, blackness claimed her. Damp cold gusted. Stumbling blindly forward, she came up hard against the base of a stalagmite. She followed the pull of the vortex toward the sound of dripping water. The earth shivered beneath her, a deep beast-bellow echoing as she fell to her knees at the foot of a stone column.

She spread her arms and lay against it, rock slippery against her face. Against a heavy resistance, one hand groped for the etched crystal on her breast. She whirled down the spiraling roots of the stone pillar. Down the black cord of the *omphalos* into the earth.

Clashing forces toss her like a leaf in a gale, winds shrieking. Titan voices howl with laughter at her puny invasion here in the realm of Chaos. Explosions tear the air, ripping her apart, flinging her pieces spinning to the ends of the earth—

All she had left was her hand. She gripped the etched lattice of her quartz crystal, a faint glow in the voracious blackness. She clutched it, pushing its harmonic light outward, but the darkness squeezed in on her with another cataclysmic roar. Icy fingers split apart the polished facets, breaking the lattice to scatter the ordered fragments in bright tiny stars swallowed by the nothingness of space.

The black fingers tightened on Ariadne. Peeling back her skin, they flung its warmth into the screaming vortex. Layer by layer, the darkness shredded her.

Memory and will, gone.

Now there was only vague identity—*helpless infant squalling hunger and terror, groping in the dark for the breast.* Ariadne groped—*a huge figure of iron-red clay and blocky face wreathed by cloud cradles her close to a mountainous swollen breast and the river of honeyed milk a nurturing sweetness*—and she touched Her.

But with a sharp pain, she was ripped from the Mother's warmth, flung through the darkness screaming and writhing. Another agonized ripping, and identity vanished, too. *A furred beast scrabbles sideways, snarling and snapping at the fingers of blackness harrying her.*

One more layer, one more explosion of pain. Another shell of being whirled away, leaving only a cold, sluggish pulse. *A lizard clings to a black rock, darting her tongue to taste threat, moving reflexively away but not fast enough.*

More ripping, peeling pain, oddly filtered now, and then merely an amorphous wriggling shape in a black salty sea. *Primitive responses ignite to chemical changes as the organism shrivels, reduced to dust blown away in the howling nothingness.*

She struggled to remember why she was here. There had to be order somewhere in the chaos, a hand gripping to an etched crystal lattice of light.

There. Warmth. A tiny spark in the frozen wastes. If only she could rekindle it....

Howling with laughter, a cyclone whirled down on her, snuffing the spark, tearing loose the walls of the rock tunnel. A serpentine form stirred deep in the earth, screaming in pain, black coils twisting upward over the subterranean roots of the stone column, shaking it. The coils tightened around Ariadne, squeezing the air from her.

The earth quaked as giant redrock hands reached down to Ariadne.

If only she could stretch up and catch those hands, climb to that haven. But she was trapped in the stone. Choking, the black serpent strangling her. She had to reach the Mother's giant hands stretched out to her, had to find her own hand gripping the crystal with its buried light—

"Ariadne!" Rough hands grabbed her. They pulled her through the blackness, fists pounding her ribs as air whistled painfully through her lungs, and then—

The hands tried to rip the crystal pendant from her fingers. *Stop!* But she couldn't find her voice. The hands tore the last spark of light from her grip.

Ariadne clawed for the crystal, but the air hurt her lungs and the beast had her in its clutches, dragging her into the roaring madness of tremors and crashing rocks. The earth split open, spitting her out.

74

"MITCHELL, YOU'VE FINALLY DONE it. Lost your goddamn mind." Peter heaved himself up from the rock rubble, wincing and working his bruised shoulder. He started up the shifting scree toward the black gap in the cliffside where Ariadne had disappeared. Pulling off his knapsack, he rummaged for a flashlight. Another tremor shivered the loose rocks.

"Don't believe this...." But of course he was going to crawl into an unstable rocky crevice in the middle of an earthquake—why not? Scrambling on all fours, flashlight held gritted between his teeth, he froze at the distant stutter of gunfire down the mountainside. What more could possibly go wrong?

He had to work himself up to duck through the narrow black opening, damp cold gusting from the cave. He shuddered. Taking a deep breath, he plunged through.

Darkness closed over him. There was a distant slow dripping. He snapped on the light, beam skittering as he edged forward. He stopped short as a dark void swallowed the flash beam. He could feel the immensity of the cavern opening up before him in echoes of the earth's shivering. Waves of urgency washed off the walls to lap over him, through him. He jerked the flash lower, caught glimpses of towering rock columns, stalagmites glinting. He swept the light over a rock wall hung with a lacy dripping curtain of rock, up toward the sharp spikes of stalactites, impenetrable darkness overhead.

A beastlike growl rolled out of the subterranean depths. The floor beneath him shivered.

Where was she? They had to get out. Pulse pounding, he ran through the cavern, beam raking wildly back and forth. A sound of water, closer now. More stalagmites. The light caught her.

She sprawled at the base of a massive rock column. His heart stopped— she'd fallen, hurt herself. She lay still. Then she stirred, moaning, and he could see she was gripping her crystal pendant.

He started forward, then froze. An icy presence breathed out of the rock pillar, oozing up from the black depths it was rooted in. But that was ridiculous. Another tremor shook the cavern, stronger, pebbles spattering around him as he staggered. Red sparks pulsed behind his eyes, pressure swelling to split him open.

"Out. Gotta get out." He dropped to his knees to grasp her shoulder. "Ariadne."

She moaned, twisting away from him.

"Ariadne! Come on." He tried to gather her up off the floor. She struggled, arching back and striking her head on the stone column.

The floor was really moving now, a deep grinding in the earth. Grappling her, he dropped the flashlight. He fumbled, found it, swept it over her face. Shock sent his heart slamming as he saw her blind, glinting eyes and features fixed in an agonized rictus, one hand clawing the air as a horrible labored wheezing rasped out of her. She convulsed, fighting for air, one hand still clenched on her quartz pendant.

"Jesus...." He caught her against him, dragging her up off the floor and thumping his fist against her back until she gasped in air. But then she was fighting him again, as he half-dragged, half-carried her through the cavern. She was still clutching the damned necklace, twisting it tight around her neck and choking herself.

The cavern jarred and rumbled. Fragile pillars snapped, rocks clattering down as he darted and dodged. He stopped to rip the pendant from her grip, yanking the necklace over her head.

She screamed, "The crystal!"

He lurched over the shaking slippery floor, almost dropping the flash as she clawed at him. The beam swerved in wild arcs through the echoing blackness. He started to fling the blasted necklace away, but then he tugged the loop over his own head. He heaved her onto his shoulder, running for it.

He jolted to a stop. Did he get turned around in the maze? He couldn't find the gap. No, there it was. He dragged them out and down the scree slope, rocks dancing like peas in a hopper. He skidded down among them. Finally hitting solid footing, he ran along the foot of the cliff, toward the solid outcrop he'd seen earlier, panting and staggering under his burden. A tremendous roar behind them. He came up short, Ariadne sliding to the ground. Peter whirled to look back along the mountainside, past the cave entrance.

A black mass burst free from a higher cliff and plunged onto the forested plateau they'd crossed earlier, swallowing it and plummeting on. Shock waves rolled up the mountainside as thunder split the air.

Ariadne screamed. She sprang to her feet and attacked him, berserk, as he staggered in the aftershocks. She clawed viciously for the necklace at his throat.

"Wait, stop it! Ariadne!"

She clutched at the necklace, choking him as she stumbled against him over the heaving ground. He managed to rip her hand free, catch a breath as he groped for her other arm, but she swung around, clawing like a madwoman. He tripped over something, lost his footing, went sailing backwards over empty air.

Pain blossomed into blackness.

75

ARIADNE WAS LOST IN the dark. She had to keep running. Was she running to, or from? The coils of the black serpent squeezed her spine, driving her on.

She'd fallen countless times in her scramble down the mountainside, but the pain in her knees and hands was numbed by exhaustion, muted by the pulse goading her on. Down, in shivering aftershocks. Into another winding ravine. Black cliffs reared against a night sky of writhing auroras. She staggered, panting, down a goat track.

The ravine opened into a valley, leaves whispering a taunting promise of rain. She blundered beneath their limbs and across a narrow stream. Tripping over slippery rocks, she fell splashing.

The cool water soothed her scraped skin and eased the maddening heat pulsing through her. She sat in the shallow current, chest heaving for air. Her hammering heart finally slowed. She bathed her face, gulped handsful tasting of windchilled heights, and pulled herself out the other side.

The beat up her spine still insisted, but now she could go more slowly, as long as she kept moving. When she tried to stop and rest beneath the trees, voices shrilled in her ears, crescendoing to an unbearable pitch. She dragged herself on, over another open slope. Her hand crept to her throat, fingers groping. They found only an absence.

The crystal pendant. Petros.

The ringing was louder in her ears, driving her on, toward a gleaming ribbon winding through the maze of dark hills below. She was running from the pursuing Furies. Petros had stolen her etched crystal. He, too, was after her. Betrayed. They'd all betrayed her, betrayed the earth. The mountainous stone goddess howled in outrage, shaking. Ariadne had to escape the raging turmoil, had to find the crystal and the refuge of its serene lattice.

She staggered over an embankment, onto the hard surface of a road. Dizzy, she planted her legs, weaving. The road hummed beneath her feet, and lights stabbed out of the night. Closing her eyes, she threw out her hands, braced for the impact.

A squeal of tires, grinding gears, backwash of wind. A voice barked, "Are you crazy? You want to die?"

She swayed in front of the harsh lights. They dimmed, and the voice called again, "You in trouble? You need a ride?"

She moved slowly around the truck cab, staring blankly at the flat wooden bed and stone slabs strapped onto it. The door beside her pushed open. In the glow of dashlights, a thickset man leaned across the seat, impatient. "You want a ride or not? Those quakes might start up again. Got to get this marble to Athens."

Athens. A memory, deeply buried, stirred. She frowned, but all she could see from a hazy distance was her mother's face, bending over her with a gentle smile. "Remember, it will be there for you, in Athens, if you need it. Your trust..."

Trust. What did it mean? She didn't know, couldn't grasp it through the sparks of pain in her head. She managed a stiff nod. "Athens." She climbed numbly into the truck.

76

DREAMS OF A PALE-faced woman
arms like white snakes
slithering cool through the leaves like the moonlight from her face.
Mouth a red well.

Her voice, insistent whisper, surrounds him and he lies helpless as the flesh rises like a tide. He's drawn, pulled in. He looks down, the crimson lips are devouring him and her eyes are slivers of ice. His thrusting hips pump blood, the spray sucked into air, and a crimson stain slowly rises over the floating white cratered features. His glassy eyes hold the image of a red moon, wicked smile tracking the night sky.

Peter's gut wrenches. The world spins dizzily and the moon's beneath him—a crimson reflection?—no, pulsing orb blurred deep in black waters, but rising as the sea drains from her shoulders. She's immense, an iron-red towering mountain of vast thighs, swollen belly, enormous pendulous breasts. And far above him, veiled in cloud, an impassive face stares down as the stone ridges of her thighs strain and shudder with the earthquake, squeezing him, crushing him in toward her core. A heavy beat pounds in his head and loins. He's trapped between horror and primal lust, and he throws back his head to scream his agony up at her.

The giant stone mask turning down to him has Ariadne's face, Ariadne's distant eyes—

Peter bolted upright, sweating, head pounding. He groaned and fell back, stars exploding behind his eyes, pain throbbing upward from his left leg and of all things a raging hard-on.

"Sonuva...." He lay there panting, trying to get a handle on the different agonies, blinking in filtered light. Where the hell was he?

Daylight glowed behind a dirt-encrusted corrugated plastic roof. He was lying on piled straw in a shack with concrete-brick walls. A goat pen, from the stink and the scatter of dried dung on the dirt floor. A thick leather strap was locked around his right wrist, chain bolted into the wall, probably an animal hobble.

Overhead, a whispering patter. Soothing, like surf. He blinked, rolling his eyes toward the ceiling and the spatter of drops on plastic. "Rain?" he croaked.

The effort made his head hurt worse. And his left leg was screaming, somehow heavy and cold and burning all at the same time. He raised himself carefully on his elbows to look under the frayed blanket draped over him. Someone had taken off his clothes and spread what looked like a tablecloth between him and the straw. His leg was propped on a wicker basket, splinted with flattened metal rods that must have come off some kind of machinery, wrapped with rags and duct tape.

"Damn." He tried to move his foot and felt bones grinding in his calf. He bit off a cry. Sagging back in the straw, he took deep breaths until the pain ebbed.

Hell of a mess all around. Who had him? Did they get Ariadne? Maybe better if they did. Gone berserk. Crazy all along? He was the crazy one, mixed up in this shit, hadn't he sworn he'd never be suckered again? Fanatics. He wouldn't think about Ariadne, wouldn't let himself see her smiling up at him beside the sail, eyes deep and purple-blue clear as the sea. *Damn*. But there was nothing he could do now, leg broken, he was out of it. And some part of him was relieved.

His hand had crept unthinking over his chest, fingers closing over her quartz pendant.

That was it—he'd pulled the blasted necklace off her. His grip tightened to yank it off. But the slippery planes and etched pattern felt good. Soothing. He closed his eyes and took another deep breath. Rain pattered overhead.

"Food." The wood door of the hut crashed open and light streamed in. A woman stood in the doorway, rifle cradled in one arm, covered basket in the other. She set the basket down, scooted it toward him with her foot, and stood back warily. "You eat now."

The English was awkward, intonation wrong, like she was just parroting the phrase. She was a short woman, probably about thirty though her weatherbeaten face looked older. Short and thickly built, she looked strong. She was wearing cross-strapped leggings and a rough wool tunic with an ammo belt. One side of her head had the usual thick dark peasant braid, the other cut short and bristly. Made her square features look lopsided beneath a black headband with a white design of a spiral and a staring eye.

He gritted his teeth and leaned over to pull the basket closer. Ignoring the hunks of bread and cheese, he grabbed the plastic water bottle and took long greedy swallows. He leaned back to catch his breath, eyeing her. Moisture glinted over her hair and shoulders. Clearing his throat, he thanked her in Greek. "It's raining? That's good, with the drought."

She looked startled. "Only a little, a storm from the earthquake." Then she caught herself, gripping the rifle tighter. "You speak Greek, yet you come from America?"

"Piraeus, now. Where am I? Why are you keeping me here?"

She frowned. "We would have killed you, but we think you're not one of the mercenaries invading our mountain. You were with Ariadne Demodakis?"

"That's right." They must not have found her.

"If we didn't believe that, we would kill you now. Though she won't need you when she joins us. We allow men only for the ceremonies." A cryptic smile. Her head tilted toward his chest. "Did she give you that necklace?"

"I— Yes, she gave it to me." He realized with annoyance he was touching the polished crystal again, and he dropped his hand onto the blanket. "What do you mean, when she joins you?" Corybantes, that was it, Ariadne had said that... last night? He racked his brain. News clips hadn't said much about them, really. But there was something....

"No more questions." Her eyes shifted uneasily from the pendant. "Take the food out and push the basket back. There's pain medicine, too. Your leg is broken, so don't think you can escape."

He tossed the basket to her feet. She picked it up and backed to the doorway.

"How long are you going to keep me here? What do you want with me?"

"Rest. You'll be questioned later." She started to pull the door shut.

"Damn it, wait! You can't just—"

"We do what we will, what no man tells us." She turned back to regard him impassively. "You look like strong stock. If you obey, we might let you recover to be crowned the vine king. To claim the throne and its pleasures for the rest of your life."

"What?" His head was throbbing again. "Vine king? But you allow no men...."

Again the odd smile, before the door latched shut. "The vine king reigns only for one night."

77

ROSE-FINGERED DAWN GLOWED behind jagged hills. Tires swished, engine buzzing, ringing in her ears.

"You had trouble in your village? Your man denounce you and drive you out?"

Ariadne's body was heavy, pulse sluggish, cold scaly coils weighing her down inside. Her head turned slowly toward the voice.

"No offense, I can see, such a beauty as you.... But you're in bad shape. Athens can be tough. You want somebody to look after you. I got a room, you can get cleaned up there, rest a little."

A thick-fingered hand sprouting black hairs moved through her tunnel of vision. It rested, squeezing. After a moment she realized it was her thigh the fingers pressed.

She had to find the commands to raise her face toward the source of the voice. The man's face was very far away, yet sharply outlined in detail—florid color beneath sun-deepened brown skin, heavy beard shadow, aggressive slope of nose, thick lips pulled into an insinuating smile. She studied it like an alien landscape.

The dark-eyed glance shifted sideways to hers. The smile turned uneasy, then faded.

In the odd diminishing magnification, Ariadne could see the pores of his face produce a sheen of sweat. The hand jerked away from her leg and gripped the steering wheel. The buzzing intensified as the truck picked up speed.

78

"...ACCELERATING INSTABILITIES. THE ONLY recent bright note, an anomalous, geomagnetically stable zone around Crete and the Cycladic islands, may also be a false hope. The zone now appears to be weakening, suffering incursions of fluctuation...."

Silent laughter rasped mirthless down the Link. Leeza's fingers twitched, feeding another channel into the box.

*** "...escalating violence of internal Palestinian—"***

Bored, she shunted to internal chip storage.

Delphi Archives Three, English Translation. Image of a big egg-shaped stone, carved with a netlike leafy design. "The omphalos stone, now removed for safekeeping to the Athens museum, marked the navel of the world at Delphi. In archaic times, the omphalos was guarded by the monster Pythia, a python or possibly a mythical dragon embodying the dark powers of the earth. In pre-Homeric times the new sun-god Apollo fought and slew it. Notice the intricate carving, symbolic of...."

Leeza made a face and yanked off the headgear, tossing it onto the master box. *"Mierda."*

She rubbed her face, took a deep breath of stale hot air, jerked to her feet to pace the shabby room. Another stifling fleabag hotel, this one right in Athens, but more of the same. Her stomach growled. She grabbed a hunk of cheese and the half-eaten loaf off the cluttered nightstand, wolfing down barely-chewed mouthfuls as she paced. She stopped again to gulp from the pitcher of lukewarm reconstituted milk she'd finally badgered Chuck into locating for her. Tilting the pitcher higher, she choked, milk spilling down her chin.

Fumbling the pitcher onto the nightstand, she coughed, dragged the back of her sleeve over her mouth, and grabbed up a handful of dried figs.

She froze, catching sight of her reflection in the cloudy mirror on the wall. An acid taste rose in her throat. She dropped the figs back in the bowl, feet dragging her over to the mirror.

"Madre de Dios...." Puffy blue eyes stared out of the chipped silvering, face without makeup mottled and sunburned—somewhere she'd lost her sunscreen lotions but worrying about skin cancer lately didn't seem like such a priority item. She was a mess, all right. Lank pale hair growing out of the style, hanging limp. Crumbs and milk stains blotching her wrinkled T-shirt. And the damned itchy rash spreading up her back, little red spots on the back of her hands now, too. Damiana had finally brought her some antifungal ointment, but it hadn't helped.

Out of control. *Todo jodido.*

Nobody was talking, only got pissed when she tried to find out about Ariadne. Things were tense since Esther and Hollywood had bit the big one up at that Delphi ambush, crazy cult women attacking, screwing the whole plan. Fucking hilarious, really, but nobody laughing. Whole scene over before Damiana had given up the roadblock and gone up there. Maybe Ariadne hadn't even gone through there at all. And now Damiana wouldn't tell her diddly, just left her locked up in here except when she could talk Chuck into taking her on a food hunt....

Leeza's bod was freaking out on her. Couldn't seem to help pigging out, she'd never been that big on food before but now her stomach was actually bloating, all her skin felt hot and swollen and she could hardly stand to wear anything tight over her breasts. She needed her stash—nothing fancy only a few uppers to get things back on a leash—but Damiana was being a complete bitch.

"Chuck!" She screamed, pounding on the bolted door. "Chuck, you asshole, let me out of here or I'm gonna scream this place down!"

Muffled voices rose in complaint down the hall. Stomping footsteps. Snap of the bolt, and the door crashed open. Chuck loomed over her, bleary-eyed in camo pants and matted black chest hair, one oversized hand clenching into a fist as he backed her into the room, his casted arm swinging in its sling.

Leeza cringed, babbling, "All right, just take it easy, I didn't mean it, it's just I'm going stir-crazy in here." She eyed him warily. "Look, I know it's a drag for you, too, stuck here watching me. Nobody said we can't go out for a while, right?"

He rubbed his face, swore, and backed up to yell out the door at someone whining down the hall. He swung back around, glaring down at her. "Turner'll have my ass, we're not here when they get back. He's pissed already over that fuckup in the mountains. We might have to move out fast again." He swung the door shut and thudded over to scoop up a handful of figs.

Leeza snatched the rest before he ate them all. Chewing, she asked casually, "So what was the big deal this morning? What are they doing now?"

He eyed her, chewing with his mouth open. Dreck, never hit brain-birth. He shrugged. "Some new lead. Bullshit, you ask me, all this big deal over some half-cracked bitch."

Leeza's hands clenched. "She's not crazy." She stared down at the Demodakis ring on her finger, deep blue gem glinting. *Eternal and unyielding stone.* She laughed raggedly. "Maybe we're all crazy, Chuck. You ever think of that?" She dropped onto the bed. "Look, maybe you want to do something to get out of the doghouse, huh?"

"Forget it." He took the last fig from her grasp, turning for the door.

"No, wait. They questioned that old Chinese guy, right? But you think he's going to tell *them* anything? Look, I've got the ring she gave me. Maybe he really knows something, and if I go in alone, who knows?" She didn't even care, she just wanted out of this stinking hole.

He frowned, wheels turning slow. Then he leaned his bulk over her, thick fingers closing around her arm and dragging her up off the bed.

"Hey, you ape! Take it easy—"

"Just listen, cunt." His fingers tightened painfully, then let her go. "All right, but if you try anything fancy, I'll kill you. Got it?"

She nodded quickly, jumping up to rummage through her bag for the frumpy peasant clothes from Crete.

79

CONCRETE BURNED HER FEET.

Athens engulfed Ariadne in its cacophony of motors, shrieking brakes, blaring horns, clattering footsteps, voices shouting arguing laughing questioning. Hands pointed, lifted, scratched, flicked rattling worry beads. Heat shimmered from sidewalks and streets, sun-glared windows, brick and cement and stone buildings. Walls closed in, hot air choking with fumes. Far above the street, a strip of dirty yellow sky.

The black serpent squeezed her inside, twisting her spine off-center. Her vision was narrowed to glimpses at the end of a dark tunnel. Groping, she stumbled against someone she didn't see, heard a distant cursing, was shoved to one side, saw an alley opening. She fled down it from the noise and harsh light.

Her feet carried her through a maze of alleys and cobbled lanes. Groping from one curb to the next, she whirled from the blare of a horn, fell against a vendor's cart, was chased into shadows by sounds of breaking glass and a furious scream. A dog barked, and she ran into the blinding sunlight again to be caught in a tangle of draped fabrics. More cursing. She flailed desperately through, coughing in the foul air.

She kept doggedly on, knowing she had to find it. *Trust. Mother's trust.* She didn't know what it was, or where to find it. But it had to be here, in Athens.

Another twist of an alley brought her out again into the glare of sunlight. Wincing, she caught glimpses, shapes and colors that had only nebulous, nearly-forgotten meanings—an open square of paving stones, women with baskets, vendor stalls, a dirty red and white striped awning and a sign advertising beer, two chipped enamelled chairs. Against one wall in a strip of shade, a bundle of dirty rags and two sticks.

Ariadne pulled herself numbly past. The bundle shifted. A small head in a scarf lifted a grime-streaked face.

The little girl's pinched face was empty of expression. Then a patched-on smile appeared, and she raised a bowl with a coin in it. "Please, *Despoina*?" She pulled the rags up to disclose withered legs, calves barely thicker than the crutch sticks beside her.

The choking coils tightened around Ariadne. She stared into the girl's dark eyes. She dropped to her knees, sucked into those shadows as she grasped the deformed legs. A frightened cry, then only the ringing in her ears as she whirled down the black tunnel.

Pain inside there. Hopelessness ringing off the walls, a black greedy presence opening up to suck it in. Ariadne is the darkness. She is the immensity devouring warped vibrations of stunted flesh and bone, oscillating with their tremor, swelling larger.

Ariadne gasped as the pain wracked her. Burning fingers wrenched her own legs and squeezed, twisting them until she screamed. But the blackness fed on her cries and her pain, feeding her as the coils of the dark serpent writhed in sparks. Electric jolts pulsed from her hands, igniting dormant cells into a madly proliferating dance.

Somewhere far away, a scream of terror and agony. Futile writhing. The crack of splitting and realigning bone.

The flesh beneath her hands swelled and firmed as the shower of sparks danced through her and the hot energy pulsed. In a final burst of backsurging, opposing charges, Ariadne was flung onto the cobbles in the sun. Fire blossomed up her spine, flooding her with a heaviness of release, exhaustion and gratification. She groaned, squirming like a reptile in the dust.

Angry shouts. Cries of alarm.

People were running over the cobblestones. A man gripped a walking stick as if to strike, staring from Ariadne to the girl slumped against the wall.

himself wondering how stable the slope was, and whether the widening cracks in the mortared cement-block walls would loosen his chain-bolt first or collapse on him instead.

"Damn...." The latest wobble subsided in dancing dust-motes, ringing in his ears. Not much this time, but he'd count it anyway. Twisting to gouge the mark, Peter grimaced as pain throbbed up his leg.

He'd stopped taking the pain meds, they were fogging him out. If he got a chance to make a break he was going for it. The metal rods they'd rigged for his splinting were pretty stable, and he could always find something for crutches. Even crawling would be better than hanging around waiting for another landslide to bury him. Though there could be worse ways to go....

He shrugged stiffly. *Etse k'etse*. But he could tell the women who'd been bringing him food were worried about the tremors, too.

He gave his chain a halfhearted tug. Still holding. He'd given up on trying to gnaw through the leather cuff. Sitting against the wall, he leaned over to press his palms around his throbbing calf. The pressure seemed to help dull the aching. Now he took a deep breath, tried to let all the jittery jostling thoughts go, and imagined cool, healing waves lapping through the pain. It worked a little, or maybe he'd just convinced himself it did, but what the hell.

He leaned against the wall and closed his eyes. His hand crept up to scratch his chest, fingers wandering higher to touch the crystal pendant. It was getting to be a habit, but somehow soothing, if he just didn't think.

Ariadne. His fingers tightened, the pain throbbing again. Damn, that was no good. He thrust it away, focused on relaxing, letting the beckoning waves lap over him.

The polished crystal felt good to his fingertips, warm from his skin but somehow cool inside, the design of the double spirals, like a DNA helix, clearly etched and pleasant to trace. Another deep breath, and he felt oddly sleepy, heavy, sinking down into warm darkness. Like a dream, sliding into a cleanly echoing place inside spiral walls. The ringing in his ears had become distant breathy flute notes, wisps of melody. The tingling warmth of that place kindled up his spine, flowing down his arms and legs.

An electrifying pulsation suddenly locked around his broken leg. Like a thrown switch on a grid, it vibrated down his bones and up the metal rods, cycling in hot oscillations. Pulsing, on and on and on.

The girl was gasping, sobbing for breath as tears tracked her dirty face. In the babble of voices, she pulled herself upright, staring at her legs stretched out before her. They were still thin, but the crooked calves had straightened, and there was a normal contour of muscle swelling around them.

"Sacred Mother of God!"

"Do you see, a miracle—"

"No, witchcraft."

"Just look at her! Where did she come from?"

Ariadne wanted to crawl, roll her belly over the warm stones, wallow in her lassitude on the sunbaked dirt. From somewhere she summoned the will to pull herself to her feet and stagger away from the frightened eyes and pointing fingers. As she reeled for balance, clawing her snarled hair out of her face, the onlookers shrank back.

Hands made the sign of the cross. A woman spat against the evil eye.

A last glimpse of the girl, staring down in disbelief as two women helped her to her feet and her legs quivered like a new-birthed lamb's, but held. The heavy, sluggish beat was driving Ariadne on, and she staggered at random into another shadowed alley.

80

PETER COUNTED THE TREMORS.

Nothing much else to do, chained in the hut, so he'd been scraping a mark on the grimy wall for each one. He couldn't figure accurate timing since they'd taken his watch, but in the three days he'd been here the number each day had increased, so the intervals between had to be shrinking. Like his cousin years ago had told him she gauged her labor pains. As he lay there, riding out the shivering pangs of the mountain, he entertained

Peter gasped, frozen for seconds—minutes?—then jolted out of it, blinking. The crystal pulsed in his grip. His leg tingled.

"Damn." He dropped his hand to the blanket, shaking his head. The energy still coursed through him, his leg feeling oddly lighter. And he thought about what he'd seen in that chapel on Crete. The girl and her broken arm, Ariadne pressing her hands around it, and then the mother's stare....

The door of the hut rattled and opened a crack. Dark eyes peered in.

Peter startled, then grinned. "Come on." He raised his fettered hand. "I won't bite."

The door smacked shut, quivered, then inched open again. A little girl, maybe six, peered in at him, long black braids swinging.

He smiled, said quietly, "It's all right. You can come in."

She nibbled her lips, then eased into the hut. Gripping her hand, a smaller boy, sandy-haired, stared wide-eyed at Peter.

"I'm Petros. What's your name?"

She jerked her gaze from the crystal pendant on his chest. "Iris," she whispered.

"Iris. That's pretty. You live here on the mountain?"

She nodded, took a deep breath, and said in a rush, "The mothers say you have a magic necklace."

He wiggled his eyebrows, touched the engraved pendant, and nodded sagely. "That's right."

She bit her lip again, staring at it.

Peter pulled it over his head and held it out. "Here, you can touch it. Won't hurt."

She took a quick breath, eyes gleaming. Clutching the boy's hand tighter, she edged over to Peter's bedding, reaching out to touch the glittering crystal. She gave him a dazzling smile.

"Iris!" The door crashed open against the wall.

The girl dropped the pendant and leaped back, hugging the little boy against her.

It was the Corybant with the schizophrenic hair again. Eurydice, he'd gotten out of one of the others. She glared in the doorway, jerking a hand at the girl. "Back to the hearths! Now!"

Iris shot Peter a look, grinned, and bolted out of the hut, dragging the gawking toddler along. The Corybant looked after them, a smile quirking her lips. Then she swerved back to Peter, scowling. "If you touched them...."

He lifted his fettered hand. "Cool out, Eury." He slipped the necklace on again.

She spat and shoved the basket over to him with her foot. Pretty much the same stuff, though they'd thrown in some dried figs this time.

"Thanks. Want one?" Chewing, he held one up toward her.

She tightened her lips and stepped back a pace, gripping the rifle, nostrils flaring like one of the New Lambs clutching her hymn book and sniffing out impropriety.

Peter gave an exaggerated shrug and took his time emptying the basket, weighing the bread in his hands, raising his eyebrows over the big chunk of cheese, sniffing a little pot of stewed greens, enjoying provoking her. "Mmm. You women know how to treat a guy right."

"The basket." She bent resentfully as he tossed it back. She started to leave, then said grudgingly, "One of our Wise-Mothers has returned. She'll come to question you."

"I'll find room on my calendar."

She frowned and came up with a parting shot. "Now she's back, we'll have a ceremony." The door latched shut.

Dread shivered through him, this time nothing to do with earthquakes. He'd remembered what the wild mountain Corybantes back in the good old days used to do to the vine king after his short orgiastic reign. Best not to think about the spears, the knives.... The teeth.

What were they going to question him about now? He'd convinced the "Wise-Mothers" he'd already talked to that he'd been with Ariadne, not the mercenaries—he thought. The lines of communication hadn't exactly been flowing:

The old crone, a white-braided Greek who looked to have survived a century of hard labor on the sunbaked hills, had sat blank-faced, dark eyes fixed on a point somewhere past Peter's left shoulder. The plump young Italian was nursing a baby as she questioned Peter. Her Greek was worse than Peter's, so they were maybe missing a connection here and there.

By that time, a persistent sensation of altered reality had settled over him. He did try. But the Corybantes wouldn't answer any of his questions, especially about the upcoming "ceremony." He'd broken their laws. He explained the logical thing to do was let him go, since they didn't want men on their mountain, but they didn't seem impressed with his reasoning. They did make it clear they believed in what Ariadne was trying to do. Something about "the Mother" calling her back. They'd seemed pretty interested in having her make another go at the cavern.

And they'd asked him about the crystal pendant. He could tell the Italian was tempted to take it, but she didn't. He'd tried to convince them he could arrange a meeting with Ariadne if they'd let him out. They hadn't bit.

Peter was still stubbornly hoping they'd find Ariadne on the mountain. He was sure they wouldn't hurt her even if they were crazy—hell, crazy didn't have a meaning any more. She could be hurt somewhere out there. Maybe it was cracking her head on the stone pillar that had made her go nuts and attack him. What would she do now? Damn. If she tried to go to her connections in Athens, she'd be a sitting duck.

Eyes squeezed shut, Peter blew out a long breath. His hand was clutching Ariadne's quartz pendant again.

81

THEY HAD BROUGHT HER food again, thrusting the chipped pottery bowl fearfully, worshipfully through the gap in the curtain made from an old coat.

She stirred in her nest of rags and straw, growling, burrowing back into warmth and darkness. Sleep. She wanted more sleep. Tired. But hunger flared in her belly, and her nostrils twitched. She growled again and pulled herself upright, groping for the bowl. Tilting it to her face, she bolted down the thick porridge and licked the bowl clean. A dented metal coffeepot by the cardboard wall still held water, and she gulped that down, too. She wanted more. *More.* She raked matted hair from her eyes and crawled around the dim cubicle, circling inside the two walls of soot-blackened crumbling masonry, the one of cardboard, the one of buckled sheet metal. She prowled around again, a heavy coiled presence stirring within her.

The draped coat was pulled aside. Dusty sunlight, and a face thrust through the gap. "Wise-Mother? You will see more now?"

She snarled, and the face hastily retreated. The blackness inside her swelled, squeezing. *More. We want more.* And a different hunger mounted.

But Ariadne shook her head from side to side, irritable, resisting. Something else, some distant nearly-forgotten voice teased her from outside the stifling den. *Light?* Pushing through swirls of darkness, she lunged across the dirt and scrambled through the draped opening.

Startled voices. She staggered unbalanced, hands groping as she winced in the sunlight. Blackened brick walls surrounded her, bent pipes protruding, window shapes empty of glass. Inside, piles of broken machine parts, stacked boxes defining cubicles walled with cardboard, metal scraps, stretched blankets or black plastic sheeting. Faces crowded into the open space—frightened, avid, blank-eyed.

Bandages. Draining sores. Crutches. Dull interest quickened inside her.

A woman with an infant wrapped in rags pushed forward. "Wise-Mother, please." She held out the squalling bundle.

Two men took the woman's shoulders and pulled her back. A gray-haired woman, layered in clashing skirts and blouses, barked at the crowd, "You all got to wait your turn. Now I want to see those numbers, and if you haven't paid up with Marcos over there, then you better see to it." She swung around, eyeing Ariadne and moving warily closer. "Now come on, Mother, back inside, you know they don't like to see the screaming, just them healed afterwards." She cautiously grasped Ariadne's arm.

Ariadne took a step back, shaking her head, confused by the noises, the colors. She didn't want the woman's hand on her. She stared down at it, focus narrowed at the end of a dark tunnel, and there was a gasp as the hand jerked away.

More voices clamored around her in an irritating buzz. She lurched away, crashed through a collapsing cardboard barrier, and pushed her way toward a crumbled gap in the masonry walls. More people blocked her way, but the black coils were swelling in her now, screaming, demanding, filling her with the power and the hunger. *Mine, they're mine.* The frightened faces shrank back from her.

The blackness wanted them, wanted their sicknesses. *More.* But there was something else, calling faintly.

She pushed her way through the warrens of makeshift shelters, through the maze of cracked streets, bare foundations, burned-out shells of buildings. Babbling voices surrounded her—shouts, pleas, commands—but no one touched her. She had to find it.

Find what? She shook her head again, the heaviness inside dragging her down. She fell against a broken-off wall, felt the warm sooty bricks against her face, stroked them mindlessly as she groped for what it was she should remember. She scrambled onto the wall, stood swaying as pigeons burst up in a stutter of wings.

Blackened ruins sprawled outward at her feet, a rat's-nest of squatters' huts crawling with movement and color. Beyond, gray concrete towers and earthquake rubble. Hazy hills. She turned, arms flinging out for balance, the charred landscape spinning around her, then settling into tile-roofed buildings lapping against a rocky cliff.

She swayed, squinting past fragments of walls, a distant billboard and buildings.

There. Through a gap, she caught a pale shimmer. On top of that high rock outcrop, a clean white geometry of fluted marble columns and sweeping cornices, impossible perfection floating above the squalid Athens streets and smog. *Yes.* Harmony and balance. She had held them once in her hands, smooth planes and angles of a crystal funneling blended pure light….

But that was gone now. There was only a terrible emptiness. *"More!"* She cried out, flinging up her hungry hands.

A roar answered, voices calling up to her. She blinked, clawing the twisted ringlets from her face to see the crowd pressing against the wall below her. They held up their hands. Pleading. Demanding. Their roar was the voice of the black serpent, coiling about her in hissing sparks, filling the emptiness as she and the darkness merged. They swelled together into the immensity of power, dwarfing the supplicants at her feet.

Mine. They're mine.

82

ANTIQUITIES.

The rest of the sign was in Chinese characters and Greek alphabet, almost as bad. Leeza frowned across the street at barred windows and scrubbed marble.

"You're sure this is it?" She held the coin above the reach of the pigtailed little Asian girl in rolled-up denims.

"Sure. Okay, you bet. Zhao Dieng." She pointed indignantly at the sign across the street, holding up her palm.

Leeza shrugged and dropped the coin. It winked in the sun and disappeared into the denims, the denims disappearing down the cobbled street. She eyed the storefront again. She'd expected a dive. It was in Chinatown, all right, but on the fringes close to the business district. She felt ridiculous in the shapeless black peasant skirt and scarf.

She sighed and turned to Chuck. "You stay over here. You can watch the door. I promise I won't climb out the back window."

He grumbled and took up a casual pose with a Greek news flyer. Inconspicuous—twice the size of anyone else on the street. Leeza walked across, shaking her head.

Inside, thick patterned rugs and ceiling fans and a lot of gleaming dark wood furniture, glass cases toward the back. They were on her like flies, deadly polite all the while edging her toward the door. When she started yelling, and showed them the ring, they whisked her into a back room. A teenaged boy appeared and bobbed his head. "If please, this way."

He took her up a spiral staircase off a dim hall, along a pale green-papered passage to a shiny wood door she was willing to bet wasn't veneer. He tapped softly, opened the door and bowed into the opening, gestured Leeza inside.

The old guy sat very straight in a black-lacquered chair, looking like a well-groomed, alert grasshopper in a silk jacket a size too big. His eyes were shiny black marbles behind antique plastic-framed glasses.

She strode over and stuck out her hand. "Mr. Dieng, I'm Leeza Conreid, a friend of Ariadne Demodakis."

The old man raised his face to study her. Just as she was about to drop her hand, he reached out. But he didn't shake it. He grasped her wrist in fingers that felt like dry twigs, looked at her ring, looked at the red bumps on her fingers, then turned her hand palm up. He held her wrist between his fingertips for a while, like he was taking her pulse. She thought maybe it would be rude to pull her hand back. She stood admiring the gem-studded ivory sheath over his three-inch pinky nail.

Finally, with a polite little noise, he released her hand and said something in whispery Chinese.

The boy bowed and translated. "He sees why you have come."

"Oh." She blinked. "Well then tell him we only want to find her and help her. She's sick, in trouble. I just want to take her home."

The boy translated, the old man nodding, shiny eyes still fixed on Leeza. She cleared her throat, gaze flickering around uncomfortably, hoping for a chair. None materialized.

He waited for her to drag her gaze back to his unnerving stare. Then he went on, pausing to let the boy fill her in. "Sickness, yes. Lack of balance. The *chi* is disordered. It is like the earth—we must respect the lines of the dragon, must not impede their flow. Now we feel the dragon's claws. He is lashing in anger, pain. You must breathe deeply, open the channels."

"No, no! Ariadne. Can you help me find Ariadne? Have you heard from her?"

But the old man was turning carefully in the chair even as the boy haltingly translated her outburst, slowly opening an enamelled box on the little table beside him. He pulled out a green stone pendant on silk cords and raised it towards her.

She shook her head, confused.

He swung it before her. The cords shimmered—red, black, and white, braided. "For the new one. Good for open ways. *Chi* flows."

Leeza shook her head again and shot a look at the boy, wondering if he was translating right. But the old man was insistent, thrusting the pendant into her hands. She took it, looking down.

She caught a quick breath. It was exquisite—translucent jade circlet carved with an arching dragon, all curly claws and tail and flaring nostrils and fringy spikes, glaring ferociously as it sprawled around the circle. It seemed to stir in her hands, spitting fire.

A tug on her arm, the boy bobbing his head apologetically. "You must go now. He's tired."

"Wait." She held the pendant back toward the old man. "You haven't answered about Ariadne."

He only sat composed in his chair, gaze fixed through her. The boy bowed to him and hustled Leeza out, pushing the pendant back at her until she slipped the cords around her neck for fear of dropping it. Before she could think, she was out on the street, door shutting behind her. Chuck glowered across the street over his newspaper.

The stone dragon warmed between her breasts.

83

ARIADNE STAYED BY THE burned wall, wouldn't let them take her away. It was warm against her back. Solid. Alive. She could hear everything, every whirring insect wing, every tiny tremor of the earth ringing in her ears, and she could hear the life in the brick wall. Scurrying, scrabbling.

She chuckled, hands tightening on the flow of power, black river swirling around her, through her, rippling up her spine.

Sharp talons dug into her shoulders as she shifted. Wings fluttered. Low cooing. Harsh cawing. Ariadne chuckled again, raising her arms, staring into the glittering beady eyes of the pigeons and crows roosting on her shoulders, lighting on her arms. The snake coiled around her neck stirred sluggishly, darting its tongue, scales whispering. She stepped forward, over the rustling earth alive, alive with the eddying ripples, the rats scurrying thick at her feet and gaunt alley cats slinking around her legs. She laughed aloud, scrambled in a flurry of wings onto the wall to join the goats waiting for her with their amber eyes.

"Wise-Mother, please...."

The dark river roared in her ears, swirling her down into shadows. Hunger. At her feet, faces looked up, arms stretched, beseeching. Festering sores, twisted limbs, wasted bodies. *Mine. They're mine.*

The darkness howled with laughter, fed, and swelled.

84

IT WAS DARK IN the hut, getting cold. Peter had finished the last of the food, was saving a little water. Wind wheezed around the walls. He had a sudden fierce longing to see the stars. No sign of the promised visitors. Maybe your friend and mine Eurydice had just been jerking him around.

He burrowed deeper into the thin blankets—they still hadn't given his clothes back—and tried to sleep. His mind kept spinning in the same uncomforting grooves.

He jerked angrily at the chain shackling his wrist, then sighed.

This time he touched the crystal pendant deliberately, stroking it, letting himself feel the pulse of warmth still tingling through his injured leg, letting himself think about Ariadne. That first bowled-over glimpse in her cove.

The way he'd edged back from her power that night in the ruined stone labyrinth on Crete. Later, her eyes like the sea rocking the boat as she sat up, splendid in her nakedness, to smile at him beside the sail.

He took a deep breath and made himself think about that other night anchored in the Ionians. Black terror drowning him, pain ripping him apart, hurling his pieces into the dark unknown. And then the light of her crystal….

He took one more deep breath, squeezing the facets of the crystal harder. He pictured himself inside it, within its glinting coils. A jolt. The electric hum ignited down his spine, snapped into crackling life around his leg. *Sparks, spraying wildly, surging and swelling. Searing, burning him.* He gritted his teeth, dizzy and lost in the darkness, clenching his fists against the pain. *Pulsing jolts cycling faster and faster, white-hot light blazing agony, splitting the dark. Pulsing on and on and on—*

The bolt of light shattered his skull and he screamed.

∞

Peter came to, sprawled half off the straw bedding in the night. His pulse hammered in his ears. His leg stung and throbbed. "Sweet mother of…." He sat up, braced himself, and tried moving his foot.

No stab of pain. Just the heat throbbing, stinging prickles like waking up after numbness. He swung the splinted leg around on the bedding. Bending his good leg, he pulled himself upright in the dark. Gritting his teeth, he put weight on the broken leg. Nothing, just a little quivering. He tried moving his foot. No grinding sensations. Heart beating faster, he took a few cautious, stiff-legged steps to the end of the chain. He couldn't be sure, maybe it was only the splint holding it steady, but it felt okay.

He started unwrapping the rags holding the metal rods around his leg, heart hammering, a shrill voice babbling panicky protests. He set the rods aside and tried another step, fist clenched on the steadying chain.

His leg ached and quivered, but held his weight. There was a wild ringing in his ears. He shook his head, turning, pacing awkwardly back to the bed. Maybe it hadn't been broken at all. Crazy women didn't even have a doctor.

The door swung open in a gust of cool wind. A burning torch thrust through.

Peter jerked back, stumbling, and caught himself with his injured leg. In the doorway, the old Greek woman came up short, gripping the torch. Her dark gaze flashed toward his unsplinted leg, up to his face, back to his leg. Without a word, she came on into the hut, stuck the torch into a crack, and spread a blanket. She sat cross-legged, going into the fixed-stare routine. The overweight Italian and a newcomer followed her in.

The Italian's eyes bulged as she raised fluttering hands, launching into excited chatter. The newcomer stood poised beside her, meeting Peter's wary eyes and raising one narrow brow.

He remembered then he was naked. A ridiculous flush heated his face. He dropped clumsily onto the bedding, favoring his leg reflexively, pulling the blankets over himself. He glared up at the new arrival.

She coolly studied him, eyes pale in the flickering torchlight. Maybe five years older than Peter, but something in her face put him back in grade school under the scrutiny of the merciless Miss Haberly. She had the standard-issue headband with the spiral and staring eye, but her red hair was cut stylishly short, not just hacked off. She wore one of the roughspun tunics, but she had a shimmery thermal turtleneck and leggings under it, and an expensive needle-gun in the holster at her waist.

Peter met her ironic eyes. He was suddenly back in the real world, and he was pissed.

"Make you feel good, locking me up like an animal in a cage? Well, I'm not planning to go along with your fun and games. So you might as well just use that thing on me, get it to hell over with."

"Let's not lose our temper, Mr. Mitchell." Crisp British accent. She held up a hand, turned to say something in Italian, then she and the plump woman sat beside the old Greek on the blanket. She eyed Peter again, gesturing toward his covered leg. "This is certainly an interesting development. If you'll excuse me for a moment...."

She turned to murmur something in the Italian's ear. The young woman waved her hands, voice rising to an insistent pitch as she pointed to Peter's legs and the discarded splinting. Red-Head conferred with the old Greek.

The crone nodded. She rose and stepped over to Peter's bedding. He edged back against the wall. She sat on the straw and fixed her glinting black eyes on him. His ears were ringing again. He shrugged and flipped the blanket off his leg.

Her hands looked like claws, but they moved deftly, lifting and examining his leg, bending the foot as she looked up at his face again. Her palms pressed around his calf, stroking, disturbing but somehow soothing at the same time. She nodded and scooted back to her blanket.

Red-Head was opening her mouth when the quake hit.

The floor shook, heaving sideways in a grinding crack of mortar. It shivered as dust spun and the roof seams split above the guttering torch flame. Peter was tossed sideways, clutching for balance at the chain. It ripped free from the cracking wall. A last sharp tremor, then it settled, rumbles fading beneath him. He scrambled into a crouch, ignoring the pulsing ache in his leg, and gathered himself to swing the chain around.

"Don't do it." Red-Head was on her knees, needle-gun pointed at his throat, eyes intent on him and not at all cool.

He froze for a second, tensed to swing at her, then let it drain. "Damn."

"Believe me, Mr. Mitchell, I won't hesitate to kill you if you don't cooperate. Mother Gaea is screaming with her wounds. The time for softness and mercy is long past." Her pale face had flushed, but the hand holding the needle-gun was steady. "We women have sat back and watched the creations of men wreak havoc for far too long. Now it's our turn. You can hardly blame some of our sisters if they're thirsty for blood."

Peter stiffened, gathering himself again for a swing.

"Listen first, Peter Mitchell." The old woman spoke in Greek.

She was standing in the flickering torchlight, dark eyes fixed on him. She held up her palms in a dignified gesture, then let them fall to her side. "We are not beasts, to kill without reason. Like your Ariadne, we seek to heal. Her place is here, with us. The mountain calls her back, may she be in time." She gestured again, past the cracked walls. "There are many ways, you see—new science and old wisdom, words and actions—and now we need them all to find a balance we have nearly destroyed. To find Gaea again. To save her and ourselves."

"You won't find any balance by killing all the men."

"That is not our aim. We have needed to be separate, to fight to protect ourselves and our place, to search for a new way. The traditions of the Wise Women, the guardians of the sacred places, are not enough against these new disruptions and pollutions, these new plagues. You have learned from Ariadne. Perhaps now a man will teach us what he has found?"

He blinked. Then he shook his head, muttering in English, "You're looking at the wrong guy."

Red-Head translated for the old woman, adding, "He's obviously right."

The crone shook her head, gripping Red-Head's arm. "Look at his leg. Is this not what you and the other scientists have tried to learn with your experiments? What the ancient sages tell us?" She turned back to Peter. "We build knowledge together. Share with us. We all have need."

"I don't know anything," he burst out. "But if I show you what I did, what then? You make me your sacrificial goat?"

The Italian interrupted, tugging at the Brit's tunic. Red-Head translated, keeping her eyes and the needle-gun steady on Peter. The Italian burst out with something else, and Red-Head said to the Greek, "She's right. The warriors are demanding a ceremony. If he can run now, all the better for the chase. And if the rest of him stands up, it wouldn't hurt to expand the gene pool." The irony was back in her voice, her gaze flickering toward Peter's groin.

He swore, standing there naked, hand clenching around the chain he was still gripping.

"Perhaps, Gwendolyn, *Kyrie* Mitchell should now remind us of that mercy we have set aside." The old woman stepped toward him.

His gaze flicked to red-haired Gwendolyn and the gun, then back to the old woman, standing calmly within striking range of his chain. She reached into the folds of her dark skirt and pulled out a key. She unlocked the leather cuff on Peter's wrist.

"There is violence and disruption on Parnassus now. There must be a ceremony to appease the angry goddess. Yet I think Peter Mitchell need not die." She reached up to touch the crystal pendant rising and falling on his chest. She gestured toward his leg, and a smile cracked the weathered lines of her face. "There can be surprises, even miracles, when one calls on the old powers."

Peter unclenched his fist and let the chain rattle onto the dirt floor. The old woman's eyes held steady on his. He touched the pendant, thought about it, and finally grinned. "One miracle—ready, willing, and able."

He turned to meet Gwendolyn's narrowed eyes. "If you've got my knapsack, I need my Lure-glo monofilament fishing line."

So it was a cheap thrill, but what the hell, he'd earned the look of total confusion on her face.

85

TIME WAS THE COILS of the serpent—endless cycles of shadow and light, ebbing and flowing. They came with their wounds and diseases, and the darkness sucked it all in, swelled with it as will and memory drained away. Exhausted then, she would sleep, and there would come the faint whisper, a catch of haunting silver melody.... Then they would wake her for more healings, and the humming voices would be drowned by the need, the glut of power, the sluggish pulsing release.

And it would begin again.

Ariadne leaned against the burned wall, soaking up the heat of its bricks through her back. Solidity, rooting her. And there was something else here, a glimpse of.... *What?* Something she needed. She couldn't remember. But she had to stay here, with the restless flutter of wings, rustle and scurry of rats, the human moans and whimpers of the sick. No beginning or end to it, lost in the maze—

Crack! An explosion ripped the shadows. Wings burst outwards in a clapping whir. *Crack!* Another shot. Shrill squeals as her rats scattered. A stutter of bullets crackled from the ruins.

People screamed, cowering or running. More gunfire erupted. Ariadne stood rooted against the wall, blinking in confusion as the white pigeons and the black crows wheeled to flail the sky. Her ears rang, hurting. She hunched, pressing her hands to her pounding head.

Someone ran up, shouting. More bullets sprayed the air. The crowd broke into panic. Hands grabbed her arms, tugging her away. Overhead, a loud pop, a whine and hiss. A small dark shape shot over the blackened buildings in a streaming trail of green smoke.

Ariadne gasped, alarm finally burning through her numbness. *Gunshots. Gas*. Memory ignited. They were after her.

Another pop, gas canister hissing over the squatter hovels. Screams, as the people shoved blindly, blundering through flimsy shelters and falling, racked with coughs in the settling green miasma. Through the haze, a glimpse of two figures in bubble helmets pushing through the pandemonium.

The tendrils curled closer. Wrenching free of the clutching hands, Ariadne ran.

Another popping hiss ahead, to the left. She veered blindly right, tripping over broken cement footings, scrambling on all fours beneath draped blankets as a choking haze clouded her eyes. Coughs racked her. She groped on, knocked over a water bucket, grabbed up a soaked rag to cover her face, blundered into a clear alley. Hacking, eyes streaming, she ran, one hand trailing a wall.

They were after her. She had to escape. Gasping through the wet rag, vision blurred by tears, she fled through broken walls, down buckled streets. Shadows fell over her. She ran on. Higher walls enclosed her now, trapping her in endless cobbled passages, doors barred against her. But the greenish haze was behind her now. She dropped the rag, sobbing for breath, lungs burning.

Behind her, a muffled shout.

Face jerking over her shoulder, she crashed into a wall and staggered back to stare at a blank cul-de-sac. She spun, searching frantically for escape. A narrow passage ran between two walls, plunging steeply down the slope of terraced buildings.

As she dove toward it, there was another shout down the dead-end street. An insect whine shot past and hit the wall by her shoulder. A convulsive leap carried her into the dark passage as a second dart furrowed the dirt at her feet. She pounded down the passage, careening off mortared walls, skidding the last stretch into a cobbled street. She slammed into a milling crowd along rows of vendor stalls, clawing her way through outraged shouts and curses. She staggered on through bartering shoppers, knocking over a cart of clattering metal trays. Commotion erupted behind her.

A clear alley magically opened to her right. She ran down it, hand pressed to the ache in her ribs as she sobbed for breath. Shouted commands rang out behind her. She bolted through traffic for the cavelike dark mouth of a building across the street.

Sunlight glare, and then shadow falling over her. Forcing her way through a wall of heat, bodies, and voices, she fell through into dimness. She faltered, blinking, numbly registering cavernous walls opening up before her. Overhead, a high ceiling of curlicued iron grillwork in flyspecked peeling white, flecked with red. Blood everywhere.

Slabs of meat dripping blood. Headless poultry hanging. Severed tongues piled. Rows of hearts, livers, brains. She staggered forward, eyes glazed, deeper into the meat market. Convoluted twists and turns carried her on through swarms of buzzing flies, between racked carcasses lining the passages. She was jostled by hungry figures haggling over the meat, mouths shouting as they jabbed fingers at the raw red cuts.

She was lost in the maze, gagging in the reek of blood. She stumbled past slashing knives, muscle and guts tossed on the scales, thrown dripping over the heads of the buyers to be wrapped. She came up short, staring at trestles of twisted pale intestines, numbly tracing the convoluted kinks until someone pushed her aside. She tried to find a way out, but the passages kept turning and twisting back on themselves. Voices shrilled, ringing in her ears, and she could hear the distant shouts of her pursuers.

The flecked white walls swayed, closing in. She looked up, straining for escape, stretching for the distant rafters and a thin slice of sunlight shimmering through them. Grisly joke high overhead, crucified on a butcher's hook, a life-sized pink naked baby doll smirked down at her.

Ariadne screamed her fear and confusion, exhaustion and despair, up at that empty leering face.

More faces turned toward her—accusing eyes and mouths—and she was running again, tripping, hands scrabbling over the slippery stained floor, scrambling up to run on.

Suddenly, somehow, she was out of it. She stood swaying on a cement platform, staring at refuse bins in an alley. A truck idled, loading door ajar.

Thudding boots and shouts behind her in the building. She scuttled across the platform and into the truck's cargo space. Gagging, she started to back out. The door slammed shut behind her, wheels lurching into motion. She fell to the floor, huddled beneath swaying racks of meat as the truck carried her off.

86

TURNER WAS PISSED. EVEN his neck was mottled, shaved flesh livid around the polished stainless insert on his upper spine. He snapped switchplates on his processors, plucked out his neural lead, and glared at Leeza in Damiana's grip. "I'll waste you right now, bitch, if you don't give me a reason not to."

Leeza stiffened, so tight she was vibrating. She darted a look up at Damiana's face set in carved lines, dark eyes cool and distant. Leeza knew she'd meant it before, she'd given her one break but she'd kill her now if she crossed her. *Think. Think.*

She swallowed, throat dry. "I just thought maybe I could help...."

"You're wasting my time." He brought his pitted cheeks and cold eyes closer. His stare shifted, past her. "Nobody's irreplaceable here." He raised a needle-gun and held the muzzle to Leeza's neck as she cringed back futilely. "You got a problem with that?" he asked Damiana.

"Nothing to me." Her husky voice indifferent, but the strong fingers dug in on Leeza's shoulders. Warning?

She panicked. Turner meant it, he was on a bloody rampage now they'd lost Ariadne *again*, here in Athens, and the *Tyrannos* had screwed Leeza over, they'd never let her go now, she was dead she was nothing but Meat—

"Wait!" She gasped. "All right, I was trying to tell you, just give me a second, okay?" Her voice shrilled and broke, and she panted, heart slamming her ribs, weight of the jade pendant like a ton of bricks pulling her down....

The Dragon. That was it. She sucked in another breath, voice shaking, "The old Chinese guy, Zhao Dieng. Like I told Chuck, I knew he wouldn't talk to you guys, but I— I convinced him I was Ariadne's friend. See, he gave me this."

Her hands fumbled at the peasant blouse as Turner pressed the gun's muzzle against her neck, and she pulled out the circle of carved jade. "The dragon, see?"

"So? What is this shit?"

Her mind had finally clicked into gear, improvising desperately. "Delphi. She told me about it, the... navel of the world, guarded by this huge dragon. That's the place, she has to go back. That's what he told me." *Carajo*. If she could just buy some time. "He told me, take it to her there." Right, that was a good touch, inspired. She held her breath.

Turner's eyes drilled her. She met them unflinching, all of a sudden crazy calm like she was telling the truth and she'd almost convinced herself, it sounded so perfect.

His lips stretched in nothing resembling a smile to show the glinting metal teeth. "A raincheck, then." He prodded her neck with the gun one more time, then lowered it, glare raking Damiana.

"All right. You run your crew up there and check in with Demodakis's men at that village. Arachova. I'll take care of the other approaches. You'll have to hike it into the ruins, over the landslides where we ran into those Corybant bitches, check all over again for personnel mines and booby-traps. Amazons might show again, so watch it. Stake out the site, maybe their precious Saint'll show. See if the bait works this time."

He lifted the jade pendant from Leeza's chest, snorted, and dropped it. "If not, feed her to the dragon."

87

"MOTHER GAEA!"

The cry echoed off the shadowed dome of the cavern.

A wordless chorus keened from the kneeling women packed shoulder-to-shoulder on the rock floor between stone pillars and spiky stalagmites.

"Hear us!" The old Greek wise-mother stretched her arms overhead, torchlight wavering from below and transforming her face into an ancient tragic mask. Echoes and rising voices blended with a deep growl from the depths of the caverns as the rock shivered beneath Peter.

Nobody else seemed to notice. Maybe it was only his strung nerves. The women were rising to their feet now, swaying in unison as they chanted to a heavy beat, eyes glinting fixed and dilated in the flickering torchlight. The rhythm was pounding in his head, his throat parched, heart slamming, and he vaguely realized someone was pounding on a drum. He'd tried not to swallow much of the bitter herb drink they'd forced him to share with them, but he was lightheaded, striped colors of the rock pillars swirling around him to the pulsing beat of the chant.

The women were dancing now, caught in the rhythm. Faster, frenzied, tearing their tunics down about their waists. Light and shadow gleamed over naked arms and bobbing breasts as they swayed like one communal creature. His own bare chest, glinting with sweat and pungent oil, heaved with his pounding heart, the crystal pendant rising and falling and flashing a sharp spark.

A shriek pierced the drumbeat. The celebrants spun around, straining upward, stilled but shivering taut.

"Hear me!" The crone raised her arms again. One hand clutched a long knife. "Great Mother, we sacrifice to you."

Faces turned hungrily to Peter on the flower-strewn bier they'd carried him here on. Knots tightened in his gut. He couldn't seem to suck in enough air.

A bleat of terror shredded the tense silence. The sinewy old hands clutching the knife swept down.

The flower-garlanded lamb bleated again, struggling against the women holding him, but his throat was severed in a bright gush of blood as the women crowded forward with ululating cries.

"Great Mother, take pity on us! Forgive us. Accept our thanks." The old woman lifted the gushing carcass overhead. She turned to smear blood over the massive stone column.

Another cry burst from the celebrants. The drum broke out again, faster now, urgent, as they flung themselves into the dance. They stomped, waved their arms, rubbed against the blood-stained rock pillar and then twirled on toward Peter. Torchlight guttered over the writhing women, burnishing their bare skin. A face swept down on him through fire and shadow. A fierce, red-smeared grin. Hands brushed his chest. The dancing wave broke over him.

Drums pounded. Faces leered, gloating. The flicker of a pink tongue, licking down his arm. Fingers clutched his wrist and raised his hand to a heaving bare breast, nipple hard under his palm. A sweaty body rubbed over him, ringlets trailing like Medusa's. Musky scents twined around and through him as arms wove a serpentine dance of shadows. A hand stroked lower, groping under his goatskin loincloth.

Peter's head swam with the drug, the undulating naked women flickering into and out of focus in the torchlight. They were circling around him now, stamping and chanting. His pulse roared in his ears. His muscles quivered with a mounting compulsion to run, race blind over the night mountain and flee the Furies shrieking at his heels. The Corybantes on their hunt….

Hands clenching around the wood poles of his bier, he tensed to bolt. He looked up and met the old Wise-Mother's stare. Jet-black, deeper than shadow in the torchlight flickering over her seamed face, her eyes held his. He dropped back into the folded animal skins, letting out a shaky breath.

Thirst raged, licking with the flames of the torches. The dancers shrieked, pounding their feet over the stone floor. And he could almost hear the voices of the Amazon warriors coming closer down the rocky slopes, wild-eyed Bacchantes howling, scenting the prey—

The drums beat a furious tattoo and died. The dancers shouted, "Gaea!" They raised their palms to the red-streaked stone pillar, then turned outward toward the darkness. An eerie wail rose through the silence, swelling, until the stone walls rang with an animal scream. The Corybant warriors rushed in out of the night.

They growled and feinted side to side with their spears and knives. Eyes glinted, hair hanging loose over strong naked bodies, third eye glimmering from the white spiral on their headbands. Their faces, streaked with black charcoal and red clay, were barely human. The other dancers shrank back against the cavern walls, teeth glinting in the shadows as the warriors stalked their prey, working closer to Peter on his bier.

He tried to swallow, throat bone-dry. He was shaking so hard the bier shuddered beneath him. No, it was the floor shaking again to a grinding tremor. The warriors froze, clutching their weapons as the cavern quivered.

Peter took a deep breath. *Now or never.*

As the tremor subsided, he bellowed as loud and deep as he could.

Echoes boomed back from the walls, ringing over the women. Savage faces swung startled up at him as he raised his head in the leafy garland they'd crowned him with, raised one hand in supplication toward the blood-smeared stone pillar. "Great Mother, grant me your protection!"

And it was weird—even as he flicked on the penlight hidden in his loincloth, and the Lure-glo optic filament snaking up through his chest hair ignited a blossom of light in the crystal pendant to flash out its polished facets—he seemed in his feverish sweat to see the rock column take on a voluptuous living shape breathing sparks into the stone over his heart.

Startled cries below him.

The warriors with their knives and spears faltered and moved back. They dropped their weapons as Peter threw the loosened splints aside and rose in the flickering shadows, the crystal blazing on his chest, to stand on two strong legs.

Saved by a miracle.

88

THEY WERE BACK IN the trucks, headed for Delphi, but this time Damiana let Leeza sit up front with her. She wasn't talking, just sat holding her stubby rifle and staring out the side widow, dashlights washing over her expressionless face. It was making Leeza really nervous.

The driver wasn't talking much, either, just following the taillights of Turner's truck up front. He'd decided to come along and supervise after they'd gotten a tip Ariadne might have escaped the Athens attempt in a truck headed toward this region. "Maybe the Conreid bitch ıs right," he'd grunted, like he was pissed he'd have to wait to waste her. "It better come down in Delphi." And he'd bared his steel teeth at her.

Now it was looking like something was already coming down. Literally. From the traffic on the potholed "highway" the last hour, everybody was headed the other way, out of the hills. Here came a beat-up truck with a bunch of scruffy-looking Greeks, easing past them. Then two wheezing cars, packed with faces. Finally a cart pulled by a donkey, piled with kids and rugs and chickens.

The driver grunted. "Looks like more villagers clearing out. Maybe the Med League soldiers had another run-in with those Corybant bitches."

Damiana didn't respond.

They swung around a turn, climbing, headlights raking more of those thick, twisted old olive trees, and they looked like evil gnome faces staring out at her, gloating. Waiting. Leeza was sweating, heart thudding, ears ringing. *Madre* if she got out of this alive, she swore she'd clean up her act.

Crazy laughter burbled up through her, but she bit down on it, hand going to the smooth curves of the jade dragon pendant, soothing. It was getting to be a habit.

A metal sign flared up on the roadside: *Arachova 1 km.*

Damiana straightened, come alert, rolling down the window and cocking the rifle. In the back of Turner's truck, more rifle barrels poked out from under the tarp.

Stone houses closed around them, narrow bumpy street switchbacking up through a ghost town, shutters over the windows. The fat crescent moon shed a watery light over the craggy steep ridge the village clung to, and Leeza craned forward, spotting a derelict clocktower stuck like a weird barnacle to the highest outcrop. *Mierda,* good material, and her camera and gear was all stashed in back. Then she saw the rifles again, tracking the dark windows and alleys, and she caught a sharp breath, slumping down low in the seat.

She started breathing again as they got through the silent village, down a dip over the other side and across some terraced fields, but then the trucks were pulling over where a landslide blocked the rutted road.

"End of the line." The driver shut off the motor. "Hoof it from here." Turner's crew was piling out of the truck ahead, all in camo, pulling out weapons and gear.

Damiana got out and curtly gestured Leeza after her, handing over the backpack they'd given her for her clothes and food. She'd managed to squeeze in her portable recorder unit. It was cold. She blew on her fingers, flexing them. The rash blisters had stopped itching finally, but her fingers had gone numb. She pulled on her gloves and knit cap.

Freddy jumped out of the back as the third truck pulled up. He headed over to Turner, smirking at Leeza perched on the bumper. "Looking glam, Ms. Media!"

She scowled and flipped him the bird.

Turner was barking out orders as the men got the gear together, Damiana in a huddle with a couple guys Leeza didn't recognize. She shivered and hugged herself in the bulky camo jacket.

A rough-looking Greek with a rifle suddenly jumped down from the rocks, onto the road beside her.

"Ah!" She scrambled back, stumbling around the side of the truck.

Damiana caught her shoulder. "Med League." She let Leeza go as Turner came over, shooting her a nasty look, and her stomach gave a sinking flop. He was itching to do her.

"Town emptied out?"

The Greek shrugged. "Some are... hide inside. The headman, too. So we still play we fight you, yes?"

Turner snorted. "Yeah, give Demodakis a show. Got the ruins secured?"

The Greek nodded. "Was yesterday... ambush by the Corybantes." He spat. "We lose one man. Kill two women, but one also we hold... hostage."

"Where?" Turner was eager. "She talk? Anything about Ariadne?"

"In the ruins. We beat her, but she would say nothing."

Turner's metal teeth glinted, silvery in the moonlight. "I've got ways. Let's move." He pulled out his radio and thumbed it, but there was only static. "Fuck. Out again." He glanced up and swore.

Leeza looked up and saw auroras writhing faintly beyond the moonglow. More geomagnetic eddies.

"Roberts." Turner gestured to one of the men Leeza didn't know. "Take your crew around the other side, back up the old Amfissa road. We don't know if she'll hook up with these Corybantes or not, which way she'll come. Don't know if we'll get radio contact back, so keep the rendezvous schedule. Get going."

Without a word, Roberts got back in the third truck. There was a hassle getting it turned around in the narrow road, but then it rumbled off.

Someone grabbed Leeza's shoulder from behind, and she jumped. "Get you gear." It was Damiana.

Leeza struggled into the heavy backpack and staggered along with a prod from Damiana's rifle, stumbling onto a rough, rocky trail winding through the landslide boulders, nasty thorn bushes, and broken trees. Turner came up behind with the Greek. "He'll go first, make sure they haven't set more booby-traps."

One of the men swore. "That's what got Hollywood. Ugly, man."

"Remember, Ariadne might be with those Amazons. No rifles until we're sure. We kill their Saint, the *Tyrannos*'ll have our nuts. Use your darts to stun."

"Shit, and they'll be using rifles!"

"This sucks, whole scene getting out of hand."

Turner whipped around, needle-gun on the nearest grumbler. "You want out, I got an easy way right here."

"Fuck. Okay, man." The man raised his hands, edging back on the trail.

Turner whipped back toward Leeza, who tried to hide behind Damiana. He grabbed her shoulder and pulled her forward, fingers digging in hard. "Better hope your saintly friend shows, you cunt. Maybe we'll hang you up in the ruins for bait, start cutting off pieces." He gave her his ugly grin. "That'll be Damiana's job."

Damiana just stood there, face impassive.

Turner let go, then backhanded Leeza hard across the face.

"Ah! Shit!" She gasped and crumpled, cheek flaring pain.

Turner pushed on ahead with the Greek guy.

"Come, girl. You got to keep up." Damiana pulled her to her feet, voice gruff, but she held her arm, guiding her down the rough trail.

Leeza's eyes streamed tears, face throbbing. Everything blurring into a nightmare. Her face pulsed pain, heart thudding, feet stumbling—they'd gone numb, too—and the goddamn backpack was wearing her down. The men took turns dragging her on around boulders, up over tree trunks and rubble, all the while craning around looking out for those Corybantes, and Leeza almost wished they'd just come screaming down out of the dark and get it the hell over with. "Are we there yet?" She staggered to a stop, swaying and gasping for breath.

"Quiet." Damiana was there, giving her shoulder a shake, but somehow in the shadows it looked like she was grinning down at her. Leeza shook her head and blinked. No, she was just staring ahead up the trail, gesturing Leeza along.

Leeza braced herself to plod on, then came up short again. Despite her daze, she caught a quick breath. "Subliminal!"

Laid out before them was a shimmering moonlit mirage. A flat little oasis of grass and blossoms and gracefully arched tree limbs, like they were bowing to the remnants of the past. Somewhere near, a soft trickling of water. The ancient ruins were mostly just footings of buildings or broken chunks of carved stone, but there on a round foundation stood three fluted columns, silvered in the night, set in a curve topped by a broken off ring of fancy marblework. The graceful remnant was ghostly, unreal, smack dab in the middle of the wilderness and earthquake rubble.

Leeza sighed and swayed, soaking it in. She didn't even think about the recording gear in the bottom of her pack until someone pushed her from behind, jostling the weight. "Come on, we don't got all night."

A sharp, bitten-off cry from among the ruins, and the men behind her ducked, going for their rifles, pulling Leeza down among some boulders.

"He said no rifles!" she hissed. "If you hurt Aria—"

"Shut up." Someone slapped his hand over her mouth, setting off the throbbing in her face again.

"Mmmph!" She kicked at him.

"Get up." It was Damiana, coming back. "Just Turner playing with the hostage."

"Chee-rist! That fucker's going out of his—"

"Quiet, now. Take positions." Damiana gestured for the men to fan out among the trees and brush. She took Leeza's pack and set it down, then pulled her toward the ruins. "He want you to see." She set her jaw, and Leeza finally realized she was pissed off, keeping a tight lid on it. At her? *Madre*, were they really going to do it, carve her up?

She was panting, a crazy roaring in her ears, then somehow they were out among the marble, Turner and the Greek guy looking down at somebody sitting bound by the waist to the base of one of the pretty columns. Damiana nudged her forward and held onto her shoulders.

Leeza gasped. It was a woman sprawled coughing there, clutching one hand to her chest, long braid matted with something dark and sticky-looking, nose broken sideways and her face all bruised and swollen. Her rough tunic was torn open in the front, breasts exposed. She was young. Turner gave her a casual kick, and she bit back on another cry.

He knelt down and jerked up the arm she was cradling. She made a harsh animal sound, her one unswollen eye glaring what even Leeza could translate as some heavy-duty curse onto Turner. She hissed and spat at him as he leaned over her, writhing and trying to kick. He swore and jerked hard on her wrist, and the hand flopped crazily, nothing but smashed bones and pulp.

Leeza gagged, a sick taste in her mouth.

"Ask her again if they have Ariadne."

The Greek shrugged and translated. The woman spat out some Greek at him, still glaring at Turner.

"She says only that we will pay for dishonoring the Goddess." He spread his palms. "We questioned her a long time, as you see."

Turner licked his lips. He pulled out a short, dull black rod from his jacket, jerking his head toward two of his crew standing back under the trees. "Hold her feet down."

They came over, one on each side, and held her boots as Turner flipped up her tunic and thrust the rod at her crotch. A snapping buzz, and the woman convulsed, head cracking back against the stone column. The men released her feet, but she kept kicking awhile after Turner stood back, blood trickling out of her mouth, eyes rolled back in her head. A wet pool spread beneath her, and Leeza's nostrils flared at the stink of shit. Her stomach flopped, and she tried to turn away, but Damiana held her there, and somehow she didn't think about closing her eyes.

The woman moaned and shook her head. Turned knelt and grabbed her hair, yanking her face up. "Ask her again," he told the Greek.

The man looked nervous, stuttering something at her.

She took a couple of breaths, coughed, then said something in a hoarse voice.

The Greek translated, "Ariadne is not with them, but she is coming. The mother is calling her back."

"The mother? Whose mother? Isn't the Demodakis wife supposed to be dead?" Turner shook the woman's head by the hair, but she'd fainted, head lolling forward as he released her in disgust.

Turner paced across the stone floor. He came back to stare down at the Corybant, then at Leeza. "Getting the picture, cunt? You better hope this Ariadne's really a friend of yours." He paced some more. "Let's send a message to those Amazon bitches, if they think they can keep her…." Sweat glinted on his face, steel teeth and the whites of his eyes glimmering, and Leeza shuddered back against Damiana's grip.

He whipped out a knife and knelt by the woman, hacking viciously. Blood spurted and the woman came to, screaming, a long drawn-out wail that raised Leeza's hackles. Turner stood back, clutching something dripping, and the woman's chest bled from the raw meat where her breast had been.

"Oh, God!" Leeza tore herself loose from Damiana's grasp, heaving.

"Hang her up. Get some ropes, haul her up against that column where they can see her from up there on the mountain."

A cut-off protest, someone swearing, footsteps around her. The Greek strode past with Damiana, gesturing. "This is not good. He goes too far."

"You." Turner grabbed Leeza's hair and jerked her head up, and she bit off another shriek, hands panic-scrabbling at the air, ears ringing. He gave her his sick smile, *madre* he was really insane he was holding up the severed breast. Admiring it. "Little offering for their precious goddess." He set the bloody tissue atop one of the broken columns, nipple pointing up obscenely. "Now she's a real Amazon."

He let Leeza go then, pushed her stumbling over the broken stone footings. "Remember, you're next, if the Saint doesn't show."

89

TOSSED ABOUT IN THE careening truck, breathing in the reek of blood as the swaying carcasses brushed her, Ariadne awoke.

Blinking, she looked around her. She looked down at her hands. She started laughing, and she couldn't seem to stop the shrill laughter, even when the truck stopped, the stupefied driver opened the back, and she climbed out filthy with ashes and blood, tangled ringlets falling over her face. She was still laughing, a hoarse crow-cawing as she staggered past stunned village faces and hands making the sign of the cross. Finally she stumbled into the shade of an olive grove.

Above the rock terraces, a spring spilled into a rock-dammed pool. She tore off her filthy rags and plunged in. She wanted to swim down forever into the clear cold, wash away the smell of blood and her own human corruption. She emerged gasping for air. Shivering, she rinsed the threadbare skirt and blouse, beating them against the rocks and spreading them over branches to dry, then huddling into exhausted sleep.

It was afternoon when she awoke. She pulled on the damp clothing and set out, her mind strangely light and clear now. But the compulsion was still there, beating with her heartbeat, shivering up from the damaged earth to fill her with a terrible sorrow and rage and pity, and she had to return to the cave on Parnassos. She knew the forces were too great for her, but that didn't matter.

She found a crossroad with signs, and set out steadily walking, raising a hand to passing trucks or the rare electric car. Silent laughter mocked her, but her feet were set on the road and there was no turning back. *Pride. Fatal hubris*. Had Oedipus known, set upon this same ancient road, it would have made no difference. Ariadne could only accept the call of the mountain, the call of her own flesh and blood.

Near sunset, a car stopped for her. The spinning wheels meshed with her rising pulse of urgency, the clash of forces ringing around her, and she wondered how the driver could fail to hear it. He let her out just short of Arachova, warning her it wasn't safe to go farther. She nodded, thanked him, and continued on foot.

Reaching the steep terraces of a village clinging to a jagged ridge, she stumbled along dirt lanes between whitewashed blocky houses glimmered with moonlight, shuttered and silent. A crumbling tower clung to the highest rock buttress of the village, the hands of its clockface stilled, the pale circle staring down like an unblinking eye. A goat jumped out from behind an empty vendor stall, stopping to fix its satyr's gaze on her. She emerged onto a steeply terraced hillside of olive groves.

A screaming whine, a popping sound and then the roar of an explosion below, near the foot of the mountain. Overhead, the writhing shapes of green and purple auroras strangled the crescent moon. A tremor shook the earth. More gunshots, another explosion below, near the ruins of ancient Delphi's columns, and even through her exhaustion, alarm and urgency flared. Somewhere Ariadne found a renewed burst of energy to hurry up the dirt track toward the mountaintop.

"*Stomat!*" *Halt*. The shouted command came from behind.

She whirled around to see a shadowed woman emerge with a rifle from the cover of a twisted olive tree.

Ariadne whipped around to run up the trail.

Two more of the Corybant warrior women stepped out in front of her, their woven headbands bearing the embroidered eye within a spiral. One held a spear, the other a rifle. The one with the spear, long hair twisted in plaits with what looked like bird bones, grabbed Ariadne's arm. "Come with us now."

"*Ohi*. I need to finish what I started. There's no time, you don't understand—"

"You join us now, or we leave you to those foreign dogs." The woman jerked her chin toward the gunfire below the village. "Do you have the cure?" Her grip tightened.

Ariadne pulled back and lifted her empty palms. "I have nothing left." Her lips twitched. "And nothing left to lose. I must try."

"Good. Then we need to hurry, there may be another earthquake." She gestured with her spear toward the looming dark peak of Parnassos.

They wrapped her legs in leather skins like they wore, and gave her a woven wool shawl, water, and some figs. Only then did she realize she had been hungry, and cold in her threadbare blouse.

Dimly lighted by the crescent of the waning moon and the writhing green and purple auroras, they followed a rough trail until it was swallowed by the chaos of landslide rubble. They scrambled over bare rock outcrops and across raw gashes, then hiked up pine-clad slopes. Moonlight still shone over the ridges as they came out onto the open mountain again. The warriors made Ariadne sit and wait, though the earth's distress was screaming its urgency now, violent forces mounting in the depths.

They pressed more food and water on her. "You will need your strength. We need to wait for the moon to sink behind the ridge. The mercenaries below, defiling the sacred site, must not see us with their rifle scopes."

A tremor shivered the slope beneath them.

"Pigs." A woman spat. "They'll pay for angering the Goddess. Let their blood slake the thirst of the *pythia*."

Ariadne shook her head. The silent cry shook her bones and filled her head, and she could think of nothing else. *Come. We await you,* a deep voice taunted, and she shivered.

∞

The moon finally sank behind the high ridge, relinquishing the sky to the coiling auroral serpents. They hiked on. The Corybantes clearly knew each twist and turn of the goat tracks. Ariadne could simply follow the sturdy shape leading the way, her feet falling into the rhythm of the pounding beat in her head. A flash of lightning tore the night, a low rumbling overhead. They climbed on in silence, the ridges steeper now, and Ariadne didn't need her guide to know the way. Another bolt of lightning, thunder crashing. A cool wind whipped the slope. The forces surged, pulling her.

A sharper crackle. Distant gunfire, below. The first warrior swung her face around. They climbed on, faster, into the storm, as if the Corybantes could finally hear the ringing summons.

Across another sheer ridge in howling wind, down a ravine, up and across a fresh rockslide. Lightning flared, the crash of thunder almost instantaneous. Ariadne hurried ahead, cutting off of the goat track and straight up the loose scree, oblivious to the rocks shifting beneath her.

"Wait! This way."

She knew the way. The mouth of the cavern was drawing her in. She scrambled onto the ledge leading to it and stood, chest heaving, wind whipping, staring at the gap of darkness in the cliffside. Dread shivered through her as the black seething flowed out to claim her once more.

"No," she whispered. She shuddered, fighting the remorseless pull. She was nothing—less than a dust speck blown in the vastness—with nothing to hold to, nothing but a frail conception of order. An ephemeral memory of a lattice of humming light. She couldn't face what was waiting, calling, swelling to tear the mountain apart and rip her puny flesh with its fangs. But it already it had her in its grip.

"Ariadne!"

She whirled around. Women in tunics and furs were emerging from the mouth of the cavern, flames of pitch torches streaming in the wind. At their head came a white-haired woman in fluttering skirts and a dark, bearded man in animal skins and strapped leggings, the eye-in-the-maze headband of the Corybantes around his brow. He held out his hand, glittering gemlike sparks in the torchlight.

The Corybantes admitted no men. Ariadne blinked. "Petro?"

He moved down the rock slope, limping slightly. He stopped a few paces away, face shadowed, and held out his hand. It dangled her etched crystal pendant, the facets trembling. When he finally spoke, his voice was husky, hesitant. "Ariadne, are you—?"

"Petro! Are you hurt?"

They broke off together. He didn't move, only stood offering the necklace.

She darted forward past the dangling pendant to hold him and feel his heart beat against her ear. His arms curved around her, and then he was holding her tightly, rocking her against him, lips brushing the top of her head as he murmured incoherently.

"Petro." She wanted to stay in the comfort of his arms. Finally she pulled back, looking up into his face, wind whipping his hair, longer now. "Petro, I don't understand."

"I know." He touched the woven headband she was puzzling at. A flicker of his old self-mocking grin, then he sobered. "They insisted. Things got a little crazy, but I think it'll work out." He turned around to face the old woman, waiting behind him. "This is Wise-Mother Eleni."

The old woman stepped closer, skirts swirling in the gusts, to grip Ariadne's hands. "*Chairete*, daughter of Gaea. You must try again to reach the goddess." Warmth tingled from her battered hands.

"There's no time to waste." A younger woman with short hair pushed forward, speaking in clipped English. "There's a significant seismic event building. And the geomagnetic fields are all over the map—the reversal seems to be accelerating. If you can do anything to ease the effects, it's got to be now."

Peter turned on her. "I told you what she did on Crete."

Ariadne looked into the old woman's eyes. "I'm afraid."

She said gently, "As are we all. Do the best you can." She squeezed Ariadne's hands and released them, beckoning her toward the cave mouth. The women waiting with the guttering torches were chanting now.

Peter draped the necklace over her head, settling it around her neck. "I don't know if you need it, but it helped me."

There was something new in his voice, his touch. "Helped you?"

A fleeting smile. "You were right. But now we better hurry."

She shuddered, resisting. "Petro, the blackness will swallow me again. You don't understand. I can't control the power." She hunched in misery.

His grip tightened on her wrist. "A little late for that, isn't it?" He grasped her shoulder, giving her a little shake. "Ariadne, what you have *is* power. You better face it now."

Startled, she raised her face to his.

His eyes softened. "I'll be there, right behind you, for what it's worth."

She took a deep breath and nodded. Pulling out a crumpled bit of cloth from her pocket, she looked down at old Cassandra's embroidery of serpentine spiral and staring eye. She tied it around her head. Her hand found Peter's as they climbed past the chanting women to the cave mouth.

A tremor shivered the stone floor of the cavern as Ariadne hesitated beneath its soaring dome. Colors shimmered in the layered rock, the sharp spires. Dark immensity echoed as urgency pulsed stronger with the quaking of the mountain. She pulled loose from Peter's hand, hurrying to the blood-stained stone column.

The blackness seethed beneath her, voices of chaos whirling through the roots of the pillar and pulling her down, but this time she held back, closing her eyes and taking slow, deep breaths. Her hand crept to the etched crystal pendant, the double-helix pattern steadying her. Behind her, Peter stood waiting.

The chanting swelled to a pulsing drumbeat. Heartbeat. Ariadne took one last breath and stepped forward to kneel at the base of the pillar, spreading her arms to embrace it.

90

COLD WIND GUSTED DOWN off the twin crags of the *Phaedriades*—the Shining Ones, she'd learned from her data cache—masses of shadow in the night, towering over Leeza. Swirling out of the cleft splitting them in two, wind moaned through the ruins of Delphi. A pale crescent moon floated above the jagged cliffs, dull pewter washing the slender stone columns below. An owl hooted, ghosting past on silent wings.

She shivered in her bulky layers. Owls meant death. But they were Athena's bird, too. Maybe it was all the same, the ultimate wisdom, just let go and give in to it, looked like it was coming down for her pretty quick here, and maybe she didn't even care any more. Turner was coming back any time now, string her up and start cutting off pieces.

She shivered again, hugging herself as she hunkered behind the rocky terrace where Damiana had put her. She couldn't feel her feet or hands any more, and the puffy swelling at the base of her spine made it hard to snap in her Link lines. Tension quivered, ringing in her ears, but it was somehow separate, outside herself, like the auroras slithering off beyond the moonglow. She was only a hollow tube, funneling it all down the neural leads and into her portable recorder.

Second night waiting here. No sign of Ariadne. No sign of the Corybantes coming to avenge their Goddess and the tortured warrior woman. When the men would come creeping by, checking in with Damiana, she could feel the strain lapping off them. Waiting. Even the ground beneath them shivered with tension, tremors clenching the gut.

Waiting. She'd already recorded shots of the Delphi ruins, straight lines of the Apollo temple and six marching columns, the stone theater with its perfect curves cupped at the foot of the cliff. Calm, cool serenity in the midst of this bloody mess of knives and guns and quake-shattered rock. Even as she was recording it, she knew the Link could never capture this. Tall marble columns shimmering in the moonlight and shadows like ghosts in graceful robes of vanished gods. Leeza could feel them dancing, slow and stately. And she didn't have to replay the Link to taste her drink from the ancient sacred spring. She could still hear it faintly, gurgling out of the cleft near the rocky outthrust Damiana had chosen for her vantage point.

Leeza thought about jacking out and burrowing down for a nap. But what the hell, she had plenty of unused chip space and maybe something would happen before Turner came for her. Maybe she'd really take Art to a new dimension, go out into blackness the last dying twitch of neurons imprinted. Though even that wouldn't be a first.

Didn't matter. She was past tired, but the edginess wouldn't let her sleep. She rocked herself, ears ringing.

Damiana's face, dark as the shadows of the ravine, swivelled down from the outhanging stone lip to check Leeza. Low voice, brusque, "You rest, girl." She went back to scanning through her scope.

Leeza hugged her belly, fist clenching around the carved blue crystal she'd stolen from the island chapel, like if she could squeeze it hard enough it would call Ariadne. Somehow she could feel her out there, and she was starting to believe her own story, all the edges blurring, believe Ariadne was really coming for the jade dragon, here at the *omphalos*, the navel of the ancient world. She wanted to see her just once, before.... Tell her. What? She's sorry?

She swallowed bitter bile. It was only that easy on the NeuroSoaps. Leeza Conreid has really blown it this time—max.

The carved crystal hummed in her tight fist, even though she couldn't feel it, but she could *hear* it, a pure tone ringing down her bones, ringing in her ears. Maybe she was losing her marbles, too. So who cared if she felt like tying the jade dragon pendant around her waist to rest over her belly button? It was like that mythological *Pytho*, guarding this birthplace. The stone circle felt good on her belly, pulsing over the faint swelling.

She could admit it now. She was pregnant. It was that stiff Peter Mitchell, she hadn't used anything except an STD bolus. Maybe it was too early, but she could almost feel a stirring inside her. And the weird part was, she actually would be glad, but the truth had been staring her in the face for too long now: The rash. The puffy bumps. The numbness. Like Kenny before he died of the new RIP-Leprosy. She couldn't save her cousin, and now she couldn't save herself, or her baby. She didn't deserve to live.

"Good evening, viewers, this is Leeza Conreid, totally fucked up—"

She gasped as the earth-shivering revved into a shaking slide. The stony plateau heaved with another tremor, a deep grinding. "*Madre!*"

Damiana slithered down beside Leeza, slapping a hand over her mouth and holding her down as the ground wobbled. A rending sound, pebbles clattering, stinging over them from the cliff at their backs. They were lifted, suspended for a second as a throbbing gathered and built and built and *Jodas* was this one It? But then it drained away in pulsing shudders.

Leeza sat up, took a deep breath, and touched Damiana's arm. "Thanks for cutting down the Corybant. That was too ugly, her hanging there bleeding."

Damiana shrugged, face vague in the shadows. "The Greek, he help I. He gone, now, getting more Med League men. I be thinking maybe the *Tyrannos*, he take over this operation."

Leeza shivered. "Was she dead?"

"No." Voice curt. She took a breath. "She ask the Greek to finish she."

"Oh." Leeza swallowed. "Look…." Her voice shook. She took a deep breath, got it out in a rush. "Look, I know Turner's coming back, he'll be pissed about the Corybant, but it's not your fault, I'll tell him, I mean he's gonna string me up there, cut me up, he's just been itching anyway, so could you…. I mean, I'd rather it was quick." She hunched.

Silence. Damiana just sat there, a still dark shape.

"Please." She whispered, hot tears squeezing out.

"Girl." Damiana gripped Leeza's wrist. "This whole scene fucked, I be thinking. Turner losing it. So you get you gear, girl, you and Damiana leaving this show."

"Leaving, you fake bitch? I knew it, I've been watching you." A scramble and thud, and he was standing over them, stun rifle pointed at Damiana's head. Moonlight glittered over Turner's steel teeth.

Damiana jerked back, arm raising fast with a pistol, but Turner kicked it away, and it clattered past Leeza over the stones.

She couldn't help it, she shrieked and cowered back, huddling.

"Don't do it. Throw it over there."

Damiana gave a choked-off growl and tossed her knife to the side.

"Stand up. Slow. Hands on your head."

Leeza rocked herself and whimpered as Damiana slowly rose to her feet, Turner backing warily, rifle still aimed at her.

"We're going down below, have us a little fun, tell the boys how you were planning to fuck them over, man-cunt." He took another step back, turning to bark at Leeza, "You, too, bitch. Get up."

In the second he took his eyes off her, Damiana was springing forward, snapping her arm up under the rifle as Turner swore and brought the barrel down across her face, stepping back as she staggered and swinging it around again, but Damiana was flinging herself onto him and then all Leeza could see was their dark shapes staggering locked together stumbling grunting over the rocks. Sick splat of a blow, glitter of steel, somebody had another knife, high whine as the stun rifle went off and the dart went zinging against the boulders past Leeza, rifle clattering down onto the ground.

Somehow she was on her hands and knees, panting, scrabbling her hands over the dark rocks, and there! Her shaking hands closed over Damiana's pistol.

They came staggering back toward her, and she scrambled out of the way, clutching the pistol, couldn't tell them apart, but then she could see it was Turner with the knife, whipping it up and Damiana cried out, she was bleeding, but she spun and kicked and Turner fell back, reaching to his waist for his own pistol, those teeth bared.

Leeza stiffened her arms, held her breath, and squeezed the trigger.

Darkness blossomed over Turner's face as Damiana yelled and jumped back, Turner's pistol firing, the ricochet whine of a bullet in the rocks, and then he crashed over.

Echoes rang in Leeza's ears. She was frozen on her knees, gripping the pistol, nausea washing over her. She stared at the dark, still shape that was Turner.

A hand fell onto her shoulder from behind, and she startled, jerking the pistol up.

"Easy." Damiana took the pistol from her, sticking it into her holster. She was panting, blood dripping from a slashed sleeve.

"Shit." Leeza started shivering and couldn't stop, legs gone jelly and she slumped to the ground.

Damiana crouched beside her, still catching her breath, took Leeza's shoulders and squeezed. "You do good, girl." A glimmer of teeth. "Now you take some deep breaths, help I bandage this arm, then you and I moving out."

Shots rang out below them.

Damiana swore, pushed Leeza down, and wormed back up over the rocks to scan below.

A faint cry from the other side of the ruins, over where Freddy and the others were watching the trails in. Damiana swore again, pulled out her radio and got only static, thrust it angrily back in its sheath. She raised her rifle she'd left at the top, scanning through its scope.

More rifle shots below. And above, on the other slope over the ruins.

A distant scream. More echoing shots. Damiana swung the rifle and fired off a stuttering burst.

Hardly thinking, crazy looped and shaking, Leeza was Linking back in, pulling on her camera goggles and scrambling up the piled rocks. Adrenaline sang sharp almost the good old taste of the high as Damiana's gun clattered deafening and red tracers spat fire down into the night

A whine, a loud popping below, and the harsh light of a flare floated over the ruins, lighting men sprinting in camo, lighting a surge of women warriors rushing down over the landslide rubble. The flare faded. Overhead, the auroras writhed. More shots, echoing ringing in her ears, and Leeza was getting it all, going out with a bang, part of the mad rush of chaos flying down the red hot sparks into the booming dark.

∞

The night was a screaming kaleidoscope, rushing ride through a Link gone crazy—spinning bits of sound, sense, sight blazing her nerves:

Red spitting trails of the tracers. Stutter of bullets. A distant cry. Stones rough under her hands. Auroras writhing faint colors. Wind howling. Damiana slapping in another clip, firing down over the ruins. White carved columns shimmering, serene and remote. Blinding flare, lightning crackling. Deafening thunder.

Holy terror, exultation, flamed in Leeza's belly.

"Down, you fool!" Damiana swung an arm to shove Leeza back.

She slid down the loose rocks onto the ledge. "Uhn." She fell against a flat boulder wedged against the cliff. Damiana was firing again. Hands shaking, Leeza slipped the camera goggles into her pouch.

The boulder was shaking behind her back. Another tremor? But then the stone slab slid sideways, and she was falling backwards.

Leeza flailed, opening her mouth to scream. Hands grabbed her, muffled her roughly and lifted her, yanking her aside as shadowy figures pushed past, leaping out of a crevice revealed in the cliffside. Women. Corybantes.

Arms held her, hand still clamped over her mouth. The Amazon warriors were rushing up at the rock shield, gripping guns and what couldn't really be spears, and then Damiana was swinging around with a startled oath, bringing the rifle barrel down.

One of the warriors lashed out with a spear, and the rifle went clattering. Flash of lightning strobed Damiana mid-air, launching herself knife glinting down on them. Darkness, thunder. Shapes struggling, a whipping slash and a bitten-off scream. Damiana kicked and spun and another warrior fell against the cliff, but then someone else swung the butt of a rifle at her head and Damiana crumpled, sprawling over the rocks.

"Mmph!" Leeza tried to scream.

More Corybantes pushed past her as she struggled. They fanned out from the open crevice, moving in fast crouches along the base of the cliffs, working stealthily down toward the fighting. Leeza thrashed, kicking, jerking forward as the woman behind her swore. A faint light-beam flickered over Damiana's prone shape. A hissing whisper, flash of a raised knife blade.

Leeza bit down on the hand muffling her, jerked her head free to scream, "Don't! Wait, we'll give up!"

The hand smacked over her mouth again, grip tightening roughly, but the knife had halted as someone else muttered angrily and the glow flickered over Damiana's unconscious face. A hand pushed back her cap and braids matted with blood, finger tracing the scarred spiral design on her forehead.

More hurried whispers, the knife gesturing emphatically, but the others were shaking their heads, arguing. A few last warriors hustled out of the crevice, darting away with their rifles and spears. Another lightning crack, a booming roar. Two grunting women hoisted Damiana's limp height and dragged her into the crevice, Leeza hustled along behind them. As she groped around tight turns and into the flickering light of a torch, she realized it was a tunnel into the mountainside.

Muffled and far away, more gunshots. A louder explosion. The sounds faded as hands pushed her stumbling on, through a slick gap to the drip of water. Into a wider cave, then up steep steps hacked out of the mountainside, worn slippery smooth. Into a steep passage. Torchlight guttered over faint chisel marks.

A deep groan. Rock shivered around her, shadows leaping, and Leeza gasped as the mountain shook. She clawed against the hands dragging her. Stone walls and darkness closed in.

"*Stomat!*" The hands yanked her and slapped her face.

Leeza reeled into the shivering wall, fell to her knees, scrambled back in panic the way they'd come as rock chips rattled and slid beneath her. Behind her, the hand caught her ankle, but the torch fell, and she kicked the hand away, blackness dropping over them as the world wobbled and spun.

"Shit." Leeza realized she was clutching Ariadne's etched blue crystal, rocking hunched over it in the blackness as the tremor slowly subsided. Heat pulsed in her fist, she realized—she could feel that at least.

"*Ela etho! Blazomeh!*" The flashlight flickered on again, wavering over a sweating face and fear-bulged dark eyes. And a third eye, staring from a spiral on her forehead.

Leeza screamed.

Then she saw it was an embroidered headband. The Corybant was grasping her wrist again, tugging, and two more were dragging a stumbling, half-conscious Damiana with blood oozing down the side of her face. One of them babbled something Leeza couldn't understand except the word "Gaea," gesturing around them and pointing frantically upward, and Leeza didn't have to know Greek to read the woman's face. She stopped fighting and gave in to the insanity, running after the torchlight streaming ahead up the passage.

The rock maze shivered again, mountain monster-bellowing deep inside. Leeza was running, eyes glazed with sweat and flickering flames. The world was upside-down, spinning around her, and she didn't know if she was climbing up or falling into a bottomless black well, but it was the way she had to go. All she could hear was drumming in her ears, an insistent beat.

Her feet pounded along to it, fist clutching the blue crystal, and she swore she could feel the carved shapes, the moon and the horns and the winged serpents, stirring into life. Heat pulsed in her grip, light captured in her palm, shattering out through the facets. Its unseen blaze pulled her on.

91

AT PETER'S FEET, ARIADNE shuddered, one arm embracing the stone pillar flickering in torchlight and shadow, face contorted as her free hand clutched the crystal at her breast. Drums and chanting pulsed to an engulfing heartbeat, echoing in the cavern.

He stood helplessly over her, hands flexing. "Can't we help her?"

Mother Eleni shook her head. "She must find the way."

Peter's jaw was clenched so hard it hurt. "She can't take this much longer."

Ariadne stiffened, gasping, face pale. Peter started forward, staring down as she screamed. A hand fell onto his shoulder, urging him back.

He tore free, dropped to his knees, and touched her.

Blackness. Lightning crackles, thunder booming with the groans of the quaking earth, icy winds shrieking in glee. He's lost. Fiery pain racks him. Ariadne–

He can't find her. No, there. Beneath his hands.

Peter groped blindly and found her hand fumbling over her breast. He guided her hand back to the crystal, then gripped his own tight around hers, holding her there.

Christ! Mother of God the pain screams through him. Her pain — his — the world's — too much to bear and he starts to let go, fall back gasping. A wail of despair tears at him. He grips tighter. If it's all he can do he has to hold her here.

Peter caught a sharp breath, whirling in darkness, the pain overwhelming. But he caught her, held her, his hand tight over her hand gripping the crystal.

She writhes, convulsing in agony and he opens his gates, lets her pain flow into him. The shock! Too much. He starts to scream but then bites down on it, holding on.

Lost in the blackness, he whispers, "Hold on. Hold on."

92

THE DARKNESS HAD SPUN her downward almost before she touched the stone pillar. Ariadne gasped, fighting for air as the shrieking forces claimed her once more, ripping away her bearings. She gripped the quartz crystal, making herself heavy as stone, dropping deeper through the turmoil. It howled around her, plucking at her parts, trying to tear her in two, but she was hard, unyielding, plummeting toward the center of the earth and the pulsing beat of its heart. Seeking Gaea.

"No. She's mine. Mine!"

The voice blasted her, flaying her open. Darkness coiled into an immense black serpent, opaque noncolor swallowing the last spark of light. It swelled about her, sucking more power from her fading strength, gaping jaws swallowing her.

She is one with the black monster of chaos, greedy for the sickness of the world. She burrows and swells, bursting through earth and stone, her roar shattering outward. And she grows, ballooning to swallow the light, writhing upward for the moon and beyond it the sun—

No. That was wrong. There *was* order, somewhere. *The lattice.* The crystal was the seed.

Ariadne, nearly lost within the voracious black nothingness, groped for that memory of solidity. Her hand was holding the stone. *Stone!* Yes, she had to be stone. Had to build the lattice.

She gripped the crystal and tried to rebuild the lattice of light within herself. But the darkness seethed, stronger, sweeping away the faint glimmer of facets, flinging her spinning away into dizziness. Eternal cold sucked up the sparks of energy linking those tiny seeds of order. Chaos screamed in triumph.

Ariadne was lost, torn into pieces, her parts scattered and flung down the whirling vortex. No voice to cry, no hands to fling out to catch herself.

"Hold on."

A jolt. Something grabbed her through the turmoil, dark forces bucking and clashing against the intrusion. Something solid, warm, gripping her. Another hand? It was holding her, letting her find her own hand within its grip, both of them gripping the quartz pendant. The blackness roared furiously as her fingers tightened on the hard lines and gleaming facets.

She caught a breath, gathering her strength to trigger the crystal's lattice again.

A mocking roar, and the crystal blazed into fire in her palm. She nearly dropped it then, convulsing in agony as flames leapt searing through the facets. But the hand around hers wouldn't let her drop the blistering torment of the stone, forced her to hold it as the weight of it pulled her back down through the dark vortex to where she could hear the world's pulsing heartbeat. Where the Mother waited.

The fire had drained away. She thought she could hear a voice distantly crying out, in pain. *"Hold on."* She shuddered, started to turn toward that suffering, but then it was muffled, shut away from her. She could hear the giant heartbeat again, Gaea calling her.

She gripped the weight of the crystal pulling her deeper. Toward the heart of the world.

Another furious shriek. The quartz crystal shifted, suddenly melting in her grip and reforming. Its transformation spread, infecting her hand. She recoiled in horror as a glowing, sparkling grid ate its way up her arm. Mocking laughter drowned out the faint, faltering heartbeat. The glinting grid transformed the Mother's song, too, into fleshless pure tones chiming distantly. That glowing, inhuman lattice burgeoned through her, burning away her skin and bones. Remaking her to an abstract, alien order....

Revulsion flooded her. She writhed, breaking the glittering lattice, and flung its crystal seed away from her.

Howling laughter, triumphant. The hovering darkness swept over her.

Ariadne was lost. Tricked by the ebony voice, and the silver song. She'd failed. Spinning in the vortex, exhausted, she gave up and let chaos take her. The void spun her outward, flung in wider and wider circles.

Circles?

She strained, puzzled. *Circles.*

Yes! There was still some pattern to the wild forces, some resistance at the center of the whirling. Now, instead of fighting in toward the core, she let herself be thrown outward. Farther. Higher. Until she could see that the black consuming vortex had the shape of spinning coils, enclosed within a shape even larger.... The world, turning in space. And she saw now that the spinning could engender its own central force, could whirl like a generator to send a beam coursing down the shattering, collapsing axis. It could transform the shifting energies into a new balance.

If she could only trigger it, kindle a burst of realigned light....

But she couldn't hold the image of the encompassing pattern, and at the same time find the light. The forces of chaos were too strong. She fought, flailing against the currents churning over the axis. She slipped, weakening. The clashing waves swept her away.

Faint, and fading, a voice whispered painfully, "Hold on."

That hand!

It was still there, steadying her. It still held her fingers cupped around the pulsing spark in the crystal. Finally she recognized that grip. *Petros. The rock.* He was there, holding the point of reference, offering his solidity as an anchor to the quaking stone pillar, to the source, to struggling Gaea.

Ariadne scrambled gratefully toward him. Toward the axis. The surge of his energy crackled around hers, sparks showering over her in images and sensation: A chestnut bull, gleaming in the sun. Her thighs tightening around him as hooves pounded the heartbeat, and they plunged together into the molten heart of the Mother.

"Petros." As she gripped with him, the flailing vortex straightened into a dark tunnel, the sleeping twin serpents stirring and swelling and twining together—black and white—to coil down its length.

Far distant, down the hollow spiral, a ponderous heartbeat labored and pulsed, faltered, pulsed again. Something was still blocking it, cutting off the vital flow of light and energy. Ariadne had to send a spark down the tunnel.

But all she could do was grip tight, Petros anchoring her as she strained to hold the spinning passage open. She couldn't let go to release the sparks of light locked in her hand.

She was exhausted. She tried to tap energy from the forces swirling around them, but they couldn't be tamed or funneled.

She could feel Peter's strength draining into her to hold the fragile alignment as the earth screamed and groaned, shivering in pain. It wasn't enough. And if she let go now, they would both be swept into the black chaos as the tunnel collapsed.

She cried out in pain and despair.

A thin wail answered her.

Where?

No, there was nothing. Only vacuum.

Wait. Again... faint but whirling closer. Another presence—two?—flailing desperately in the dark tunnel as the coils started to warp, twist out of Ariadne's control and squeeze in on themselves, earth trembling and screaming.

93

DARKNESS. TERROR AND THE earth shuddering beneath her feet, insistent beat goading her on.

Leeza's running up that dark tunnel in the mountain, running with the Corybant warriors for her life. Running for the life of that pounding heart of the earth. But the tunnel kept twisting back on itself and she was lost in the maze. She was gasping, screaming in pain, but she had to keep running, the drumbeat wouldn't let her stop and the sapphire crystal clutched in her hand throbbed with heat, pulling her.

She looked down in the darkness as she stumbled on and she could see the blue pulsing light glowing out through the cracks between her fingers, illuminating her fist with its X-ray light so she could see the pattern of the bones, scintillating hot sparks like the waters of the radioactive Hot Zone. And there was a thread of light, laser-thin, connected somewhere else to the stone and pulling her on through the darkness.

She ran on. Shapes swelled around her in the dark turmoil of the quaking earth. Flashing curved horns, and a sleek bull pounded ahead up the passage, muscles bunching in neck and haunches as his hooves struck drumbeats off the rock. The sound of waves surged and ebbed in her ears. A bone-rattling roar as the winged serpents launched into the air, flying circles around the spinning earth. She kept running, and far in the distance, floating pale and fragile in the void, hung a crescent moon.

But it was too late. The black chaos was rending the moon, tearing the earth into pieces and swallowing the light. Frantic, Leeza looked down and saw the blue glowing crystal had died to a cold lump of coal in her fist. She was ice, stiffening, lost as the darkness spun her away into nothingness.

"No!" Leeza panted, chest burning, red swimming in her eyes as she tried to scream and only got out a faint whimper. But the curtain of darkness over her eyes rippled, and for a second she could see through it to a confusion of guttering torchlight, shadows leaping over cavern walls and a massive stone column. Sprawled at her feet, Ariadne clutched the quaking stone pillar and convulsed in pain. Peter, eyes rolled up into his head, held her down and screamed.

The curtain of blackness closed over Leeza again. It whirled her away into the cataclysm, but she could feel their pain echoing through it, feel their need as the distant laboring heartbeat faltered and failed.

She clutched the cold dark coal in her fist, shook it furiously, screaming, "Fuck this shit!" And she hurled that last bit of solidity at the whirling emptiness, flinging herself after it like flying blind down the singing electric lines of the Link—*what a rush ultimate flight down the spinning walls*—laying herself bare and throwing everything she had at that voracious blackness.

A furious sizzle. Out of her heart bursts a smoldering ember of pain and loss, fanned by the winds to a crimson spark.

94

DESPERATELY ARIADNE PULLED ON the coiling lines of force with her last strength, tugging them open again as Petros dug in against the dark whirling chaos. That lost wail again, louder now, and then a sharp cry of defiance. A spark of light burst into the blackness.

Silence.

The roar of chaos hung suspended for an interminable Now:

Flame blossoms within the spinning vortex. It burgeons into the glinting form of a carved sapphire crystal flashing with light, hovering in the vacuum. Crescent moon glimmers over the bull's horns, hooves pounding the heartbeat, and the winged serpents rise, hissing and spitting fire. The lattice ignites.

Three forces—elements of stone, fiery air, water—three separate frequencies and wavelengths join and twine into one coherent lasered stream. A brilliant burst of white pulsing light and—

How can this be possible?

It is so—

Hot what a rush ultimate scream down

the flying spinning walls of the Link and

bloody wild it's—

Serpents and mouth a red well no a black abyss that terrible drowning voice calling, tempting but damn we're plunging in now and through it, beyond to—

*One. The music crescendo a white blazing chorus
of perfect harmony and I/we are inside, treading
the labyrinth in the lapping rhythm, deep inside
dazzling light-gem-music, looking out through the
angles the magic the music, flung fearless all/one
to the heart of the maze*

∞

The pulse lasered down the whirling tunnel to explode in dazzling illumination.

With a cry of pain, the frail catalytic spark died. But the core was spinning with its own light now. Lapping waves of energy merged into humming blended white, pushing back the voracious darkness. Denying chaos.

The light merged into the steadying beat of a distant heart—a massive presence holding them, rocking them as the pulse floated them slowly upward. Ariadne gasped, drained. She floated limp, buoyed by the rhythm and the cradling warmth.

Then she remembered.

She sent searching tendrils for the source of that desperate cry, the spark of defiance that had burst out of the darkness. And she recognized the stilled presence floating up after Peter and herself.

She should have known—that blind reckless leap into the void. Lisa.

Limp, lost, her presence floated closer. Ariadne reached out to catch her and tug her unresisting upward as Petros pulled them both higher through the surging light. Dismay filled Ariadne. Lisa was cold, empty. She'd thrown life itself at the dark chaos.

In grief, Ariadne pulled Lisa's frozen shell closer, rising on the tide. She touched the stiff form carved in blue ice, fingertips shuddering away from its empty cold.

95

ICE.

Leeza's sheathed in ice, locked in a frozen void. She isn't breathing. No heartbeat. Eyes closed, frozen tears sealing them shut, but she can see though the transparent lids. Cold weight presses down.

She's dead, then.

It's odd, though, not like she'd imagined. Somewhere a vague thought drifts: is she still Linked into her recorder? Will it make sense to anyone else? But it isn't important. She can see a little clearer now, and she thought you were supposed to be floating above your body looking down, but she's still inside it looking out. And there are translucent lines above her, like a grid. Leeza frowns inside, face frozen, realizes she's tracing the planes and angles of the block of ice encasing her. It glows dimly blue in the empty place, and she can just make out some sort of designs.

Wait. It isn't a block of ice, it's the sapphire crystal. She's inside it, and now she can trace the etched figures—crescent moon, waves and winged serpents, sharp curved horns or a womb-shape....

A cold jolt. The baby inside her. She can't hear its heartbeat. More tears well up, but they only freeze, too, and now the heaviness is tugging with gravity, spinning her down as the shape of the crystal rotates around her. Sharp light glints off the angles of its facets, each one an image flashing memory bytes, and one suddenly swells to engulf her—

And for an eternal Now

bloody wild it's

>> *drowning tempting plunging on beyond*
>> *crescendo of harmony I/we dazzling light/gem/music*

she's no longer alone, but all one, all light, all song, joined dancing—

But that's it, Leeza's shot her bolt. She drops, frozen, heavy and empty. Sinking.

Ice. She's sheathed in ice, spinning down. Dead.

"Come back!"

A voice, outside the ice. But she was sinking, dead, and she wanted to go now as the ice started to crack and let her slide away from her body. She didn't want to hear that voice.

"Lisa, come back." The voice kept insisting, a familiar irritating authority to it. Warm hands tingled with the pulses of white light.

The hands touched her heart, touched her belly, warming the disk of carved jade. The dragon circled, stirring with a cry. It was curled in the womb, heart pulsing with her pulse in the white egg-shaped throb of light. The egg trembled, cracking, and a shattering light lanced her eyes.

96

"LISA! COME BACK." ARIADNE flattened her palms over the carved blue ice, summoning the last of her own warmth to give. Was it enough?

"Here." Petros was still with her, joining his strength to hers.

She felt a faint tingle under her fingers, their fingers. A spark of life still pulsed at Lisa's core. Part of her, but somehow separate?

Now she could see a faint trail coiling outward and down from Lisa's form—a glowing streamer of green luminescence in the sea of darkness. Touching it, she touched mossy rock and flowing water.

A jade dragon uncoiled to dart its bright tongue of flame, spreading its wings. They were floating upward within a hollow white egg, life stirring, suffusing them. They floated higher, and the brittle shell trembled and cracked.

Part III. LATTICE

Tear yourself loose from the unfaithful time
And sink.
Needs must he sink who carries the great stones.

—George Seferis, *Santorin*

1—WE FEEL DIFFERENT. The world feels different.

Lisa gasps and blinks, pushing blindly at the hands stroking her head, stroking her hands, to sit up and take long deep breaths. Dazzled by the light, she blinks again.

She's staring out over a rocky plunge into the sun rising from a rose-glimmered haze. Far below, green-and-silver-leafed slopes ripple down to the distant blue glint of the sea. Swallows dip and dance the sky. Scrubbed clean—it's rained in the night. She sucks in another deep breath, greedy for the cool clean bite of it, like the sunlight and colors and tingling air could nourish her all by themselves. She stretches, humming. And she realizes the rocky mountainside is humming with the same current of well-being. She's never heard its song before, but now she can feel the smooth waves of harmonics lapping up from below, and she wonders if she'd always been deaf.

She laughs in delight, pressing her hands to the earth to feel the waves sing through her bones, sing through her hands and she can feel again, the leprosy puffiness gone. She presses her hands over her belly to feel the Dragon breathing there. And it's all right, the child, channels somehow cleared out now like the old Chinese guy told her.

"She'll be fine now, just let her...." Vague words float in the singing haze, voice familiar and tugging, but it's more important to sit here and relearn the wordless song.

"Of course, this is only the start." That vibrant voice, drifting gently over Lisa with the breeze. "Peter is right, we need to get the word out. It will take a great communal effort. We must go out from here to create a global network, using the old sacred sites as rectification centers to realign the energy fields, ease the transition of the geomagnetic reversal. To bring us back into connection with Gaea."

"That's it." A new voice, clipped British syllables. "Something on the order of the ancient *feng-shui* energy grid. The dragon lines over the earth."

"Well, now that the gals have agreed to let some men in," a deeper voice cut in, "I know some people who might come on board, help us disable the rest of the microwave towers. Make the big shots pay attention."

Lisa laughs. "Maximal!" She fumbles to stand.

A hand reaches down to help her up, steadying her as she swings around, laughing and touching the jade pendant resting on her belly. She blinks down at the cluster of Corybantes in spiral-eyed headbands sitting on the slope below the cave mouth. Off to one side of them sits tall Damiana with a bandage around her head, looking warily up the slope. Lisa grins and waves to her. The dark face just watches, waiting, but it doesn't matter right now, Damiana's smart and they'll work it out. Lisa dances around to find Ariadne, but she loses her balance on the rocky hill and a strong hand steadies her again.

She turns to see Peter. "Maximal." Good old Stiff Mitchell grinning at her, looking great in a wild, animal-skin outfit and beard. She smiles right back at him. She takes his hand and puts it over her belly and she can feel the warmth of his palm. He looks surprised, then his grin widens.

He takes her arm, real gentle, and leads her over to where Ariadne stands with her back to them, talking to a wrinkled old Greek with lustrous dark eyes and a woman with beautifully-cut red hair. Ariadne breaks off and turns around.

She gives Lisa her grave, studying look from those sea-deep eyes.

Ariadne looks tired, dirty and sweat-streaked and rumpled, but then she slowly smiles. And her beauty comes shining out without mask or filter, and she's positively glowing. Lisa flinches at the pure force of it hitting her, gaze flickering to Peter and the old Greek, and she can see now they have faintly glowing auras, too. Peter's smiling at Ariadne and his glow intensifies, and then Lisa braces herself to meet Ariadne's eyes again.

"*Chairete*." *Rejoice*. Ariadne's voice is low and clear, resonant.

Intense warmth floods Lisa, and she's so light she could float out over the mountain into the sparkling air. She finally recognizes the sensation: Joy. The earth beneath her feet hums with her, vibrant hues swimming in her eyes to blend into a shimmer of pure harmonic white. She dances over the stones, dancing the true colors.

∞

ADDENDUM: The Major Players

NeuroLink NewsEntertainment Network

FIELD ASSIGNMENT: 5 March 2027

NEWS CELEBRITY AGENT: Leeza Conreid, Hostess of "Celebrity Smackback"

LEADLINE: *Where is Ariadne? Who is Ariadne?*

SUBJECT: "Saint Ariadne," rumored healer of New Plague leprosy victims.

MEDIA SATURATION: 53% and growing.

QUOTABLE: Gaea Speaks cult leaders: "Mother Earth is fighting back against the pollution of the patriarchal corporate technocracy. Only Ariadne can save us now."

GLOBAL SNAPSHOT:

Audience crossover potential high with existing media coverage of global dramas:

Climate change—rising sea levels and coastal population migrations; new storm patterns, drought, famine, pestilence.

Geomagnetic pole reversal—increasing instability of global magnetic field as it prepares to "flip," impacting electronics and media communications.

"New Plague" leprosy—Rapid-Proliferating Hansen's disease now classified by the World Health Organization as Number One public health threat.

REGIONAL SNAPSHOT:

High NorthAm audience-engagement potential, largely untapped:

Post Gulf War Three political instability, border skirmishes, lingering Mediterranean "hot zones" from tactical nuclear weapons.

Med League aggression—self-declared Cycladic Islands nation claiming control of shipping lanes, enforcing No Entry zones militarily.

Drought, population relocations, and food/supply shortages incite uprisings and terrorists.

Earthquake frequency increasing.

THE PLAYERS:

Saint Ariadne: spiritual healer, possibly an urban myth gone viral. Stories originating in the Med region claim she heals RP-Hansen's leprosy by "laying on hands."

Constantin Demodakis: self-anointed Tyrannos of the new Mediterranean League. Is his secluded daughter Ariadne Demodakis in fact "Saint Ariadne"? Med League spokesmen deny it.

Gaea Speaks: (aka "Rock-Heads") worldwide feminist, nonviolent religious group claiming to channel healing powers of Mother Earth through crystals. Seeking "Goddess-Incarnate Ariadne" to lead them.

The Corybantes: (aka "New Amazons") feminist eco-terrorist group based in Greek mountains, claiming responsibility for recent bombing of Turkish nuclear fuel facility. Reportedly attempted to kidnap Ariadne Demodakis.

Sons of the Prophet: regional terrorist group gaining traction. Have declared *Fatwa* and death sentence against the blasphemer Saint Ariadne.

Pharmaceutical consortium: officially denied, rumors of PharmCo-hired mercenaries seeking Saint Ariadne for exclusive licensing of RPH cure.

ASSIGNMENT TECHNICAL CONSTRAINTS:

Electromagnetic interference during unstable shifts of the geomagnetic reversal prevent direct data transmissions. Newsstims will be recorded on data chips.

EQUIPMENT:

Field agent Conreid is issued the *ImmerseTech™* model X3bt NeuroLink portable cam-senscorder, now enabling on-the-go recording of Newsstims via direct interface with operator's spinal cord receptor implant for high resolution image *and* sensation. Enthusiastic audience response to the latest generation high-res: "No more static interface—I can totally *feel* it! It's like I'm *being* her!"

ASSIGNMENT DANGER RATING: High. No data on risk factors for illegal penetration of Med League border. No weapons or training provided.

INITIAL FIELD CONTACT: None established. Field agent is advised to scout Athens's Piraeus Harbor taverns for one Peter Mitchell, AWOL NorthAm Navy. Current occupation: smuggler.

Author's Note and Reading List

For those readers curious about the story behind this story, here are some sources that launched me into the labyrinth:

- First and foremost, an enduring fascination with Greece, since my earliest reading of Greek mythology, *The Illiad* and *The Odyssey*, *The White Goddess* by Robert Graves, and many more. I spent four months—back when time, that precious commodity, was more abundant—rambling around the islands and mainland with my backpack. I visited historical sites, rode ferries and hiked around the islands, camped in ancient ruins on Crete, and generally inhaled all that I could of the land and culture, old and new. Go there, if you can.
- *The Greek Islands*, by Lawrence Durrell. This is a wonderful compilation of Durrell's musings about his beloved Greek islands, enhanced with gorgeous photos.
- *The Body Electric,* by Robert O. Becker., M.D. A fascinating discussion of Becker's work, starting with his U.S. military research into bioelectric healing. He went on to explore possible side effects of exposure to electromagnetic fields, as well as connections between organisms and geomagnetism.
- *Occult and Curative Properties of Precious Stones*, by William Fernie. This book details some myths and traditional beliefs about crystals and jewels.
- *The Way of the Shaman,* by Michael Harner. An introduction to the traditions and practice of shamanic healing worldwide.
- *Zorba the Greek,* by Nikos Kazantzakis. A wonderful novel that captures the Greek spirit.

If you enjoyed reading *The Ariadne Connection*, please consider posting a brief review on Amazon.com or Goodreads.com. I appreciate your support.

About the Author

Sara Stamey—novelist, independent editor, and Senior Instructor of Creative Writing at Western Washington University—has returned to her Pacific Northwest roots after years of wanderlust. Her journeys include teaching scuba diving in the Caribbean and Honduran islands, trekking around Greece, New Zealand, and South America, operating a nuclear reactor at Hanford, and owning a farm in southern Chile. She stays grounded with her native-plant restoration project in her expansive Squalicum Creek backyard, which she shares with wild creatures, her cats and dog, and very tall husband Thor.

Find her other novels at www.bookviewcafe.com and visit her website/blog at www.SaraStamey.com

About Book View Café

Book View Café Publishing Cooperative (BVC) is a an author-owned cooperative of over fifty professional writers, publishing in a variety of genres including fantasy, romance, mystery, and science fiction.

In 2008, BVC launched a website, bookviewcafe.com, initially offering free fiction and gradually moving to selling ebooks of members' backlist titles, then original titles. BVC's ebooks are DRM-free and are distributed around the world. BVC returns 95% of the profit on each book directly to the author. The cooperative has gained a reputation for producing high-quality ebooks, and is now moving into print editions.

BVC authors include New York Times and USA Today bestsellers; Nebula, Hugo, and Philip K. Dick Award winners; World Fantasy and Rita Award nominees; and winners and nominees of many other publishing awards.

www.bookviewcafe.com

Also by Sara Stamey
from Book View Café
Islands

Romantic suspense and adventure in the Caribbean. A *ForeWord* Book of the Year Finalist. "Superior mystery and suspense—a stomping, vivid ride." (*Statesman Journal*)

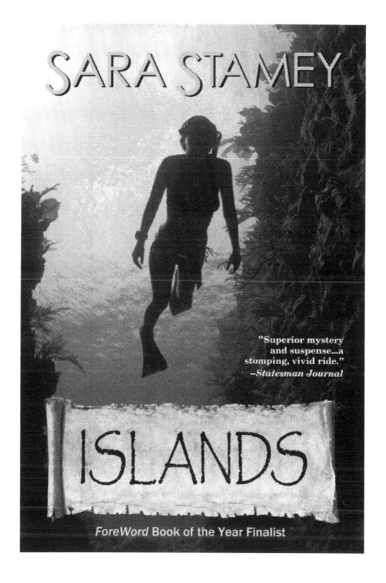

Made in the USA
Columbia, SC
31 August 2017